ONE

LITTLE

SPARK

**Also by Ellie Banks
writing as Maisey Yates**

*The Lost and Found Girl
Confessions from the Quilting Circle
Secrets from a Happy Marriage*

For a complete list of books by Maisey Yates,
please visit www.maiseyyates.com

ELLIE BANKS

ONE LITTLE SPARK

CANARY STREET PRESS

CANARY
STREET
PRESS™

ISBN-13: 978-1-335-60097-4

One Little Spark

Copyright © 2023 by Maisey Yates

For questions and comments about the quality of this book, please contact us
at CustomerService@Harlequin.com.

Canary Street Press
22 Adelaide St. West, 41st Floor
Toronto, Ontario M5H 4E3, Canada
CanaryStPress.com

Printed in U.S.A.

It takes a village to write a book, and I'm so thankful for mine. To Jackie, Nicole and Megan, for always seeing me through.

ONE
LITTLE
SPARK

Tenmile Wolf Scouts Guide to Building a Fire

1. Place a support stick in the ground at a thirty-degree angle.
2. Place a tinder bundle beneath the support stick.
3. Place a few small pieces of kindling against the support.

Take your fire starter (be it a match, a flint, or a lighter) and ignite a spark at the tinder. It doesn't matter what the fire starter is as long as you have enough fuel for it to burn.

1

The Day of the Fire
Ignition Point—

Jenna

JENNA ABBOTT WAS late and she didn't have time to get gas.

She pulled her car up to the pump and waited. The attendant was inside and not paying attention and this was Oregon, and she couldn't do anything about it.

He was on his phone.

Dumb kid.

She had to pick Chloe up from dance and Aiden from football, and if she was five seconds late, her ex-fucking-husband would make a trauma out of it, and then she'd have to murder him. If she was in prison for murder, she would have bigger problems than being late for practice.

It was *almost* appealing.

If she were in prison, someone would cook for her. And do her laundry.

And Ryan would be dead, so there was that, too.

She didn't actually want Ryan dead. *For the children.*

That was nearly convincing.

She was so grumpy today, homicide seemed like a reasonable outlet for her feelings.

It was the smoke. Her eyes hurt. It made her cough.

She hadn't seen the sun for two weeks, and this hotter-than-hell midsummer nightmare, which brought about the kind of seasonal affective disorder usually reserved for the dead of winter, was beginning to get under her skin.

She was tired of it. Wildfire Season had become a thing in Southern Oregon and she was heartily sick of the weeks and months from as early as June all the way through October when the brown smoke blotted out the sky and turned the sun orange. Smoke that blew in from Northern California and got trapped in the little soup bowl of a valley, giving residents even more reason to curse their neighbors to the south.

Her eyes were scratchy, the stench of the smoke coming through the vents. And *she was late.*

"You little asshole, get off your phone." She tapped on her steering wheel and glared into the office at the kid, who didn't look up, even when she waved. She honked, which she hated doing because it was a small town, and while she was having a small tantrum, she didn't want everyone to know it.

The honking didn't even get his attention.

Everything was annoying today. *Everything.*

She got out of her car, about to turn and walk toward the office and pound on the kid's door, when she stopped. There was a woman standing across the street holding a sign. She had dirty hair and clothes and was looking away, like she was ashamed. And Jenna felt compassion for another human being for the first time in four months.

For the first time since Ryan had walked out. For the first time since he'd confessed to his affair, and that the woman—

if a nineteen-year-old could be called a woman and not herself a fetus—was pregnant.

Jenna had been sitting in an air-conditioned car on butter-
soft leather seats, despairing, and this homeless woman was out
in the triple-digit heat, asking for a few coins. And honestly,
even if it was a scam, there were easier ways to make money,
so Jenna had to assume there were reasons she was here on
the roadside, in the tiny town of Tenmile Creek.

It was the ability to feel something that made her do it.
That made her go back to her SUV and open the passenger
door, lean in and unzip her purse, dig until she found a five-
dollar bill.

As she started across the street, she heard the door to the
office open—dammit, she was going to miss that kid—but
she was on a mission now.

Standing with a healthy amount of space between herself
and the woman, she extended her hand and smiled. "Here
you go."

The wind whipped up. And it was hot.

Not like the air around them had been. It was more.

She looked up, across the street, and she saw it. A wall of
flame.

"But there's an alert system."

She knew because she'd helped get people to sign up for it.
There was an alert system. And it was supposed to warn them.

It hadn't.

Then the flames touched the gas station. And the world
ignited.

2

TENMILE FIRE DESTROYS HOMES, BUSINESSES—
DEVASTATING LOSSES, MIRACLES ABOUND
AMONGST THE ASHES

WINEMA COUNTY, OR (KWTV)—Law enforcement has launched a criminal investigation into the start of a wildfire that devastated the Southern Oregon town of Tenmile. The Tenmile Police Department, the Winema County Sheriff's Office and the Oregon State Police are conducting a criminal investigation, including into the resulting deaths of the fire.

The state of Oregon has been besieged by wildfires as temperatures soar and rainfall dwindles. But fires in densely populated areas have been rare. Until now.

There have been five confirmed fatalities from the fire that ripped through the town during the record-breaking heat wave this September. The identities of the deceased are being withheld pending identification and notification of the families. Thirteen people have been reported missing.

The burn unit at Winema Regional Hospital is at capacity. Citizens abandoned their cars on the highways as they found themselves caught in traffic that wasn't moving, only to run into the path of the flames. One resident, Alexandra Coleman, 42, is the wife of one of the missing residents. She is being treated for second- and third-degree burns.

What's being seen as a failure of the Emergency Alert System is also being investigated. Town Councilwoman, Jenna Abbott, the person responsible for establishing the alert system, spoke briefly to reporters.

"The alert system was tested as recently as two weeks ago, and we had no reason to believe it wouldn't function as planned. We have escalated this to the parent company of the system and they are conducting an internal investigation to see where the failure occurred."

An estimated twenty-six hundred homes and thirty businesses were lost in the blaze.

There are miracles amid the devastation, including the preservation of Old Town Tenmile, a strip of historic buildings on the original town's main street, established in 1880.

Chelsea Goddard, 41, owner of Thistle and Rose Florist, credited a water leak with saving her life. "I would have been home," said Goddard. "But there was a leaking pipe at the store flooding the basement and I drove there to handle the emergency. That's where I was when the fire started." Goddard's brother is among the missing.

Even amid death and destruction, life goes on, and even grows.

Morgan White, 19, was home the afternoon of the fire when labor pains woke her and prompted her to go to the hospital, where she gave birth to a premature baby girl, who is stable, but in serious condition in the NICU. The father of her baby remains among the missing, but Morgan gives thanks for the life of her child. "If not for her, I probably would have burned along with the house," says White.

Law-enforcement agencies have stressed that, while there are no current suspects, this is an active investigation.

"We have determined that this is a human-caused fire and we are seeking information," Fire Chief Derek Ray said. "If you saw something out of the ordinary that day, we encourage you to speak up. In a situation like this we will look at every angle, at every possible scenario, no matter how unlikely."

Anyone who may have information about the origins of the fire is encouraged to contact the dedicated Tenmile Fire Hotline.

3

Alex

THE ENVELOPE HAD no return address. Alex's home address had been printed on the outside in a neat, nondescript font.

She nearly tossed it straight into the junk mail pile, until she realized it had something more than paper inside.

There was something heavy in the bottom right corner.

She opened the top of the envelope and tilted it, holding it over her kitchen counter. A metal chain slithered onto the counter, and the heart-shaped locket came out last.

She started to pick it up, then froze.

It was a gold heart, with vines twining around the edge, and on the left side of the locket the design was worn down, like the wearer had reached across to worry at it with their right hand.

Alex knew that because it was exactly what her mother had done.

Alex knew that because this was her mother's necklace.

And Alex hadn't seen the necklace since she was seventeen, when her mother had walked out the door to meet with friends for dinner, and hadn't come back, more than twenty-five years ago.

4

Afterburn—

Jenna

WE'RE REBUILDING YOUR COMMUNITY!

THE CHEERY SIGNS, which were shaped like the sun, were posted in the front yards of nearly finished homes all across Tenmile. The name of the contractor was bolded beneath the enthusiastic slogan, as if the guy needed more work.

He'd rebuilt the whole town.

She wondered if anyone had looked into an arson conspiracy involving contractors.

She shouldn't be *that* cynical. But cynicism was just so much easier than anything else. Jenna had never been a big rebuilder.

She had always liked a little scorched earth. She'd done it with her toxic parents; she'd done it with her ex. She'd never seen the point in going out with quiet dignity and grace.

Nope. If she was going down, it would be swinging. And screaming. Loudly.

It had been called a *lack of decorum* by some, like her dear friend, Alex, who had been her sidekick since ninth grade at Tenmile High—Go Tigers—when Jenna had thrown a whole bottle of iced tea at a boy who'd snapped Alex's bra strap while she was trying to eat a sandwich.

You didn't mind my lack of decorum then, Alex.

Of course, the scorched-earth analogy felt a little on the nose now, all things considered. There were parts of town that were still scorched earth and nothing more. Chain-link fences surrounding burned-out cars and blackened trees.

There was a lot of cleanup yet to be been done.

The fire had ripped right through town, devastating the mobile home parks along the main highway in particular, a perfect fuel to amp up the flames as they headed to the apartment complexes, and then fast food restaurants, grocery stores and finally, the larger homes in neighborhoods on the other side of town.

It was Old Town Tenmile that had been spared.

The little cluster of historic shops that forked off to the left of where the flames had done most of their damage.

Jenna had lost her home, but her business had stayed intact.

She'd lost less than a great many people.

And more than others.

But she wasn't thinking about loss today; she was thinking about rejuvenation. About the Harvest Festival the town council was planning to celebrate the restoration of Tenmile.

This was the fresh start Jenna had been waiting for.

The new beginning. She was so tired of being in limbo, and it had been a protracted one for her, starting with her divorce. She had been drifting, and Jenna didn't drift. Jenna *did*.

She'd been a late-in-life surprise to parents who—she

assumed—must have thought it would be an interesting experiment to try and raise a child, but had lost interest quickly.

From the time she was small, Jenna had never accepted anything. Including a life of neglect. She'd joined every extracurricular activity and figured out how to get herself there. She'd been the pet of every teacher. She'd been on every organizing committee for school. She'd learned to make herself important, essential early on, and she had woven herself so tightly into the fabric of the community—though reviews on her were occasionally mixed—that she'd become necessary.

Something she'd never been to her parents.

She'd never been one to sit in discomfort. But over the past two years, it had been forced upon her.

She was ready for that to be over.

The new houses were almost complete. Many businesses had been rebuilt, and the entry to Old Town was no longer gnarled, blackened branches and a charred sign. It had been relandscaped, repainted, renewed, and a host of little plaques were stuck in the ground down there, surrounded by flowers.

Restored by The Wolf Scouts, Pack #457
Planted by the Tenmile Rotary
Maintained by the Tenmile Town Council

All that glorious community involvement made it beautiful again.

And in certain pockets, it was like nothing had happened, or even worse, the neighborhoods had been improved. The houses that were being built up around the community were better than the rows of trailer parks that had existed before. Although, Jenna couldn't help but wonder what was supposed to happen to the people who had lived in those places. They'd probably left town.

At least they'd gotten a piece of the settlement money. Everyone had. For damages from the faulty alert system. And Jenna'd had a hand in that because she'd had detailed knowledge of what the system had been meant to do, and how it had failed to perform.

So even if she didn't know what had specifically become of everyone touched by the fire, at least she knew she'd... done something.

Something other than feeling sorry for herself, anyway.

Today wasn't about looking back. It was about looking forward. A meeting with her favorite portion of the Main Street business coalition. At Alex's shop, Tenmile Treats. Which served amazing baked goods, and lovely coffee drinks and the kind of sanity that Jenna was happy to throw money at any day of the week.

The shop was situated across the street from Jenna's own, Hidden Gems, and two doors down from Thistle and Rose, the florist shop, owned by Chelsea Goddard, her former sister-in-law.

They'd known each other in high school, but hadn't exactly been friends. In fact, Chelsea had been a little rude to Alex when Alex had started dating Paul. Ancient history, though. No one was mad that Ryan's little sister hadn't handled losing her crush to Alex back in ninth grade. Not anymore.

Even with the divorce, Jenna had maintained a connection to Chelsea. Chelsea definitely seemed to be on Jenna's side, but Chelsea also seemed skittish about letting her mom know they still maintained a connection.

As far as Melinda Abbott was concerned, Ryan could do no wrong, even when he was *doing* a nineteen-year-old.

The weight of performing perfection in that family was heavy. Though, Ryan's affair had exposed that they didn't need *him* to perform. They would bend perfection to fit around their golden boy. Jenna was confident they would never have done that for Chelsea.

Jenna was familiar with dysfunction. Enough that she didn't judge Chelsea for letting her family assume their interactions were merely business meetings and not a continued friendship.

Even if it did hurt her feelings a little bit.

She pushed that thought aside and parked her car in front of the cheery red-brick building right in the center of Main Street. Old Town truly was untouched. A miracle, many had called it.

Jenna didn't know how you could claim a miracle in a situation like this. That made it sound like some were more worthy of miracles while others weren't, and she just didn't think that was right. Or the truth of it.

But then, she wasn't in charge of the universe, something that constantly confounded and enraged her. But no one had ever offered her the position. And she was open to it. She felt she had made that very clear.

She got out of the car and pushed open the door to Tenmile Treats, where Chelsea and Alex were already sitting at a small table by the window. For a moment she was caught off guard by how…formal their expressions were. She wasn't often the last to arrive, so it wasn't typical for Chelsea and Alex to be sitting there by themselves in the first place.

"Hey!" As soon as Jenna greeted them, she could see them physically relax.

There was an array of goodies sitting on the table, and a drink already occupied the space in front of the empty chair waiting for her, since they knew what she liked.

She unwound herself from the wrap she was wearing— completely unnecessary because, even in September, it was hot as hell, but she liked fall, and she liked autumnal clothing, even when it seemed ridiculous—and slung it over the back of the chair. "Have you started without me?"

"Yes," Chelsea said.

She offered nothing other than that.

"Well—" Jenna took an oatmeal square off the plate at the center of the table and took a bite "—then I hope that you've solved every issue that might arise."

"We left all the problems for you," Alex said, rearranging the stack of napkins so they made a fan.

Alex was one of those very careful women who moved a bit like she had a headache and was afraid to unnecessarily jostle herself.

"Rude," Jenna snorted. She was tempted to mess the fan up. She didn't.

"You *like* problems," Chelsea pointed out.

And Jenna couldn't even be mad, because it was true.

It was strange to watch her friends age. Because sometimes, when she thought of them, she pictured them exactly like they'd been in high school. Not as women in their early forties who had lived whole lives since they had wandered the halls of Tenmile High, but she could see Alex, her hair a darker shade of blond, wearing a beaded flower choker and holding a notebook with a pink fuzzy pen shoved into the spiral edge.

That wasn't her *only* pen, of course.

She had an entire pack of them, all different colors, so that her notes would be organized in a very specific fashion. Whatever Alex did, she did right. Down to the smallest of details. She had been the head cheerleader, a straight-A student, valedictorian. Her perfectionism manifested itself in an easy way that people seemed to find delightful. Which was not the way that people tended to see Jenna.

Jenna was not a perfectionist.

She was insistent.

If something needed doing, she would do it. And where Alex tended to slip into spaces where help was required, Jenna made the spaces. She was the one who created something from nothing. Who chewed her way through fences erected in her way. Who would ferret around in things until she found a way forward, and fashion solutions out of nothing.

People often found her abrasive. A *little much*. And there had been a time in her life when that had really bothered her. When she'd tried to soften herself after the inevitable explosions that would occur and a friendship would implode, or a working relationship would become challenging because of Jenna's *muchness*.

But she was forty-three now. She didn't give a fuck. A combination of age and life had left her absolutely fuckless.

There were things that needed to get done, and if somebody wanted an easy friend, they were simple to find. But if you wanted a friend who got shit done, that was Jenna.

You don't need me to take care of you…

She did not need to think of him. Not right now.

She directed her focus instead across the table to Chelsea, whose hair was always on a journey through the auburn spectrum. It had been burgundy in high school. She'd been that burgundy hair type of girl.

Chelsea had been so *different*. So different from her brother, who had been on the football team, headed to medical school…

Shared the position of Most Likely to Succeed.

And Best Couple.

That was almost funny now.

Then she took a sip of her latte. Which was delicious.

"There really shouldn't be any problems. We want to set up different displays out on the sidewalks, and that will clear up space inside the shop for the expected influx of people."

"Unless the weather is terrible," Chelsea said.

"You're such a pessimist."

"How are you…not?" Chelsea asked. "Anyway, being concerned about a little rain in Oregon in October is hardly pessimism."

"So says the pessimist. Anyway, I don't think it's going to rain. Because it's just as dry *this* year as it was *last* year."

The corner of Chelsea's lips twitched. "Then maybe the real thing we should be worrying about is a fire tearing through Main Street."

"Hey, it didn't last time."

Jenna looked at Alex, aiming for a conspiratorial smile, and Alex returned it, but there was something hollow in it.

"When will you be moved into your house?" Chelsea asked.

The house. That would be the ribbon cutting of her brandnew life. A house she hadn't built with Ryan. A house filled with things she'd chosen herself, because it was just her and the kids now, and this house would be the full acceptance of that.

In that sense, she supposed the fire had been helpful.

An enforced clean slate.

"We should be in next week."

"Me, too," Chelsea said.

Alex's house hadn't burned down. It was weird how that worked. The way the fire had spared certain things and not others.

"I think we should run a bouncy house," Jenna said, charging on, past the awkwardness and the urge to shrink. "There needs to be something for kids to do, or it isn't going to be a draw to families. And Lord knows all anybody needs is bored kids to turn this into a nightmare for the adults. In fact, we could do a whole play area, and the kids can wear wristbands, and some of the high schoolers could help watch them. I know that I can get Chloe to…"

Alex's lips parted, and then closed again. She always did

that. Always took an extra moment to speak. Like she was thinking carefully about what to say, which was something Jenna never did. "You're going to get resistance on that," Alex said. "This is supposed to be a beautiful return to the town. I think if you introduce screaming children at any point on the block, Courtney is going to take issue."

"Courtney is a po-faced cow, and utterly power hungry since Tom… Well, since he's been gone."

Alex looked down at the napkin fan and shifted one slightly. "It does seem a little strange she's just in charge now. We never did find out who took the money. It could still be anyone on the town council."

The concern about money that had been stolen from last year's charity dinner seemed to have burned up along with so many other things in the town. Understandable, but Alex had a point.

"It could be anyone," Jenna pointed out. "The settlement from the alert system company is enough to build three new high schools. And we're starting fresh again, anyway. New charity events, new money."

"Same Courtney," Chelsea pointed out.

"I don't really care if she takes issue. In fact, I consider an idea a *success* if she takes issue with it."

"You could also not be obstinate for the sake of being obstinate," Chelsea pointed out.

And it felt weighted, as if she was making commentary on Jenna's former marriage. So maybe the distance she sometimes felt with Chelsea wasn't just her performing for her family.

But that could be in Jenna's head. That was a problem she had. If she didn't stay busy, her mind got needlessly crowded. She overthought things, turned them over until they were smooth and shiny, polished anxiety rocks. Which she kept in her mental pockets.

One of those was a rock that told her Chelsea was secretly quite judgmental of Jenna and Ryan's marriage. Because of course, as a friend, Chelsea was all too familiar with Jenna's foibles. Which Chelsea might have accepted, but that didn't mean everyone else had.

"I just think that broadening the audience is actually going to result in a bigger turnout." She took a sip of her latte and set it down decisively. "I'm willing to fight for it."

"You're willing to fight for literally anything that smells like a cause," Chelsea said. "That's all I'm saying. We don't need to turn every town council meeting into a brawl."

"We can have Alex present it," Jenna said. "People respond well to her."

Alex's blue eyes met Jenna's.

She was still that girl with color-coded notes. She had been taking down everything Jenna had said in a notebook. Because of course she had.

She was pristine, her soft blond hair lighter now, and though she never said it, Jenna assumed it was because it was easier to cover gray with that shade. When it started to grow out, people didn't notice. Of course Alex colored her hair, but she would never talk about it, and no one would ever know. Because again, her perfection was always effortless. Jenna had a feeling it was designed that way. They had known each other for twenty-seven years.

"I'm fine presenting the idea, but I wonder if we should speak to the other Main Street Business Coalition members…"

"Why? They'll all be at the meeting."

"Yes. That is true."

The town council had various subsets, some official, some not. The doctors were definitely their own voter bloc, with their own concerns, even though they weren't an official committee. As were the PTA moms. The Main Street Business Coalition, MSBC, was an official committee within the broader town council and, theoretically, Jenna probably should consult all of them before she made a plan about the festival to submit to the council, but...she didn't want to.

Because she didn't like a great many of the people who were part of the MSBC. So that complicated things.

In fairness, they were no particular fans of hers.

"Has anyone ever told you that you catch more flies with honey than vinegar?" Chelsea asked.

"Repeatedly," Jenna said, grinning broadly. "Throughout my life. Can't figure out why."

She said it cheerfully, and she knew that neither Alex nor Chelsea would ever be certain whether she was serious. She actually was.

She was a results-driven person. It was her results that made her valuable. When everyone in town who'd lost property, or a business, or a family member had received a check from Emergency Alerts, the value in her methods was easily seen.

In the day to day, she might have conflicts with certain people in town, but even if getting there was bumpy, she got there. That was what mattered.

She knew Alex was driven far more by process than product. She wanted every step of the routine to be perfect.

Jenna just wanted to stick the landing.

There was a flash of movement outside the window and she saw Ethan, the owner of a local coffee roaster and stand, walk by. And she was momentarily very, very distracted. He was tall, broad shouldered, with very big arms. He had a beard and a man bun, which she would've said she didn't like at all, but on him, it brought nonchalant lumberjack energy, not cultivated hipster vibes.

Being single was so damned weird. Her brain had definitely not caught up with the fact that she was not thirty years old, or twenty-five, and she just continued to check out men she would've checked out twenty years ago, and it was…unseemly.

She would like to pretend she didn't know exactly how old Ethan was, but she did. He was thirty-five. She'd known him too long not to be aware of the age gap. And for it not to be weird.

This should not be something she was worrying about.

She wasn't supposed to be single.

She'd said *I do* so that none of this would ever be a concern for her, ever again. But Ryan was gone. If he'd never left her, if he'd never had an affair…would he still have died in the fire? Or would he have been somewhere else? Somewhere safe?

She noticed that Chelsea and Alex were staring at her.

And she didn't want to get into the sticky, tangled thoughts that swamped her. Chelsea and Alex had too many of their own problems.

"He's hot," she said.

"Well, sure," Chelsea said.

"It's just so weird, having a man's hotness not be philosophical. I could do something about it if I wanted to." She blinked. "I don't know how to do this whole thing. This… dating thing."

"Who's dating?" Chelsea asked.

"I'm not dating, I'm just…going to have to eventually."

"*Are* you?" Chelsea asked.

"I miss sex," she said.

Chelsea sighed. "Right. Well. I get that."

Chelsea and her husband, Mark, had separated last year, before the fire. He'd taken a job overseas; she'd stayed. And she hadn't shared the details with Jenna. Their relationship had been even more uncertain back then, since Jenna was still in the throes of her divorce.

But she had a feeling Chelsea would have put caution tape

up around the subject of her marriage even without the circumstances.

Jenna was fond of crashing through caution tape.

"You aren't dating, then?" she asked.

Chelsea shook her head. "No. I'm *married*."

Well. That was interesting. She found herself looking at Alex, whose eyes widened.

"Don't look at me," Alex said. "It's too soon. I would've thought it was for you, too."

"Why?"

Alex looked at the plate of goodies, but Jenna had a feeling it was only to hide the disapproval in her eyes. "It's only been a year."

"No. It's been a year for *you*," she said. "I'm not a widow, Alex. You're a widow. My *ex*-husband died."

Every so often she wished she could shove words back into her mouth. This was one of those times. Because Ryan had been Chelsea's brother. And the father of Jenna's children, and she really shouldn't have brought up Alex's husband, Paul, like that.

Because everyone had loved Paul. Most of all Alex. But their pain wasn't the same.

"I didn't mean it like that," Jenna said.

"You never do," Alex said, resigned and accepting, which made Jenna feel worse. Like she was a child whose bad behavior had to be borne by those around her.

"I *really* didn't. I only meant that our pain isn't the same… It's not equal. I'm not… When it comes to romantic stuff, I was healing from a divorce, and I started that more than a year ago. I was sorry about what happened. Of course. I didn't wish him dead." *Mostly.*

"Right. Well, I'm not thinking about dating," Alex said. "They're missing, anyway. Missing, presumed dead." She picked up a napkin and started to put neat folds across the edge. Back and forth. Back and forth; her movements meticulous.

"I'm not interested in dealing with another man," said Chelsea, reaching into her purse and rummaging around. She took out her pack of cigarettes and a lighter and set it on the table. "I couldn't deal with the one I married. Hence the separation."

"Sure," Jenna said, her familiar urge to dig in once she'd made an ass of herself and just go all out deciding to kick in. If you broke it, sometimes if you kept smashing till the pieces were little and manageable, it was somehow better. "I'm not in a hurry to ever be in a long-term relationship again. My last one ended badly."

Chelsea huffed a laugh. "Yeah, it did."

"But he's so hot." She winced. "And a child."

"He is *young*," Alex said.

"He's a hot man in his thirties," Chelsea said. "I liked them when I was nineteen and I see the appeal of them now. It's not a crime, Jenna."

Alex frowned. "But what would you actually say to one out at dinner?"

"Maybe I don't want to go out to dinner," Jenna said, lifting a shoulder. "Maybe I just want to fuck."

"Hmm. I mean, I can see that." Chelsea tapped the edge of her lighter. "Do you just want me to join your single ladies club?"

Jenna sputtered. "No."

"You like a club, Jen," Chelsea said.

Alex was carefully not looking at Jenna.

"I don't need you to be in a club with me," Jenna said, narrowing her eyes.

Except, it might make them closer again.

That thought sent a kick of guilt sailing straight up against her ribs.

"Good. Because I don't join clubs. I sit in the town council meetings to support you, and to witness the chaos firsthand so I can later inject spite-filled commentary into our conversations. I don't give a shit about that stuff and you know it."

"Seriously, Chelsea, you need to figure out what you're doing with your marriage."

"Don't you need me to figure out what I'm doing with the Main Street Harvest Festival first?"

"Such a clubby statement," Jenna said. "One wonders if you're really just here for spite or if you secretly love it."

"I do not."

"Well, I don't care. Because I do need you. Fall is the season of renewal. *Rejuvenation*. And that's what the festival is. Rejuvenation for the town. With a damned bouncy house."

"You're going to end up pitching the bouncy house over the top of me," Alex said.

"I will not. Unless you do it wrong."

"How would I do it wrong?"

"If you do it without passion."

"Everything you do could stand a little bit less passion, Jen," Chelsea said. "People find it alienating."

"Well, people are ridiculous."

"I hope you lead with that at tomorrow's meeting," Chelsea said.

"I might."

"I thought you wanted your initiatives to succeed?"

"Please. I don't fail."

Except for all the times she had. Except for her marriage to Ryan. No. She wasn't going to think about that. She didn't fail. She wouldn't. Not with this new beginning that meant so much. It felt good to care about something like this. It might be a bouncy house, but it was definitely better than not caring at all. She ignored the great feeling around the edges of her heart.

Yeah. A bouncy house was definitely better than that.

5

Alex

"WHO IS THAT?" Jenna looked across the room and homed in immediately on the young woman who had just walked through the door.

Alex followed her friend's gaze. Jenna was clearly doing a complex math equation in her head to determine if the new person was friend or foe. "I don't know. I've never seen her before."

She was a human dewdrop. Glowy and soft. The kind of beautiful that was annoying to Alex now, though she was loath to admit it. The longer it took to look the way she did, the more irritating she found fae creatures who wandered around glowing by virtue of the fact that they were in their twenties—and she knew this woman was in her twenties from the moment she walked in.

Aging was a particular challenge.

Not for her husband, Paul, who had been physically perfect for as long as she'd known him, and seemed to be aging into something even more astonishingly beautiful as time wore on. Tall and fit and blond, with a chiseled jaw and the kind of blue eyes random women would comment on when they were out together.

Sorry to stare, but your eyes are just so beautiful.

Like Alex wasn't standing there with a ring on her finger. Like she was invisible. And that was the weird thing, being married to a man who seemed to get more attractive as the years marched on, and she sank into this unwelcome over-forties insecurity that women seem to find themselves in…

He got *more* attention. She got less.

And sometimes she wondered what had happened to the girl she'd been in high school. Who had been pretty confident and often got whatever she'd put her mind to.

Not that there was anything wrong with her life. She was finding the empty-nest thing to be a bit of an adjustment, but it was an achievement. Her kids had made it. They'd graduated high school, gotten into college.

No one had done drugs—that she knew of—and no one had gotten pregnant or gotten anyone else pregnant in high school.

Unlike her.

She had been a perfect rule follower, except when it came to Paul. Much to no one's surprise. Because who could resist Paul?

Pretty Paul, as they called him in high school. She told him that once, and he had laughed himself silly and had walked around with a ridiculous swagger for three weeks afterward, so she'd never mentioned it again.

She'd been so careful her entire life. An only child with parents who had lovingly handed her their every hope and dream, like a fragile figurine she'd had to carry around everywhere she went. A difficult task for a child. But she'd done it.

Until it hadn't mattered anymore.

Until her mom had shattered everything.

And one night she'd let Paul gather up all those pieces and turn them into passion in the backseat of his car. And nine months later, Ruth was born. Just one month after high school graduation.

She could still vividly remember that day. That pregnancy test she'd taken in Jenna's bathroom.

"You just…have pregnancy tests?"

"Yes. I mean, I take the pill like it's a religious ritual and Ryan always uses condoms because I make him, but if I'm ever even slightly late, I need to know."

Alex didn't even have to ask if she was worried her parents would find them. Jenna's parents wouldn't care. Jenna could probably have sex with Ryan on the living room couch in full view of everyone and they'd just be mad she was blocking the TV.

"Thanks." She stared down at the pink box. She felt stupid and naive. She hadn't thought about protection at all.

"Hey. Whatever happens, I'm here for you. If your dad kicks you out. If Paul doesn't take care of you." She paused for a second. "I'll hunt him down and kill him."

She was sure Jenna would.

She was less sure what Paul would do.

Paul was on a path. A very specific and prestigious one. He was going to be a doctor, and she knew nothing would get in the way of that.

The test had been positive. But Paul had surprised her. Not only had he promised to be there for her, he'd also proposed.

He went to med school, where they lived in married student housing. They'd had their daughter, Ruth, and he'd become a doctor. And his success had eradicated the debts that they'd accrued being a foolishly young married couple who had children far too soon.

It was strange to be on the other side of it already. To be forty-three and have no kids left at home. That was part of her problem. She'd been very involved with the PTA, the school board; she had been involved in everything. And there was just less to be involved in now. Less to make herself feel…visible.

The new pretty girl looked lost.

It was annoying to see her innermost soul reflected so artlessly on such a beautiful face. Alex had learned never to look like that, never to walk into a room and look around like she was desperate for a safe haven, with her mouth slightly open and her hands pulled up to her chest like she was a nervous rodent.

Alex wanted to tell the girl to buck up. Stop showing everyone how soft she was.

"I'd better take my place," Paul said, leaning in and kissing her.

He wasn't one of those men who just dropped a perfunctory peck on his wife's cheek like it was a habit. Paul always kissed her right on the lips, like he would rather be at home in their bedroom than here.

Like he was proud to be with her. Proud to be seen with her.

Some of her insecurity faded. He was good like that.

He left her side and started across the room. He stopped and talked to people on the way, shaking hands and smiling. She took a breath, her pride expanding in her chest.

After he was done running the greeting gauntlet, he went to sit near Jenna's husband, along with the other doctors. Jenna, Chelsea, Alex and the other members of the MSBC took their seats in their segment of the room.

"Paul should be a politician," Jenna said.

"Oh, please no," Alex said. "I don't need him to be gone even more."

"But he's so good at it," Jenna said. "Everyone likes him. If I were a man, everyone would appreciate my skillset rather than thinking I was abrasive."

Privately, Alex didn't think that was true. They would probably still find Jenna abrasive if she were a man. They'd just all sink to their knees to offer blow jobs, anyway.

"Everyone's an idiot," Chelsea said.

That seemed to mollify Jenna.

The new girl went to the edge of that segment, sitting on a chair that left three spaces between herself and Jillian Armitage.

Alex would like to leave three spaces between herself and Jillian at all times.

She wasn't overtly mean, just one of those women with very stiff posture and glassy eyes, and Alex could never work out if it was from a prescription pain pill addiction or an actual dislike for the people around her.

It was very hard to say.

Jenna was vibrating at Alex's side. But that was very Jenna. She had an agenda, as she always did. A new initiative to introduce to the town council, and she had been gesturing wildly about it in the coffeehouse only a couple of days prior.

She wanted to put together a loyalty program for people shopping local, maybe even an app. As usual, Jenna was incapable of starting small with something like a punch card; she wanted apps and stars and rewards and prizes.

It was part of her charm, but starting small was not in her wheelhouse. Being friends with Jenna meant accepting that about her. Alex admired it. She was always worried about doing the wrong thing. Jenna never seemed afraid of being wrong.

Her house had been filled with silence, and Jenna had always seemed to take that as a challenge to fill it. Her parents hadn't let Jenna's existence crowd their lives, so Jenna had expanded outside the house and made her presence felt everywhere else.

Alex didn't know very many people who could have done that. Somehow found all that confidence in themselves when their parents hadn't given them any.

It was almost as if their total hands-off approach to parenting had placed Jenna in such a way that she simply didn't see boundaries. She'd had to be self-sufficient and self-reliant her whole life. But she didn't do it reluctantly. She did it with verve.

Jenna had been seething at the coffeehouse the other day because her husband had gently pointed out that perhaps she should start analog since the members of the city council, in large part, still did not know how to use smart phones.

Jenna had been incensed by his lack of support. Alex and Chelsea knew that they could not oppose their friend on this, or speak any sort of measured response to her when she was like that.

They would leave it up to Ryan to try and wrangle her, though they didn't think he had ever successfully managed to do that.

In total fairness to Jenna, she had gotten everybody on board with a text alert system for wildfires, which had become a concern in recent years. Of course, they'd been able to use existing warning systems to get it off the ground, but she had amassed a robust list of people who would now receive texts if there was an emergency.

That, too, had been received with a certain amount of skepticism, as she had gestured broadly at the meeting where it had been broached, about fires, floods and any other potential natural disasters.

"What about earthquakes?"

"If there's a way to alert for earthquakes, I'm sure we can arrange it, but I think the essential issue with earthquakes is that you don't get advance notice."

"Well, Oregon is expecting The Big One to hit anytime. We are overdue."

"How can you be overdue for something you can't predict?"

"I listen to the science, Jenna," the woman said, sniffing.

"There's no reason not to warn people about fire just because we can't also warn them about earthquakes. We could use the system for tornadoes, too."

"We don't have tornadoes."

"We have," Jenna insisted.

Alex had said nothing, but surreptitiously pulled her phone out of her purse and googled it. She'd discovered that Jenna was, in fact, correct. Though she imagined anyone living in parts of the country that had real tornado danger would consider what they'd seen to be more of a strong breeze moving in a circular fashion. But still.

Ultimately, Jenna had managed to get the alert system instituted, and Alex felt better for it. So, she supposed, even if her friend swung wildly for the fences, it was often to great effect.

New business at the meetings was sent out ahead of time in a newsletter, so the basics of Jenna's proposal were already out there in the community, but it wouldn't be officially on the table until it was pitched at the meeting.

As soon the meeting began and the question of who had business was introduced, Jenna was up like a bolt of lightning. She began her pitch with a dramatic flourish, and Alex sometimes wondered if even half the words Jenna used were necessary, or if they were simply there for enthusiasm, to add cadence to her pitch as her hands gestured in rhythm with the rise and fall of her voice.

Excitement always seemed to electrify every part of her—her shoulders, her hands, even her hair.

"Thank you for your pitch," Courtney, the acting treasurer for the city council, said, but it was difficult to tell if she was being sincere, as her mouth turned down in a frown, her dark hair a perpetual tangle. Almost as if she dared people to dismiss her because of how disheveled she was. But it was a mistake to dismiss her. She was mean. One of the meanest people Alex knew. The unfortunate thing about city councils, and all other assorted types of boards, was that they tended to be populated with the mean and the petty.

But Jenna wasn't cowed. Jenna was never cowed.

"You're welcome."

"Do we have any direct opposition to Jenna's pitch?"

Very few people ever directly opposed Jenna.

So there was a ripple that went through the room when the new fairy creature in her white dress stood up. She had a folded piece of paper clutched in her pale fingers, her eyes round. "I do. I am Morgan White. Marjorie White's granddaughter."

Marjorie's granddaughter?

She looked at the girl and tried to decide how old she was. She'd pegged her as being in her twenties. She could be Cody's daughter.

Cody…

She looked immediately over at Paul and tried to catch her breath. She didn't think about Cody.

There was no point thinking about Cody.

"She can't be here tonight," Morgan continued. "But she asked me to speak on her behalf. So the objection isn't mine. It's… It's my grandmother's. And… Anyway." She unfolded the piece of paper, which Alex could see had been folded and unfolded multiple times already. "With regards to the pitch made by Jenna Abbott, I would like to remind the council that it was promised that the sidewalks that run along C Street, which impact walking conditions in front of many shops, including Wool Gathering, were supposed to be repaired some years ago, that other initiatives continually jump in front of the renewal project. So I would like to voice opposition to this initiative until the promise to fix the sidewalks has been kept."

The girl sat down quickly, and Jenna popped up. "Who are you again?"

"Marjorie's granddaughter."

But who is your father?

"If Marjorie wants to push an agenda, then she needs to come in person to do it."

"She's sick," Morgan responded.

Alex watched as Jenna's eyes darted back and forth, clearly deciding if there was any way for her to continue pushing without looking like a heartless monster. The thing with Jenna was that she was the furthest thing from a heartless monster, but when she got an idea, all she really wanted was to see it through. And sometimes she could seem insensitive. Just a little. Or maybe a lot.

Alex knew that Jenna meant well. A great many other people did not.

"I hope she feels better soon," Jenna said. "But the sidewalks on C Street are not that bad. And our primary concern should be building incentives for people to shop locally and resist the tyranny of internet conglomerates and big-box interlopers."

"The sidewalks," began Terry Pritchett, her finger held aloft.

"Haven't caused any harm," Jenna finished. "If no one is walking on them, what's the point of worrying about them at all?"

"You had the floor already, Jenna," Courtney said. "The objection is registered, as is your initiative."

As soon as she was done speaking, poor Morgan slipped out the side door.

Alex could only feel sorry for Morgan, who had made a very big mistake. She had been there for only a few minutes, and had already opposed Jenna, which Jenna would find an unforgivable offense.

Even though it was on behalf of Marjorie, Jenna would associate it with Morgan forever. Alex wasn't sure how this feud was going to play out, but she knew it was a feud. Even if poor Morgan didn't know it yet.

6

Afterburn

Chelsea

"I SENT SEAN cookies at school."

Chelsea looked across the dinner table at her mother. The curve of her brow told Chelsea that this was not a benign comment, but the lead-up to a monologue.

Great.

Her father had already gone into his study; to do what, Chelsea didn't know. He was retired, and had been for nearly a decade. But still, Doctor Michael Abbott found ways to keep himself busy, and away from his wife, and by extension, his daughter. It was deeply on brand for the man. When he wasn't in his study, he was golfing.

And that left Chelsea to be the subject of her mother's laser focus.

It made her want to reach into the beyond and elbow Ryan right in the gut.

At least if you were here, we would be talking about your many achievements. But you died. You asshole.

Even his affair hadn't dimmed their mother's admiration for him.

What must it be like to live a life where your mistakes weren't held against you? Chelsea had no idea.

"Great," Chelsea said. "Thank you."

Except that she knew it wasn't that simple. Knew that wasn't why her mother was telling her. "He hasn't sent a thank-you note," she said.

"Mom," she said. "That's a very old-fashioned thing to do." Though, she did think that her son *should* thank her mother. "He should text you. I'll talk to him. He's nineteen and not in touch with his better instincts sometimes."

Her mother looked appalled. "A text?"

"Mom, it's how kids do things." And just saying that sentence made her feel about a thousand years old.

But here she was, a woman with a grown child. So it shouldn't *shock* her that she was firmly very much an adult.

Except it still did.

Sometimes she felt so disoriented. She wondered what had happened to the girl who had arrived at college, unexpressed rebellion burning inside her, with burgundy hair and an early-established nicotine addiction? She'd been the quiet, artsy weirdo who had written things in her diary that might have gotten her put on psychiatric hold if anyone had read them. She'd poured her anger out there; her dreams.

But she'd been too afraid to do anything more explosive than sneak cigarettes and dye her hair unapproved colors. Everything else had remained written down, not shared with anyone.

But then she'd gone to school—art, horticulture and floriculture—and while she'd loved being immersed in the things she was so fascinated by, what she really loved was the freedom.

The feeling that she wasn't performing anymore, or making up for a mistake.

She'd cut loose.

She'd tried everything, and everyone, making sure her rebellion became real rather than simply imagined.

Then, her first year at school, she'd met Mark. He didn't even go to her school. He was twenty-three and working in finance downtown. She'd met him at a bar with her fake ID. It had been the most amazing sex she'd ever had. They'd gone to a fancy hotel, which had felt illicit in a luxurious way that sex in the backseat of a car never could.

But she'd been sure it was a one-night stand.

Once was never going to be enough.

She could still hear him saying that. Could still hear the intensity in his voice, see it on his face.

Mark…

Always the dangerous choice.

Right then she remembered the moment he'd walked into the flower shop after the fire…

"Chelsea." His voice was rough. Like smoke.

"How did you get here so fast?"

Always the dangerous choice.

Her stomach pitched.

She needed to get a grip. Whatever had been…that wasn't the life she was living now. Her husband had moved across the world to get away from her. And now she was sitting at her mother's house for one of her twice-weekly dinners.

She was no rebel. She'd just been off leash for a while.

It shouldn't surprise her, either. This wasn't new.

It was just that Sean's going to college, the separation from Mark, the fire, Ryan's death—it had all disrupted the comfortable life she'd made. It shone a light on her. And she'd never liked that one bit.

"I'm surprised it's how *your* son does things. Because I certainly taught you differently than that."

"Mom…"

"Mark's influence, I imagine." Her mother did not sniff disdainfully, but it somehow felt implied.

You would think that after twenty years of marriage, her mom would have made peace with Mark. But no.

"Mom…"

"I do wish that you would let me set you up with Anna Beth's son…"

Oh, good God.

"No, thank you," she said. "I'm not single."

She'd just had to tell her friends this earlier today. Now she had to tell her mother? She wanted to yell, but Chelsea didn't yell.

Just like she didn't rebel.

She took care of things. She fixed things.

It was infinitely better than breaking them.

She wondered if it was time to bring it up. It had been a year. And her mom was still so firmly fixed in denial, it was beginning to worry Chelsea.

Her mother could be rigid. Her mother lived life with blinders on, maybe because she needed to. But more than anything, she loved her family.

She cared about her children. She *needed* her children.

Ryan was dead.

It sometimes made Chelsea want to apologize, that she was the one left.

That was pathetic. It was just… She'd nearly broken her family once.

She'd skipped school at fifteen. She'd taken the bus to the

larger town next to Tenmile and gone to the movies. And then she'd seen her father, leaving a hotel with a woman she'd never seen before in her life.

She'd had no choice but to tell her mother.

Her mother had packed her bags and left. The fight had been epic.

And her father had called her into his home office, his face a livid purple.

She could remember staring at the rug on his floor, tracing the lines of a vine with her eyes because she couldn't look back up at him.

This is what happens when you break rules, Chelsea. You see things you don't understand. It was a business meeting, and look what you've done. I have to repair what you've broken.

But he'd put his hand on the woman's lower back, and she had touched his chest and laughed. She was sure. Almost sure.

Dad...

You don't understand what you saw. You're wrong.

Eventually her mother had come back.

It was a misunderstanding.

Chelsea had still been afraid it wasn't.

But everyone said it, so firmly, and her mother had come back. She'd been wrong.

That, unfortunately, was a theme in her life.

Being the idiot who read the situation wrong.

She'd spent years after, trying to make up for it, then years running full tilt into everything her mother had warned her not to do.

It hadn't worked, and she'd come back.

Because if Chelsea had learned one thing over the years it was that she couldn't trust herself.

A misunderstanding.

For some reason she saw Mark again. In the flower shop.

She blinked.

"Mom, I did want to talk to you about…doing a memorial. For Ryan."

Her eyes went soft and dewy and Chelsea knew a moment of real regret. "Chelsea… He isn't… They haven't…"

"Mom," she said gently, "if he were alive, he wouldn't be gone, would he?"

"He could be injured or…"

"I don't think so," she said. "And we need to think of his children. They deserve to have some closure. Chloe and Aiden deserve to have some closure. We deserve it."

"Did Jenna ask you to bring this up?"

She and Jenna *had* discussed it, though not recently. "I think that she would like this, yes. And you know you haven't made it so she can talk to you…"

"I didn't know that I had to speak to my son's ex-wife."

"You don't speak to his current partner, either."

"A *partner*." She said that with such disdain. "She isn't a partner. She was…"

"How long can you be mad at all the women in his life without ever being mad at him?"

She knew this was pointless. She did. She also knew she could push, just a little. And then she'd have to back off. She was an expert at managing her mother. She had to be.

"Ryan was special," she said. "He just…"

"He made a bad choice. But I think that Morgan and her child could probably use support."

Saying that made her feel disloyal to Jenna. But she couldn't help but feel some sympathy for the girl.

She *was* a girl. She was maybe twenty now. She'd been nineteen when she'd started dating Ryan. Just barely. She had a baby, and the baby had been born so prematurely… Ryan hadn't met the baby.

"She does need support," her mother said. She looked down for a moment, then back up at Chelsea. "I asked her for custody."

"You did *what*?"

Her mother could barely manage keeping track of herself these days, much less a child. And how had that interaction gone? She couldn't imagine it going *well*.

She wasn't known for her tact.

"I asked her for custody of the child," she repeated as if it was Cheslea who was insane, and not the question.

Her mother's blue eyes—the same color as Ryan's—filled with tears. "She's a piece of him. Another baby. His baby. My grandchild. And I want her. I don't want her living with that…that creature."

"Do you hear yourself?" Chelsea couldn't access her usual patience, or managerial skills, not right now.

"You know she can't offer anything like what we can."

"I imagine she'll be entitled to some of Ryan's life insurance policy once he's declared…"

Her mother had gone frozen. "Don't talk like that."

"Did you really try to take this girl's baby from her?"

"What other choice do I have?"

"*Visiting*. Visiting would be good."

"I have nothing to say to her."

"You can't keep on living like this. Like everything is society stuff and…doctors' wives games. Morgan isn't *beneath* you just because she's…young and doesn't have money. Just because she's Marjorie White's granddaughter."

"I didn't like her uncle either, back when he was running with Ryan and Paul. He wasn't anywhere near their class of person."

Class of person.

What class of person were *they*? Her father wasn't interested in them; her mother was desperate to feel better than everyone around her.

And Chelsea?

She was everything Mark had ever accused her of being. A yes woman, caught between her desire to live her own life and please her family, never quite finding a balance between the two.

And she resented the hold her mother had on her sometimes.

Yes. There was nothing she wanted quite as much as her mother's elusive praise.

She was pathetic. But in that sense, who wasn't? Didn't everyone want that?

When she was finished with dinner, feeling completely defeated since she hadn't made any progress with her mother and, in fact, just felt worn down and uncertain, she staggered into her empty house.

She was tempted to pour herself a glass of wine, but the whole drinking alone thing was probably not her best urge.

Instead, she went to the fridge and got a can of sparkling water, opened it and sat down on the couch with her laptop. It was time for Facebook and zoning out.

She did not look at her husband's profile while she scrolled through. They hadn't unfriended each other or anything like that. That would imply a level of vitriol that simply didn't exist.

She moved her finger over the trackpad, hovered over the search box for a moment and considered typing in his name.

Okay. Maybe she had hidden him. So that he didn't just show up.

Sometimes she could forget about him. Almost. Sometimes she felt like she was living a weird, new life. The family home that they had raised Sean in had burned down less than a month after Mark had gone to Europe. Sean had been away at school for his freshman year. Now he was a sopho-more, and was going to be headed to Germany to visit his dad for Christmas rather than coming back to Tenmile. She couldn't blame him.

Dad in Germany wasn't going to be a permanent thing.

More or less. The whole place had burned to the ground since both of them had left.

She finally clicked over to her notifications and winced when she saw the first one. Chad Staley. She clicked it.

It was a photo of Ryan, and she was tagged in it.

Back in the med school days. Missing this guy today. Went to the bar and had a beer, and tipped an extra one back for Dr. Savage!

She clenched her teeth. She also had a message. From one of her mother's friends.

I think about you daily. Praying for you, Chelsea. And Mark and Sean. If there's anything that you need…

Without thinking, she fired off a response.

Ryan meant so much to all of us. Thank you for the prayers.

Being polite in the face of condolences she wasn't in the mood for had become a habit. It was too bad she'd left her rebel self behind years ago. She'd reverted to her original form. Burgundy hair and cigarettes, but still mostly doing what was expected of her.

Then she went back and liked Chad's photo.

She shut her computer and leaned back against the couch. It was weird, dealing with grief in this internet age, where you could be in one place during the day, but someone else was thinking of him, and so you had to bear witness to their grief. These people who didn't even know Ryan. Ryan was *her* big brother.

Ryan was maddening. Perfect. Except when he wasn't. And she had loved him. Regardless of what he'd done in the last year before his death, she had loved him. And sometimes she wondered if she should contact…

And then she froze up, because she was loyal to Jenna, even when Jenna was annoying. Because Jenna had been Ryan's loving wife for all those years, and her niece and nephew had been so badly hurt by his midlife crisis that hadn't been midlife at all.

"Ryan, you fucking idiot. Couldn't you have held on for one more year? Couldn't you have kept it in your pants for *one more year*? Because you fucking died."

He'd died and her house was empty, and why not shout F bombs at the ceiling at her dead brother. Why not?

He would've had a different legacy. A different story. He just wouldn't have… If you just wouldn't have done that. She wanted to protect Ryan, like her parents always had. Because he was golden. Because he was this perfect specimen, and she couldn't help but want to preserve his myth. Ryan was so great, and she would always smile and say that he was, and never talk about the fact that he had once given her a noogie until she had to elbow him in the nuts to get him to let her go.

It was all regular older brother stuff, of course.

But she had never even wanted to badmouth him by telling a story like that.

And Ryan wouldn't have cared.

Would he? What about the pills?

Okay. There had been the incident with the pain pills in high school. When she'd been accused by her parents of being a pill popper because they'd found a bottle in the house, when they absolutely hadn't been hers.

What about the cigarettes, Chelsea?

Fine. She'd been a smoker since she was fifteen. There was that. But she hadn't been on pills.

They were Ryan's. She was sure of that.

And he hadn't defended her, the weasel. Hadn't confessed.

Her mom and dad certainly hadn't believed her. She'd been proven a liar once before. Even if she hadn't lied about her father on purpose.

No one would believe that Ryan would put a foot out of line.

She was a little more sympathetic to that now, though. Her own kid had been caught with pills he shouldn't have had in his senior year, and as an adult, she'd watched how he'd shut down. Frozen. How could she stay angry at Ryan for not throwing himself on the pyre for her?

Ryan was easy to like. Easy to forgive.

Mark wasn't easy. She had never needed him to be. He'd been strong, and wonderful and they'd had so much baggage…

She missed Mark. But she had broken that. *They* had broken it.

For twenty years she and Mark had barely had a fight. But the feeling of walking on glass had intensified in the last few years. And suddenly, Mark had decided to smash all that glass.

"You let them walk all over you. You let them turn you into a robot. You don't even look at me. You won't fuck me."

"Stop it."

"It's true."

"It isn't anything to do with my family," she said.

"And what is it?"

She couldn't answer him. She couldn't tell him. Because telling him would destroy everything that they were.

"Maybe it's you. Maybe it's you and your secrets."

"Don't give me that."

He was angry. And he had every right to be. He didn't even know how much.

Because she had no right to throw secrets back at him.

"Mark…"

"I swear to God, sometimes I think it's this town. You're the one who wanted to come back here. You're the one who wanted to be near your family. Your life revolves around running between your mother, Jenna and managing your brother's drama. Sometimes I want to burn this place to the ground, do you know that? And then what would you be left with? You wouldn't have anything left to hide behind. Would you?"

The truth was Mark had come back from Germany the day after the fire. And she had no idea how he had made it back that quickly. How he had known. She hadn't told anyone he was there.

She told herself she wasn't sure why. Or that it was emotional.

But she was worried. Because Mark had always been a man of his word.

And Chelsea was wrong about things all the time, after all.

A very small, dark part of herself wondered if she had ever really known her husband. Wondered whether he'd kept his word about burning everything to the ground.

7

Afterburn

Alex

THE HOUSE WAS BEAUTIFUL. As beautiful as it had always been.

Her street had been spared. The houses behind them had burned to dust. Ash.

Like Paul?

The thought made her dizzy. Even a year later.

She couldn't think about that. She hated it. She couldn't think about any of it at all.

It was too hard.

And the locket felt heavy in her apron pocket.

Why now? Why had she gotten it now?

She'd felt fractured since the fire. Had spent the past year trying to cope with flashbacks. With fear. With spiraling PTSD. To have two people in your life go missing—whether or not they were presumed dead—was enough to destroy a person's fragile grip on their control. She knew that for certain.

She did a good job not thinking about it. About that day. About what might have happened. She'd done a good job sweeping away the messy, broken pieces of her memory and deciding they didn't matter.

She'd been burned, but she'd survived. Paul was gone. Nothing else mattered.

But the locket had shattered everything.

She'd begun having dreams that felt like memories. Impossible memories.

Her mother standing in the flames.

She shook her head.

She didn't tell anyone about the necklace. How could she? She already felt crushed beneath the weight of what she didn't know. Beneath the weight of her dreams and fears and flashbacks. Things she wasn't sure were dreams or memories.

It was the *not* knowing. The not knowing was so destructive.

Not knowing whether her mother was gone had haunted her since she was seventeen years old. And now her husband was gone, and there was no body in his case, either.

No closure.

She knew Jenna thought she was being overly optimistic by saying Paul and Ryan were presumed dead. But there was nothing optimistic about it. Not knowing wasn't optimistic. It wasn't about hope. It was the wondering. It ate at you. She knew that for a fact. And now the necklace ate at her. Made her wonder what was true. If her mother… Had her mother sent this to her? Why? Did it have anything to do with Paul's loss? Was it some kind of olive branch, reaching out because of what Alex had been through? She doubted it.

If her mother was out there…

Why would she make contact now? Why only after a tragedy? Not her marriage, or having her first child, or...

She didn't have answers.

And she didn't have time to find them today. She was very, very good at compartmentalizing. Good at looking serene when she wasn't. She had to be. It was how she'd weathered losing her mother, getting pregnant in her last year of high school and still graduating with honors. She could shut out what she couldn't control, and focus on what she could. It was her superpower.

She had baking to do. With fall on the horizon, there was any number of pumpkin treats that needed to be procured, and she enjoyed that. She loved pumpkin spice. Alex Coleman was a basic white girl, but she knew exactly what she was.

It was funny. She *had* known who she was. Dr. Paul Coleman's wife. Baker extraordinaire, former commander of the PTA. Now she had her bakery. She wasn't Paul's wife. Just his presumptive widow. She struggled against that knee-jerk rage inside her. It was just unfair.

He saved people's lives. It was what he did. Daily. And now he was... He was dead. He was dead.

Paul Coleman was dead.

She tried to force herself to truly believe that.

He was one of the unidentified dead. The heat from the fire destroying the ability to ID via DNA or dental records.

She felt like she was being stabbed in the chest. But it was necessary. She had to believe it. Because if she didn't, then it might get lost in the mists of time, and when she got home, she would open the door and expect to see him sitting there on the couch.

She might expect him to come back.

She'd played that game already. For years. She'd hoped her mother would come home for so long and...

She couldn't do it again. She couldn't.

The locket was a cruelty. A mockery of her acceptance.

Why don't you put some tears in the pumpkin spice?

She gritted her teeth. There was no point dwelling. Not on anything. She went into the kitchen and put on her apron. She had a collection of them. Linens in all different colors, elegant gray stripes. But today she chose a lime green apron with oranges on it that said *squeeze me*, because Ruth had bought it for her during her epic graduation trip to Disneyland a few years ago, and Alex liked it.

The ties on the apron wrapped around her waist twice now.

She was a baker. One might expect she would eat her feelings, but her feelings sat in her stomach like a brick and didn't leave room for anything but misery.

Except she wasn't 100 percent miserable 100 percent of the time. Grief was weird like that. It was a long game. So some days everything was good. Some days everything was bad, and some days she was completely fine until that thought would pop into her head. Paul Coleman was missing, presumed dead. And then she would have to press her hand over her mouth to keep herself from screaming.

And the useless, selfish words would echo in her head, over and over.

Why me?

Why me again?

She rubbed her arms, her fingertips brushing over the rough scars there, and bent down to take out some cans of pumpkin. Pumpkin strudel was on the menu today.

She didn't scream. She hummed to herself, all her anguish buried deep inside. The methodical motion of the can opener, the scrape of her spatula against the side of the corrugated can. She watched the pumpkin tumble out into the bowl, dumped cinnamon on top, eggs, sugar, then began to mix it all together. She poured herself into that moment. So that there was nothing else. And she nearly didn't hear the sound of the bell at the front of the shop.

She wiped her hands on her apron and exited the kitchen. The dining room was empty except for the man who had just walked in. She was struck by two things almost simultaneously. First, his looks—because he was handsome. Dark hair pushed back off his forehead, his lean, muscular body hugged by the dark suit he was wearing almost as if it were a second skin. And second, she knew him.

It was *Cody*.

Cody, whom she had thought about more since Morgan White had come to town two years ago than she had in all the other years since she'd seen him.

Cody, who was more beautiful now than he'd been in high school.

And she was standing there in an apron that said *squeeze me*, suppressing screams she'd never let out.

But when she looked at him, she wasn't brought back to the present. It was a hot day, so long ago. Warm brown eyes and a comforting hand on her face…

He'd looked at her like she was the only thing.

She had been young then. Very pretty. And not in this apron.

"Cody. Cody White," she said. Like he didn't know his own name.

"Alex?" The way his eyes squinted when he said that made her want to crawl into the giant mixing bowl in the back and turn on the whisk. Just blend herself to death. Or at least into unconsciousness, so she didn't have to marinate on the fact that Cody White hadn't recognized her. Probably because she looked like a limp dishrag with bags under her eyes.

Tragedy bags. Her constant companions these days. A re-minder that nothing could make her world perfect again.

There was gray in his hair. Right at the temples, and it was sexy. She would like to feel that it was very unjust, but it looked too good for her to even be mad about it.

What is the matter with you? You haven't had thoughts this shallow since…

"Yes," she said.

"Alex Wheeler."

"Coleman."

"Right," he bit the word out. "Sorry."

"What are you doing here?"

"I came to get coffee. It looked like there was coffee here."

"There is. And…goodies. I… I was in the back. I was bak-ing."

"You made all this?" he asked, gesturing toward the bak-ery case.

"Yeah. I did. I do. All of it. From scratch. I mean, I have employees. Who are here occasionally. Just not midmorning on a weekday. We're busy early. Then there's a lull. It'll pick up again in the late afternoon when kids get out of school."

"If only we'd had a place like this to hang out in when we were in high school."

"We still would've smoked cigarettes under the bridge."

That bridge where Paul, Ryan and Cody had jumped into the river, and made Alex afraid they'd die every time. Stupid kids doing stupid things.

"*You* never smoked a single cigarette, Alex, and you know that."

She laughed. Because it was true. She had kept nervous lookout, and had scolded all of them. In contrast to Jenna, who had tossed her hair back and laughed as she'd shared cigarettes with the boys, especially edgy because she'd put her lips where theirs had been.

Alex had simultaneously been so judgmental and so jealous of Jenna.

"I haven't seen you since…"

"Graduation," he finished.

"No. A couple weeks after that. But not since you left for college."

He shrugged. "Yeah."

"Why are you back? This is kind of a… Did you move back? Are you…?"

"No. I'm investigating."

"Investigating?"

"I'm Agent Cody White now. With the FBI. We're investigating the source of the fire in Tenmile." His voice changed when he said that. It was a practiced line, like he was on a cop show.

"*The FBI?* You are FBI? And you're investigating the fire here… The FBI is investigating the fire?"

"Yes. There are no leads and the local agencies have exhausted their resources. So I'm here to look into it. Talk to some people. Do a little bit of digging."

"Oh."

Silence lapsed between them. Very deeply uncomfortable silence. Alex searched for the right thing to say. Because the adult, together version of herself would know what to say.

The frazzle she was now didn't really know. And the teenage version of herself hadn't been able to form a coherent thought around him.

"Have you seen any family since you've been here?"

She realized too late what a loaded question that was. His mother had passed away. Morgan was the only one and she was…

She didn't know what Cody thought about his niece's present circumstances.

That she'd had a baby with an old friend of theirs from high school.

An old dead friend.

The thought was like cannon fire.

"No," he said. "I've just been getting settled and communicating with my department head. Getting the lay of the land."

There was more to it than that, she knew. She also knew she had no right to ask.

"I understand that." She wasn't sure which thing she was claiming to understand.

"I'll probably see you again. I'm in a vacation rental above the place across the street."

"Oh. That's...that's nice." She would see him again. She hadn't even been expecting to see him once.

"Yeah. A big improvement over what the department often springs for."

She lifted a shoulder. "The worst motels burned down."

He chuckled. "I guess that's a win for me?"

"If they hadn't burned down, you probably wouldn't be here at all."

"Good point. Can I just get a black coffee?"

"You're going to come into my bakery after all these years and get a black coffee? You're not going to let me give you any baked goods?"

She looked at him. He was in better shape than he'd been when they were in high school. He been on the slim side then, and now he was well muscled, like a man who spent a decent amount of time in the gym. Not a bit of fat on him. He probably didn't do baked goods.

"Sure. Throw in whatever your favorite is."

"You didn't come back for the funeral."

She shouldn't have said that. It had come out sounding like a mom lecture, and she really hadn't meant to do that.

"Yes, I do know that I didn't come to my mother's funeral."

"Sorry," she said, pressing her hand to her forehead. "It's been a lot. A lot. And I wasn't expecting to… It's been a lot."

"No," he said. "I'm sorry. About what happened to Ryan and Paul…"

"We don't know for sure what happened to them."

"I doubt either of them would leave town."

She bit the inside of her cheek. Jenna was the kind of person who said anything that came to her mind. Alex wasn't. She was much more careful. She always had been. But Cody had always made her want to tell secrets that she never shared, and apparently, twenty-five years apart hadn't changed that.

Looking at him made the locket feel hot in her pocket.

"Ryan did a lot of things in the end that I never thought he'd do," she said slowly. She watched his expression, waited to see his response. Did he know that Ryan had left Jenna for Morgan? She couldn't tell. So she just thought she'd ask. "Did you know that Ryan and Jenna had split up?"

He looked surprised. "No."

"Oh. Well, they did. And… I wonder…"

Cody's expression sharpened. "You wonder what? If he left?"

"I try not to engage in wishful thinking, but sometimes it's hard not to. Maybe he and Paul… I don't know…left together and decided to start over? Not that they were—just because they were friends, you know? It's easier than the alternative thought."

Than accepting that her beautiful husband had been burned beyond recognition.

"Anything is possible, and I'm here to explore every avenue. I have all the documentation from the various agencies but… I'm coming at it from a fresh angle. New set of eyes. So…information like this is valuable."

She poured him a cup of coffee, then reached into the bakery case and took out one of her apricot oat bars, which everyone liked. She knew he would enjoy it.

"Here," she said. "No charge."

"You don't need to give me free coffee."

"It feels weird to charge an old friend." The word was so inadequate. Dishonest. She could see that reflected in his eyes. "I'll see you."

His gaze flickered behind her and she fought the urge to look over her shoulder to see exactly what he was seeing. "See you."

He turned and walked out of the coffeehouse, like he hadn't been there. She looked around at the red brick walls, the shelves with little ceramic animal figurines on them and the bistro tables. It was empty.

And she might have hallucinated Cody.

Except she had spent twenty-four years basically not thinking of him at all. So why would he appear now?

He had to be real.

All of this was real. Cody and lockets and Paul's being gone.

Thankfully, she was very good at compartmentalizing.

8

Afterburn

Morgan

MORGAN WHITE OFTEN wondered why she was still in Tenmile. Maybe because she felt like she had a to-do list from her grandmother. Maybe because she felt like she had to oversee the rebuilding of the farmhouse on the property Marjorie had loved so much.

Marjorie had loved her. Unconditionally. Even after everything with Ryan...

Living in Tenmile had its downsides, but Marjorie's friends had rallied around her.

Anyway, she didn't have another idea for where she might want to raise Lily.

Her own childhood had been a series of shitty apartments and dangerous situations. Men with alcohol on their breath and hands that did what they wanted while her mom was passed out in the corner.

She wanted something more. Something better for Lily. Here, she had a job. A business. Land, too, when the house got rebuilt. All inherited from Marjorie. More than she'd ever dreamed she could have.

There might be issues here, sure, but she just didn't have the heart to start over. Again.

At least here she had the yarn store. The little community had grown up around that. Years ago. And sure, they were all in their fifties and sixties with the exception of a few hipster girls that were very into the fiber arts, but it was something. And it had given Morgan something to pour herself into. She loved the shop. She loved the business. Moving it would be risky when her client base was here.

It was a beautiful, idyllic little town.

Except for the people who hated her.

Except for all the places that were burned to ash.

She blinked and turned back to the shelf full of yarn. She'd been rearranging stock all afternoon. It was soothing. The colors and textures of the yarn were sensory delights, and she found it incredibly mindful to move the different skeins around to different bins, different shelves, different displays. Organized by weight or color, brand or fiber. Sometimes the old ladies got snippy with her for moving stock, but mostly, they enjoyed seeing something new.

"Mama!"

"Morgan, dear?"

The two voices called to her at the same time.

One was Lily, from her playpen, because she was mobile now and while she tried to just keep anything little off the low shelves, it was a lot of work to have a toddler running around a yarn store.

The other was Edna Wilson, who had been her grandmother's friend and a longtime patron of the store.

"Yes, Edna?"

"Go get Lily. I can talk while you hold her."

Morgan went over and picked Lily up from her playpen, the smell of her, the warm weight of her body, sending a wave of longing through Morgan. A longing to be able to just feel an uncomplicated, unpainful love.

But it always hurt.

"I need something dark, in worsted, for a sweater I'm knitting for my grandson."

She had met Edna's grandson a few times. Tall, with green eyes and an easy smile. "How about this?" She went to a shelf with merino wool and took a forest green skein from the shelf.

"Oh, this would be perfect for Tyler! I need six skeins," she said as she examined the yardage on the tag.

"Okay. Do you want it wound?"

"Only if I can hold Lily while you do it."

She transferred Lily to Edna and felt a small, guilty sense of relief, then went to the swift with the skeins to start the process of winding them into balls.

It was a soothing task. She loved to watch the swift spin and the ball grow.

But it also gave her time to let her mind wander.

There was a town council meeting tonight, and it was so difficult for her to bring herself to attend. She could clearly remember that first disastrous meeting, when she had first made an enemy of Jenna Abbott and her friends.

It had been the beginning of the end as far as her inclusion in that social circle.

It had only gotten worse from there.

And now she had a rock of anxiety in her gut before every meeting, and if it had not been so important to her grandmother, she just wouldn't.

But she didn't know where else to raise Lily.

She lived for the little old ladies. For her knitting projects. For the simple pleasure of reorganizing a bin of yarn, because there just wasn't much else.

She hadn't figured out how to live for herself.

So yeah. That was why she stayed. Because there would be an equal amount of nothing anywhere else.

And here, there wasn't...nothing.

But there was a town council meeting.

It was weird. Living.

She shouldn't be alive.

It was...

She'd been so close to not making it through the fire.

She should have been at home. Likely asleep. She should have burned alive in that house. But she hadn't. And she was struggling to figure out why. Why she was here. Not just in town, but here at all. The fire hadn't killed her.

But the wondering might.

9

Kindling

Chelsea

"YOUR MOM WAS in rare form tonight." Mark's tone made it clear this was not an isolated comment, but the beginning of a whole conversation she didn't want to have.

Chelsea bent down and took a bowl out of the bottom drawer of the dishwasher. It gave her something to do, something to keep her hands busy.

What made her angriest was that Mark wasn't wrong. Her mom was taking the pressure of an already difficult situation and turning it up, but part of her couldn't help but wonder if she was right, and…

"Maybe she has a point," she said.

"What? That he had prescription pills in his bag because he goes to public school? That if we would've just sent him to Saint Mary's, everything would be fine?"

"I don't know that *everything* would be fine," she said, still reeling from the discovery that her son had pills that weren't prescribed to him. He'd played it off, said that they were messing around with them in a group, and that it wasn't an ongoing thing, it was just that he'd ended up carrying them because he had trusted his parents not to go through his things.

He'd said this wounded and accusatory. Like she was the bad guy.

She had told him that trying to make sure he hadn't left a disgusting water bottle in his backpack was hardly *going through his things*. And if he wanted to rebel then maybe he should be a little neater and cleaner.

Sean was so *close*. He was a senior in high school. He was doing really well. The drugs seemed entirely out of character.

And worse, Mark was not panicked about it. *She* felt panicked.

She knew how important it was to make good decisions. How life could spiral out of control if you didn't.

She knew how important it was to stay on the straight and narrow.

And she felt like having a fight. She wouldn't yell. He would. And she wanted to push him there.

"Maybe we *should* have sent him to private school. We were being stubborn about it, and we didn't want them to pay…"

"I don't need your mom to pay for our kids to go anywhere. We decided that he should go to public school because we went to public school and we turned out fine."

"Yes, I know…"

"I don't get that. You and Ryan went to Tenmile High School, so why is your mother suddenly so opposed to it?"

"Because when they moved Saint Mary's, it became more feasible for the kids to go there, and it has a great reputation for being an elite school and if it hadn't been a half hour away when we were younger, Mom definitely would've sent us there."

"I don't like that elitist bullshit. You know that."

"Well, maybe a little bit of elitist bullshit would've kept opioids out of our son's backpack. That is really serious. The opioid crisis—"

"Right. The opioid crisis that the doctors are responsible for prescribing us into."

"Are you really making this about my dad and brother right now?"

"No. But I am a little bit making it about the influence your family still has over you."

"Mark…"

"I'm surprised they didn't come out and say they blamed me for this. And by the way, you shouldn't have told them about the pills. That should have been between us. We don't need your parents inserting themselves."

"I tell my mother things," she said.

"Why? Why the fuck do you put yourself through this, Chelsea?"

The angrier he got, the calmer she purposed to be. She had to temper her reactions, in case they were the wrong ones.

Whatever her first instinct was, Chelsea had learned to question that.

"They're my family," she said slowly. "I love them. You act like they're monsters. They're just used to things going a certain way and—"

"They treat you like shit. They treat Ryan like a god. They hate me because I'm not the kind of man they thought their daughter would end up with."

She felt like she was going to explode, but she kept her voice measured.

"How can they have had lofty goals for me if they don't hold me in any kind of esteem? Make up your mind." That was a lot more snappish than she usually got, but she was tired.

She was tired and she hated fighting. She tried to avoid it as much as possible. For most of their marriage, they had managed.

When things had been difficult, she just… She pushed it down. And she kept going. She didn't deserve to be upset.

Lately, it was harder and harder to keep it at bay.

And her worries about Sean were only making it worse.

"You weren't like this when we met." He couldn't have shocked her more if he'd hit her. "You were… You were wild. You were pushing back against them, and then you decided you wanted to move back and open your flower shop here. That you wanted to come back to *this*. And you've been… Sometimes I see *you*. The woman that I married. And sometimes… I don't know."

His words caused a trickle of fear to wash through her. Ice-cold.

"What are you saying?"

He shook his head. "Nothing."

"Except, it seems like you were saying something."

"What if I confirmed it for you? For your parents? That this is my fault."

"What are you talking about?"

"I went through a rebellious phase in high school. You know my home life was shit." He let out a long, slow breath. "I have a record, Chelsea."

She just stared at him. Like he was a different person. "What?"

"Well, I don't actually have the record. I was a juvenile, and it was expunged when I reached adulthood. At that point I had scholarships to go to school, and I had turned things around."

"What did you… What did you go to jail for?"

"Possession. Robbery. If Sean is going through something, maybe it's me. Maybe it's that bad blood shit."

"Why didn't you tell me this? How could you—in all these years, this never came up."

"I told you I had a bad childhood."

"And in none of those conversations did you mention that you had gotten *arrested*."

"More than once, too. Does that change how you feel about me?"

He was daring her to call him a lowlife. A deadbeat. To fling everything at him that she knew her mother would think. He thought she was her mother, somewhere deep down. She knew that, too.

She'd always wanted Mark. Everything he was. It wasn't fair that he didn't believe that.

"No. I don't care about that. It's the fact that you had a secret."

The words pressed hard against her chest. Called her a hypocrite.

"I didn't think of it that way. I put it behind me. I never thought of it again. I have never given anyone specifics about it. It's not part of who I am now. There's not anything about me that has happened since you and I met that you don't know about."

He was sincere. She could see it.

"Don't tell my mother."

"That's all you have to say? Don't tell your mother?"

"I'm sorry. But don't. I don't... I need time to process it. Not because it bothers me that it happened, but because you didn't tell me."

"I intend to tell Sean. I intend to tell him that I didn't work this hard—you didn't work this hard—to give him a good home and good opportunities to have him fuck around just because he's looking for fun. I got into that stuff because I was desperate. It's not an excuse. But I didn't have the opportunities that he has. And if he needs to hear my story to absorb that, then fine."

"I don't know. Considering how successful you ended up after your little stint as a criminal, I'm not sure it's a great deterrent."

"I just want to be honest with him. I only have one chance to do right by my kid. God knows my parents didn't do right by me. And neither did yours, Chelsea, whether you can see that or not."

"Please," she said. "One issue at a time."

"That's one more than usual," he said.

He left her standing there, a half load of dishes in the dishwasher and a bowl in her hand.

She hadn't known that her husband of nineteen years had a criminal record.

Yet again, she'd been wrong about one of the people in her life she should know best.

She set the bowl into the dishwasher, then gripped the edge of the counter.

If she couldn't trust Mark, she couldn't trust anything.

10

Ignition Point

Morgan

SHE WAS ALONE in bed, which was unusual since Ryan had moved in. Actually, she couldn't remember if Ryan had come to bed at all last night.

And everything hurt. Her back, her stomach… She wasn't that pregnant. Well, she was fairly pregnant, but not so much that everything should hurt. Not yet.

It was early afternoon, but she hadn't managed to rouse herself yet.

She put her hand on her stomach and felt it get tight. Impossibly tight. Along with it came a stabbing sensation low in her stomach.

Braxton Hicks. She'd heard of those. False labor. But this felt too…

Suddenly, the pain came on impossibly sharp and hard. And she leaned forward, unable to breathe.

This wasn't right.

She called out for him, because he should be in the house.

No. Maybe not? She didn't know when he was supposed to go to work today. And her grandmother wasn't here, either. Because…she was gone.

The pain of grief was blunted by another pain that shot straight through her stomach.

She had to get to the hospital.

She picked up her phone, but she didn't have any service. There should be service. All she had was four dots where the bars should be.

She grabbed her keys and, clutching her stomach, made her way out to the driveway. To her car. She started the engine. She was only five minutes from the hospital. It would be okay.

It would be okay.

She repeated the mantra to herself as she drove the harrowing few miles down the highway to the hospital.

The emergency room? Did she need the emergency room?

She parked her car out front and got out, and then another pain shot through her abdomen. This time worse. Going deeper and deeper. She couldn't help it. She screamed. And that was when a nurse came running out of the sliding glass doors.

"How far along are you?"

"Only… I'm only twenty-eight weeks."

"Okay, honey," the nurse said. "Let's get you inside."

11

Afterburn

Jenna

IT HAD BEEN over a year since she had been able to turn to Ryan and ask if her meeting outfit was appropriate. The right amount casual, the right amount put together, the right amount professional. Effortless, but thoughtful. Dressing was an art form as far as she was concerned. And the worst thing that she could ever project was the idea that she was attempting art.

Alex had always been one of those women who was beautiful without effort. She woke up like that, and it was as irritating now as it had been in high school. Alex complained about what the years had done to that beauty, but Jenna still thought her friend was drop-dead gorgeous. She was always telling Alex that the perk of age was realizing your looks were for you. She'd believed it, too. Turning forty had been great for Jenna. She'd never felt more confident. Until Ryan had left her for a nineteen-year-old. That had put a dent in things.

In general, she didn't care anymore if her weight fluctuated a few pounds—she looked great for a woman in her forties who had two children. Or maybe she was just a woman in her forties who had two children, and therefore didn't have the ability to care what anybody thought about her weight.

She had learned that if you carried yourself with the right kind of self-assurance, people were drawn to you, and it was less about the arrangement of the features on your face, or if you had lines by your eyes, and more about your smile, and your confidence.

Granted, the word *confidence* had been weaponized against Jenna many times in her life, but her thirties had been a journey to reclaim that word, and her forties would be all about owning it.

She didn't need everyone to like her. She was happy with the people who *did* like her.

Of course, the sad truth was, part of her confidence had come from her long-term relationship. She'd been secure in it. And when Ryan said she looked good, she believed him.

She had.

Rage had carried her through the separation. But his dying... That was so unsatisfying. There was no character arc. None. That was what made her angriest. He had done the worst thing he had ever done to her—the worst thing he had ever done—and he had died just a few months later. However, it all might've worked out...

You were not seriously considering taking that man back. Even if he came crawling on his knees on broken glass, you would not have taken him back.

She felt off-kilter then. It was pointless to think about. She wanted to believe that she wouldn't take him back. But they'd had two children. And twenty-six years as a couple, eighteen married. That was annoying. To not even have made it to twenty.

She didn't know why that was annoying. It just was.

She looked at her reflection critically. She had to be her own husband. Okay, that was a weird way of putting it. But as a metaphor, it stood.

She took one last look at herself. Black jeans, ankle boots, oversize sweater. It made her look softer. Maybe that would make her words seem softer, too. Which she didn't care about, except when it came to whether she got her way. It wasn't about what anyone thought about her.

Her phone flashed a text, letting her know that Alex was in her driveway. They were carpooling tonight, but Chelsea was coming directly from the flower shop, so she was meeting them there.

Jenna was living in a row of town houses about thirty minutes outside Tenmile. Rental options were slim in town, but soon, the commute situation would be resolved. The town houses were okay, but they were cramped, and Jenna didn't really care for sharing the wall with her boisterous neighbors who were prone to loud fights and louder sex.

She grabbed her purse and went downstairs. "Bye, kids," she shouted. "I love you. There's Cup O' Noodles and frozen chicken pot pies."

Nobody answered. So she unlocked her phone and pulled up the family group text, which was signified by a frog emblem and the name *Bleh*, which Jenna was reasonably certain Chloe was responsible for, but she didn't know how to change it.

She was walking out the front door while she texted the exact same thing she'd just shouted.

Kk from Aiden.

And a thumbs-up emoji from Chloe.

"Really too bad that I'm leaving, because I'm sure we would spend some quality time together tonight." She was still muttering when she got into the car with Alex. Then she straightened and looked ahead. "Onward!"

"What were you muttering about?"

"My children. And their general lack of interest in my existence. You know, you would think that, given their recent trauma, they would want to cling to their remaining parent?"

"It comes with maturity," Alex said, pulling away from the curb. "Jack and Ruth check in on me like it's their sacred duty. Of course, neither of them live here, so they're much more interested in speaking to me when they know it can be a quick phone call or a text, and I can't actually tell them what to do."

"I'm not sure I can tell mine what to do. It might all be a farce. They could be sneaking out every night. Doing drugs and giving blow jobs behind the Minute Market by the freeway entrance. I wouldn't know."

Alex's eyes never wavered from the road. It made Jenna want to shout *blow jobs* and see if she reacted. "You really think they're doing that?"

She wrinkled her nose. "No. Or I probably wouldn't joke about it."

"Tough to say, Jen. You might," Alex said.

"Are you mad at me?" It was a knee-jerk question she hadn't meant to ask. Because she was trying to own all that confidence, but when it came to her friends, she still did worry about whether her mouth had run away with her too many times over the past few days.

"No," Alex said.

Alex reached into her purse—no kidding—and pulled out a bag that had a turnover in it, and started to eat it as they drove down the road.

"And you didn't offer me one?"

"It's my dinner," Alex said.

"Are you taking care of yourself?" Her friend was eating pastries at 6 p.m., which wasn't really alarming. It was the fact that she was eating pastries at 6 p.m. *and* still looked thinner than she ever had in the time that Jenna had known her. She had a feeling the pastry was the only thing she'd eaten. And she wondered for how many days that'd been true.

"That's a loaded question," Alex said.

"It's not. Or at least, I don't mean it to be."

"I'm keeping my business going. I'm not lying around at home, buried beneath a pile of candy bar wrappers. So…"

"Thanks for coming to get me. I'm sorry. I'm probably the reason you had to eat pie for dinner."

"Don't feel sorry for me because I ate homemade pie for dinner. I certainly don't. I'm not normal, Jenna. What does normal look like right now?"

"I don't know. And I handle that by being irreverent. I hope you realize that. And I also understand that you…do that a little bit less. So I'm sorry if I am sometimes so busy making fun of my life that it rubs up against your pain."

"Jenna, I know you. I don't take it personally. I understand that you're not talking about me."

"No. Paul was a great guy." Jenna felt suddenly overcome by grief. It was a strange thing. Because usually, she was just so mad. And she could keep her focus on her own pain, and then her desire to activist her way out of that pain, that she didn't marinate too much on the rest of what had been lost.

That her children had lost their father, and that their relationship with him had been bad, so much so that their grief was challenging and complicated in a way it shouldn't be. She hated that. She hated him for that, and she hated herself a little bit for it, too, because maybe, if she had kept some of her own pain under wraps, they wouldn't be quite so angry with him.

And then there was the rest of the loss. So many people were touched by those who had died or who were yet to be identified…

Maybe if Ryan had left.

Left left. Not just her.

She wondered sometimes. If he had just decided to up and leave everything. Including his lover.

Except… He wouldn't do that.

It was the weirdest thing that she thought it. Because he had done something to her that she had never imagined he would do. Somehow, in his head, he had twisted whatever he was doing into something that was okay. What she couldn't imagine was him doing the mental gymnastics that would be required to do it again so quickly after having done it the first time.

You don't know it was the first time. Maybe he cheated on you all through your marriage.

Well. She wasn't going to think about that.

But Paul… She'd known him as long as she'd known Ryan. He had always been a good friend. A good man. A good husband to Alex. He was just… She'd been friends with him in her own right, since high school, and he'd been loyal to Ryan, even after the divorce, and she couldn't hate him for that because it was, well, it was loyal. And he'd never been unfriendly to her.

She felt far too aware now that she was predictably stuck in her own malaise and pushed other people's pain to the side so that she could wallow in her own.

"I'm not a very good friend sometimes," Jenna said.

"You're the *best* friend," Alex said. "You're always there when anybody needs you. Ferociously and fiercely."

"And I always say whatever pops into my head."

"Yeah. We never have to guess where we stand with you. It's part of your charm."

"This was not our dream, Alex. It just wasn't. Those girls who graduated Tenmile High and had so many dreams about what they were going to do… It was never supposed to end this way. Paul should be here with you. And, you know, Ryan should have been with me. I should be grieving him the way that you're grieving Paul, and I'm kind of mad that I can't. Not that it looks fun. But I'm stuck in this weird place where… I miss him. I did. I mean, I've missed him ever since he left, in spite of the fact that I also wanted to rearrange his face. But it's like I never got to fully accept the fact that he wasn't with me anymore, and now he's just not here."

They moved from the rentals to the new construction and into the skeletal trees, the burned-out mobile home park signs. The debris from the houses was long since cleared, but ghosts still lingered.

"It's okay for you to feel a lot. And to not have any idea what you feel. And you don't have to say that your pain isn't the same as mine, or isn't as much," Alex said.

"It's all a little bit too much. If I think about it. I wasn't in love with him anymore. But he was the father of my children and I loved him more years than I didn't. And I loved Paul, too."

"Yeah," Alex said, shoving the last of the pie into her mouth. "It is all a little bit much."

"Is there anything not depressing happening in your life?"

Alex shook her head and stuffed the plastic bag back down into her purse. "No. I mean, there are plenty of neutral things. It's just that… You know."

"Yeah. You know, you don't have to be the one to pitch the bouncy house."

"I know."

"I can do it."

The corner of Alex's mouth twitched. "You're going to do it, Jenna."

"Oh."

Alex laughed and shook her head. "I never figured I would. You're going to get nervous I won't do it right, and you're going to do it for me."

"I don't have to."

"No. You do. I won't do it right. And I don't want to have to deal with the fallout of your disappointment."

Jenna shook her head. "There's a moratorium on disappointment between us. We've had too much disappointment. We are living broken dreams."

Jenna had been living broken dreams going on eighteen months, and she was really tired of it. Really tired of overlapping grief on top of grief. Really tired of everything.

"This is a good outfit?" Jenna asked, right as they began to drive by the section of road that was still all twisted and burned.

"It's a great outfit."

She looked over at Alex. "You didn't look."

"I'm driving. I saw when you got in, but also, your outfits are always good."

"Thank you. I try."

"It never looks like it. It just looks like you…are magically fashionable."

Jenna smiled and let her head fall back on the headrest.

12

Afterburn

Alex

SHE REALLY SHOULD'VE told Jenna about running into Cody. And she didn't know why she hadn't. It was just the thought of saying Cody's name out loud made her stomach do this weird sweeping thing that it had done in high school, and it made her feel like a child, and it made her feel ridiculous, and she didn't want to feel ridiculous.

Cody White would forever occupy a very difficult spot in her memory. He had been one of her closest friends at one point in time. But it had gotten twisted up in teenage hormones and her own grief. He was bound up in a time in her life when everything had gone wrong, and she had behaved badly as a result.

At least with him.

She'd really done things wrong with him.

She and Paul were meant to be, obviously. She'd gotten

pregnant. And they had two beautiful children. She could never regret that.

And if she had entertained a fantasy or two of what would've happened if she and Cody had ever...

She was human. And she had been married for a very long time, which consequently meant that sometimes she indulged in an illicit fantasy or two.

Jenna just told the group things like that. That sometimes she thought about Aquaman or Jamie from *Outlander*, because cheating in your head wasn't a thing.

Alex never talked about things like that.

She thought of Cody, standing in her bakery, wearing a suit. He was... Well, he still pushed all the buttons for her. Maybe he wasn't *pretty*. He was *rugged*. That was the thing. He had always been off-limits. He had always been...

You are not a teenage girl.

She had dropped Jenna off at the front of the country club and was searching for a parking spot. She was glad she had managed to extricate herself from giving that presentation. She had known that Jenna would do it. Mostly. But she had been nervous it would fall to her to do it. And she really didn't want that.

She had been the valedictorian of her graduating class. But that had been easy.

Except, she could still see that empty chair next to her dad. And that was never going to be easy.

But she had known what she was going to say.

Empty chairs. There were way too many empty chairs in her life.

Cody had felt like an empty chair in a lot of ways. He shouldn't. Just another person who had left her life when she didn't want him to.

She pulled into the parking spot and flattened her palms

against the steering wheel and tapped it four times. Not really hitting it, but trying to do something to get the nervous energy out of her system. Trying to do something to…stop her thoughts for being quite so tangled.

Then she looked into her rearview mirror, fixed her makeup, fussed with her hair and got out of the car. She didn't bother to lock it.

Paul had hated that. They had those cars that started with the push of a button, and she was notorious for leaving the remote inside the car, so if anybody wanted to steal it, they would just have to get in and push the button.

He'd told her that the insurance would probably take a dim view on that should their car ever get stolen.

We live in a small town. Nothing ever happens here.

That memory, that thought, immobilized her, right there in the middle of the parking lot.

Nothing ever happens here.

Until the whole place burned to the ground. And burned her husband along with it.

You didn't know to be worried about that. Just the car getting stolen.

Her feet felt like blocks of cement. And she was worried if she took a step forward, she might fall down.

"Hey."

She looked up to see Chelsea walking toward her.

Chelsea was finishing what looked to be the last of a fast food burrito and trying to tie her red hair up into a ponytail. Chelsea was an odd bird. Alex liked her well enough but she'd always had the feeling her husband didn't like Paul very much. Whenever they invited them to a barbecue, there had been a fifty-percent chance of Mark's avoiding it.

As far as Alex went, she liked Chelsea. They just didn't actively hang out without Jenna. She was Jenna's sister-in-law and that was how Alex thought of her.

Plus, if she was honest, Chelsea still had alt-girl vibes and Alex half expected her to call her a preppy and scoff at her hoop earrings or something.

She'd been like that. All snotty when Alex started dating Paul. They were fine now, but she sometimes had the feeling those early interactions had cemented the fact they'd never be BFFs.

She was fine talking to Chelsea casually. But she also suspected, if not for Jenna, nothing would have kept them connected.

"The empty-nest life is treating you well, I see," Alex said.

"Why do you say that?" she asked, her mouth full as she crinkled up the paper the burrito had been wrapped in.

"Because you're also eating dinner on the run like I am rather than sitting down and taking care of yourself."

"Hey, I live for myself. I can. We can," she said.

"Yeah," Alex said.

Except she didn't have any practice at that. She had lived to do right. To make her parents proud. She had lived to make her dad proud after her mother...

She had lived to make the town proud, too. Or maybe envious. With her kids being such overachievers, who had gone on to their top schools and were doing great there, in spite of what a terrible year it had been.

"I'm bad at it, too," Chelsea said. "My version of self-care is a steady stream of reality TV and food that I can cook in the microwave." She pulled a cigarette out of her purse and lit it with the lighter that followed.

It was funny. Alex hated the smell of cigarette smoke. But it just felt like an extension of Chelsea. It didn't bother Alex when it was Chelsea.

Alex was basically only eating what she made at the bakery, because she certainly couldn't be bothered to cook for herself. And she had a feeling that Chelsea could see that, but was also not going to say anything.

"I want to figure out how to embrace what I have left." She didn't have to say the *but*. She figured that Chelsea would be able to guess what all of them were.

"It's not going to change anything if you don't."

That wasn't true for Chelsea, though. She could call Mark and reconcile with him today if she wanted to. And for some reason, right then, Alex was unreasonably enraged that she didn't. That she wouldn't. Because Jenna hadn't chosen to lose her husband. Alex hadn't chosen to lose hers. But Chelsea had.

That wasn't fair. You didn't know someone's marriage if you weren't in it.

And she did her best to push that out of her mind. To not think of it again. And to keep a smile on her face. She really hoped that Chelsea hadn't noticed. She really hoped that Chelsea had picked up on the fact that, for a moment, Alex had been so viscerally angry with her she couldn't breathe.

Chelsea chucked her barely smoked cigarette onto the asphalt and ground it precisely under the toe of her boot.

"Let's go." She scrunched her nose and pursed her lips. "Do I have burrito on my face?"

"No," Alex said.

The area around the country club was immaculate. Flowers planted in little rows with fine bark in between them, giving it all a lush, uniform appearance. The building itself had stately wood columns, and an overly grand entryway.

Alex had always felt like any and all attempts to climb the social ladder in Tenmile were laughable at best. It was a stepladder. Or maybe one of those stools that little kids used in front of the bathroom sink so they could wash their hands.

Their town council meetings were always held at the country club, which, in Alex's opinion, spoke volumes about just how *not* bougie Tenmile was. The country club couldn't survive on membership alone. It was also available for rent.

School fundraisers, weddings, town council meetings.

Jenna didn't take it seriously as a status symbol. For Jenna, it was all about making the town the best that they could. Chelsea and Alex supported Jenna, and also, given that they owned businesses on the main street, they were absolutely invested in the different ordinances that came across the desks of the town council.

But there were a lot of people who were overly involved in the whole thing, and wanted to be there, making decisions because they thought it made them special or gave them some kind of clout.

Oh well. At least the meetings were never boring.

It was just too bad she didn't thrive on conflict in quite the same way that Jenna did.

Jenna was already sitting in her seat. Perched on the end of it, in fact.

"She's in a mood," Chelsea said.

"You don't have to tell me that. I drove over with her."

She felt a little mean for having said that. Except, both of them would have said it to Jenna's face. Happily. And Jenna wouldn't have minded.

"We should have made banners. In support," Chelsea said. "It would have pissed everyone else off."

"If we start bringing banners, that's a precedent I'm not sure we want to set." Though, she had once had a great many reasons to make banners. Her kids' football games, bake sales, spirit rallies. Maybe it would make her feel engaged again.

Now, that was getting a bit weird. She didn't need to channel her maternal angst into Jenna. She couldn't tell what was maternal angst anymore, what was grief and what was just…

"I should've brought more pie," Alex said.

"Hell, yeah, you should have," Chelsea said, elbowing her. "I want some pie."

"Sorry."

"It's supposed to be a compliment." Chelsea looked at her, her expression growing more concerned, and that made Alex feel even angrier. "Let's sit down."

And then she looked up and saw a dark figure wearing a perfectly cut suit walk into the room and take his position at the back.

13

Kindling

Morgan

SHE HAD TRIED to tell her grandmother that she didn't think she should go to the Harvest Festival assembly event at the country club. Not today. Not after what had happened when she had gone to the September meeting.

But her grandmother had insisted. And given that, other than an uncle who always remembered to send her a card on her birthday, Marjorie White was the only person who treated her like she mattered in her family; she had to do what she said.

There were just so many rules here and she didn't know any of them. She'd clearly run afoul of Jenna Abbott from the moment she'd opened her mouth, and while she hadn't been mean… She was the kind of woman who intimidated Morgan.

She was so confident, the kind of person who knew the rules, but probably chose to break them, anyway. Which was infinitely better than doing the wrong thing because you had no clue at all what you were doing.

Right now she had no clue what she was doing.

When she walked in, there was a passel of women all standing around a table, doing things with…dried straw and glue guns?

Jenna was giving instructions to the group on how to assemble scarecrows.

Two months ago Morgan would never have believed she would be doing shit like this. Suburban housewife stuff. Community involvement. She'd never had a community before; therefore, had never had community involvement.

When Jenna clocked her, Morgan had the instinct to turn and run. But Jenna did something so completely shocking, Morgan just stood there. Frozen.

She smiled.

She started to walk quickly toward Morgan and turned her ankle slightly, wobbling for a second before righting herself, and never once slowing pace.

"Hi," she said, brightly. "Morgan. Right?"

"Yes," she said. "I wanted to come and help out. I'm…"

Jenna's brow wrinkled. "Are you officially taking your grandmother's place on the MSBC? Because we will have to have a referendum."

"We do not have to have a referendum," said a woman standing next to Jenna. She had auburn hair—clearly not natural—and matching lipstick. "She's grandfathered in. *Grandmothered* in?"

"Yes. Of course," Jenna said, but she looked worried. She looked around for a moment, then back at Morgan. "We could really use help with the spiders. They're made with puff balls and pipe cleaners. There's a sample one over there on the table."

"Do I need a…spider referendum to do that?"

That had come out a little more sarcastic than she'd intended.

Jenna looked like she was trying to decide whether she was offended. Whether to answer seriously. Or smile. "We don't need… There's no… We don't need a referendum for individual crafts."

"Good to know."

She did that. Got a little prickly when she felt unsure.

Jenna didn't seem to notice or care, though. She just waved Morgan off to the spiders with a newly fixed smile. It was a sparse group over there. Jenna had been welcoming, but she hadn't brought her into the scarecrow group, which she thought might be top tier Tenmile ladies only.

But Morgan was completely fine with working on the spiders. She didn't need to make friends. Her life was a mess. But she wasn't so desperate she needed to befriend the queen bees of the…quilting circle or whatever this was.

This wasn't her life.

Except…isn't it going to be? Isn't this your plan?

Maybe. Maybe not. Maybe she would leave after Marjorie…

Well, she was here taking care of her grandmother, so presumably when she died the inheritance would be Morgan's. And maybe some people would think that was a little bit craven. Thinking of it like that. They didn't know what she'd been through.

They didn't know what it was like to sleep on the streets. To wonder if you were going to survive the night. She needed this connection. And she needed to not mess it up.

She went over to the table filled with black puff balls, googly eyes and pipe cleaners. And she was actually pretty grateful to have been given this task. It did look simple. And she was by herself. She was totally comfortable with that. Completely and totally comfortable with her own company.

In fact, living with Marjorie was kind of weird. It was good. She liked it. The farmhouse was lovely, warm and historic. The lighting inside was soft and yellow, and there were floral patterns all over everything. The lampshades, the couches, the curtains. It was nostalgic, even though Morgan was pretty sure the last time she would have been to the house was when she was two years old. The last time her mom had really been in contact with her own mother.

But then, her mom was only intermittently in contact with anyone. Meth was her primary contact. The main thing that she kept in touch with. The rest of them? They were incidental.

Marjorie had always kept in touch, but it had been a surprise when her grandma had asked her to come.

I don't want to spend my final days alone…

"Do you want something to drink?"

She turned around, and for a moment she was struck… dumb. The man who was talking to her was quite possibly the best-looking man she had ever seen in her life. His eyes were brown and kind. He was too old for her. Probably in his early forties. But the connection that she felt was electric and instant all the same.

His eyes flickered up and down, the only real indication that he might've felt it, too. Had stopped to look her over. She was familiar with men checking her out. It was a common thing, but usually, it made her skin crawl. Made her feel threatened. Made her wonder how much it was going to cost her. Not him.

"I didn't know there were drinks."

"Oh yes. The harvest punch begins to flow freely at the assembly parties and doesn't stop until the actual event. I promise you, these are supposed to be fun."

"I'm a little lost," she said.

"Don't worry." He smiled. "I've got you."

He walked across the room and went over to a punch bowl she hadn't noticed before, then dished out a generous portion into a clear plastic cup. He brought it back and her fingertips brushed his. It made her feel overheated.

And of course, when she looked at his hands, she noticed the left one. He had a wedding ring.

Well. Dammit. That seemed about right. That seemed about right for her life. That was probably why he was nice. Because he wasn't looking for anything. Because he already had everything.

It was so stupid, but it made her want to cry.

"My wife means well," he said. "She can be a little bit intense."

His wife.

His wife means well…

She followed his gaze back over to Jenna. Of course that woman had him. Of course that woman had everything. She was beautiful, and she had great clothes, and she had this man. Some women really did get everything.

Morgan had never gotten a damned thing.

She was shocked by her response to that. She had seen the guy less than a minute ago. It was just that… She had forgotten who she was for a second. She had thought that maybe she was the kind of woman that men talked to, and offered things to, just because they wanted to, because maybe they liked her.

"Don't worry about it," she said, taking a sip of her punch.

"I can help you with your spiders."

"You don't… You don't need to do that."

Part of her wanted him to leave. Badly. She had no idea why she'd reacted so strongly to him, but she didn't like it.

"Hey, I want to. You're new. I get that jumping in the middle of that clique isn't all that appealing. It's a small town. People get used to new faces. But it takes time."

"You don't seem to have any problem getting used to me," she said.

"I'm a doctor," he said. "I deal with new people all the time. I'm Ryan. Ryan Abbott. Though, in med school, they called me Dr. Savage."

"Why?"

"Because of my behavior when drunk. It wasn't really meant to flatter me."

She laughed. And it felt good. It felt good to stand next to him.

So maybe she wouldn't worry about his wedding ring. Or the fact that he wasn't being nice to her for the reason she had initially hoped. Maybe she could just count him as a friend and that would be enough.

Morgan White didn't have a lot of friends. She certainly couldn't afford to reject Ryan's friendship.

Anyway, she really didn't want to.

14

Chelsea

MORGAN STILL CAME to every meeting. She came to every meeting and she sat there, staring straight ahead, even when Jenna gave presentations. Even when Jenna gave her the cut direct, which of course she did. And Chelsea couldn't blame her.

In Jenna and Ryan's divorce, Ryan was the villain, and Morgan had been an accessory to the crime. It couldn't be ignored.

But in the fire? She had lost. Like the rest of them.

Morgan had loved Ryan. However that relationship had started, this woman had loved Chelsea's brother. They had that in common.

She'd also had to contend with Chelsea's mother. Another thing she and Morgan had in common.

And she had a baby.

A baby from Ryan.

A little girl.

She loved Chloe and Aiden. Loved Ryan's kids like they were hers. Being an aunt to them was one of the greatest joys of her life.

And there was a new baby.

A baby she didn't know.

She was trying to be loyal. She was trying to do the right thing, but she didn't know what the right thing was. Not when there was so much pain to go around.

Morgan slipped out into the hall before the meeting adjourned, and Chelsea looked at Jenna, who was engrossed in the current speaker, and slipped out.

She went out the side entrance, like Morgan had, and went straight for the door that led outside. Morgan was already halfway to the parking lot. Chelsea quickened her pace.

"Morgan," she called out.

"What?" She turned around, and her expression shifted into one of shock.

"I'm… You know who I am," Chelsea said.

"Yes," Morgan responded, her expression guarded.

"I just… I want to know how you're doing. I didn't know whether anyone else has checked on you."

She shrugged. "I'm okay."

"Good. That's good. I… I don't want to say."

"That's okay. Nobody does."

She turned and started to walk away again.

"No," Chelsea said. "I'm not like everybody else. I'm…his sister, Morgan. And I loved him."

Morgan turned back to face her. "Are you here to try and take Lily from me?"

Her heart felt bruised. "No. Oh, honey, no. That's…my mom isn't well." She closed her eyes. "I'm lying. She's always been like this."

"Ryan talked about her like she was a saint."

Chelsea couldn't help it. She laughed. "Ryan was her favorite. He couldn't do any wrong. Not even…"

Morgan lifted her chin. "Oh, do you mean me?"

"Morgan, no, I didn't…"

"I don't want to change what happened. I would never trade my time with him for anything. He was the only person who ever…" Her voice broke. "He was good to me. I'm not sorry I was with him."

Chelsea felt…relieved. Relieved that this woman wasn't standing there feeling regret over what she'd done, because that would almost make it pointless. Pointless when it could be…

He was the only person who was ever good to her.

That made her feel so resolved in reaching out to Morgan like she had.

She was the mother of Chelsea's niece, and obviously loved by her late brother. And right now she was going to trust herself in this one small thing. Morgan needed someone.

"Was he happy?"

Morgan's eyes filled with tears. "I think so."

"I'm so glad. I am."

"Really?"

"Yes." She looked down. "How is Lily? I know you had a difficult birth and…"

"Why do you care about that?"

"I did, too. When my son Sean was born, I… I had a bleed that was so severe I needed a hysterectomy. I know how traumatizing it is when birth doesn't go how you planned."

Morgan looked stunned, and Chelsea was a little shocked herself at having told her all that, but she felt like she wanted to connect with her. This woman her brother had loved.

"Sorry," Morgan said softly.

"It's okay. I mean, it really is now. I just… Lily is doing well, right?"

Morgan nodded. "Yeah. She is. For all I know about babies."

"It's okay to feel like you don't know what you're doing. That's normal."

"Is it? That's a shock. I don't feel like anything about me is very normal."

"It is. I'd love to come see Lily sometime."

"Yeah I, well, I'm in the store six days a week."

"Okay."

"I have to go. Edna is watching Lily and it's getting late."

"Okay. But I'll come see you sometime?"

Morgan nodded.

Then she turned and left Chelsea standing there, her heart pounding hard in her ears. She watched until Morgan faded into darkness in the parking lot, and she heard a car door close.

She went back to the door and found it locked.

"Shit. Hell. Dammit." She quickedned her pace and went around to the front of the country club, where the door wouldn't be locked to the outside, and nearly ran into a tall man in a suit.

He reached out and steadied her, and her mouth fell open. Because while this man wasn't a ghost, he might as well have been.

"Cody White?"

"Chelsea Abbott," he said, using her maiden name.

She didn't know if she should correct him. If she should say if she was married or not.

You aren't really. Are you?

You're separated.

And you think your husband could have done something really, really bad.

"Yeah," she said. "Good to see you."

15

Afterburn

Jenna

"CODY WHITE WAS HERE," Chelsea said.

"What?" Jenna asked, putting both hands flat on the table to brace herself.

She hadn't seen him. And surely, if one of her oldest friends in the entire world had shown his face for the first time in more than twenty years, she would've noticed.

"Right," Alex said, suddenly looking guilty. "I forgot to mention…"

"You forgot to mention what?" Chelsea asked.

"I saw him. Yesterday. He came into the bakery, and I gave him coffee and an apricot square."

"And you didn't think that that bore mentioning?" Jenna asked.

There had been a time when Paul, Ryan and Cody had been best friends. Alex and Jenna, too. For a long time Ryan

and Jenna had been the only couple, but she had been buddies
with Paul and Cody. And she had been almost certain there
had been a little bit of something between Alex and Cody at
one time, before she'd ended up with Paul.

Not that she could be absolutely sure. Alex was very prim
in her way, and she was pretty tight-lipped about all things
sexual, and always had been.

Cody White had been an odd addition to the group from
the beginning. They were all overachievers. All on a path.
And she could see now that a certain amount of that stemmed
from relative financial privilege. They expected to go to college. Even Jenna, whose parents basically looked at her twice
a year, once on her birthday and once on Christmas, had expected them to pay for her to go to school. She'd been wary
of Cody at first, because he seemed like he was beneath them.

She'd repented of that.

Her–a culpa.

But the fact remained that he had been a strange addition.
He had lived on the outskirts of town in that old farmhouse
with his mother, who was a deeply unfriendly woman.

Cody had played football with Ryan and Paul; otherwise,
their paths never would have crossed. The school had provided
the fees and the uniform for him. She knew that because Paul
had told her one time, and in hindsight…

It was kind of mean that he'd done that.

Ryan was probably the one who had befriended Cody. Ryan
liked strays. For better or worse.

She thought of Morgan. Her stomach went sour.

Yes. Ryan liked a stray.

He always had.

Paul? Not so much. In fact, she had often related to Paul. It
was one reason they had never been interested in each other
in *that way*. They were too much alike.

There were good things about it, her personality, which was also quite similar to Paul's; and there were bad things, too.

She was good at categorizing people. Good at figuring out weaknesses so she could get the results she wanted.

The problem with that was when you tended to categorize people rather than getting to know them, you often set the tone for the interaction before you ever had one.

It could be an issue.

But eventually, she had forgotten that Cody didn't belong. That he hadn't been one of them. Eventually, he had just been. Eventually, he had just been Cody.

But he had left town after graduation, never to return. And she had never really known why.

It hadn't been clear. Exactly why Cody had forgotten about them. He wasn't even on social media.

"He's an FBI agent," Chelsea said.

Jenna's mouth dropped open. She noticed that Alex's didn't.

"Excuse me," she said, turning her laser focus to her friend. "You knew that Cody was back in town, and also that he's an FBI agent, and you just kept that to yourself? We drove over here together. I watched you eat pie. And get a little pie filling on your skirt."

"Why didn't you tell me?" Alex asked, looking down at her skirt.

"Why didn't you tell me that our former friend, who is *an FBI agent*, was back in town? You didn't really spill pie on your skirt. My point is we should tell each other things, and I just proved that you think that, too, and you had every opportunity to tell me, but you didn't."

"Talking about Cody is weird for me."

"Really?" Chelsea asked. "I know that I was never as close to you guys as you were to each other back in the day, but I didn't know anything happened between you and Cody."

"It didn't. Not really."

"When you say not really…"

"I mean I didn't have sex with him." Jenna watched as Alex's face turned beet red. Like they really were in high school.

And she was about to say something when *he* walked by.

Carrying a big, giant thing of coffee.

Mellow Coffee Roasters provided drinks for the council meetings, and that meant she came into contact with Ethan on a fairly regular basis.

And it hadn't been a thing. It had been nothing at all until she had found herself single.

It made her feel weird and wrong and like she was trying to get back at her husband a little bit by *being* her husband, and of course she was never going to go after a nineteen-year-old, because nineteen-year-old men were like cakes taken out of the oven too soon. There was literally nothing exciting about that. It was just flat and soupy.

Plus, her husband was dead. Like ninety-nine percent for sure dead. There was no getting back at him, anyway.

But Ethan and her fascination with him felt less like revenge and more like a compulsion.

And this was her fresh start.

New house.

Harvest Festival.

Fling?

Maybe.

She turned her focus back to the subject at hand. "But there wasn't *nothing*."

"It's ancient history," Alex said.

"That you didn't tell us about."

Alex looked down. "What happened with Paul…happened. And Cody and I never really were anything. Why talk about it?"

Jenna couldn't understand that. Talking always helped her.

"He's investigating the fire?" Chelsea asked.

"What has to happen for the FBI to get involved in investigating the fire?" Jenna asked. "Isn't it most likely that somebody from one of the homeless encampments set it? I'm not saying they don't need to follow up on that. I am saying it's going to be very difficult to find the culprit. They're probably long gone."

"I don't know what makes them decide to investigate," Chelsea said. "But there has to be something, right? And whoever set it…they're a murderer."

"I know *that*," Jenna said. "I am well aware that whoever set the fire is a murderer. It's just… I don't know if they're ever going to find anything. I don't know…" She took a deep breath. "What I want is for this town to heal. And I don't know how we are going to do that if we can't move on."

"You already have a bouncy house," Chelsea teased. "You can't be pleased."

She had won the bouncy house battle. Truth be told, it hadn't been much of a battle. Maybe everybody wanted a little bit of fun. Even the joyless assholes on the town council.

"Jenna." Matt, who owned the farm and garden store just off the main drag of town, approached her. He had a strange look on his face, one that did not speak of council business. "Can I talk to you for a second?"

"Sure," she said.

In spite of herself, she found herself looking back at Ethan. But even so, her feet moved forward to follow Matt.

He had a beard and a Patagonia fleece and a tendency to wear sandals and shorts when it was far too cold to do so. Otherwise, he was a decent person. And she supposed those other things didn't make him not a decent person; they were just of note.

"I was wondering if you might be interested in getting dinner sometime."

Dinner. Dinner. That was a *date* thing.

A whole *meal* with somebody. Her first thought was that it was an incredibly ambitious ask. It seemed to her that something like that should start with coffee. Then maybe happy hour. Hors d'oeuvres.

A whole dinner?

It wasn't like she didn't know Matt. She did. They had interacted casually many times about town and at these kinds of meetings.

He didn't raise any red flags. Well. That wasn't true. He did sometimes wear jorts. She considered that a pink flag. So yeah, no *red* flags.

Most importantly, he had come down on her side in the great charity dinner drama of last year. That explosion that had happened just before…

Well. Just before everything had caught on fire. She remembered everyone who had been on her side.

And everyone who hadn't.

She would never forget.

She wasn't the kind of person who forgot.

She kept grudges like other people kept cats.

When you had spent your life being your own best advocate, you had to.

So yes. That was acceptable in that regard.

And she didn't have to marry him. Just because she had dated one guy and ended up marrying him, didn't mean that she needed to date this guy and marry him.

He was also age-appropriate. Exactly the kind of man she should be interested in.

"Sure," she said. And she wondered if the words sounded robotic or strange. Because she felt robotic and strange. Like she was doing a series of complicated computer equations in her mind.

"Friday night. If you are available."

She knew beyond a shadow of a doubt that she was. Because, unless there was a town council meeting, she was always available. That was a little embarrassing. "How about Saturday?"

A counteroffer seemed entirely reasonable, and made it sound like she was in demand.

"That works fine for me," he said.

And he looked happy. She wasn't happy. She was weirded out. But also felt like this was something she needed to do. Because if she didn't...then she never would. This was that first opportunity.

"Great," she said.

"You have any dietary restrictions?"

What a weird question. Did people have to ask that now? So you could say that you were gluten-free. Or vegan. Or keto. The last time she had dated, it had been fast food drive-through and sex in the backseat of a car.

That made her want to recoil. Because she did not want to have sex with Matt in the back of a car. She didn't want to have sex with Matt at all. That was the thing. There was no amount of dinner that was going to change that. She was a forty-three-year-old woman. She was well aware of who she wanted to have sex with. There was one man in this room that she wanted to have sex with.

It wasn't the one who'd just asked her out.

She wasn't extraordinarily picky; it wasn't that. It was just chemistry. You had it or you didn't.

Of course, her chemistry with the inappropriately aged Ethan was probably one-sided. So maybe that was just called being creepy. Not chemistry.

But sex could be separate from dinner. The pursuit of sex, the need for sex, could be different than taking this step into trying to have a date with the first man who wasn't Ryan since she was sixteen.

So yeah. She had gone on like four dates that weren't with Ryan. In her whole life. And they had really just been dates. To ice cream.

Ice cream! That would have been another good introductory-date length.

But she was committed to dinner.

She realized she had been standing there for a long time, not answering. "No dietary restrictions. Though I only eat fish if I can literally see the ocean. So no seafood. But that's because I'm picky."

"That's fair," he said. "I think I have your phone number from the roster. Is it all right if I use it?"

Wow. So courteous. "Sure."

"Thanks. I'll… I'll see you Saturday."

She could feel Chelsea and Alex staring at her. She turned slowly.

And they approached. She was thankful that the rest of the country club was mostly empty. "Do you have a date?" Chelsea asked.

"Yes. See? I told you my situation was different. Nobody asked Alex on a date."

"That's because I'm out to pasture," Alex said.

"You can't actually think that," Jenna said. "Men stare at me all the time. They certainly stare at you."

"I don't know about that."

"This is about how you feel about *you*," Jenna said.

She wondered if it was the burns that made her feel this way. They were visible. On her arms. But they were just scars. They didn't have anything to do with how beautiful Alex was. And she didn't want to ask, because if they didn't have anything to do with it then she didn't want to introduce the idea that they should.

"It's just getting older," Alex said. "And you know, there are those naturally dewy girls…"

"Like the one my husband left me for? I'm familiar. But here's the thing, Alex. Your problem is that you *were* one of those girls. Some of us were always trying to enhance and cover up our looks. So the fact that we continue to do it now? Not a surprise. The fact that you suddenly have an inclination to do it for the first time in your life? Well. Again. Has more to do with how you feel about you than how anybody else does."

"So you're saying I'm sad, not ugly?" Alex asked.

And Jenna guffawed. "Yes. *Tragic*. But very beautiful."

Alex looked amused by that.

They said goodbye to Chelsea and got back into Alex's car.

"Do you *want* to go on a date with Matt?"

"I do not, Alex," Jenna said, stretching back in the seat. "But I'm going to. Because sometimes you have to take steps forward, even if they are not in the shoes you would have chosen."

"That's almost profound, Jen," Alex said.

"Thank you. I tried. But I think you are focusing on the deeply uninteresting fact that I have a dinner date with a man who looks like he's about to break out into a hike at any minute, rather than the fact that you revealed—just casually—that maybe something happened between you and Cody in the olden days, and also that he's back in town."

"It was just…you know. I felt… I was interested in him. Fascinated by him. Because…he was different, you know? They lived in the trailer park until his mom inherited the farmhouse from her dad. And even then, he didn't have everything everyone else did."

"You had everything," Jenna pointed out.

"For a while. And Cody didn't have his dad." She looked out the window. "I didn't have my mom. I lost myself for a while in that."

"You didn't tell me…"

"I couldn't stand letting you see me struggle, Jenna."

"Why not? Don't you think I would've been a good friend?"

"I do. I think you would have been a great friend. Because you are great friend. I realize now that it was silly. Immature. But you admired how easy things were for me. And when they weren't easy for me, I was afraid of losing your admiration along with everything else. When I didn't have my mom to perform for anymore, I… I questioned why anything mattered. Because I wasn't good enough to make her want to stay. She just left. She took her phone and her purse, and she left. She left me and everything else behind, and I have never been able to figure out why. Or what I could've done differently."

Jenna swallowed hard. It was a shame when things like that happened and you were young and insensitive. She had felt awful for Alex, but she didn't think she'd had the ability to come with real empathy. Not when she was just a teenager. A teenager who was also an idiot, because teenagers often were. Wrapped up in her own sayings, her own life.

She was pretty sure they had been seventeen… Yes. Seventeen. The day that Alex's mother—her beautiful, polished suburban mother—simply hadn't come home.

It had created a scandal. More than a scandal. And the only thing that had ever…

They had received a postcard. Once. From California.

It did not say, "wish you were here."

And for Jenna, who had taken her parents for granted, who

had always known they would be there... She hadn't really been able to fully imagine the horror of it. But she could now.

How could you leave your kids?

Her own daughter was the same age they would've been when Alex's mom had left.

How could you do that?

"Alex, it's so easy for us to avoid talking about these things. Because I know the history of your life. I was there when it happened. I know how you feel about it now, but I'm sorry I didn't know then."

Alex nodded. "It's okay. I wasn't ready to share. I'm not sure if I am now." She laughed, but there wasn't any humor in it. "I was really hurt when Cody left the way he did. Because of everything I did share with him. We were close. For a time. But it obviously didn't mean the same thing to him. And maybe the whole thing with Paul was…"

"Did you break his heart?"

"I didn't think that I did. I thought a couple of kisses didn't mean anything to him. You know the reputation he had."

"I don't," Jenna said, feeling rocked.

"Well. He had one," Alex said. "A lot of girls liked to mess around with him. And more. Apparently, he was a very good time."

And Alex had been a very good girl. It had been the most shocking thing in the entire world when *Alex* had been the one to get pregnant before she got married. But then, it was Paul, so people had been pretty forgiving.

What mortal woman could resist?

"But when he left," Jenna said. "He *left*. Very definitively."

"Yes," Alex said softly. "Very definitively."

"And he showed up in your bakery."

"By accident," Alex said.

Jenna laughed. "Okay, Alex. The FBI agent had no idea where he might find you."

Alex didn't say much after that, but Jenna wasn't repentant. At least maybe she had observed that correctly.

She would take it. Considering that everything else felt just a little bit messy.

16

Kindling

Jenna

"YOU DON'T NEED to be mean."

Jenna turned and looked at Ryan. "I'm not...mean. Anyway. Mean to who?"

"That poor girl Morgan. The one that you sent over to the pile of pipe cleaner spiders."

"I needed help with them. I wasn't being mean. I know I got off on the wrong foot with her, but it's not actually about her. Marjorie took advantage of her by throwing her in to read that statement. The businesses on Main are struggling because of seasonal wildfire smoke and—" He wasn't listening. He had that vague look he got on his face when she talked about her business, and all the businesses.

It wasn't that he didn't support her; it was just that...her business was an uneven income base, since so much of the town's economy centered on tourism. She made the "fun money." The trip to Hawaii money. She didn't pay the bills.

But it had been her dream. Always. To buy a little piece of the town, a metaphor for her desire to be permanently part of something. She got to make jewelry and sell it. It gave her an outlet for creativity, and for her business mind.

Ryan often saw it as a distraction. A drain on her time.

But he sure enjoyed a mai tai and a trip to Honolulu, so…

Also, she loved it. Didn't that matter?

That was where that fight always went. And he always said *of course it matters*. But then he went right back to spacing out whenever she talked about it, so whatever.

She looked critically at herself in the mirror, then back at Ryan. "Is this outfit okay?"

"You look great, Jen. You always do."

It sounded a little more tired and a little less sincere than usual. But sometimes, after you'd been with somebody since you were sixteen years old, it was just valuable that the person knew what to say, even more valuable perhaps than their meaning it, even if he couldn't seem to do it convincingly with the MSBC.

But this… It was a testament to everything that they'd built.

Just like when Ryan asked her if his forehead was beginning to win a battle against his hairline. She said *no, honey. Not at all*. Even though, *yes. A little bit*. But it really was only a *little bit*. The kind of thing only Ryan would notice about himself. Or that she would notice. Because she looked at him so often.

Except, suddenly, she remembered he had just called her *mean*.

She turned around. "I wasn't mean."

She hated that more than anything. The idea she was mean. She wanted to get things done. She wanted to *help*. She was good at the big picture, and maybe sometimes she wasn't great at smoothing over details along the way, but she was…effective. And there were certain people who would always be more worried about her *tact* and *niceness* and wish she could be *softer*, and that the fact her husband was suddenly saying the same thing made her so…so *mad*.

"I just don't think you need to attack everything with quite so much vigor. It's a small town council. If the thing you want to do doesn't get off the ground right away, what's the big deal? You can always introduce it later."

The thing? Like he couldn't even remember what it was?

"It's a big deal because our businesses might die, Ryan. Tourism in Tenmile is seasonal. And these fires… Having a fire season every year is killing us. People don't want to come walk around in a town when they can't breathe. And we've been under smoke an average of at least a month out of every summer for the last three years. I don't know how much longer my business can survive."

"We don't need your business," Ryan said.

She looked at him, and it was so strange. It was like all the familiarity from the moment before had evaporated.

Like there was none of it left.

Because now he'd said it. Said what she knew he thought. She'd really believed he knew better than to say it.

"*I* need my business," she said. "I love it. It's all the work I've done my entire adult life."

"It's always been difficult," he said. "You're always busy. And you don't have to be. You don't have to be on all these committees. You don't have to own a business. I make enough money."

"I know you do," Jenna said. "But…shouldn't I have something for myself?"

"The kids and I aren't something for yourself?"

"Oh, don't say that," she said. "That's completely ridiculous. You have a career, Ryan. You understand what I'm saying. It isn't confusing. Stop acting like it is."

"I'm sorry. That isn't what I meant. Not really. You have a lot of anxiety about this, and the anxiety isn't necessary."

"Says you," she said. "I have owned this business for fifteen years. And keeping stores open on Main Street has never been easy, but when you introduce the fires, and you look at e-commerce…"

"You could use e-commerce to your advantage."

"Sure. I have to an extent, but people have to know the store exists. To want to order jewelry from me. I need people to come to town and find out about me, and then they think of me sometimes. But other times, huge retailers with lower prices that sell crap outpaced me. Because they have fast free shipping and, well, cheap garbage. And I want to do something to encourage local shopping. This town needs to care about itself."

He smiled. "Maybe this town wants big-box stores and fast food restaurants."

She grimaced. "Stop. You're depressing me." Then she took a deep breath. "And you know what? You're wrong."

"Good God, Jenna." But it didn't have a lot of heat. Just…

He didn't get it.

She rarely felt out of step with him, because usually, they didn't get deep into things they didn't see eye to eye on. But here they were.

"I'm serious. It is what people want. They just don't realize what's going to be the end result of their actions. And that is why I want to introduce the loyalty program. Thank you for giving me a new angle to approach this from. Which I will give at the next meeting."

"That wasn't actually what I was doing."

"Well, I don't know what you're doing. I thought maybe you were on my side."

"I am. I could invest some money in the shop if you want."

That didn't sit well with her, or right. "It's self-supporting. It's just tight."

"I can take the stress off you. I can fix it, and then you don't have to get wound up about all your initiatives."

"It doesn't solve the broader issue with Tenmile. Do you remember how it was back when we were in high school? All those stores were empty. It was dying. And then all these people banded together, opened shops, found ways to support each other, support the community. There is only one empty building on Main Street where, twenty years ago, there were fifteen. I care about the whole thing, not just my store. I care about this place because I love it."

"I just don't get what the point of loving this place is if it makes you…"

She frowned. "Don't say *mean*."

She wasn't *mean*. She just cared so much about everything. She always had. When Ryan had needed a champion in med school, and the kids had needed her for art projects and homework and school events, she'd had such a great way to channel all that energy. But the older they got, the less they wanted her. They still needed her, but it was an uphill battle to get them to let her help.

When they forgot something at home, she had to wait in the school parking lot for them to come out and get it from her because God forbid anyone ever see their mommy at school.

This community had raised her, and her kids, and watching it come alive and flourish soothed something in her soul.

What she cared about mattered. She'd spent all of her childhood being told she was too loud, too pushy. Bossy. The kinds of adjectives that got handed out to girls when boys got to be leaders for exhibiting the same behavior. She'd just stayed herself, anyway. Because she didn't know another way to be.

One time in sixth grade the whole class had been talking, and her teacher had singled her out and punished her. She'd later asked why.

You're a leader, Jenna. Whether you like it or not, people follow you and you have to be held to a higher standard.

It hadn't seemed fair. But it had crystallized something for her.

She was going to be singled out because she was a confident, loud woman. Whether she deserved it or not. People would take her wrong. They'd place blame.

She'd decided she'd try to actually be a leader, then.

She'd thought she'd found her place, thought she'd found a way past all of that.

And her husband, the person who should have really understood where she was coming from, thought she was mean.

When she was younger, sometimes someone would say something about her voice being too loud, and she'd spend the next two days trying to keep the volume down so she didn't force her parents to have to contend with her when it was so clear they didn't want to.

Until she forgot, and just became Jenna again.

She'd decided a long time ago she could never be anything but *Jenna*. Her parents didn't care about her either way, so why bother? She'd thought she'd found acceptance. But now…

Suddenly, Ryan made her want to whisper.

17

Kindling

Morgan

HE WAS STILL being nice to her. He helped out with the Harvest Festival thing, and tended to act as a go-between for her and Jenna, which alleviated a lot of her concerns. Jenna hadn't done anything to her; she just made Morgan nervous.

And you like him.

The warmth and shame she'd felt ever since she'd first met him sat heavy in her chest now. She liked him. She wanted to be near him. She knew she shouldn't want that.

Ryan was polite and apologetic. He was friends with another doctor who was absurdly handsome and—she'd found out—was married to one of Jenna's best friends. Alex was her name. But she hadn't really talked to any of them.

Just Ryan.

He was easy to talk to, and he was so…

She shook her head and tried to stop…obsessing.

The Harvest Festival itself was adorable. There was a petting zoo and animals everywhere, and a band, snacks and it honestly was like the kind of thing that she had only ever seen in movies.

So much of this town was like things she had only ever seen in movies.

She had grown up around Portland, and while there were parts of the city that were just fine, where she had grown up really wasn't.

It was all a little too gritty, particularly compared to this.

She was working one of the game booths. A fishing one. Where kids put a little fishing pole with a clothespin over the top of a wooden divider, and she gave it a tug like she was a fish, and then flipped it back over the top of the divider with a piece of candy clipped to it.

She didn't have a lot of experience with kids, but this was actually fun, and it allowed her to give them candy without deeply interacting with them. Which was exactly perfect in her opinion.

About twenty minutes after the game started, someone opened up the black curtain that concealed her from the outside world and slipped into the booth with her. Ryan.

She felt like all the air had been taken out of her lungs.

"Just came to check on you."

"It's going good," she said.

He looked at her for a long moment, and she knew. She knew that she wasn't imagining this. Her making it up. It wasn't just her. He was attracted to her.

And he had a wife.

He hadn't done anything. And he probably wouldn't. What was the harm in letting them be friendly? What was the harm in letting him be close?

"We can open up two lines. I'll help."

He exited and she heard him giving instructions to the kids to form two lines before coming back around to her side again.

And for the rest of the evening, they stayed back there, talking and laughing.

"So you're living with your grandmother?" he asked.

"Yeah. I don't know her that well. I was raised by my mother in Portland. She's… She's a drug addict." She waited for him to recoil. If he was going to, this would be the moment. It always was. Which was why she tended to say it early, when people were trying to get to know her. "Sorry. That tends to freak people out. But I'm just used to it. I mean, it sucks, but it's how it is. So I spent time being homeless and, ever since I turned eighteen, I've been working really hard to change things. I found out that my grandmother needed somebody to help take care of her, and I quit my job and came here. Because I had a place to stay and a chance to have something different. To do something different. It seemed like a good idea."

"And you're staying in that old farmhouse?"

"Yes. I am. Marjorie moved into an assisted living facility. She wanted me to be around so she'd have a visitor, and so I could… She wants me to have it. When she's gone."

"Is it habitable?"

"Yeah. It's good. I mean, it needs a few repairs. And I'm figuring that out. There's not really a budget for anything. She owns the yarn store, and it does okay business, but…"

"Hey. You just let me know whatever needs doing. I'm a pretty good handyman. I'm happy to come over and help with things."

"Really? I thought you were a surgeon. I didn't know you fixed things other than people."

"Sure. If I can cut a human being open, I can most certainly handle whatever's going on in an old house."

"You say that. But you haven't seen it."

"Let me give you my number. If you have an emergency, you can give me a call."

"Okay," she said.

It was dangerous. She had that feeling in her stomach that warned her when something wasn't right.

But she gave him her phone number, anyway.

18

Kindling

Chelsea

"ARE MARK AND Paul on their phones all the time?"

"Yes," Alex said without missing a beat. "He's always checking the football scores."

"No," Chelsea said slowly. "Mark…"

And then she realized she didn't exactly know. They sat in the room together sometimes, and she would be on her computer and he would surf channels. Maybe he was on his phone. She wasn't exactly sure.

"Ryan has been on his phone a lot lately. I mean a lot more than usual. And I don't know if he's just being a busybody or… I think he's texting. He looks like our teenagers."

"It might be the hospital's fantasy football thing," Alex said. "Paul is overly invested in that."

"Maybe. He's not loud about it. It's weird."

Chelsea *did* think it was weird. But she didn't want to say anything. Because that had plunged her into her own sense of disquiet.

Not just that Ryan's behavior had changed, but Alex's blind belief that Paul could only be doing what he'd said.

Was it weird that she didn't just…trust Mark?

Did that mean something was wrong with her?

She didn't think she'd be able to say, definitively, what Mark was doing on his phone or otherwise.

She couldn't remember the last time they'd had a conversation that didn't center around Sean. He was graduating this year. He was graduating, and it felt like such a huge thing. A huge thing that neither of them were really ready for. They agreed on that.

Yeah. They agreed on that.

They agreed on a lot of things.

Though, recently, they'd been disagreeing more than usual. He was saying things about her parents. There was the whole thing with Sean and the pills.

The revelations of what Mark had done as a teenager. That he'd…been to jail.

And sometimes she looked up and saw him sitting on the couch and she felt like she was staring at a stranger.

It was hard to even let him touch her anymore. It made her feel like she was…

Cheating on her husband.

They were so disconnected, it felt like being touched by a stranger.

It made her feel like a lead weight was pressing down on her chest.

"Are you guys happy?"

"Yeah," Alex said. "Are you?"

Chelsea felt like she was having an existential crisis while staring down into a pumpkin spice latte, and she genuinely couldn't think of anything more depressing.

The Harvest Festival had gone so well. But Mark hadn't gone to it. Mark often didn't go to these things, because he was busy. He wasn't part of the doctor group. Frankly, he disliked Ryan and Paul. Which kept Chelsea a bit distant, because she only ever hung out with Jenna and Alex when it was just the women. That was fine with her; it just meant there was a different dynamic.

She'd often thought her mother hadn't warmed to Mark because she'd been hoping Chelsea would marry Paul.

Paul.

Ryan's best friend, the undisputed most popular guy on campus at Tenmile High. He charmed people effortlessly, and her mom was definitely one of his devotees. That was the problem with places like this.

She'd be lying if she'd said she hadn't had a crush on him back then, though. He was always in their house, hanging out with Ryan, and yet he'd always been completely inaccessible to her. He'd barely looked at her and it had only made her more fascinated by him. Of course. Wasn't that the most teenage girl thing?

She'd been beneath his notice. His friend's little sister, who had chipmunk cheeks and weird hair, and was never going to register to a guy like him.

But then she'd gone away and met Mark. And while she'd moved back to be near her family, so Sean could be with his grandparents, and she could be near her niece and nephew, she had also taken some pride in bringing back a super-hot husband who was very successful at his job.

"I… I think so," she answered. She wanted to be.

Maybe she should ask *him* if he was happy.

And suddenly, her stomach lurched. Like she'd just been startled. Because the idea of asking him if he was happy felt… Terrifying. Because what if his answer was no?

They were screeching toward not having a child at home.
People stayed together for the kids.

That was what they did.

What happened when your kid was gone? When your reason for keeping it all glued together wasn't there anymore?

"Mark is a great guy," Jenna said. "You're great together."

Were they? Because apparently, Mark had glossed over his past to a degree that made Chelsea feel like she had no idea who he was.

And it hooked into dark fears she'd had for years.

That she was just wrong.

About everything.

About her life.

Maybe they weren't happy at all.

If he could hide all that about his past, what else could he hide?

"Why do you think that?" Chelsea asked. "You don't really…know Mark."

Jenna hesitated. "Sure, but…but you love him."

"Yes," she said, looking down into her coffee. "I do."

"I'm *sure* it's the fantasy football thing," Jenna said.

She was relieved to have Jenna change the subject back to *her* marriage. "You know Ryan," Chelsea said. "He's the nicest guy. He is the greatest guy. He would literally never do anything to hurt you. You know that."

"I do," Jenna said. "You're totally right. Anyway, I'll just steal his phone next time he's obsessing over it if I'm really worried. We don't have secrets."

Secrets.

She knew Jenna was wrong there. It was, in fact, one of the very few things she was certain about.

Everyone had secrets.

The only question was just how dark they were.

19

Afterburn

Alex

SHE DIDN'T EXPECT to see Cody the morning after the meeting, but there he was. Her head hurt and she felt drained after another night of getting very little sleep.

She'd dreamed of her mother again. Standing on the streets in town with flames burning behind her.

She couldn't get the image out of her head. And when she'd gotten up, she'd put the locket in her pocket again.

Now Cody was here. If Jenna and Chelsea hadn't also seen him, she might have thought he was another dream.

Another hallucination.

Whatever it all was.

"I'll have the usual," he said.

"You've only been here once. You don't have a usual."

"True." The way a smile tugged at the corners of his mouth set off a chain reaction inside her.

She shut out her thoughts about last night. She shut out everything but him. "So you came to the meeting last night. Did you hear anything interesting?"

"No. Though, it's interesting how much Jenna hasn't changed."

"She hasn't. That is true."

"My most vivid memory of her is the time that she forced us all to sign a petition to stop seal hunting in Canada. And I think one of the teachers asked her why she wasn't more involved in local activism, and she came back the next day with that same petition, but also one to stop clearcuts in Oregon."

"Yep. That's our girl. It doesn't really matter what the cause is. As long as she can rally behind it."

"So she and Ryan had divorced?" he said.

"I guess they were technically still in the process, but she called him her ex-husband. Are you asking me as a friend trying to catch up on his old friends? Or are you asking me as an investigator?"

His lips twitched. "Does it matter?"

She realized that it did. Because one meant that he was an old friend. And given the way he had left town, given the way that he had left her, she often wondered.

"Functionally? Maybe not. Personally? A little bit."

"I can't promise that something you tell me won't end up as part of an investigation. But considering Jenna's hardly a leading suspect and Ryan is dead…"

"Missing," Alex pointed out.

"Missing."

And she knew that he hadn't forgotten that, so she had to wonder why he wasn't being pedantic about it.

"Do you know something that I don't?" she asked.

"I probably know quite a few things about this case that you don't. But if you're asking if I know the truth about Ryan

Abbott, no. I was just stating the most likely and widely accepted theory. But I haven't discounted the fact that he could be alive. Seeing as we haven't identified his remains. But—" he paused for a moment "—I'm going to tell you something. It's entirely possible that no one is actually missing. I mean, in the sense that they're out there, walking around alive. Fire can incinerate bone. There's a reason people get cremated after death. And while a fast-moving wildfire doesn't always consume a body completely, identifying remains via DNA is impossible. It can render dental records useless. We could have several bodies in one location, and it would be difficult to say."

She went ahead and detached herself from this commentary. Considering that her husband was one of the fire victims. She had gone out of her way not to imagine things.

Not to imagine what fire could do to flesh and bone.

"I'm sorry," he said. "That was very insensitive of me."

She didn't know if he meant that, or if he just knew it would be a nice thing to say. "I think about Paul, and what must have happened to him, a lot. I finally don't think about it every day, first thing, when I open my eyes. But at some point during the day, I do. He was killed by the fire. You aren't putting anything in my head that isn't there already."

He nodded, the gesture definitive, like a check on an invisible list. "Going back to Jenna and Ryan. They were divorcing."

"Yes." Unkind as it was, she was much happier to linger on Jenna's life. She was surprised Cody didn't know, given that Morgan was his niece. None of them had ever known his older sister all that well. She'd been older than their group, and always struggling with drug addiction.

"Ryan had an affair," Alex said slowly. "He got the woman pregnant."

"Was she a local woman?"

He really didn't know. She looked down at her hands, then back up slowly.

"It's your niece, Cody. Morgan."

Right then, the FBI agent cracked, and she saw the boy she'd known.

"Shit. Are you kidding me? Why haven't I seen anything about her in the case files?"

"Because she...isn't a victim of the fire? Or a suspect of anything. I mean, the farmhouse burned down, but I assume you know that. Morgan wasn't home. She was at the hospital. She had a baby, who was born very prematurely. She was in the hospital for a couple of months."

"Fuck," he said, rubbing his hand over his face. "I really had no idea. I haven't been in touch with her... I didn't talk to her after she came here."

"Because of your mom."

"It's ironic," he said. "That Mom died after the fire. The stress, I guess. If she'd been in the farmhouse, she might have died there. But she just...died in her sleep in the home the next day." He cleared his throat. "Maybe if she hadn't, she'd have told me that Morgan was in the hospital. That she had a baby. Dammit. Poor thing. She was by herself, wasn't she?"

Alex nodded. "Yes. With Ryan gone..."

He shook his head. "This isn't about me. But I would have tried to be there for Morgan. When I have an address for her, I send her birthday cards. When I don't I send them to my... She forwards them. But I haven't seen her in a few years. Maybe four?"

"You're not close to your sister, either."

"Nobody is. I tried. I really did. With Morgan. But I was young when she was born, and I was just starting out. Just starting my life. I tried to be a decently involved uncle. I'm the afterthought kid," he said. "I was a mistake for Mom. You know that."

"You weren't a mistake to me."

That sounded as needy as she'd felt at sixteen. And here she'd gone and dropped the Morgan bomb on him while he was trying to work.

"I'm sorry," she said, and she really was. She hadn't meant to be the bearer of all that news. Not like that.

"You didn't mention this yesterday. When you asked if I'd seen anyone in my family." Now he sounded accusatory, and it was almost fair except…it wasn't her family; it was his.

"I didn't know if you knew. I was afraid to be the one to tell you because it's…messy. But when the subject came up directly I couldn't lie to you. If you'd gone to see her right away you'd have known, anyway."

"Family is complicated," he said.

"I get that. You didn't see her at the meeting last night?"

His face went blank. "I don't know. I… If I did, I didn't recognize her. She was a kid last time I saw her. I can't believe… Ryan was such a fucking bastard."

"No argument from me," Alex said.

"She has a baby?"

"Yes. Well, a toddler now, I suppose."

"I need to go see her."

"She's staying above the yarn store, I think. Your mom's store." She watched his face for a reaction to that. She wondered if it would be hard for him to go there. But Marjorie hadn't owned the store when he'd been a kid. So maybe it meant nothing to him. "I think… I feel like we weren't actually nice to her. Not welcoming, at least."

"Sounds like she didn't give you a lot of reason to be."

"I mean when she first came to town. Ryan was friendly to her. I wasn't. I didn't reach out. I feel like, as far as she's concerned, Ryan was the only person who was there for her. Ryan, though, well, there's nothing for him to be proud of there. I blame him."

"Yeah. That's my *baby* niece."

"It's so weird. You know, Ryan was a god here. Amazing doctor, amazing dad. And people really do love Jenna. She's a strong personality, so of course there are those that don't always click with that type of person. People who want power or influence, and wish she did, too, so that she'd be malleable, and not...genuine. So there were definitely those who decided Jenna was the problem, and not Ryan, mostly because it was politically expedient for them to take up a cause against her. But it still dented Ryan's glow."

"As it would."

"Paul stuck by him." She cleared her throat. "But he's a good friend, you know?"

His expression went sharp. "Right."

She paused for a breath. Then another.

"You didn't like Paul, did you?" she asked.

She knew what had happened between her and Cody, and then her and Paul, had probably soured Cody's feelings on Paul. But her, too, she would have imagined.

Right then, though, it was like she was seeing the past with clearer eyes. Had Cody *ever* liked Paul?

There had been an edge to the way Paul teased Cody, that she'd accepted as boys being boys back then. Now it seemed mean.

It had been so easy to write off because when Paul did something that could be perceived as mean, he was quick to smile after. To laugh. And then you looked at him and forgot. He had that way about him.

He drew you right in.

"Alex." He said her name as though she were very stupid or very young. Either way, she didn't like it.

"Everyone liked Paul." She paused for a second. "But not you. Not ever."

Was she so good at putting things in neat little boxes that she'd separated Cody and Paul in her mind and hadn't been able to see the truth?

"First of all, everyone doesn't like Paul. They're in awe of him. Second, do you really not know why?"

It was like the years dissolved. And the brown eyes she was looking into could have belonged to eighteen-year-old Cody or forty-four-year-old Cody and it was all the same to her body. Everything went tight. She'd thought she was way past the *can't breathe, can't speak* kind of thing. But suddenly, she couldn't do either.

"Alex," he said again, but this time softer.

And she was glad the counter was between them. But she realized he'd been in her shop for fifteen minutes and she hadn't gotten him anything.

"Did you want that coffee to go?" she asked, her throat dry.

His lips curved into a wry smile. "I guess so."

She turned and grabbed a cup, then filled it up with coffee. "Black, right?"

"Yep."

"I'm not trying to get rid of you," she said.

She handed him the cup and their fingertips brushed. She tried not to react.

Breathless. But she could still speak.

Probably.

"You seem like you are."

"Because this is complicated. Because of Morgan. You didn't even know about her and Ryan and her baby. Because of me. Because I'm filled up with new feelings, so the idea of introducing old ones to the mix feels like too much. And complicated seems…impossible."

"You're right. I didn't like Paul." He took a sip of the coffee and took a step back. "He had everything I wanted."

She couldn't move, just for a second. The emotion in Cody's eyes was something she hadn't seen since high school.

No one had ever looked at her like that, except him.

Not even Paul. Never Paul.

Then Cody turned and walked out of the bakery.

Alex didn't have to try and compartmentalize then.

His words were all she could think about.

20

Afterburn

Jenna

RALLY AROUND ME. I HAVE A DATE.

AS INTENDED, Jenna's text brought both Chelsea and Alex to her rental. She was so sick of this house.

How was her life supposed to start over if she was living in a temporary house?

One more week. That was all.

"Do Chloe and Aiden know you're going on a date?"

"Hell no. And you can't tell them, cool Aunt Chelsea."

Alex frowned. "Don't you think your kids deserve…?"

"I do not. Whatever the rest of that sentence is. My kids owe me, not the other way around. I have fed them, clothed them and not had a mental breakdown this past year. I don't need to say, *hey kids, Mom needs to see a naked man. You aren't going to call him daddy but if it goes well, I might.*"

"Please don't ever say that to your children," Alex said, wincing.

"Ever, ever," said Chelsea. "Also, don't say it to me. You are not calling that little marmot daddy."

"That little…what?"

"It's what he looks like and I'm not explaining it."

"Just because he isn't *your* fantasy, Chelsea, doesn't mean he isn't mine."

Chelsea squinted. "Is he, though?"

And suddenly, Jenna just felt exhausted. Because she didn't want to do this. She didn't want to be single. She didn't want to date. She didn't want to go to the trouble of trying to get to know a new person. She didn't want to go through the trouble of trying to figure out what to talk about, trying to assess which little stories were well-practiced bids that amounted to lies, and which were carefully crafted covers for red flags. She had never done this.

Not really.

In high school, liking boys, dating them, felt like a game. And then she had met Ryan. And she had won the game. And she had intended for that to be it.

"I just need to do it," she said, more to herself than to Alex or Chelsea. "Because if I don't do it, I'm never going to do it. And it doesn't matter who he is. It doesn't matter. I wouldn't want to marry the first guy I went out with, anyway. Because I just… I'm just so angry that I have to. I'm so angry at him. And it doesn't even matter because he's probably dead, anyway, so the fact that he left me is— And you know what? The worst part about not having his body is not knowing where he died. Why. How. I mean, I can assume that it was at the farmhouse that burned down, because he was staying there with her. She wasn't there. She was at the hospital, so why was he there? Why wasn't he with her? Would he have died even if he had stayed with me? Because I would really like to think that if he had just never left me, he would've lived. But this was his karma. Is that a horrible thing? Am I a horrible person?"

She looked between Chelsea and Alex. And it was Alex who reached out her hand. "You are not a horrible person," Alex said. "Of course you think about those things. Of course you do."

"If he had just stayed with me, maybe I wouldn't feel like a widow and a woman scorned all rolled into one, but the problem is that I do. Because I was already mourning our marriage. I was already grieving this thing, and I hadn't finished. And then the idiot went and got himself burned up." She cleared her throat. "I'm trying to rush into the moving-on part. Because I didn't do that when we split. I thought it could wait. And now I feel like I'm grieving everything. It's too much and I want to be done."

"There's not a timeline for it," Chelsea said. "It's okay to not know what you feel."

Jenna looked at her. "I know you loved him. I did, too. Even if it doesn't seem like it sometimes. I think that's what frustrates me the most. If I could just not love him, all of this would've been a lot easier."

"I know," Chelsea said.

"I do not want to call Matt *daddy*. I don't think I want to call anyone that. I am just trying to be funny and make this less horrifying than it is. I would rather joke about sex than face going out to an actual dinner with an actual man that I have to get to know and treat like a human being."

"Well, it's tough when the guy is just a symbol," Chelsea said pragmatically.

"You're not wrong. He's just a symbolic marmot."

Chelsea snorted. "Well. Then you might as well just get it over with. And your outfit looks great."

"Really great," Alex said.

"Thank you," Jenna returned.

Her friends left, and Matt pulled into the driveway, and she knew her kids would never realize who she was going with, where, or why.

"Text if you need anything," she said.

And then she sent a follow-up text to that effect, since she figured nobody would actually engage with her.

It did not surprise her to learn that Matt drove a Subaru. His choice of restaurant felt right on brand, too. A micro-brewery. That had hamburgers and other foods in deconstructed formats.

Dinner was fine. It really was just fine. It was actually a relief that she wasn't attracted to him because it made the whole thing feel more like a pantomime. And that was about the level she was at. He was really nice. He was actually fairly interesting, and he didn't try to kiss her when he dropped her off at the house.

And she realized that she hadn't worried about how she looked the whole evening. So there was something to be said for that. It was never going to be the same as dating in high school, in part because she wasn't a teenage girl. If a man wasn't interested in what she was bringing to the table, then he just wasn't. It wasn't personal, and it wasn't anything that she should feel bad about.

She stood out in the driveway for quite a while after he left, because she was just sort of marinating in the vanity of it all. She could do this. Go on dinner dates. She wasn't going to be able to spend the night with some guy. Wasn't going to be able to bring him back to her house. She shouldn't get seriously involved with anybody until the kids went off to college. That seemed reasonable and fair.

They were too old to do a stepparent thing. Whoever she was with… It was just going to be this.

She walked over to the front step of the rental house and sat, a little too hard. She looked down the street that still didn't feel like her neighborhood, even after a year, and it didn't have to, because the community was being rebuilt, and she was going to get to move into a new house in just a couple of days.

Almost everything was packed, and all boxes were prelabeled, because that was who she was, whether she was ready or not.

She wasn't ready.

This was supposed to be her fresh start. And here she was, suddenly wishing she could hide from it.

She still hadn't accepted the fact that her life was different. New. That Ryan wasn't going to walk through the door, handsome and the father of her children. All hers.

She couldn't accept that their marriage wasn't what she'd thought.

That he wasn't who she'd wanted him to be.

"You can't fix it, Jenna. You finally met a problem you can't solve. You can't make a husband who doesn't love you, love you. You can't unburn the town. You can't unfuck your life. You just have to start new."

And there was something to that, to the grim acceptance of it that made her stand up and finally take her ass into the house.

Her daughter Chloe was standing in the kitchen when she went inside. "Where were you?"

"I went on a date," she said, not seeing the point in lying to her kid.

"Ew," Chloe said. And then her whole face contorted with horror before being schooled into something overly placid. "I mean… Did you have a good time?"

"It was fine." She flung her purse down onto the counter

and it tipped, her lipstick rolling out. She shoved it back in. "Just friends."

Except it was way too strong of a word for what had happened. It had been a conversation at a shared table while both of them had eaten food. It was actually perfect for what she needed. And maybe he would be disappointed. But she didn't want to waste time on this. She didn't need to get to know him over a series of dinner dates to see if there was a spark between them. She was a grown woman. Besides, a spark would be inconvenient. She could say whatever she wanted to about wanting sex, but it was all a lot of big talk.

Except it made her think of Ethan, who seemed to be the only man she was actually attracted to. A man she'd known since he was a literal child, and she'd been a teenager.

And then she just felt irritated.

"Good. I don't think… I don't think I can handle that."

"Well, I appreciate your honesty. I don't think I can handle it, either. A guy on the town council asked me out, so I thought that I should say yes because…"

"Because you're still mad at Dad?"

Jenna walked over to the freezer and jerked it open, pulling out a quart of ice cream. "Damn right. I'm sorry."

Chloe shook her head. "You don't need to be sorry. You didn't do anything wrong."

She paused over that for a long moment before taking the lid off the ice cream container. "I probably did. I was with your dad for more than twenty years. I'm sure I did a lot of things wrong. I didn't cheat on him. But that doesn't make me perfect. And you know, that last year and a half doesn't…" Her eyes filled with tears, and she hated that she was putting this on her kid. "It just doesn't erase all the other ones."

Chloe looked down and started to peel the dark polish off her thumbnail. "You were really angry."

"Yeah. I am really angry. But if I regret anything, Chloe, it's that he died, and you never got to keep having a relationship with him because you were so on my side. He was still your dad." She swallowed hard. "And I want you to never blame yourself. For anything. If you need to blame somebody for that last year, please blame me."

And she wondered how many different ways she'd messed up. If she should have hidden her feelings completely. If she should have been more gracious.

If she should have had the kids meet their half sister.

She was their half sister, even with their dad being gone.

And Morgan was still a factor in all of it, even with Ryan gone.

"I don't feel bad about it," Chloe said. "I was mad at him. She's three years older than me, Mom. It's gross. I can't understand how...he did that. How he was here with us, and then he wasn't."

"Me neither."

There was nothing else to say.

"I know we talk a lot about how sad you and Aiden have been," Jenna said. "But I want you to know that I'm actually sad, too. About all of it. I was angry, yes, but I was sad that he left. He broke my heart. That's the thing."

Chloe's face scrunched up. "Mom..."

"I don't want to tell you that to hurt you. I just want you to know... I don't hate him. It's okay that you love him. I do, too."

A tear rolled down her cheek and she grabbed a spoon and jammed it into the ice cream before taking a bite straight out of the container. "I'm gonna stop being so sad, though. I want to enjoy this. The new house. The new...everything. I didn't ask for it. We didn't ask for this. But surely, there are some things we can enjoy."

"It's my senior year," Chloe said.

And Ryan wouldn't see her graduate. But she took that bit of grief and folded it up like a secret note she might've passed to a friend when she was her daughter's age. And she tucked it into her own heart. Because she would do anything she could to shield her kids from the worst of it. She hadn't done the best job during the divorce. Now all she could do was try to carry as much as possible.

"Have you started packing?" Jenna asked.

"No."

"I get it. I got all those boxes and labeled them, but my heart wasn't in it."

"Your heart wasn't in a project that involved a label maker?"

"I know. But… I'm ready now. Really. Not just physically."

Because this house was temporary, but a lot of the pain that they'd encountered over the past year was going to be based around something permanent. The new house represented that. Because it was where they were going to live their lives from now on. And she just had to accept that. Or at least, start working on accepting it. She had a different life than the one she'd dreamed of. But she still had her kids. She was still her.

She was Jenna Abbott.

And she had no idea what that meant. As a mostly divorced widow who had been dealing with stuff she didn't want to deal with; a woman who had been throwing herself into initiatives rather than her own life…

She had known who Jenna Abbott was at sixteen. When Abbott hadn't been her last name, but a fantasy that she had doodled on her notebooks. She had known she loved Ryan, and it was the life she wanted to have; the life she wanted to build.

She had been standing next to him for so long that when he had removed himself, she had tipped to the side, because she wasn't built to stand on her own anymore.

She had to change that. She had to figure out who she was.

It wasn't enough to just…move all these physical things around and make a fresh start on the outside.

She had to figure out what it meant inside.

"Let's start packing your things tomorrow," she said.

"Okay," Chloe said.

"You're a good kid."

"You're a good mom."

And after that, she went upstairs, lay across the bed and cried.

21

Afterburn

Chelsea

SOMETIMES SHE THOUGHT it was strange that Mark hadn't been involved in the construction of the new house at all. But then, maybe that was part of the separation. They hadn't really talked about it being an official separation. Of course, she had basically told her husband she didn't love him. She had drilled down in her silence while he had come unhinged. It had been a power play.

And she had been wrong to make it. She had all the same.

Maybe this was his way of punishing her. Of letting her know just how much he didn't care.

She needed coffee, even though she wasn't sure she was in the right headspace for Alex.

That wasn't fair. Alex had never done anything to her.

The issue is what you did to Alex.

Their dynamic had never been great.

She had been a little bitch when Alex had started dating Paul.

That made her want to laugh.

Look how things turned out.

She went into the bakery and saw Alex standing there, looking...bruised. She had dark shadows under her eyes and she was looking thin. She knew that couldn't be a sudden thing. The weight loss. But she was ashamed to admit she hadn't really noticed it. She'd been so lost in her own stuff.

"Good morning."

"Morning," Alex said.

"Are you okay?"

Not only did they usually rely on Jenna as a buffer, but they always kept it to small talk. The weather and whether or not Chelsea had burrito on her face before a meeting. Not genuine, deep inquiries about each other's well-being.

Alex was just always so reserved around Chelsea. She didn't know if it was led by Alex and her holding on to Chelsea's bitchy behavior years ago, or something else. She didn't know if it was her. Or maybe Mark, and the way that he'd so obviously disliked Ryan and Paul.

But none of the people who'd created the distance between them were there anymore. Except for the two of them. So she supposed it didn't matter.

And somebody had to ask the question. Because Alex did look terrible.

"Um...fine," she said, a smile tugging at the corner of her mouth.

"Alex," said Chelsea, "I am usually the first person to just back off in situations like this. But I'm trying. To do something different. To make something a little bit different. I'm trying to be there for Morgan. And I know that's going to freak Jenna out... But someone has to. Jenna has her new life and her crusades. And good for her."

"You have to do what feels right to you."

Chelsea looked at Alex closely. She was always so perfect. So reserved. She seemed brittle right now. She had, ever since the fire. But right now it was so pronounced. "How are you?"

"I'm not great." It was the quavering note at the end of the sentence that really alarmed Chelsea. Because Alex was nothing if not steady and serene. And this wasn't that. Not at all.

"What's going on?"

Alex looked away. "No offense, Chelsea, but why... Why are you asking me? It's outside our boundary."

Normally, she and Alex didn't address that they had a harder time getting along, but apparently, Alex was in a mood. Chelsea was almost proud of her for that.

"I know. But you look really sad today and I don't see the point in letting you be sad. Yes. I was a little bitch to you in high school, and I'm sorry. So what's going on?"

Alex let out a long breath that seemed to unravel the tightness in her posture, and her shoulders sagged. "I haven't slept for a few days. I can't think clearly. Grief is one thing. Losing someone is one thing. But not even having a body, not even knowing what happened..."

"I'm sorry."

"All this stuff—all the stuff with Cody is dredging up all these things and...it's making me question some things."

"Like what?"

Alex looked away. "Do you ever just... It's like I'm starting to distrust the way I remember my life before the fire. Sometimes I'm worried I can't trust myself. I have all these memories..." She looked away. "You don't want to hear all this."

"I do."

"Please don't tell anyone."

"I won't."

Alex swallowed hard. The movement careful, like everything else. "I'm telling you because I know we haven't always been close. But you knew Paul. In a way that other people probably didn't. Because you're Ryan's sister, and Paul was in the house with you a lot. And also… I know you're not going to try to solve this or turn it into a campaign like Jenna would."

"Yeah. She would." Her stomach felt queasy.

"I don't know if Paul loved me. I don't know how to explain it. Sometimes he would tell me that he did and I would believe him, but then there would be something… I don't know. It's just a feeling. But how could that be? Isn't my life evidence of how much he loved me?"

Had everyone's life been a lie? Chelsea felt numb. "I'm questioning everything, too. I found out something about Mark. Before he left. It was about his past. But he never told me. And it makes me wonder… Alex, I have never trusted myself." She had an acrid taste in her mouth, and guilt washed through her. "I accused my father of having an affair when I was fourteen. He said that I got it wrong. That I misinterpreted things. And ever since then, I felt like I was in danger of doing just that. I don't believe him, though. Looking back, I just don't. I don't think it was me. It was him."

Alex took a step back from behind the counter. But she didn't say anything.

"Sometimes I wonder who it benefits. This whole keeping women quiet thing. Jenna is like Cassandra of Greek Myth, isn't she? She goes around and she tells the truth. She is so *confident* in that truth. And people don't like it. And here we are. We can't even say for sure if we knew the men we were married to for all those years. Why do people like uncertain women so much?"

"I don't know."

She felt shaky and scraped raw, and like she had breached all kinds of things by engaging in this conversation with Alex.

"Can I have a coffee?"

Alex nodded. "Sure."

"So it's... Cody that's triggering this for you?"

Alex nodded slowly. "He's part of it. Memories of being with him back then are getting mixed up with my life with Paul. Some things he said about him the other day got in my head and then he..." She swallowed hard. "Seeing a guy you liked in high school shouldn't feel more intense than your whole marriage, should it?" She shook her head. "Listen to me. This is insane. I was happy. For twenty-five years, I was happy with Paul, and he was a good husband, and I'm losing sleep rewriting history because the guy that got away showed up looking gorgeous."

Chelsea huffed a laugh. "I mean, he's pretty hot, Alex. That's fair."

"I'm not a teenager, though."

"But you're a human. And this past year has been really hard."

Alex closed her eyes for a moment. "Yeah. It really has been."

Chelsea bit her lip. "Maybe that's why you and I aren't so comfortable sharing things."

"What is?"

"We don't trust ourselves. How can we share what we feel when we aren't even sure what it is?"

Alex nodded. "I guess. Thank you. For this. I'm sorry. I'm sorry that there's been weirdness between us sometimes. There doesn't need to be. What we did years ago doesn't matter."

Chelsea's stomach felt sour.

She wished that were true. But she knew that what she had done years ago couldn't be erased so quickly. So easily. But what did it matter? She couldn't change that. All she could do was build something new over the top of it.

Yeah. That was what she was going to do.

22

Kindling

Morgan

IT ONLY TOOK three days for her to call him the first time. He came over right after a work shift and brought food. Which seemed above and beyond. But she wasn't complaining. It was nice to have somebody think of her. To have someone think of her basic needs. And more.

The old house was creaky, but it was homey, and Ryan set takeout on the table before he went to look at the pipes underneath her sink.

"The pipes really are leaking," she said.

"I didn't think they weren't," he said.

She had kind of been trying to flirt. But she probably shouldn't. No. She knew she shouldn't. It hadn't come across, obviously. So she just left it. It was for the best if she left it.

"Thank you for dinner."

"I was being selfish," he said. "I haven't eaten."

"You weren't being selfish. You didn't have to come over right after work. But I really appreciate it."

"Go ahead and have some food."

"I don't mind waiting for you."

She lingered in the kitchen while he got underneath the sink with tools that she didn't know the names for. But he seemed to have everything working perfectly within just a few minutes.

He had to have suspected it wouldn't take that long. But still, he brought food.

He had an excuse to stay.

"You can sit down."

He did. And she came up with a lot of different excuses, a lot of different things to have him come fix. Not that they didn't really need fixing; they did. The excuse was in breaking it up. Not giving him a whole list of things, but parceling it out so that she could extend those visits.

And during that time she found out a lot about him. He didn't talk about Jenna. He talked about life before. About high school. About being an amazing football player. And the things that he did with the guys he hung out with. Really stupid things, but she loved the stories.

He talked to her like she was important. He shared with her like she was a friend.

She'd never experienced that before. Ever.

He told her how they'd driven way too fast in the middle of the night in his friend Paul's muscle car. Jumping off bridges into the water below. Taking people's light-up Christmas reindeer and maneuvering them into sexually suggestive positions—that story was her favorite.

"That isn't a thing that people do."

"It is," he said. "We call that deer humping."

"That's horrible," she said, but she was laughing. She couldn't help it. It was objectively pretty hilarious.

"Yes. We had fun. There isn't a lot to do here, so you have to make your own."

"Believe me. Growing up in the city is only fun if you have money. Though, I am very good at shoplifting."

"You're kidding," he said, looking at her with…openness.

Like he was interested, not judging her. No matter the answer to his question as to whether she was kidding.

"Not at all. We would catch public transit—it's free—and go to different neighborhoods where they didn't know us, steal candy, things like that. Basically, stuff that didn't cost money." She blushed. "I was pretty bad. Except…some things. I haven't… I mean…"

He lifted a brow. "You haven't what?"

Her heart gave an extra hard beat. "Um. I haven't like… When it comes to experience… I haven't…been with anyone? Not like *that*. It's, like, the one bad thing I haven't done."

But she was testing things.

She had been for the past couple of weeks. Just slowly. Just carefully.

"I see. And why would that be bad, Morgan?"

His voice was lower, intimate now. She had pushed, and he had gone willingly.

"Maybe *bad* is the wrong word. Maybe I just…have been protecting myself."

"You need someone to protect you, so that you don't have to do all the work."

She wanted that. She wanted it to be him.

He could talk about Jenna if he wanted to. But he didn't. He never did.

It was two visits later when she noticed he didn't have his wedding ring on. Maybe they were going through a separation. Or a rough patch. She didn't think so. In the same way she knew it wasn't accidental that he was coming and hanging out with her in a place where no one could see.

She knew what this was. She did. She wasn't an idiot. She wasn't.

He was a married man, and a comfortable one. He had a good job and a great standing in the community, and she was…a nineteen-year-old stray.

But he was so nice to her. And kind of like a stray, she couldn't resist being scratched behind the ears if it was on offer.

Fall bled into winter, and the aggressive gray of the beginning of December seemed oppressive, even with Christmas lights. She should be used to this. To the Oregon gray, but it always got her. Maybe because Christmas had never been particularly happy.

And then Ryan brought her a tree.

He showed up without making any kind of announcement; just with a giant tree.

"What is that?"

"I thought the place needed a little bit of cheer."

"I… I've never had a Christmas tree."

"That's outrageous."

"I don't have any decorations."

"That's outrageous, too. We have to get some."

"Ryan, I don't have…"

"It's my gift to you," he said. "You don't need to have anything. I want to give it to you."

And that was the first time he took her out. They didn't go to Tenmile. He drove her an hour away, and she didn't need to question it. She knew. He was hiding this. Because it wasn't innocent. She had known that for a while. And while they were out in the store, he touched her sometimes. Putting his hand on her lower back and guiding her through the aisles of Christmas decor.

She wondered what other people thought when they saw them. If it looked like what it was. Or if years of watching sitcoms and movies where the age gap between the male and female actors far exceeded the age gap between herself and Ryan, made it so that they weren't even notable.

Just twenty-three years. That was all.

But that would never have been a barrier. That wasn't the barrier.

She shoved an image of the barrier aside.

They paid, and he played Christmas carols in the car the whole way back. He sang and she thought he had a much nicer voice than was reasonable. Some people really did just have everything.

"It's nice to be able to take care of someone," he said.

She didn't question what that meant, because it was nice to be taken care of.

It was late, and she really wanted to ask him if Jenna was expecting him, but they didn't ever speak her name. Never.

Sometimes Morgan thought of her. Of how bright and confident she was, and sometimes she felt guilty. Because she knew what this was.

But then she let the guilt turn to envy. Jenna had it all, as far as Morgan could see. Friends, a business in town and, well, Ryan. But if Ryan was happy, he wouldn't be *here*, would he?

If he thought about Jenna as often as Morgan thought about him, he would talk about her.

Morgan was in love with him.

No one had ever looked at her and seen what she was missing, or tried to be the one who gave it to her. But he had. From the moment they'd met.

He'd been friendly when no one else had been. He'd helped at the Harvest Festival. He'd bought her a Christmas tree.

He saw her.

And she knew—*she knew*—that this mattered.

It couldn't be reduced to right or wrong.

She'd felt connected to him from the first moment she'd seen him, and that had to matter.

She had never in her whole life benefited from fate. Fate had given her an addict mom who didn't love her. And then suddenly, fate had given her him.

It might not be easy or clean, but nothing in her life ever had been.

At least she wanted this.

She had noticed him on his phone, texting a few different times, and she assumed that he was covering his bases. She also was fairly certain he didn't say: Took Morgan out to buy Christmas decorations because I got her a Christmas tree, and that's why I'll be late.

He helped string lights around the tree, and they decorated it together. And when it was done, she just felt the most irrepressible, wild impulse. And she turned, wrapped her arms around his neck and kissed him. He held her still, and his face went serious. He looked at her for a long moment, and she thought that he was going to set her back. That he was going to tell her that she had the wrong idea.

But then he put his hand on the back of her head, held her like she was something special and he kissed her. Really kissed her. And it was better than anything. Better than any kiss. Better than any dream.

It was like she could hear an orchestra playing. And for a moment she might as well have been flying.

Because she was in love.

And she knew what she wanted. She wanted him to be the first.

It was what she'd been waiting for.

He was what she'd been waiting for.

"Will you… Will you come upstairs?"

"Yeah," he said, his voice sounding tight. "Yeah, I will."

23

Kindling

Jenna

IT WAS THE most spectacular Christmas they'd ever had. Ryan had catered the food, and it was exceptional. The Christmas tree was over-the-top, twelve feet tall and decked from bottom to top with glowing lights. Ryan had bid on it at a charity Christmas tree event, which made Jenna fall in love with him all over again. Because really. It was just the greatest. Not only did the money go to charity, but she also had something completely extra in the window that the neighbors could drool over.

And given that jewelry was her thing, what she sold in her store, having spent tons of time perusing artists and designers online, it was very difficult to get her jewelry. But he got her a Sammy Daniels original cuff, made from hammered gold with sun stones, and it was just the most incredible thing she'd ever seen.

"I haven't even seen this," she said.

"She made it especially for you," he said. "I commissioned it."

"Thank you," she said.

He had gone overboard with the kids, too. It was just the most magical.

"We should do a vacation," he said. "For spring break."

The kids were still on Christmas break when he proposed that.

"Absolutely. Where?"

"Hawaii. You always talk about how much you love it, and we haven't been back in years."

"That sounds great. You never take vacations. What's gotten into you?"

"I'm just realizing how fast time moves. The kids are basically grown up. They're not even going to want to hang out with us soon."

"They don't want to hang out with us now," Jenna said.

"No. True. But they won't even go on vacations with us soon."

"I'm looking forward to that," Jenna said. "Imagine when it's just you and me and Hawaii. The possibilities."

She leaned in and kissed him and was a little surprised when he didn't take it deeper.

"So, March?" he asked.

"Sure. Sounds good. I'll figure out what to do with the store. I'll either get someone to cover or go to reduced hours."

"Great."

He was working himself to death. It was a little bit intense. He had accepted a couple extra shifts at the hospital because they were shorthanded, and while she absolutely appreciated what a great guy he was, committing to things like that, it was still difficult for her to share him.

But they had a vacation planned. And it was going to be wonderful.

Anyway, she had a new project baby keeping her busy. She wanted to have a huge fundraiser dinner at the country club for some of the local schools. There were severe budget issues that were impacting classrooms everywhere. Music and art were going to be a casualty the following school year unless they did something.

The teacher who'd told Jenna about it of course knew Jenna would do something. Because doing something was her specialty.

"I'm proposing dinner with the local stars."

She stated her pitch at the February meeting, excitement making her fingertips tingle.

"Local stars," said Tom, chair of the council and constant skeptic.

"Yes. We, of course, have Jonathan Nesbitt." He had been the star of a science-fiction series in the nineteen sixties. "And Gary Cooper." Much more niche, and star of some low-budget cult-classic zombie films. "Mary Anderson, Martin Stevens." Both from sitcoms in the late eighties. "And of course, Joseph Parker." A comedian, and brother of an arguably more famous comedian who had died of a drug overdose in his peak. "Oh, and Lydia Stapleton." The reclusive mystery author would be a little more difficult to ferret out, but Jenna had yet to meet a person in the arts who wasn't swayed by flattery. It was why they did it. At the end of the day, if all you cared about was the art, you'd keep it to yourself, rather than sharing it with the world. Even if it wasn't about money, it was about acknowledgment.

"Okay. And what exactly do you think that's going to accomplish?"

"People can buy spots at tables with their chosen celebrity.

We can charge a certain amount of money a plate, and all the proceeds will go to the school. I know that I can get people to donate their skills to this. We'll do raffle baskets, have an auction. It'll be great." She heard a groan of skepticism. She cut it off. "Not only will it raise funds for the school, but it will provide this town with something much needed. A little bit of culture. A little bit of *something*."

"The farm and garden festival really is quite cultured," said Courtney.

"I am glad you feel that way, Courtney." She did not give a damn what Courtney felt. "But this is something slightly different than our usual festivals. You know I love a festival. I am a festival champion. But this will give us all a chance to dress up—"

"Does anyone want to do that?" Tom asked.

There was a slight ripple in the room, a murmur of agreement. Agreement with Jenna.

"Yes. I think they do. And here's the thing. We'll sell all the tickets in advance, and we can give the ticket sales to the school before the school year starts. I think, ideally, we can hold the event over Labor Day weekend. And then all of the auction proceeds that we collect that night can go in as an additional gift. But the presales can go toward the organization of an art and music program."

"All right, Jenna," Tom said. "You win. And you're also in charge."

Truly, the seven greatest words that Jenna had ever heard.

She was going to need all hands on deck for this. It was a good thing they had that new girl, Morgan. She was young. She'd have the energy for it.

"Hey," Jenna said, waving as she crossed the room after the meeting. Morgan stopped and looked at her like she'd been caught in a spotlight. "I was thinking that maybe I could enlist you to be part of my charity dinner committee."

Morgan looked shocked, and Jenna felt...bad. Had she really been so difficult when they'd first met?

"I'm not an ogre," Jenna said. "Promise. I just... I get tunnel vision. I'm sorry I don't always think about how that looks to other people. Especially when they don't know me at all."

Morgan's face turned pink. "Oh. Don't worry. I... I'm just... Sure. I'll be on the committee."

She looked down, and Jenna noticed a necklace sparkling in the low light.

"Is that Sammy Daniels?" Jenna asked, reaching out and touching the stone.

Morgan jerked away from Jenna and took a step back. "I don't know."

"Oh. It's just... I got a bracelet like that for Christmas. I make jewelry, and I carry work from other designers, too. I do a lot of sourcing for stones and metals... Anyway, I carry her work in my store. She's a great designer."

"I don't know anything about jewelry," Morgan said. "I didn't know it was...a thing."

"Oh. Well, I do. So if you ever want to know who made something. I probably know. You should come into my store sometime."

Morgan looked away. "I've been...busy. Busy figuring out the yarn store. You know Marjorie isn't doing very well."

"I'm so sorry to hear that." She was. She liked Marjorie, even if they disagreed about sidewalks. "We aren't far from each other, though. Stop by sometime and I'll show you Sammy's other pieces that match the one you have."

"Yeah," Morgan said. "Okay."

"Well. I'll get in touch with you about the dinner. When we

start organizing committees and meetings." She wrinkled her nose. "I know. Committees within committees. It's a hazard."

"Okay. Great."

She had won the charity dinner initiative, and she had a family vacation coming up. It was like her hard work was paying off. She felt…integral. To all of this. Like she fit. Like she mattered. Tom and Courtney taking issue with her didn't matter. As long as she wasn't invisible. And she wasn't. Not anymore. Not like she'd been as a kid in her own home.

She felt like she was finally laying that demon to rest.

Jenna couldn't help but feel like she was going to have one of the best years ever.

24

Kindling

Morgan

EVERYTHING WAS RUINED in March.

She and Ryan were their own world. They talked. He helped her with things around the house. He came and ate dinner with her. And they had a lot of sex. Sometimes he spent the night, and she never asked him how he got away with that. She assumed it had something to do with his schedule at the hospital.

But still, they hadn't talked about Jenna. At least not for two months.

She didn't want to ask him. She just wanted to hold him close in her bed and pretend it was the whole world. She was like a little kid, afraid to dangle her leg over the side of the mattress, because there were monsters out there.

Because the bed was the only safe place.

She didn't have a right to be possessive of him. Not considering what she was doing. Not considering she was the one in the wrong. She knew that. But still, when Jenna had approached her at that meeting and said something about her necklace, and how she had a bracelet that she'd gotten for Christmas...

She'd felt so idiotic. She hadn't known it was something special. In her world, a person couldn't just drop a thousand dollars on a bracelet, and in her world, that bracelet would have come from Target and not been distinct at all because ten women in the room would have also had it.

She hadn't done it on purpose. She'd just...

Sometimes she really forgot. That he wasn't just hers. That this world here at the farmhouse wasn't the whole world.

But the bracelet thing hadn't just been horrifying; it had *hurt*.

It had forced her to reckon with the truth of them.

You really got your girlfriend and your wife the same kind of jewelry?

That was stupid. I'm sorry. It's... I actually went to get something for you. And I realized I needed to get her something. I feel awful... I feel awful.

She believed him. That was the thing. Maybe because she was really gullible.

But at least that had led to some honesty. Some real stuff. About his guilt; about the fact that he couldn't continue living a double life.

And when he said things like that, it terrified Morgan, because she knew that she was the one who was expendable. Not the mother of his children. Not the woman who lived in the real house, who matched the kind of man that he was. She would rather talk about his high school days.

She would rather connect with him over those stories. Because they were relatable. She didn't know anything about suburban living. Didn't know anything about having a family. But she understood being a stupid teenager, so when he talked about that, at least she felt like she had something to contribute.

She knew a reckoning was coming. She knew there eventually had to be one. That Jenna would find out. Or that Ryan would leave Morgan. Something would have to change. Something would have to give.

She just hadn't expected it to give like it did.

A missed period.

And a pregnancy test. One that ended up being positive.

She'd broken a rule. She knew it was a rule, even if they'd never talked about it. They used condoms. *Mostly*.

She'd tried to never dwell on the *mostly*. But sometimes things got so hot, she couldn't think and…he probably couldn't, either.

She went to the hospital. Because he was on shift. And she felt like an idiot, standing at the reception desk, clutching her purse strap like it was a lifeline, and realizing that she had just stepped into a part of Ryan's life that she had never been invited into before.

"Can you just…page Doctor Abbott for me?" she asked.

"If he isn't in surgery," the woman at the front desk said.

She eyed Morgan with way too much knowledge. Morgan didn't like it. But she waited. And when he did appear, he was wearing scrubs, and for some reason that made her want to turn and run away more than anything else.

"You can come into my office, Morgan," he said.

He looked unhappy, but she could also see he wasn't going to register that, not in front of anybody. She followed him down the pristine halls, her shoes squeaking on the floor.

"I'm sorry," she said. "I didn't realize how dumb this was until I was already here."

"What is it?" This was the first time he had ever sounded

irritated with her. At her house everything was great. At her house it was like they lived in another reality. But *reality* reality had come home to roost today, so if she was ever going to find him at the hospital for anything, it was this.

"I'm pregnant," she said.

And she prayed. The biggest thing she prayed was that he would not ask her whose baby it was. Because if he thought…

He's sleeping with two women. Do you really think he just hasn't had sex with his wife in three months?

That made her feel sick. And she deserved that. Right then, she felt small and ridiculous. Because she was about to really see it. The truth of it.

"How far along?"

"Not very," she said.

He rested his elbows on his desk, and she looked down at his ID badge.

Ryan Abbott, M.D.

Surgery.

It reminded her of who he was. And who she was. A nine-teen-year-old who had barely passed high school.

"You have options," he said, sounding like a doctor now. "You know that, right? What do you want to do?"

And she realized that it really depended. And she told him that… Well. She told him she was pretty sure what his answer would be.

"I think I'll keep it," she said slowly. "I don't really have a lot of family."

"You don't have a lot of stability right now, either."

That hurt. He wasn't wrong. But it hurt.

"No. It's true. Though… Marjorie has promised to leave the house and yarn store to me."

She could hear the buzz of the fluorescent light above their heads and she wanted to jump up on the chair and punch it down. She hated that sound. It reminded her of being in the principal's office, or waiting in police stations or CPS offices.

It reminded her of how young and helpless and sad she was, and how dependent she was on…

Well, *the adult* sitting at the desk across from her.

This wasn't different. Not really.

"I'll leave her," he said.

"What?" Morgan nearly collapsed.

"Sit down," he said, suddenly coming around the desk, his strong arms guiding her into the seat. "Yeah. I'm not happy with her. If I was happy with her then this wouldn't be happening. I don't think… I don't think I've been happy for a long time."

"You're going to leave your wife. For me?"

He let out a slow, long breath. "Let's give it a little time."

That reservation… He wanted to make sure she wasn't going to have a miscarriage. She realized that. "Right."

"I have a vacation planned. With her and the kids. It's next week. I can't…"

He couldn't bail on that. Because he cared about Jenna or because it was paid for? She didn't know what kind of math rich people did on that kind of thing. He might say he wasn't rich, because most of the people around him seemed to be part of the same economic tier. But he was definitely rich as far as Morgan was concerned.

"Of course," she said.

"I'll come over after work. We'll talk."

They didn't talk. They went to bed instead. Even if he had sex with Jenna on his vacation, it wouldn't be this. He was leaving her. He had chosen Morgan.

She'd known they were special. It wasn't just an affair. She wasn't on the side. He cared for her. More than anyone else ever had.

It was okay that he was taking the time to say goodbye to his other life.

Because then they would start something new. Together. With their baby.

25

Afterburn

Alex

WHEN CODY CAME in for his coffee, she was ready this time.

"Good morning," she said as she sprung into action, grabbing the cup, moving it beneath the coffee urn, and pouring the scalding liquid into it.

"How do you know I wasn't going to change it up?"

"Well, if you were, you're going to have to wait until tomorrow."

"I wasn't," he said.

"Somehow, I figured that."

"I have a couple questions for you. I've been going over all the documentation about the fire. And there is, of course, a section on you. So I just would like to talk about it. But we don't need to do it here."

"This is like…questioning?"

"Unofficially. I guess. It's more trying to get clarity about certain things."

"I've talked to the police."

"I know. Everything is in the file. I just… We know each other, Alex. I want to talk to you. Because you went to do something really awful, and I want to understand it."

She couldn't figure out whether this was actually friendship or if it was just the FBI. And she wondered if she was supposed to be able to tell the difference between the two.

"We can… We can do that."

Questions. He had questions.

There were several flashes in her mind then, of fire and her mother, and Paul's blue eyes.

The locket.

Broken. Disconnected.

She hadn't been honest with Chelsea. She'd given her a piece of the truth.

About her concerns.

About Paul.

But not about the rest.

"Good. I'd like to. Is there a place we can talk where you'd feel most comfortable?"

"You can come to my place," she said. "After work."

Her throat was dry.

"Okay. That sounds good. Are there other people you think I should talk to who might not be in the files?"

"I don't think so. I don't have any… I don't have any insight. Have you been to see your niece?"

"I'm on my way."

"Okay. Well. Good luck with that."

But after he left, she just stood there and stared at a single spot on the counter. He was coming to her house tonight.

For some reason, that spurred her into action. She would bake something. She would bake many things.

She would find something to say to him.

She would try...

She would try to find a way to piece together all the images in her head.

Dreams. Memories.

Flashes of things. Her mother in a wall of flame. Her husband. His electric blue eyes, so real she thought he was there. That she could touch him.

The locket.

She didn't know what was real. What was made up.

She hadn't told anyone this. Because it made her feel crazy. Because it made her feel like she wasn't all right at all.

She didn't remember the day of the fire.

All she could remember was waking up in the hospital.

26

Afterburn

Morgan

SHE HAD JUST deposited Lily into the playpen and turned the open sign on the yarn store when he walked in.

"Wow. I haven't seen you since..."

"It's been a while," she said.

She knew exactly how long it had been since she'd seen him. She'd been fourteen. He'd hand delivered her birthday card that year, along with a unicorn balloon. They'd talked in front of the apartment complex and he'd given her a hug, but he hadn't come in.

He wasn't on speaking terms with her mother.

For some reason she wanted to run to him and away from him at the same time. She was just so...alone right now. And he had always been there for her, even if it was distant. And he was distant. She didn't think that was anything but by design. She could understand that.

"What are you doing here?"

She felt a deep sense of shame, suddenly. What would Cody think of this?

For God's sake, Ryan had been his friend in high school and she'd had a baby with him.

"I'm investigating the fire." He walked over to the playpen and stood there, looking down at Lily like he had no idea what to do.

"The FBI sent you to investigate?" she asked.

"Yep. I'm afraid so. So here I am."

"How long have you been in town?"

"Longer than I should have been without saying hi. I'm sorry. It's…"

"You don't like to come back here," she said.

"I don't. And I need to tell you… I didn't know about you and Ryan. I didn't know about Lily."

"Oh. I don't want to talk about that—"

"Morgan, I'm not mad at you."

For some reason that replaced the shame with anger of her own. "No offense, Cody, but I don't need you to weigh in. You weren't here. I haven't seen you in six years."

"Has it been six?" He looked ashamed then.

"Yes. Marjorie was there for me, and you weren't there for her. Ryan was there for me, so I don't need you to tell me anything one way or the other."

He cleared his throat. "Simmer down, kid. I really wasn't judging. I'm sorry, okay?"

She wanted to fix it. Immediately. Because whatever she'd felt right then…

Cody was Cody.

He mattered to her.

Ryan and Marjorie were gone. They were dead.

She couldn't afford to lose Cody.

"I'm sorry. It's just been… It's been a hard year."

"I know that. It's not easy for me, either. Getting sent back here to do this… It's hard for me, too."

"You didn't come back when Marjorie died."

"I know. It was shitty of me." He bent down and held his hand out toward Lily, who leaned forward in that haphazard toddler way, and grabbed the edge of his hand. "But I have my own stuff with her, with this place…"

"Well. Whatever. It all got left to me."

He looked up at her. "I didn't mean for it to."

When she'd said it, she didn't know if she had meant the farmhouse, and all of the assets, which was a good thing, or the work, which was a less good thing. He had interpreted it as the work, clearly.

"I got the farmhouse, too."

"There's no farmhouse anymore," he pointed out.

"No. But I have the property."

"And you can have it. I don't need it. I don't want it. I'm not staying here. This isn't a happy place for me."

"Like it's a happy place for me?"

"Then why are you here?"

"Because I have a business here. And it's going well. Because… Because maybe I am going to have to start over, but I don't feel strong enough to do it. I had just done it. And I had everything… And then it all got ruined." She walked to the playpen and scooped Lily up, taking her in her arms since he wasn't going to do it. "Thank you, though. For the birthday cards."

"Oh. Yeah."

"You don't have a girlfriend or something who sends them, do you?"

"No. I sent them."

"It's just that, sometimes those birthday cards were the only birthday present or acknowledgment of my birthday that I got. I imagine if you're going to move around a lot, and have a mom who's hiding from people, having an uncle in the FBI is probably the best way to get birthday cards consistently."

"I can neither confirm nor deny that department resources may have been used to get you those cards."

"She's not a good mom, Cody."

"Yeah, she's not a good sister, either. Or a good daughter. But I'm kind of an asshole son, so it's fair."

"Are you a good brother?"

He paused for a long time. "I tried to be. I tried to be."

"How long are you here for?"

"Until I get some movement on this. I'm staying right here in town."

"Me, too. There's an apartment just upstairs. I'm really fine. I'm probably just going to sell the land, then. Marjorie… Grandma…"

"Was she good to you?"

The question caught her off guard. "She took care of me. And yeah. She was pretty good to me."

"Good."

"She wasn't good to you, was she?" This was her first time seeing Cody as an adult, and understanding…

Well, she supposed the one good thing about having had a relationship with a man who was in his forties was that she'd seen him as a human.

Not at first. At first, she'd seen Ryan as a god.

Then they'd actually moved in together. His laundry had become part of her life, along with him. His bad habits had been shared with her, not just with his wife.

It had become real.

She'd loved him, in spite of it all, but it had definitely been a change.

They'd still had passion; they'd still had fun. But she'd also seen his temper, his insecurity. He became such a bro when his best friend was around.

That, however, allowed her to see Cody as a person now. Not someone so much older than she was that he should just… know everything, or be perfectly together.

But as someone who probably had a reason for being as distant as he was.

"You know, people and things change a lot over the years. It doesn't really matter. My childhood days are ancient history. I left here so that it could all be ancient history."

"So you must be the friend that Ryan talked about. He didn't mention you by name. He mentioned Paul because I had met him, but…he mentioned another friend, too. One he did a lot of dumb stuff with. Jumping off bridges and things like that."

"That was definitely me. Me and Jenna and Alex."

"Jenna. Yeah. She's not my biggest fan."

"Fair enough, right, kid? I'm not mad at you, but I figure it's not really outrageous for the guy's ex-wife to dislike you."

"Yeah. Well. I figured his marriage was his responsibility." She held her chin up and stared him down. She'd had plenty of shame in her life. Being poor. Occasionally in foster care, never in the nicest clothes. Having a mother who was a drug addict… People had tried to shame her for those things for years. Things that were out of her control. And yes, what had happened with Ryan had been completely within her control. She had done it fully knowing that he was a married man. But she didn't feel ashamed. There were so many things she hadn't gotten. So many things she hadn't been given. She couldn't feel bad about one thing she had, not even for a little bit.

She did feel guilty, though. It was different than shame, she discovered. That sadness that she'd caused someone else pain.

But she'd just loved him so damn much.

"I really…didn't want to hurt her, and I don't blame her for hating me," she said. "But the thing is I just didn't *care* about her. I didn't care about what would happen later. I just wanted what he gave me then, and until I found out I was pregnant, I really didn't think about…his life away from me, or what would happen in the future. He was good to me," she said. "Better than anyone ever has been."

And she ignored the complicated things. The sticky things. The nagging thought that he'd have kept her tucked away in a farmhouse in the woods forever if she hadn't gotten pregnant.

The fact that he'd been able to somehow go home and pretend they weren't happening when he was with Jenna.

That was what ate at her the most now. Without him sleeping beside her, without his voice, his smile, his touch. It was easier to worry at the loose threads.

To wonder what kind of man so successfully lied when he was with the woman he'd been married to all that time. And what kind of man could so easily pretend that part of his life didn't matter at all when he was with his new girlfriend…

"Well, good. Look, I've never been married. Jenna was a friend back then, and I care about her, but with him gone, I guess none of that stuff matters all that much. He was always a good friend, too."

She felt jealous of him then. That he'd known Ryan back then. It was all so complicated, because while she might have had a whole year to think about the problems in her relationship with Ryan, she also had a daughter who had his eyes. And she wished, more than anything, that she'd had a right to him. That she'd had more time with him. "If you had such good friends here…why did you leave?"

"I did have good friends, but there were also a lot of… complications."

"What kind of complications?"

"Like…complications like you and Ryan."

"You were sleeping with an older, married woman?"

"No. But I had feelings for somebody. And it was impossible. And at the time… Look, I had to go to DC to do my training. There was no way I could get to the level I wanted in my career living here. But yeah. There was some personal stuff. All water under the bridge now. No big deal. Anyway, I need to go." He backed away from her, heading toward the door. "We should get together and have dinner while I'm in town."

"You don't have to do that," she said. "We don't have to pretend that family matters. It never really has for us."

But she had saved his birthday cards, so it was pretty obvious she was lying.

He hadn't come to his mother's funeral, but he couldn't pretend it was because family didn't matter to him, either. Because he had sent all those birthday cards. Without fail. For twenty years. Wherever she was.

"We'll have dinner," he said. "See you later."

And he walked out of the shop. She impulsively walked over to a bit of yarn and started moving skeins around. Rearranging them by what she didn't know. Just touching them to touch them, because she had found that yarn and knitting contained a certain level of solace that she couldn't find anywhere else. Cody was in town. And he was looking into answers about the fire. The fire that had killed Ryan.

Maybe that would bring closure. Answers. *Something*.

She needed *something*. She just didn't have a clue what it was.

27

Afterburn

Alex

ALEX HAD MADE two types of cupcakes, a strudel and a crumble. It was a little much, but Cody White was coming over. And ridiculously, she wanted to text her friends like they were in high school. But what was there to be said?

She had shared everything with Jenna once upon a time. Everything except Cody. He had been hers. The sacred space that no one had been allowed to tread.

Of course, this girlish giddiness was just a nice place for her to live while she grappled with the fact that he was going to ask questions she didn't know the answers to.

When he showed up, he wasn't in that dark FBI suit. He was wearing a navy blue sweater and a pair of jeans. And for some reason it threw her off. Made it difficult for her to find her feet. Thankfully, she was able to see him walking from the curb up to the front door, and then gather her wits.

She walked over to the door and pulled it open, smoothing her black dress down as she did. "Hi. Come on in."

"This is nice."

There was something heavy about those words, and she looked around, tried to see the house the way that he might see it. Tried to look at it like she had never seen it before. With the knowledge that she had about herself and Paul from high school.

He probably looked at it and saw that kind of snobby rich person that he had sort of resented. Even while he hung out with him. She had called him on that once.

We're your friends. If you hate rich people so much why do you hang out with us?

It's in spite of it. Definitely not because of it.

Well. Maybe you should be less bigoted.

Spoken of course with the ferocity of youth, and all the idiocy that went with it.

Yeah. That bigotry against rich people must be really rough.

She had always hated it when they fought. They hadn't often fought seriously.

"Thank you." She gestured toward the living room. She had all the snacks set out in there. "Have a seat. Can I get you a drink? Coffee? Beer?"

"You don't need to serve me."

She pushed one of the plates to the left, just slightly. "I'm sorry. I was unclear about whether or not this was a personal visit."

"I'm probably mixing things a little bit, to be honest with you." His eyes met hers, uncomfortably direct. "But I find that I have a difficult time keeping things strictly business with you."

Her breath stalled out.

"Right. Well." She touched the top of the mug she'd set on the bar. "Drink?"

"I'll take coffee. But I'll go with you."

He followed her into the kitchen, and she felt embarrassed to have him in her house, picking up clues about her by the way she had arranged things. The white on cream on beige. Which she'd thought looked clean, but now she wondered if it was like being the person who liked vanilla the best.

He made her feel sixteen.

"There was no fire damage on this street at all." It bothered her, not having any idea what he knew and what he didn't.

It was all in folders she'd never seen.

She'd lived through it and there were things she didn't know.

Mostly, she'd accepted the memory loss. It was part of the trauma of the day. In the grand scheme of things, it didn't matter. Paul was gone. What did it matter if she'd lost a few hours?

Fire.

Her mother.

Paul's eyes.

The locket.

It didn't matter. She was having dreams.

It had nothing to do with those lost hours. And it wouldn't change anything.

"No. It was a miracle. Not one I'd have asked for. But you don't get asked, do you?"

He cleared his throat. "Can I walk you through what we have in the documents?"

"Whiplash, Cody."

"Sorry. I'm trying not to get distracted."

"Do I distract you?"

And that had sounded way more flirtatious than she had intended. She hadn't meant to be flirtatious at all. He had stubble on his face at this hour. She wanted to reach out and touch it. The last time she had touched his face, he hadn't had anything quite so mature as whiskers. She was fascinated by it now. But Cody was a man. She wondered what he saw when he looked at her. When he looked around the house, he clearly saw an upper-middle-class housewife's dwelling. She was pretty sure there was something in here that said *Live, Laugh, Love,* bought by her before it had become a joke on the internet. Her kids had informed her she was "basic."

He was probably thinking she'd been prettier back then.

Or he was just thinking about the case, and not her at all, because she suffered from middle-aged invisibility. Which Jenna could claim wasn't a thing all she wanted, but it sure felt like a thing to Alex.

She wasn't sure if it seemed silly or gloriously human that she could worry about all of this given the reason for his visit.

"Let me get the coffee." She turned and started to pull shots on her espresso machine, going straight over to the hot water tab and filling the mugs the rest of the way with that. Instant Americanos.

She handed him his, leaving it black, and poured a generous measure of cream in her own.

"Let's go sit down," he said.

He had taken over immediately. Like it was his house, not hers.

But she followed him into the living room and sat down in a chair across from the one he chose.

"There isn't much to tell. I was burned. On my hands. And my arms." Absently, she ran her fingertips over the lingering scars. "I was found walking down Dark Hollow Road. They found my car later. Or they think it was my car. Burned out. I must have left it, and run."

"Alex," he said, looking at her directly. "This is all information that I have. Tell me from your perspective."

She didn't have a perspective. She didn't have anything. Her hands started shaking and she tried to make them stop.

Why couldn't she remember?

She did her best not to dwell on this. She'd decided it didn't matter.

And then the locket had come in the mail and her dreams had started.

What was she supposed to say to him? *I don't remember anything but sometimes I wonder if my supposedly dead mother came to town and started a fire? Or she came to town and...*

I started one.

Because maybe my husband didn't love me?

No. That couldn't be it. That couldn't be it.

She had to tell Cody. He was the FBI and if she lied, there would potentially be legal consequences.

But if she was honest, she would probably end up a suspect.

And she had no way of knowing if she should be one or not.

"I don't remember," she whispered.

"What?"

She shook her head and tried to keep her hands steady. "I don't remember," she said again.

"What part?"

"I—"

"Walk me through that day. September eighth. Everything you know."

He was Cody. So it seemed okay.

He was Cody, so she looked at him, and she felt safe.

She let out a long, slow breath. "I haven't told anyone."

"What?"

"That I don't remember. Everyone knows I got hurt, everyone knows I got rescued and everyone has their own...

trauma from that day. So it's not like we've asked each other to sit down and relive it."

"Why haven't you told anyone, Alex?"

"Because I hate it. I hate not knowing and I can't help but…" She tried to catch her breath. Her heart was pounding too hard. "If Paul were here, he would help make sense of things. He was always sure."

"Start at the beginning," he said.

She nodded. "I got up that morning. I remember that. I *think* I remember that. Or maybe it isn't a memory? Maybe I just know what I do most mornings. Maybe it's any Tuesday morning."

"That's okay. Tell me as best you can."

"I got up, I went to the bakery. I… I don't know after that."

"Who did you talk to?"

"No one. Except my employees. Jason and Lori were there for opening. I went in the back…"

"You don't remember seeing Paul that day?"

"No," she said. "I don't know where he was."

"And they found your car on the highway?"

"Yes. I was driving back toward town."

"Was that part of your normal routine at that time of day?"

She waited another beat. "No."

"Would Paul's normal routine have included being anywhere in the path of the fire?"

She shook her head. "No. Not at that time."

"You were both behaving out of character?"

She looked at the back wall like it might provide some answers, but it was blank. Like her brain. "I don't know that I'd say that. There are all kinds of reasons people deviate from their routines."

"No one else knew where Paul was at that time?"

She could see Paul's eyes. Like in her dream.

And the reflection of flames in his blue eyes.

"No," she said. "All his colleagues at the hospital were questioned."

"How were things between you and Paul?"

She looked at him. Directly. "How were things between me and Paul? That can't be an FBI question."

He lifted a brow. "I'm FBI. Therefore, it is."

"Good. Normal. The same as always."

"Which was?"

"Good," she said, not hesitating at all. "He always treated me like I was a priority. He was attentive and he was… He was so charming." She faltered then. She didn't know how to explain Paul. And why should she? Cody knew him.

Cody's jaw went hard for a moment, then softened. He looked around the room and she wanted to hide things from him. Her wedding picture, family photos, knickknacks. She didn't want him to see her so clearly.

"Paul was the same as he's always been," she said, her voice softer for some reason.

"An asshole, then."

The bluntness of the words shocked her. "That wasn't my experience of him."

Cody looked at her, a little too sharp. A little too knowing. "He was a narcissist."

She looked away. "Probably a little. But most surgeons are. They all think they're God. You know the old joke."

He leaned back in his seat. "I don't know. That probably plays in different circles than I run in."

"What's the difference between God and a surgeon?" She pressed her fingertips together and looked down at her hands. "God doesn't think he's a surgeon."

Paul *loved* that joke.

"That tracks."

"So yes. Paul could be arrogant. But it's not unique to his field. They have to be arrogant, right? You don't want an insecure person to cut you open."

Cody chuckled. "I think I'd have passed on having Paul cut me open."

Those words landed heavily.

He shuffled through the paperwork, but she didn't get the sense he actually needed it. It was a prop. He already knew what it said. And what he wanted to say in response.

"What do you know about the money that was stolen from the charity fundraiser?"

"Nothing," she said, that word coming out quickly.

His gaze was too hard. He was too much law enforcement here, and not enough Cody. "I think there's a link. Between the fire and the money. Everything about it seems too coincidental to me."

"Paul didn't need money."

"Ryan?"

She took a breath. "Maybe. He did have a new woman to support. I can't speak to what was happening in Ryan's life. *I* was not in contact with him. Paul was still socializing with him. They were friends. That's fair. You shouldn't have to pick sides."

"You wanted him to, though?"

He was still asking in his FBI voice. And that was not relevant, she was sure. "I was upset on behalf of my friend. I did think that Paul should…have words with Ryan about what he did."

"He didn't?"

She shook her head. "No. He never outright refused to speak to Ryan about what had happened, but I'm almost certain he didn't."

"You didn't ask?"

"I did. But he… I don't know. He was good at… He's so charming, you know? He can talk circles around anyone. It was a weird thing with Paul. You could talk to him for hours and not realize he'd never shared a single thing and you'd told him everything."

This was why she was careful.

So she didn't say things like that.

But she'd said it.

Of course, to Cody. It was always Cody.

"I always end up telling you my secrets. No matter how close I am with Jenna or Chelsea…or Paul. I always end up telling *you* my secrets."

And the FBI agent was gone then. She could see something dark in his eyes. Resentment.

"Yeah. I really like that. What boy doesn't want to be the confidant of the girl he really wants to—" He cut himself off. "Sorry. Maybe I have a little bit more resentment than I thought I did."

She looked down at her bracelet and straightened it. "I don't believe that."

"You don't believe that I'm resentful?"

She met his eyes again. "I don't believe you're unaware of it."

He chuckled. "Maybe you have a point."

He stretched back in his chair, his long legs flung out in front of him. He put his hands behind his head, emphasizing the broad musculature of his chest. He was a good-looking guy. He always had been. But there was more to it than that. He had always called to her in a very specific way.

She hadn't had a chance to speak to him after she'd found out she was pregnant. She hadn't spoken to him since the night in the woods when…

She owed him something. An explanation.

"I was a coward when I was seventeen," she said. "Just so you know. Everything in my life was falling apart. I clung to what made sense." There was more than that, but she didn't know how to say it.

"I was always there for you," Cody said. "And then I kept being there, and I don't know why you stopped wanting me to be."

"Because it was too much."

"Was it too much or did you want him instead?"

It would be easy to say yes, she had. It was the story she'd built over the top of the truth for years. She'd wanted Paul so much she'd been swept away.

Because no one knew the truth. No one except her. And the man sitting across from her.

That she'd been caught up in passion once before, and said no because it was too much. That she'd felt something more—something deeper—and she'd run away from it.

That Paul was the easier choice.

"Paul wasn't too much. Paul was the one that I should've been flattered to get attention from. Because wasn't he the best-looking guy in school? And he was going to be a doctor, and definitely everything that my mom would've wanted me to have. She always liked Paul."

"Your mom left you, Alex. Why the fuck did it matter what she would want you to do?"

"I can't explain it, Cody. I only know that it did matter. And I was afraid. Because my life didn't look like I had thought it was going to. Because everything around me was falling to pieces and I thought if I clung to something that looked whole, then maybe I would be okay. Because my mom was supposed to be there for me. For everything. She was supposed to be there when I graduated, and I sure as hell wasn't supposed to get pregnant before I walked out of that school. At least if I married Paul, I could see a way toward having everything be normal. Not everything. But something. I could still see the future I was supposed to have. And I was desperate for that."

"And you couldn't see that with me?"

"I was already pregnant with his baby, Cody. I made my decision."

"Right. Just remember that was your decision. Not mine."

"Are you telling me that you would've been with me? Even though I slept with him? That after you and I kissed, after we almost…that you would have been okay with me sleeping with him?"

"I wasn't happy about it, Alex. But I wanted *you*. Not an idea. Not a fantasy. Not a virgin. I wanted you. And I would've taken whatever you came with."

God, it was like getting stabbed in the heart.

"That sounds really nice, twenty-six years later. But you didn't say that then."

"I was hurt."

"And I was scared. And bleeding out from my mom's abandonment. From the fact that life was changing and moving in the direction that I didn't want it to. And he was there for me."

"He probably just wanted to sleep with you."

He'd said it. The thing that she carried, deep inside her. The thing that gave her doubts even now.

"I realize that. Now. It doesn't matter what he wanted then. He married me." She laughed. "I still talk about him in the present tense. Like he isn't gone." She took a deep breath. "Cody, the truth is, I was in love with you. I was in love with you even when I gave Paul my virginity in the back of his car."

His lips twitched. "That stupid fucking car."

"It's a cool car. I still have it."

"I always hated it. And now I hate it even more."

"I thought you didn't care?"

"I care. It just wouldn't have stopped me from being with you."

He said that. But there was no way of proving it was true.

"Well, now you're a big FBI agent. And you don't have a wife, do you? How do you think that would've gone? You and me. We would've struggled, wouldn't we? It must be really hard for people to have relationships in your line of work. Or you do have one?"

"I *have* had them." His voice made it clear they were few and far between.

"Ever been married?"

"No."

"Any kids?"

"No."

"Well. I think that says a lot, don't you?"

"I'm not here to suggest I know how things would've turned out. Not at all. But I do want you to understand why I left."

"You left for your job."

He nodded once in acknowledgment. "I guess the real thing isn't why I left, but the fact that I left without you. And the fact that Tenmile hasn't felt like home for all these years."

His words hit something deep inside her. It hadn't felt like home. She looked at him and felt something expanding in her chest that she hadn't felt since she was seventeen and the world still seemed full of possibilities. She wondered if this place had felt like home to her even once since Cody had left.

"I wasn't mature enough to handle it," she said.

"Seventeen-year-olds aren't supposed to fall in love," he said.

And it was the truest thing. But they had.

She was careful. Always.

So careful she'd run from him and jumped into a mistake she couldn't take back.

Because at least *that* mistake wouldn't break her.

After her mom had gone, she'd felt far too close to broken.

"You probably thought it was because he was better-looking than you. Because he was rich. Because he was going to be a doctor. But that wasn't it. Not for me. I never thought he was better-looking than you."

He laughed. He actually laughed. "It's just… You know, even straight guys around the school talked about how pretty he was."

"Pretty. But that's not chemistry. It was never that I felt more for him. It's that what I felt for you was impossible. Too big. After my mom was gone, too big. And I wanted something I could manage. Someone I could manage. And it was never you. He felt like the safe choice. Like the choice I was always supposed to make. And so, in the end, it was the choice I made."

"Were you happy with him?"

How did you distill so many years into something so benign and simple? She thought about Ruth and Jack. This house. Family vacations and barbecues.

"Yes," she said.

"Have you seen a psychologist about the memory loss?"

"No."

"Memory loss is a pretty common part of PTSD."

She resented that. Resented him peeling her skin back and exposing all of her regrets, her feelings, and then reverting back to being an agent interrogating her with his very next breath. "Glad you're an expert."

He looked at her hard, and she suddenly realized she was looking at a stranger. He had been in the FBI for going on twenty years. What did she know about the things that had given him PTSD?

They didn't know each other anymore. She had just given

him a lot more information than anyone else in her life had; the truth about her marriage. But she didn't actually know anything about who he was now. It was like she had started talking to him as if they were still in high school.

The same people they'd been.

But there was a lot of extra wisdom in his eyes. More lines around them, too.

Deep grooves of concern worn between his eyebrows.

"I'm sorry," she said. "I realize that I don't know enough about you to comment."

"I chose the job that I chose. There's no use pitying me. I've seen a lot of things that no one should ever see. We live in a world where astonishingly horrible things happen. And unless somebody is willing to wade into those things, there's never going to be justice. I've chosen to be that person. I'm going to be that person here. I'm going to fix this. As best as it can be fixed. I know that you can't rebuild from ashes, but you can build something new over the top of it. You're not broken, Alex. It's not broken."

"How do you know that?"

"Because I need to believe it. Because one thing that kept me going all this time is thinking of you. And thinking that you were here. And safe. And I hoped you were happy."

"I was." They'd had a life. A beautiful life. She'd chosen that life. Somewhere, deep down, she'd known she might not have chosen the wildest love.

Cody would have burned her alive.

Now you know what it's like to be burned alive. Isn't it tempting to try?

Her husband's body had never even been found. It had only been a year. How could she even think she wanted that?

Because there was never a moment in her whole life, in her marriage, when she hadn't wanted it.

She'd wanted Cody all along, and the sudden conviction in that thought, the strength of it, rocked her. He was here now, and there was nothing standing between them.

Except the same fear she'd always had.

"Why didn't you come back after the fire?" She hadn't meant to ask that. Cody made her speak by accident and no one had ever done that but him. "You said you'd have been there for me in high school, if I'd have let you. But you could've been there for me after the fire. And you weren't."

He really did look like Cody from back then now, not FBI Cody. But a kid. A kid who'd gotten called out and refused to admit it. "Yeah. I suppose." He cleared his throat. "You know, maybe all of this is kind of bullshit. Me lecturing you about anything. I don't have a single connection outside of work that I've maintained in the last twenty years. I have been called emotionally unavailable by more than one woman, so…"

"And are you?"

He looked at her for far too long.

"Entirely." He stood up and grabbed a cupcake off the tray. "I'm going to take this with me."

"Okay."

She didn't know why he was leaving so quickly. But she had a feeling she needed to let him.

He walked toward the front door, then stopped. "I'm emotionally unavailable because my emotions have been tied up elsewhere since I was about fifteen years old. And I never did figure out how to get those back."

Then he walked out, and he took all the air in her lungs right with him.

28

Kindling

Jenna

THE VACATION HAD been so awesome. Ryan hadn't been on his phone at all, which was so unusual lately. The kids had a great time. They had swum with *turtles*.

And Ryan had organized all of it. She hadn't had to do anything. It really was a surprise for *her*.

Truly the best.

But after that, Ryan had seemed distracted. And he had picked up even more shifts at the hospital.

"You're only one man," she said. "You can't do everything."

"I know. It won't be forever."

She hoped not. In the meantime, things with the charity dinner were going amazingly. They had confirmed all of their celebrities, and interest in spots for dinner was high. People wanted to come, even from surrounding areas, and the presales started the following day. She was just so excited. She had a feeling it was going to be a massive success.

"You're in a good mood, Mom," Chloe said.

"I am. Because everything is great." And she hummed, wandering around her kitchen, which she loved. It was such an expression of her. Of course, she wasn't the best cook. She had a whole business to run. But she was very good at setting out takeout. And buying prepared meals that tasted great.

Chloe was off to a friend's, and Aiden was going out for pizza after football practice, which meant tonight it would just be her and Ryan.

That inspired her to put on a particularly fitted dress and a pair of high heels. Because why not? She put in an order for his favorite Chinese food and got it arranged in actual bowls on the table, because her presentation was good, even if she didn't do the preparation.

She liked to put something into it. Another way of making herself important.

"Something smells good," Ryan said when he walked in.

"It's me," Jenna said, grinning.

His gaze slid away from hers. He didn't laugh.

"It's obviously dinner," she said. "Are you tired?"

"A little. I didn't know you were getting dinner."

"Yeah. I got your favorite."

"Thanks. I... I need to talk to you."

"Okay," she said.

She wondered what the hell was going on, because Ryan never looked serious like this, and he certainly never looked nervous. Ever. He was one of those overconfident guys. And genuinely, it was kind of an annoying trait that he had. He never... Ever.

"I just want to start by saying... I am really sorry."

The kitchen tilted. Or maybe that was impossible. But she

wasn't sure what was impossible now. Because there was nothing good that could follow what he'd just said. Nothing. It wasn't possible.

"Okay," she said.

"It's my fault, Jenna. It wasn't you. It wasn't *you*. There was nothing… It's me. And… And then the situation…"

"Oh my gosh, Ryan. You have never taken this long to get a sentence out in your entire life." And she felt completely destabilized, and she hated him for that. Because how dare he? She was standing in her kitchen. Her beautiful kitchen, where she didn't cook. But it was hers. This was theirs.

"I… There's not an easy way to say it. And I was kind of waiting for there to be an easy way. I got someone pregnant."

And of all the things, that wasn't what she expected. Of *all the things*. Maybe dirty texts. Errant dick pics going out to another woman, perhaps. Maybe—*maybe*—a one-night stand. Maybe a one-night stand *with a man*.

Hell, with *Paul*.

She could have seen that.

All of that had crowded her head right before he'd spoken.

But getting another woman pregnant?

She put her hand on the edge of the counter and tried to keep herself from falling.

"Not even… I found someone else? Not even introducing me to the idea that you had perhaps stuck your penis in another woman, *but you're leading with the pregnancy*?"

"Because it's why I'm telling you," he said, and he couldn't look at her.

She wanted to scream at him to do it. To meet her eyes. To look at her like he'd done at their wedding when he'd made vows to not do this very thing.

He continued, his voice heavy. "I'm going to be really honest with you, Jenna. The longer it went on, and the longer you didn't find out…the more I told myself I was going to stop. And that you would never know that it happened at all. Or maybe that I could…do both. I thought that for a while. And then I realized I couldn't do that, but I knew what choice I would make. You don't choose the other woman, not when you have a home and kids. But she's pregnant. And it forced me to be honest. It's forcing me to make the honest choice. I haven't been able to breathe for a while. I'm just not… I'm not happy."

Ironic he would say that because her lungs didn't work. She was gasping.

"You can't breathe? *You* can't breathe, because I'm smothering you? Or… What?"

"It's not that. I told you it doesn't have anything to do with you. I met her, and it's like, all we ever needed to talk about was…growing up. And dumb things we did when we were teenagers, and it was…"

"Not sharing a life with someone? Not sharing bills and children? Because what you're talking about just sounds like… dating? That thing you do when you first meet somebody. It's not… It's not deep."

"Well, maybe I needed to get away from deep."

And her bracelet caught the kitchen lights. Her Sammy Daniels bracelet. And there was one other person that she could think of that had a Sammy Daniels piece. And she didn't even know that's what it was. Because it was a gift.

"You are sleeping with that child, aren't you?" He was still looking at everything but her and her control snapped. *"Look at me, you fucking coward."*

He did. She wished he hadn't.

"She's not a child, Jenna."

"Ryan. You…" And she was about to tell him that he was a cliché. Her high school-football-playing doctor husband, who had been Most Likely to Succeed. Who had been voted best couple along with her, was having an affair with a woman closer in age to their daughter than to his wife.

She was about to tell him that he was a cliché. But she couldn't do that.

Not without admitting that she was no less of one than he was.

A woman with a business her husband saw as a hobby, who had been popular and pretty in high school, and had a white kitchen with roosters all over it, and who was completely and utterly blindsided by the fact that her husband had slept with a younger woman. That he had slept with anyone else. That he would ever...

Yeah. She could call him a cliché. But it was her. The cliché was her. Just as much as it was him.

"Who knows?" she whispered.

That was the thing she couldn't face. How many people knew. When she walked into her meetings, when people came into the store... Did everyone know but her?

Had she been so busy trying to be important to the town, to make changes, to run her business that Ryan didn't even think mattered, that she'd missed something obvious?

"Paul knows."

She couldn't help but think of every time she'd seen Paul in the past few months. Those sharp blue eyes of his, the way he looked at people like he could see into them. He'd known. It made her want to throw up. "Did he tell Alex?"

"No," Ryan said.

"How do you know? They're married. He probably tells her everything. Because that's what people in healthy relationships do." If her friend knew...

"Believe me when I tell you, Paul Coleman does not tell his wife everything."

And she decided to go ahead and skip right past that. Because her thoughts were a blur, and so was everything around her.

"Do I have an STD?" she asked.

"No," he said.

"You're clearly not using condoms with her, and I don't recall you ever once whipping one out to use with me. And we had a lot of sex in Hawaii, Ryan. Was it just because you were cut off? Because you've been having it with two women and suddenly you were stuck with one?" At home they'd had a little less than usual because he had been working so much, but they'd still been having it. Enough that she would never have thought there was a red flag.

"You don't have an STD. She's not—"

"Do not tell me what your mistress is and isn't."

"She's not my mistress. I love her. I'm sorry. But I do. I didn't mean for it to be that. I didn't mean for it to be this."

"You love her." And that felt like a bullet wound she would never recover from. She was going to bleed out. All over her white kitchen. It hurt so much she couldn't breathe. It hurt so much that when a red wave of anger appeared, she grabbed on and rode it because if she had to feel nothing but pain, she was going to die from it. "You love her. Wow. *Wow.* You love her. That is really something. It really is."

"I was going to stay…"

"You were going to *charity stay* with me? For what? For appearances? Well, thank God you got her pregnant because I would rather die than be your quiet martyrdom."

"Jenna—"

"I'll make this easy for you. I don't want you to stay. I want you to leave. And if she loses that baby, don't come back here. I don't care. You made your choice."

"She's twelve weeks. I waited to tell you."

The cruelty of that took her breath away.

She looked at his face. His perfectly handsome face. Those lines worn into those familiar features, which were so…familiar. And he might as well have been a stranger.

He had been lying to her for months.

Maybe longer. Because apparently, he could cheat and as long as she didn't find out…

"Get out of my house. This is *my* house, Ryan. This is my house, and you can't be in it. You cannot move her into this house."

"I won't," he said.

And there was no reason to hold anything back. Because this was broken.

This was her chance to say it all, to smash it so it could never be repaired.

To burn it all down.

Because he didn't get to walk away from her like she didn't matter. She would make it so he couldn't come back. She would make it so she had a hand in it, too. She would push him out, because she couldn't be…

Nothing.

"No, you are not the best husband," she said. "And I…have never slept with anyone else. Ever. Because I've been with you since I was sixteen. I gave you all those years. And you have never even bothered to figure out how the washing machine works. You think because you make the most money that your job is the only one that matters. You think my store is a hobby. That my jewelry is a hobby. That what I love, what I spend my time on, doesn't matter the way what you do does. You don't think I'm as smart as you are, do you?"

"I never said that," he said.

Which wasn't a denial. But he also seemed to be refusing to shout recriminations at her, and that was just annoy-

ing. She wanted him to. At this point she needed him to. She
wanted him to blame her. Say all the ways that she had failed
as a wife, so she could get even more indignant, and feed off
it. She could tell him how wrong he was. So she could… So
she could fight.

How did she fight with this man standing in front of her
right now, with his shoulders hunched? Like a dog that was
just waiting to get hit with a rolled-up newspaper?

She looked away for a second, and when she looked back,
she just saw Ryan. Who she would've said would *never*. And
it made her want to scream.

That isn't true, though. You were worried about the texting.

"Everybody thinks you're great," she said. "You walk into a
room and they *assume* you're going to be amazing. And you've
learned to walk into every room being six feet tall with a doc-
torate and accepting all the accolades your existence brings
you, but over the years you stopped doing anything that proved
you were all that special. But you still got the benefit of people believing it. I think you forgot what being exceptional
means." She wasn't even sure if that was true. But it felt good
to say it. And she didn't have to be fair.

"We can talk about this more."

"There's nothing to say." And even as she said that, she
wished there were. Wished that this could be an endless night.
They'd had a lot of those during the early years of their marriage. Arguing until their voices were hoarse, quietly and into
the wee hours of the morning. Not over anything that mattered all that much, she realized in hindsight.

Or maybe they had mattered more than she realized. Maybe
the key to what was happening now existed in those long
midnight conversations, and the resolutions they hadn't actually come to.

She didn't know. She had no way of knowing.

Because she wasn't going to have another endless conversation with him.

Because he wasn't her husband.

Not anymore.

And she couldn't stand to have him there. Couldn't stand to have this liar standing in front of her anymore.

"I should talk to the kids," he said.

"You can do that. But not here. Because you're not coming back here."

"I have to get my things," he said.

"Great. You can do that. You have two hours to do that." She walked over to the table, picked up one of the bowls of Chinese food and dropped it onto the floor. The bowl shattered, and the food went everywhere. Then she picked up the other one and did the same thing. "And you can clean that shit up. When I'm back you better be gone."

And she walked out of the house. And she knew that the next time she walked back in...it wouldn't be the same house.

It wouldn't be the same life.

She would never be the same again.

29

Chelsea

"RYAN LEFT JENNA."

Chelsea was still in total shock after her visit with Jenna. Of all the things, she had not expected that. Not ever. It just didn't... It didn't make any sense.

Everyone has secrets.

You can't know anyone.

You were wrong about Ryan, too.

"He what?" Mark looked genuinely shocked by that, and she watched his expression to see what kind of shock it was.

"He was having an affair. He got the other woman pregnant." The words sat like a lump of sand in her throat.

She continued to watch Mark's face. Was he judging Ryan? Did it seem unfathomable to him that Ryan could have broken his vows like that?

Mark breathed out, hard, and shook his head. But didn't say anything. So Chelsea kept on talking.

"I'm… I'm *livid*. He's my big brother. He… I never thought he would do something like that. He was always perfect."

"He was never perfect, Chelsea. You all just think he is. Your parents tell you that he is, all the time. But he isn't. He's just… He's basic. Honestly."

"Are you upset that he did that? Or are you just wanting to trash my brother?" She started hunting around for a cigarette. One her husband wouldn't let her smoke in the house.

But why did he get to decide that?

Who were they, anyway?

He was this good finance guy who thought cigarettes were bad but had committed robberies, apparently, and he got to judge her?

"Are we not supposed to trash your brother when he leaves his wife for another woman?"

"Of course we are. But I haven't even talked to him. I only talked to Jenna. I don't know if I can talk to him. I just… I can't believe that they're going to get a divorce. Ryan and Jenna. *Ryan and Jenna.* I can barely think of one of them without thinking of the other." She shook her head. "This is just… It doesn't make any sense. They're great together."

Mark just stared at her. And she couldn't figure out what he was thinking.

Because she didn't know him. So how could she guess?

They'd built this perfect life, but the house was starting to cave in around them.

There were cracks in the foundation.

And there was no one to blame but herself.

30

Kindling

Alex

"DID YOU KNOW?"

Alex had a strange, cold feeling in the pit of her stomach when she went home after Jenna had come to the bakery. After she'd explained what had happened with Ryan.

Paul looked at her. "What are you talking about?"

"He's leaving Jenna. He had an affair."

"Honest to God," Paul said. "I had no idea. I'd have kicked his ass."

She looked at him, and she wanted to believe him so much that his words settled into her bones. Helped her calm herself.

"Of course you would have," she said, setting her purse down. "Of course. I can't believe it."

"I can't, either. I'll call him and ask if he can meet up. Find out what the hell he's thinking."

"Yeah. Do that."

She went to the bottom of the stairs and stopped, her hand on the railing. Then she wanted to say something else to him. But she didn't know what. So she just let it go.

31

Jenna

"SO HOW WAS the date?"

"Just god-awful," Jenna said, clearly distracted—and not even able to hide it—by Ethan's presence.

He was moving giant bags of coffee beans, and his muscles were on display.

"Why was it awful?" Chelsea asked.

"You know what? It wasn't. It just wasn't the right thing. But that was…"

She realized that the only thing that really mattered that night was the conversation she'd had with Chloe.

"I am not living the life that I wanted. And I need to get over it. I need to live the life that I have. We're all ready to move into the new house. And I'm trying to be excited. I'm trying to embrace the fact that my life is different."

"That sounds difficult," Alex said.

"Yeah. It does. I don't know that I really want to. But I don't see another option at this point. I need… I need something to change. Because I can't keep living in the worst eighteen months of my life. And that's what I'm doing. I'm just living in it. In him leaving. In him dying. I can't make my whole life about him, either. He had chosen to make a new life, and I need to do that, too."

"The problem is," Alex said slowly, "your feelings don't magically change." She worried her lower lip, and Jenna could only stare. Alex wasn't one to make big, declarative statements. She wasn't really one to share. And Jenna could feel that she was on the cusp of…something. "I had Cody over yesterday," she said.

"Really?" Chelsea and Jenna asked at the same time.

"Yes. To talk about the fire." She sighed. "Not that I had anything new to tell him. It's more that he makes me want things. And I'm realizing I've always wanted him." Alex's eyes suddenly shone bright with defiance Jenna had never seen from her. "Time didn't change it. Being married, loving another man, it didn't change it. If Cody had come back ten years ago, I don't know. I might have been Ryan."

"You wouldn't have been," Jenna insisted.

"I wanted someone else while I was married, and I can't be sure I wouldn't have acted on it."

"Hey, Jenna?"

She turned and looked up—way up—at Ethan, who was standing over the table. "Yeah?" she asked. Her heart did a crazy jump up into her throat, and she could remember this feeling. Sadly, far too well.

Oh, for God's sake.

She was acting like she was in high school.

It wasn't like she didn't know him. He had grown up across

the street. She'd babysat him when she was fourteen and he was eight and their parents had been drinking in the backyard.

And she knew him as an adult, too. They had mainly talked about the town council thing, just casually.

He had created a stir when he'd returned from college a whole man, who had clearly experienced the kind of growth spurt and injection of testosterone boys prayed for, and started a coffee-roasting business that had grown exponentially in just a couple of years, with major chains and supermarkets picking up his product. He'd caused hot flashes and Hail Marys about town, as people had grappled with the boy they'd once known turning sexy. It had been funny. A topic for the local Tupperware parties—as long as his mom wasn't there.

She'd been married, not dead. She'd noticed he was hot then. And maybe she had found herself spacing out and imagining what it might be like to run her hands over his biceps, if she were a different woman. A different woman entirely, and not one happily married to a wonderful, handsome man.

It was just that all that had gotten twisted up when she wasn't happily married to a wonderful man, and had discovered that she was married to a very flawed man, and she didn't know how long he had been flawed.

Forever. He was just a man.

"Can I talk to you for a second?" he asked.

She gestured to her planner. "We're um… We're talking."

"Sorry," he said. "It can wait."

"Thank you."

"No," Alex said, reaching across the table and stealing her planner. "You're fine. We're fine. Go talk to him."

Well, she didn't have her planner now, so she might as well.

She slid from her chair and stood up, and she only came to his shoulder. He was just so tall. It made her feel fragile and feminine and she liked it.

How your feminism has fallen.

Hey, feminism was about equality. And choices. She chose to think it was hot that he was tall. Her choice was valid.

She stepped off just out of earshot of her friends, who were pretending to talk but were clearly paying attention to her and Ethan and really, it was high school.

"I was wondering if you'd like to grab coffee sometime," he said.

She blinked. "Um. To talk about the Harvest Festival?"

"No," he said, his eyes never leaving hers, the confidence inherent in such an extended gaze giving her heart palpitations. "To have coffee."

She felt like her brain was stuck loading. "To discuss…"

"I want to take you out. I thought coffee would be a good place to start."

Oh. *Oh.*

He…he liked *her.* He *liked* her.

Or wanted to take her to coffee, anyway. Coffee was hardly a booty call.

Well. It was for her. It was actually much better for her if she met with someone early and on…a weekday. When her kids wouldn't be home.

She felt obligated, though, to make absolutely certain that he knew what he was doing. To make sure they were clear on things, because the idea of getting it wrong…

She couldn't handle that.

"So I just want to be clear. Because I'm not totally certain that you're intending to ask me on a date, and I'd hate for either of us to be embarrassed."

He looked her up and down. Slowly. "You aren't certain I meant to ask you out?"

"It's just you're younger than me."

"Oh, is that so?" he asked as if nothing on earth could bother him at all.

"Yes, which you know. Because I once babysat you."

"I think more than once, actually, Jen."

Her palms were sweaty. "So you did mean to ask me out?"

"Yes."

"Are you…sure?"

He laughed and it made her feel…a lot. "I'm always sure about what I want."

"Oh. Oh. Well. Okay. So coffee, then."

"Could be dinner if you want."

"No. Coffee."

It's almost like you have a better chance of getting laid if you go out for an early coffee, when your kids are at school.

Because he knows what he wants.

He might want you.

"How about 9 a.m.?" she said. "We can meet right here."

"Sounds good."

"*Tomorrow.* So we're clear. Not on the weekend." The kids needed to be at school.

"Okay."

"Good. I'll see you then."

And she turned. And she felt like something that had been connecting her to her old life, holding her back, had been released.

This was that new thing. That new life.

It wasn't sad. Yeah, there was plenty of sad behind her. But this step forward didn't feel sad. Alex had actually shared her feelings with them, and Ethan had asked her out. That was change.

As for the date, it might not be anything. It might not be significant. But she felt good about it. And there were spare few things that she'd felt really good about in the past year and a half. So she was going to take it. She was absolutely going to take it.

32

Afterburn

Chelsea

CHELSEA DECIDED TO go to the yarn store, her mind still spinning from her earlier conversation with Alex. She was uncomfortable with the conclusions that she had drawn. But she was trying to be more certain of herself. Of certain things. Alex wasn't somebody she needed to keep her distance from. And Morgan was nobody's enemy. She was just a sad girl. And Chelsea wanted to see her niece. Chelsea wanted to begin to repair things between Morgan and her mother.

When she walked into the yarn shop, Morgan was behind the counter, holding Lily on her hip. It was the first time Chelsea had seen them both. Morgan looked so different holding her daughter. Happier. Brighter.

"Oh…" Morgan looked up. "Chelsea."

"I'm sorry. I didn't mean to startle you. She's… She's beautiful."

She really did look so much like Ryan. And it made her smile, her heart squeezing tight for her complicated, ridiculous brother.

She loved all his kids. And in that moment she knew Lily was no exception.

She was uncertain about so many things. But she was not uncertain about this.

"I know it's a while from now. But I was kind of hoping you would join us for Thanksgiving this year."

"What?"

"Yeah. My kid, he'll be coming back from college. For Thanksgiving. And I will have the new house finished, and my mom and dad will be there."

Morgan shrank. "Your mom…"

"I'll deal with her. I know that she's difficult. But you just… I know. And I'm really sorry. But she's actually not completely unreasonable. She's not completely horrible. She'll come around."

"You seem confident."

"I'm trying to be. I spent a lot of time questioning things. But one thing I do know is what's right here."

"Jenna's not going to like you befriending me."

"Jenna's my friend. And her ex-husband was my brother. It's complicated. And it'll have to be. Jenna's going to have to deal. She's a strong woman. She'll sort it out."

Morgan bit her lip. "I don't want to be difficult for you."

"Morgan, the situation is difficult already. We can't hide from it. Actually, that's something I have learned watching Jenna. At least she explodes. At least she says what needs saying. And she doesn't hide. We don't need to hide."

"Why are you being so nice?"

"Because what happened happened. Ryan's gone. But you're here. And Lily is here. That's what matters. And from everything I've seen of you, it's not actually hard to be nice to you."

"I'd love to have Thanksgiving with you. As long as your mom's okay with it."

"She will be. Trust me."

Chelsea was going to make sure of it. And she wasn't going to let her mother, her father, or anyone else tell her what was right or true.

She wasn't letting other people decide that anymore.

33

Kindling

Jenna

THE TOWN COUNCIL was divided. Not along its typical lines. But along Ryan and Jenna lines. There were a lot of
people who might not be particular fans of Jenna's, but they
were not okay with infidelity.

Her friends were shocked anyone was on Ryan's side. She
was not, sadly.

Ryan was a man, after all. So nice. So handsome. And important, too. A doctor!

And just maybe Jenna hadn't been a very good wife.

Of course they thought that.

It was easy for Jenna to wonder, too.

That they felt like they could show their faces here...

She didn't have time for this. For the feelings. She had shit
to do.

The charity dinner, which was going to dovetail with the

Harvest Festival, was so close now, and the last thing she needed to be dealing with was feelings about her soon-to-be ex-husband and his mistress.

Mistress.

She wasn't even that. She was his... She wasn't the mistress. Because he had left Jenna.

She had that pregnancy glow. That happiness.

She had a pregnancy glow that had once belonged to Jenna. Because she had been expecting Ryan's babies once upon a time. And now she was old, and he was starting over, and...

She turned away from them and took her position at the front of the room. "Ticket sales are complete," she said. "With generous donations from our foundational families, the Coles, the Barneses and the DuPonts, we have raised $300,000, with more pledged for the auction."

"Jenna," Courtney said, looking down at her phone, then back up. "The account is empty."

"What?"

"The account. That the money was in. It's empty."

"Well, there has to be a record of what happened to it." Jenna really did feel like the floor was lava. How could this be happening?

This was the one piece of evidence she had right now that she was important. This charity event, her brain child. She'd lost her husband. He'd left her like she didn't matter and—

"I don't see one."

"What do you mean you don't see one?"

"It's a withdrawal."

It was after hours, and the bank wasn't open, but they did have one of the bankers on the town council.

Her umbrage over Morgan and Ryan was somewhat forgotten in the panic. Everybody in the room was yelling at each other. And all she could think was…all of this had started when Morgan had first shown up.

And if Morgan wasn't responsible for this, she would be shocked. Because they never had money go missing before, and her husband had never cheated on her before. But both of those things had happened for the very first time once that bitch had rolled into town.

"What happened to the money?" she asked, directing her fury toward Morgan.

"Why would I… Why would I know what happened to the money?" Morgan asked.

"Jenna, get it together," Ryan said.

"I'm sorry. She's the only new person here. We've never had money go missing before."

"It was probably a hacker," Janice, the banker, said. "And if so, it'll be insured. It'll be okay."

"It had better be okay," Jenna said.

Anxiety rolled through her. This was the only thing she had. This project. It was what she had been working on. It was the only thing that mattered. Because Ryan was gone, and her kids were busy and the only thing that made her relevant at all was that she had been doing the best job—the very best job—at this charity dinner. And it was going to be the biggest success that she had ever achieved. And there was already a homewrecker in this room that she knew of for sure. So why the hell wouldn't she have wrecked this, too?

Maybe it wasn't rational. But she did not feel rational.

"You like to take things that don't belong to you," Jenna said.

"Jenna." This came from Chelsea, her tone stern as she reached out and put her hand on Jenna's arm. Chelsea, who didn't have her wedding ring on, and whose husband was in Germany. Chelsea, who let go of things without a fight.

But that wasn't Jenna. She *fought* for things.

"How can we be missing money?" she asked.

"I'll call the banking line," Janice said.

She went off into a corner of the room, and Jenna began to pace. "This is impossible. There was over a quarter of a million in there. We have never raised so much money."

Ethan moved from the coffee urn over to where she stood, and handed her a cup. Her eyes met his, and for a moment she felt a bit steadier.

"Thank you," she said.

Then, suddenly, she pictured him when he had been a little snotty-nosed boy, running around her parents' front yard. His mother had come over for something. A Tupperware party? He had been eight. And she had been about fifteen. And she hadn't had any use for him at all.

Her lips twitched. "I just think we should be particularly on guard around outsiders."

"You're biased," Courtney said. "I think even you have to admit that."

"I don't have to admit anything, Courtney. Maybe you took it? You're the treasurer. And you have access to the account."

"Right. And I chose to announce that the money was gone in the middle of the meeting."

"I don't know how the criminal mind works."

"Just settle down," Alex said, reaching out and grabbing her, pulling her into a corner. "Wait until she gets a hold of the bank."

Alex was on her side. Paul seemed to land somewhere in the middle. Which made Jenna kind of mad. Because Paul was friends with Ryan, yes, and they were both surgeons at the hospital, but they had known each other since high school also. So he could maybe be a little more supportive of *her*. But in this instance, he did come over to where she was and stand.

"You okay?"

"You want some alcohol for that coffee? I mean, it's cute the kid was trying to help you, but you need something a little bit stronger."

The kid. As if the thirty-four-year-old man who had given her a cup of coffee was more of a kid than the nineteen-year-old her ex-husband had gotten pregnant, whom she was pretty sure Paul had never called a kid.

"You're kind of an asshole, Paul," she said.

His lips tilted up on one side, and there was a glint of humor in his eyes, as if nobody had ever said that to him before.

They probably hadn't.

Because Paul Coleman was tall and handsome and rich and the kind of person who succeeded at everything he did, so even when he was an asshole, people didn't intend to call him out on it.

But Jenna was in a *calling out* mood.

"It appears that an untraceable wire transfer was made from the account. So it was someone who had access to transfer the money out. It could've been a hacker…"

"But it could've been someone here," Jenna said. "Who has access to the account?"

"I don't," Morgan said, her wide blue eyes looking impossibly wide, and impossibly innocent.

And no wonder her husband had wanted her. She was like a little doll that needed to be picked up and protected, and Ryan was a sucker.

"We'll call the police. It's going to take some kind of digital crime team to look at it… But obviously, the bank accounts here will be looked at," Janice said.

Tom, the chair, rubbed his hand over his thinning hair. "This is… It's all quite irregular."

"That is my point," Jenna said.

"But that doesn't mean you can go around accusing people," Janice said. "Just because you have an ax to grind with somebody."

"I have not begun to grind my ax, *Janice*. If I were to grind an ax, it would make contact, and heads would literally roll."

It occurred to her that she should maybe ratchet back the physical threats if the police were going to be called.

"Yes, well, call the police," Courtney said.

"All right," Tom said.

The police came and questioned everybody. About their access, their bank account numbers. Some people, of course, loudly refused to talk without lawyers, and Jenna made deep note of all of them.

But the police released them all, which incensed Jenna, because she felt that Morgan should absolutely be handcuffed. Which, she had to admit, was maybe a little bit bloodthirsty even for her, considering the girl was like six months pregnant.

And you care?

She felt awash in uncertainty then. Ryan's baby.

Her kids' half sibling.

Half sibling.

They weren't supposed to have one of those.

They weren't *those* people.

They weren't supposed to be.

When they started letting people go, she stormed outside, ahead of her friends.

"Jenna."

It was Ryan.

She turned around. "You know what? Fuck you, Ryan. *Fuck you.*"

"Jenna," he said. "Leave Morgan alone. She didn't have anything to do with this."

"Well, she had plenty to do with you and me. I already

know she doesn't have any respect for anything. And neither do you. Maybe you stole the money, too."

"I don't need the money."

"You didn't. Until you had two full households to support. Have you thought about that, by the way? That you have to pay for her and for me, and our kids' college? And this kid's college? I have. Your life suddenly got a hell of a lot more expensive. And as far as I know, you weren't actually picking up extra work. You were just having sex. *Asshole.* You were having sex with her while you were having sex with me, and coming home to me every night, and coming into our house. Our house, Ryan. *Our house.* And you... You dare to just be...*fine* with all of this. You dare to be reasonable. And levelheaded. And try to take all of the shit onto yourself. *Oh, it's not you. It's me.* And it isn't even fair. If you would insult me, then at least I could scream at you. But you're acting like you're the nicer person, when you're the one who destroyed our family. You destroyed *us.* You aren't nice."

"I know that. I know... But what do you want me to do? She's having a baby."

"Maybe fucking stay with the woman who had your babies already? I had two of them. And I've raised them. I did everything. I made their lunches every day. I helped in their classrooms and I made dinner for all of you every night. How was I not good enough? How did I not win this contest? How? It's bullshit."

She wasn't trying to win. She wasn't trying to be the most polite, the most serene. She wasn't trying to be anything but *furious.* And she didn't care if everybody heard it. Because they should hear it. It wasn't fair. It wasn't fair that anybody was on his side, just because he was Ryan Abbott and everybody liked him. He was wrong.

Didn't anyone care about that?

"It isn't really helping our kids that you're behaving like this."

"Honestly, fuck you," she said. "How dare you? Do you think it helps our kids that you left them?"

"I want to be in their lives. But they're angry with me because…"

"Because of your actions. I don't have to tell them that their dad leaving me for *a child* is wrong. They just know it. They know it because, by some miracle, they didn't inherit your denial gene. Whatever thing that you have that is allowing you to recast yourself as the wounded party here. Because you aren't. She isn't. Grow up. If you can't handle a woman scorned, don't scorn one. Jackass." And she looked at him. At that man, that man whose bed she had shared for all those years.

That man she had loved so fucking much.

"I could light you on fire and not feel the slightest bit of regret about it right now."

Then she turned and walked away.

34

Chelsea

SHE WAS SPIRALING. There was no other word for it. And she felt like she was losing her shield. Sean.

God, she felt like that was just such a terrible thing to admit. That her son was her shield.

But he was leaving. Going to school. And everything was just… It was falling apart. She couldn't bear to let Mark touch her. Not now. Not in the wake of everything.

This feeling of disquiet and distrust had been growing and growing. The whole thing with Ryan had tipped it over into something ugly. Something darker than they had ever experienced before. And she hadn't said anything. She was shrinking herself, smaller and smaller, because it was the only thing she knew how to do. It was that or implode. Those were the two things. The two things that she knew.

Her anger was dangerous. She knew it was. Her anger destroyed things. She knew it did.

She and Mark had been brilliantly volatile once upon a time, and look at what that had gotten them.

She had stopped fighting, because it just made sense.

And now she didn't even know how to speak.

"We need to talk."

She looked up from where she was scrubbing the kitchen counter.

"Do we?"

"Yes. We do. I know that must be a shock to you, since we haven't spoken at all recently."

"Mark…"

"Chelsea," he said. "What is the matter with you? Remember when we first got married and we used to fight and then we would…"

"Yes," she said. "Yes, I do. And it didn't solve anything."

"And freezing me out is solving something?"

"I'm not freezing you out."

"Yes, you are. Ever since you found out about the robberies."

"You lied to me," she said. She looked up at him. "I feel stupid. I feel stupid for having not known. For having lived with you for that many years without knowing. Don't you know how that makes me feel?"

"There you go," he said. "Be honest. Is it that you actually care about the robberies, or is it that you care that I didn't tell you?"

"I don't know. Because it's all big, and you didn't give me a chance."

She felt horrible. Just disgusting. And wrong. In every way. About everything.

But she didn't shout. Instead, she got quieter.

"I'll tell you. I'll tell you everything. You already know that I was raised by my dad, and he was a drunk. There was never any food in the house. I started stealing things when I was little. I started running with a bad crowd when I was thirteen. We held up a couple of stores. Armed robbery. That's it. That's the story. I got out of it when I was a sophomore in high school, and I started taking things seriously. I met a guidance counselor who helped me figure out that I could have a future but only if I worked for it. I was good with numbers. I excelled at it, and that's how I ended up getting scholarships. By the time you met me I was years removed from that kid. By the time you met me, I was in the life I wanted. I wanted to be successful, and I was. I didn't want to be a criminal, so I stopped. I wanted to meet a woman and fall in love and get married. Have a child. I wanted a normal life. We have that life." He shook his head. "But I thought it would be… I don't know. You were wild, Chelsea. You remember…"

"I was nineteen when we met. I'm not nineteen. Maybe the problem isn't me."

"Is that all you have to say? I just told you *everything*. I held up a store with a gun. How do you feel about that?"

She looked at him, and she just felt tired. This was honesty, she supposed. And it wasn't fixing anything.

"I don't know." She looked at him, and she tried to see a stranger. Or the man she'd met and fell in love with.

But it was like she couldn't even look at him. Not in the face. Not right now.

"Why don't you fight with me?" he said. "Yell at me? Hit me?"

"I'm not going to hit you."

"Why not? It would be better than this. You looking sad while you dry dishes. Fight for this."

He reached out then and grabbed the bowl, threw it across the room. It hit the wall.

"Mark."

"I can show you. Everything. Everything that I am," he said. "If it would make you fucking wake up."

"I'm not asleep," she said. "Maybe you just don't like who I am."

"You let them walk all over you. You let them turn you into a robot. You don't even look at me. You won't fuck me."

"Stop it."

"It's true."

"It isn't anything to do with my family."

"Then what is it?"

She couldn't answer him. She couldn't tell him. Because telling him would destroy everything that they were.

"Maybe it's you. Maybe it's you and your secrets."

"Don't give me that."

He was angry. And he had every right to be. He didn't even know how much.

Because she had no call throwing secrets back at him.

"Mark…"

"I swear to God. Sometimes I think it's this town. You're the one who wanted to come back here. You're the one who wanted to be near your family. Your life revolves around running between your mother, Jenna and managing your brother's drama. Some days I want to burn this place to the ground. Do you know that? And then what would you be left with? You wouldn't have anything left to hide behind. Would you?"

"You don't even make sense," she said, something inside her snapping. The thing that needed to protect itself rearing up into position. "It isn't them. Did you ever think that it's you, Mark? That you are why we're having these problems? Or maybe the way I feel about you?"

He took a step back, looking like he'd been punched in the face. "You don't love me? Is that it?"

"I didn't say…" He moved forward, grabbed hold of her arms.

"Say it, then. Tell me you love me."

She couldn't. She just turned away.

He released his hold on her and took a step back, looking down at his hands like he didn't trust them. Or didn't trust himself.

She knew the feeling. She knew it well.

"I got a job offer in Germany."

"What?"

"They've been after me for a while. But there's been no point in it. But now Sean is going to be done with school in a month. We don't need to be here. He's moving away and I want to take the offer. It's a temporary contract. It will be a year. I'm going. Whether you want to come with me or not."

"Mark—"

"I can't stand it anymore. You moved back to this town and you got small. I thought you wanted to be here. You were happy here. This was your dream. The flower shop on Main. You wanted it so much, and I gave up my job for you. For this. To be embroiled in the middle of your fucking family. So you come away with me and see if we can fix this—or you stay here. But if you stay here…"

"I'm not going to Germany," she said, panic clawing at her insides.

"All right. That's as good as saying it, then."

35

Alex

ALEX WAS STILL feeling raw from her admission the other day. Her house felt extra empty, and the bakery didn't feel like a very sufficient escape. Admitting she had wanted Cody, had feelings for him, felt like a betrayal.

Why did it feel that way? Because Paul had been so good to her?

But then she thought again of what Cody had said. Did everybody like Paul? Or had everybody been enamored with those attributes of his that were so valued by society? Handsome, over six feet tall, rich. Confident. Was he seen as inherently wonderful because those things simply dazzled people?

He had been good to her.

It still hadn't been enough to eradicate what she felt for Cody.

He'd been good to her.

He hadn't shared anything at all…

She stood there in the back kitchen, her apron tied firmly around her waist, her heart hammering like an insistent child knocking on a door.

Maybe it was the memories of that day.

Or maybe it was something further back.

But sitting face-to-face with Cody was making her look at her marriage in a way she hadn't.

She didn't think she had ever really loved him. Not in that all-consuming, forsaking all others, kind of way. She might never have had an affair—or even ever thought about having an affair—but she had never felt the same way for him that she had about Cody. And she had told herself if she ever had that little sensation of doubt—that little nagging feeling—it was because wanting someone that you never had at seventeen was vastly different than being married.

Cody had been there for her after her mother's abandonment.

But that was when Paul had started paying more attention to her, too.

And when she had been crying in the back of his car, he'd kissed her, and she'd kissed him back, and that moment had been written in her memory as a blaze of fate and glory.

She'd used it to blot out the memory of another kiss, another touch, secret meetings in the woods that no one but herself and Cody had known about.

She had retreated to Paul. And she knew that no one else in this community would understand that. He had been the most sought after boy at Tenmile High. But he hadn't been the one for her.

And that had been okay for a lot of years, when the one wasn't there. When he wasn't there the same as he had been before.

Frightening and just far too much, and everything she wanted all at the same time.

She had been in such a gray space since Paul died, but she had been in a gray space before that, too. If she was honest with herself.

Oh, she'd been happy; she wasn't rewriting things.

She and Paul had had times of intense, beautiful happiness. She'd been so scared when she'd gotten pregnant with Ruth. But she'd been the most beautiful, perfect baby. They'd lived in school housing in Washington, and she'd walked all around campus with Ruth in her stroller.

They'd had Jack during Paul's residency. It had been chaotic but wonderful. She'd been so proud of everything they were accomplishing together.

And Paul had been…such a proud dad. He'd shown pictures of the kids to everyone. He'd been in the front row at every play, every recital.

She has my eyes.

Kid has my football skills.

He'd loved them.

Whatever had been between them, whatever her feelings for Cody, Paul had been the father of her children. Whether they would've stayed together forever or not. She knew it was the thing that hurt Jenna so much now. Her kids' grief.

And Alex felt that keenly.

But she wasn't entirely sure she was the tragic widow everyone thought her to be. Just like she wasn't sure she had ever been the lovestruck young girl who had given in to passion and gotten pregnant too soon, and become a young bride.

She'd clung to that story. With everything she had.

And now it was slipping through her fingers.

It was closing time, and she decided to save some of her

duties for tomorrow morning, because suddenly, she was in a hurry.

Because suddenly, she really needed to see Cody.

She walked down the street, the wind blowing her coat. And it reminded her of that day. That fire day. It had been hotter last year at this time. So hot. It almost felt like fall already this year. Everything was so fickle. So fragile. Except her feelings for Cody, apparently, which could endure across space and time, or maybe it was just an illusion, because the truth of it was it was easier to fantasize about someone than it was to live with them. To actually endure life day in and day out, and maybe that was the actual issue with Paul. Her mind playing tricks on her in a completely unfair way. Her mind looking for an out. A way to grieve a little bit less. To magnify little moments where she'd looked at him and seen a stranger. To magnify feelings for an old spark that had never had a chance to become a flame.

To make it a bigger deal than it should be that he was somewhere he shouldn't have been the morning that fire started.

She stopped in front of the yarn store and looked inside. She saw Morgan lift Ryan's baby up out of a playpen. She smiled at the baby and spun in a circle. She looked young. And there was just so much love on her face as the warm light in the shop made her hair glow like a halo.

Maybe life was just a lot more complicated than anybody wanted to believe.

She kept walking until she came to the building she knew he was staying in, then went around the back of the red brick facade where there was a narrow, wooden staircase that went up the side of the building, creeping vines lining the wall up to the red door at the top. She swallowed hard, then knocked.

It took a moment, but he opened it. He was wearing a white shirt, open at the collar, the sleeves pushed up past his forearms. His jaw had dark stubble on it, with just a bit of gray. It was incredibly sexy.

"Is everything okay?"

"Yeah. I came to see you."

"As opposed to coming to see my front door?"

"I just meant I'm not here to talk about the fire or anything like that."

"What are you here for?"

To talk about their past. To talk about her feelings. And then she realized there was time to talk. It wasn't what she wanted.

She had been afraid for years. So careful. So restrained.

And she was done.

She remembered Jenna saying she had to start living life, the one she had now.

And Alex was ready to do the same.

She stretched up on her toes and bracketed his face, and leaned forward, kissing him.

It was like a wave of relief and desire washed through her.

Cody.

She wanted to cry. Cody.

One strong arm wrapped around her waist, and she found herself being pulled inside, the door shut tight behind them. Whatever she had intended, this wasn't it. This was nothing she had experience with. This was something she hadn't thought existed outside of movies. Desperation. The thrill of being with the new person. Clothes coming off at a record pace.

He pushed his hands beneath her shirt and pushed it up over her head. Cast it onto the floor, and along with it, the insecurities she'd been carrying around for years.

Because Cody White looked at her like she was a treasure. He didn't look at her like she was less beautiful than she'd been in high school.

In his eyes, she saw a raw hunger. And it thrilled her. She felt an answering hunger within herself, and she put her hands on his chest, hard and masculine and like every fantasy she'd never let herself really have. Back when she'd first wanted him, she'd been a virgin. She hadn't known anything about sex. About her own body, about her desires. She was a woman in her forties now. And she knew exactly what she wanted. Knew exactly how to get it. This was better than anything she could've dreamed up at seventeen, and he was everything. He had been so handsome back then; she thought he was cute. But now he was *hot*. He was a man. And she was a woman who knew what to do with one.

His hand skimmed over the burns on her arms, and she shivered. There was concern in his eyes, but still desire. They didn't turn her into an object of pity. He took his shirt off, and she marveled at his masculine beauty. Many people would say, she knew, that she had certainly gone for quality with the lovers in her life, even if she hadn't been able to have quantity. Paul had been in great shape until the end. But this was still different. It was still more.

It was elemental. Fierce. It was all those years of denied longing. It was chemistry. It was need.

Grief and desire and teenage love combusting into this perfect moment. Where there was no thought. Where there was no worry about consequence or the future. Where there was nothing but achingly glorious need. Her hands went to his belt buckle and she stripped him completely, and he did the same to her, before gripping her hips and lifting her as he sat down, bringing her over the top of him on the couch. She kissed him as he drove into her, and her climax was so intense, so instantaneous, it took her breath away, a raw cry escaping her. It was fast, and furious and left her spent and breathless and clinging to him.

"I will be more impressive next time," he said.

"Any more impressive and you might kill me."

She looked up at him, and suddenly, all of the uncertainty and embarrassment she probably should've felt before she took her clothes off creaked in. She felt her face get hot.

"What?"

"Well. I don't know how common of an occurrence this is for you… But it's not for me."

"Right."

"I was married for a long time," she said.

"Sure."

"What I'm trying to tell you is you're literally the second man I've ever been with."

"Wow."

"You are very monosyllabic."

"Yeah. My brain's not really working."

She laughed, kind of hysterically, her face buried in his chest, because…

"Holy shit. Cody White. I just had sex with Cody White on a couch."

"Does that mean I get to say I just had sex with the girl of my dreams? I want to go back in time to tell my eighteen-year-old self that it *will* happen."

"Don't get into that. If you have to go back in time, then you'll have to warn us all about the fire. And then…" She shook her head, and then all she could do was laugh more. "I'm sorry. I was literally about to say you can't stop my husband from dying because then this couldn't happen. I think something is messed up in my head."

"You're allowed to be a little messed up right now."

"Maybe it's not just right now. Maybe I'm kind of messed up. Period. I spent all my life trying to be so perfect, Cody. And I was afraid of everything. My mom leaving… That broke me. It broke me in ways I wish it didn't. I wish I were stronger than that. I really do."

"Stronger than what, Alex? You went through something that nobody else your age did. I never had my dad in my life, and that's its own shit. It's not thinking that you have a perfect life and then losing it."

"I know. I do. I can't regret my life. And I don't. So much of it was good. I love my kids. But sometimes I wonder…"

"There's no point. Believe me. I've spent a lot of time thinking about what-ifs."

"I guess it doesn't matter, because here we are. You know, time going fast used to make me sad. And for this last year, I've been grateful for it, and resentful of it. Because the settled, easy part of my life was over. And I couldn't get back to it. But this makes me kind of glad. Glad the time moves quickly, because now it doesn't seem so long since the last time I saw you. It seems like I was waiting for you for just a little bit."

"Still felt like *for fucking ever* to me. But I'm glad you got that out of it." He groaned. "I didn't use a condom," he said. "Sorry."

Well, this was a conversation she hadn't had since she was seventeen.

"I have an IUD," she said.

"Thank God."

That made her a little sad. Which was dumb. She didn't want to have more kids. She was too old for that nonsense. But maybe it was just how definitive he was about it.

"Yeah. Well."

"I spend a lot of time on the road," he said.

"Are you telling me about your life, or is that a euphemism for how often you have anonymous hookups?"

His mouth curved upward and she melted. "This isn't anonymous."

Which didn't answer her question really, but she decided she was going to let silence be the better part of valor here.

"Do you want to stay?" he asked.

"Yes. I didn't know I got to choose."

"You're not a hookup. You're Alex."

"Meaning if I was a hookup, I wouldn't be invited?"

"No. You wouldn't be."

She was trying to decide if that made her feel special or not. She decided it didn't matter. It could be whatever she chose to make it. She wanted to be here. She wanted to be here with him. It was special to her. That was what mattered.

"I could offer you refreshments…"

"That's okay."

"Good. Because I have beer."

She wrinkled her nose. "That's not very healthy."

"I order in. Or I go to your bakery."

"Well. I appreciate that."

"I wasn't here for this. It really was just supposed to be work."

"But they assigned you knowing that this was where you're from, I assume."

The house was adorable, neatly appointed, and she was certain that if it was genuinely his place, it would look nothing like this at all. At the end of the hallway there was a sign that said *Live, Laugh, Love*. She started laughing.

"What?"

"Nothing."

Completely naked, not caring at all, she walked into his bedroom.

She slipped between the covers and he groaned.

"What?"

"I was enjoying the show."

"Well. I'm enjoying being warm."

"I take that as a challenge," he said, grabbing the bottom of the blanket.

"That's fine with me."

From her position in bed, she stared at him, took a leisurely visual tour of his body. Yes. For the first time in a good while she was feeling perfectly happy with her circumstances. And her choices.

"To answer your question," he said. "You're right. They did ask me to come here because I knew the place. And the people. They thought I might be disarming as a local."

"And have you found that to be the case?"

"I'm not really supposed to share details."

Of course not. He really shouldn't share the details with her. There were things she wasn't sharing with him.

She couldn't be trusted.

"Right."

"I'm going to the ignition site tomorrow," he said. "Do you want to come with me?"

"I… You just said that you can't…"

"I'm going because I want to look at some things. But it's not a crime scene anymore. I can bring you if I want."

"As long as you don't tell me why?"

"It really is nothing but wanting to see it. I've been all over the areas with burned outbuildings. I've seen the new construction. I just… I just want to see it."

"Yeah. I'll go with you."

"Have you been?"

She shook her head. "No."

"Will you be okay?" he asked. "The fire is what changed everything. I don't know if you really want to see where it started."

She let her head fall back on the pillow. "I don't know. But then, if you would have asked me a year and a half ago if I would've been okay if my life as I know it changed forever, I probably would've said no. I think I would have said that I couldn't imagine life any different than it had been for the last two and a half decades. And I would've told you that I couldn't survive losing…him. But here I am."

"You're doing good, Alex. You really are."

"Yeah. I want to go."

"Okay, then. We'll go."

He got into bed next to her, reached beneath the covers and put his large hand on her bare hip. "But until then, we have all night."

"I like the sound of that."

He kissed her instead of talking more. She had the feeling they were going to have to really talk. Someday. About the timeline of everything. About how exactly she'd ended up in the backseat of Paul's car that night. About what exactly had been going through her mind when she'd decided to choose him instead of Cody.

But not tonight.

Tonight they were done talking. And she was grateful.

36

Chelsea

SHE WAS AT the new house bright and early that morning. The furniture delivery was set to come, and she was trying to be excited about getting everything pieced together. But then she paused. Because it was difficult to get too excited when you had no idea if this was actually a new start. Or what a new start even meant.

She'd had the very unpleasant discussion with her mother the night before, that Morgan was coming to Thanksgiving and they were all going to have to be nice. Her mother had thrown one of her classic tantrums and said something about other women and on and on.

Chelsea had snapped.

"Is it because you can't blame Dad for his affairs that you can't blame Ryan?"

Her mother had looked stricken. "Chelsea, you were wrong about that…"

"I wasn't. I wasn't and you know it, and my own parents have spent all these years gaslighting me… To the point where I have felt like I couldn't trust myself."

Her mother's eyes had filled with tears.

"But he did it to you, too, didn't he?" Chelsea asked. "You knew. You knew but you couldn't know, and that's why it all felt so precarious. And that's why you were angry when I called it out."

It had been such a difficult conversation. Because her mother had had to admit that she had chosen to simply accept the affairs because she couldn't handle the idea of starting a new life.

"It's why I got so angry at Jenna," her mom whispered. "She did what I could never do. And it made me feel so small."

Poor Jenna. She did the honest thing. The real thing. And it made people so angry. So afraid.

"Well, maybe you owe Jenna an apology, too."

"Your father…"

"You could leave him. You could move in with me. Mark isn't there. I have this big house. I don't have anyone else."

Her mother hadn't been able to commit to that, but Chelsea honestly wished that she would, not because she wanted to live with her mother, but because her mom needed to stop living with somebody who made her feel like she had to doubt herself.

She stood in the middle of her new living room for a long moment. She had blamed Mark. For lying to her. For making her doubt herself. It wasn't Mark. It never had been. She had been looking for things and reasons and ways that he might be a villain. But it was only because she didn't want to face herself.

She didn't want to face the much scarier, deeper issues. Because she hadn't wanted to know if he was happy because the answer might be no. Because she hadn't wanted to fight when he had decided to leave. Because she had decided not to go to Germany because they were at a point where change had to happen. And she had known that it would be a painful, hideous change that she didn't want to confront.

She was standing there, turning circles in the empty room of a brand-new, beautiful home she wasn't sure she even wanted to keep, when she heard a car door in the driveway. She turned, and her heart slammed against her breastbone.

It was Mark.

Mark was there. Wearing a suit like he was going to a big corporate building in Germany, his dark hair pushed back off his forehead. She could see how blue his eyes were all the way from inside the house, and it still made her stomach turn over.

She'd been in a daze when he'd come back during the fire. But she wasn't in a daze now. And she felt...everything when she saw him. Felt like a teenage girl. Terrified, yet excited and hopeful, even while she was terrified.

Even while she had doubts and suspicions and everything else rolling through her.

Do you ever wonder who it benefits that we don't feel like we can be certain of ourselves?

She'd asked Alex that. And she was wondering how very true it was.

She went to the front door and opened it.

"What are you doing here?" she whispered.

He looked raw. Ragged. Resolved. It terrified her. Because this was the brink of honesty. She knew it was. And she had to be prepared for what would come with that.

"Chelsea," he said, his voice rough. "Do you honestly not know?"

"No."

"I'm here for you."

Her stomach went tight. "For me?"

"Yes. I've been waiting. I've been waiting for you to tell me what you want. I've been waiting for you to end it. For you to ask me to come home. I've been trying to give you the space that you wanted. That you needed. But you just didn't talk. Ever. You froze me out, like you do. What am I supposed to do with that, Chelsea? What do you want?"

What do you want?

She wanted to fling herself into his arms. She wanted to cry on him like she was a child. She wanted to yell about how unfair it all was. She wanted… She wanted something big. She wanted something new. She wanted…

She wanted.

And he was making her say it. And it frightened her.

But it had been eighteen months of not saying it.

It's been years of not saying it, and you know it.

And she didn't know why. She felt like she had a blind spot where they were concerned.

Like she couldn't see down to the root of whatever their problem was. And she was afraid.

She was afraid because if she asked him if he wanted to be together then he might say no. If she said that they should divorce, he might agree.

And if he knew how much she loved him, she might find that the love he felt back wasn't big enough. It wasn't a match. Wasn't the same.

She had told herself he could have started the fire, for what? So she could keep on lying to herself? Keep pretending that his secrets were the problem?

"I told myself you might have started the fire."

"What?" he asked, his face stone.

"You got here so quickly…"

"I was already here. I missed you, and I came back. It was a coincidence."

"Why didn't you say that?"

"Because you didn't want me here."

He was…afraid. She could see that now. He was as afraid as she was. That maybe this was the end. That she didn't love him.

"Why aren't you angry with me?" she asked.

He laughed. "I am fucking furious at you. But I want you, Chelsea."

"Do you want a divorce?" She finally brought herself to say it. To ask.

"No," he said.

And her knees gave out. Went weak. And she found herself dropping to the hardwood floor, shiny hardwood floors that nobody had walked on. And she felt like he could see her. Really see her. Like somehow he could see past the brash red dye in her hair and the dark lipstick she wore. She felt exposed and terrified and small, and she hated it. "I don't want one, either," she said, shaking.

She didn't want to cry.

And she didn't know why.

Why she was broken in quite this way.

But he bent down, right there with her on the floor, and he wrapped his arms around her without her having to ask, and for the first time in a good while, she could remember why she had thought they were meant to be. Because this felt meant-to-be. It felt right. It felt honest.

"I don't want a divorce," he said. "But we can't go back, either."

She nodded. "I know that."

"I rented a place," he said. "I'm not going to move in here. I want… I want us to get to know each other again."

"Okay." But she felt tremulous and rocky, because she had gone from feeling for a moment like everything might be fixed to feeling like they were just seeing if they could. And none of it felt quite that certain. She wanted certain.

She had lived. She had survived that fire, and for what? She was still terrified.

And she wanted to kiss him. She hadn't kissed this man in over a year.

Her husband.

"I'm really sorry," he said.

"For what?" she asked.

"For where we ended up. Look how much you don't trust me," he said. "You think I could have started that fire. What did they do to—"

"It's me I don't trust. And I love you. And if I can't be trusted…"

The words were there. She knew the words. But what if she could fix this without them? She'd been spared in that fire. Maybe that meant she was okay. Maybe that meant she deserved him.

"Trust *me*," he said.

Oh, she wanted to. She really did. But she was paralyzed. It was one thing to try to start making changes. Another to do it when the stakes felt so high.

It seemed absurd to say goodbye to each other while they were still sitting on the floor. But they did. Then he lifted her up, stood himself up along with her and walked out the front door.

And she stood there, asking herself questions in the hollowness of her chest.

That hollowness that was surrounded by a wall.

She couldn't dispute it. He wasn't wrong.

She just didn't know how to break it down without breaking everything else. Including her.

Including them.

But there was no way she could truly ask him if he'd burned
down the town without breaking them.

And there was no way she could ever tell him the truth.
About her, about their marriage, about everything.

37

Afterburn

Jenna

IT WAS COFFEE TIME. She was on a coffee date. With Ethan. Alex wasn't working at the bakery, which was strange, but she also kind of appreciated that, because it meant that she didn't have to endure the date under her friend's watchful gaze.

She wanted to be able to tell Alex about the date without Alex having any sort of added perspective on how it had gone. Jenna wanted to be able to at least fantasize about how good it had gone.

Ethan was tall. Maybe six foot five. It seemed excessive. Broad shouldered, very big hands, muscular forearms. His face was sculpted, chiseled. And on most men, she found the man bun laughable, but his dark hair tied back was compelling.

As was his beard.

Maybe it was mostly the being six-five.

She had always struggled with the "is he hot or is he tall?" conundrum.

Ethan was decidedly both.

"Thank you for agreeing to meet with me."

Oh, Lord. She sounded like she was conducting a board meeting. Or was at another town council meeting, rather than on a date. She didn't know how to do this.

"I think I asked to meet with you," he said, his dark eyes sparkling with amusement.

He also had a sense of humor. It was a little excessive for one man to contain so much.

Maybe her bar was low.

"Yeah. Okay. It has been a very long time since I've been on a date. I don't actually know how to do it."

She had just been on a date. With Matt. She was lying. Well, no. She wasn't *lying*. She just wasn't counting that, because it had been bad. And she had known the whole time she didn't want to sleep with him. And really, the tone of a date dramatically shifted when you wanted to see the other person naked. Then she was forced to wonder if Matt had wanted to see her naked; she assumed that a man only asked a woman on a date because he wanted that. So that maybe meant Ethan wanted that, unless there was some inverse nudity effect when the woman was a certain number of years older?

This was the world's shittiest math equation. She did not like it. She didn't know why anyone would choose to be single.

"I'm going to start over," she said. "What's your sign?"

"I don't know," he said.

"You don't know?"

"No."

"When is your birthday?"

"December sixth."

"Well, you're a Sagittarius. Which explains a lot."

"Now you have to tell me what it explains."

She put her hands flat on the table. "I don't actually know. I have just found that when you say that following the revelation of someone's astrological sign it either intrigues them or makes them very angry. I thought I'd see which you were."

"You fascinate me."

His words stopped her cold. She was pretty sure she was blushing. From the roots of her hair down past the collar of her shirt. "I fascinate you?"

"You always have, Jenna. You say whatever you want. You run around town like you're going to single-handedly fix everything. And sometimes I think you might. It's impossible to ignore you."

"I have heard that before. Usually not a compliment."

"I would think it would only be an insult coming from somebody who felt threatened by you."

"I knew I liked you."

"Good."

"Okay. I'm going to be really honest with you now," she said, her heart thundering. Even while her insides were warning her. *Jenna, don't do it. Keep your mouth shut.* It was like she had been telling herself this entire time not to be too honest with him, because she was afraid she would. Because she knew herself. She was in a chaos stage and if nothing else, what she really liked to do was throw the bomb out there and see what happened. She couldn't help it. Even while it terrified her, she wanted to do it. Wanted to see what happened. It was how she was, and she didn't know how to make herself any different. So she had been warning herself. Literally for weeks while she checked him out.

Don't say that you think he's hot. Don't say that you want to sleep with him.

And she knew that the honest truth was about to come out of her mouth, and… She just decided not to stop it.

"In theory, a coffee date should be safe," she said. "And you did ask me to coffee, not dinner. A coffee date seems to mean there is less of a chance of…pressure for sex after."

He didn't laugh at her. Instead, one eyebrow shot up, and he tilted his head to the side. "Does it?"

"Yes. Because of the timing."

"I didn't know there was a specific time that made sex less likely."

She stared at him. "Oh. Because you haven't been married. So you don't know the whole, *well, we're already in bed so we might as well…*"

He shook his head. "No."

"So that's not why you asked me to coffee?"

"To avoid sex? Hell no. I asked you to coffee because I wanted to make it easier for you to bail on me if you needed to."

"Well, that is… That is very… Look, the truth is, it is actually a much better time for me to have sex with someone now than after a dinner date. I have kids. And they're in school right now."

He lifted one dark brow. "Are you propositioning me?"

"I wasn't going to. I was going to let you keep running this because that is a novel experience for me, let me tell you. But I'm also just really… I'm alive. I didn't die in the fire. And I don't have time to sit around and marinate in subtlety when I have things I want to do, so yes. I am."

"Is having a conversation with me so boring that you want to skip ahead?"

"No. You're just that hot."

"I actually want to get to know you," he said. "I want to make that clear."

Oh, boy. That wasn't what she expected. She'd figured it was one of two things: either he was indulging her because he didn't hate her, or he was looking for a quick hookup. She had not expected him to be interested on a level that was deeper than nudity. For him to want to have sex with her *and* for him to want to get to know her.

"You are not following my script."

He looked her over. Slowly. And she felt like he'd put his hands on her. "I bet that doesn't happen to you very often."

"It doesn't. Because you know what I'm really good at? I am really good at pegging exactly what kind of person someone is. So they don't usually surprise me."

"Interesting."

"I am also very good at holding my breath. For like a whole minute at a time. And I can tie a cherry stem with my tongue."

"Jenna, you don't have to keep trying. I want you."

He wanted her. "Want to go back to my place?"

She sounded so calm. She sounded like she did this all the time. She did not. She wasn't calm. She was freaking out. She had sat down with the guy for all of ten minutes, and then fully propositioned him. It was crazy.

"Should I…"

"I'll drive us," he said.

Like he didn't care if people saw his car in the driveway. Of course, she was still living far out of town. And things were in boxes.

"My place," he said.

She instantly calmed down, and then got nervous all over again. Because she wasn't in charge of this. She was not in charge of this. And she didn't know what to do with that. She was so used to having the control. She was often the instigator of sex in her relationship with Ryan. She always knew that he wanted it, but it was usually on her terms. In fact, a lot of things were on her terms. Not because he didn't have opinions, but because he let her run the show.

But she wasn't going to think about him right now.

She found herself standing up, and suddenly, she felt very small standing next to Ethan, whose whole demeanor had changed. He did not seem younger now. No. There was a protective vibe to the way he put his hand on her lower back.

He didn't seem concerned about whether somebody saw them. Not at all.

Suddenly, she was having a hard time breathing.

But they kept walking down the sidewalk, and he opened the passenger door to his truck, parked against the curb. Held it for her as she got inside.

She buckled, her heart pounding in her throat as she waited for him to round the driver side and open the door.

And it became clear to her why she did the thing she did. Why she said the thing. Because then there was no guesswork. And she either burned it all to the ground or she opened up the door to things like this. But rare was the moment when she felt like she was no longer driving. And right now she was literally not driving.

"It's just five minutes up the road," he said.

"Great."

"Your husband was a dick, Jenna."

"What?" She looked at him sharply.

"That's how I feel about it. I couldn't believe it when he left you like that. I couldn't believe anyone sided with him at all, and I know it's because, for some reason, everyone is more willing to believe there's a problem with a woman than with a man they admire. And I really couldn't believe it when he showed up at the town council meeting with her. I took him to task for that."

"You *what*?"

She really hadn't known about that.

"At that meeting. I took him to the parking lot and I lit into him. Asked him what the hell he was doing and for who. What a fucking performance."

"Why did you do that?"

"Because you're a really special woman. You care about this place. You care about your friends. And he was just... Those doctors. Coming to the town council meetings in their scrubs. Acting like they're better than everybody else. Because why? Because they had parents with enough money to send them to medical school? He seemed to think he could do whatever he wanted and not face a single damned consequence. He acted entitled to everything. Including you. Even after that acting like it was wrong you should forgive him. It was more of the same thing."

"Why did you care so much?" she asked, looking down at her hands. Looking down at her blank wedding-ring finger.

"Because I wanted you."

Right then, they pulled up to a small, neatly kept house just outside Old Town.

"Since when?" she asked.

"You've been kind of a secret fantasy of mine for a while. Dirty stuff, Jenna. Fantasizing about a married woman."

"An *older* woman."

"I'm not going to lie. I find that pretty hot."

"Why?" she asked.

"Why do you find it hot to hook up with me?"

"Because you are objectively hot."

"So are you."

"Yeah, but you are like a dark and wonderful Viking who could literally get any woman he wanted. And I'm a gently used middle-age woman. I feel like the resale value on you is higher."

"Bullshit."

He leaned across the cab of the truck, wrapped his large hand around the back of her head and dragged her toward him, kissing her. Hard and deep and holy shit. It was just so much better than she had even imagined. Was it the insane self-esteem boost? Was it that he was so hot? Was it that she hadn't been kissed in almost two years? Who was to say?

But after that they scrambled quickly out of the truck and into the house. She went for the buckle on his jeans, and she found her hands moved away decisively, pinned behind her back. Her cheeks flushed with heat. "You first."

He grabbed her shirt and pulled it up over her head. And she gasped.

She felt like an inexperienced virgin. And that really wasn't how she expected the dynamic to go in this relationship.

His hold was firm, and he kept her in place while he methodically stripped her bare, her whole body burning beneath his appraisal. "My bedroom's back that way," he said.

"And?"

"I'd like to watch you walk there."

Her breath was coming in short, sharp bursts, but she turned and obeyed the command, walking slowly down the hall. And she could feel him looking at her. Her breasts felt heavy, her nipples beaded tight, and not from the cold.

No. It was from this. This thing that she had never even known to fantasize about. This thing that she hadn't even known she wanted. She felt out of control. And somehow stronger for it. Because she was out of her element, and there she was, keeping her head above water, anyway. Who had ever thought that midmorning, after-coffee sex would be the kinkiest, most exciting thing she'd ever done?

She heard the door close firmly behind her. And she turned. His gaze was hot, and she could feel it like a touch.

Then he grabbed the hem of his shirt and wrenched it over his head, his body—damn, sculpted and glorious and perfect—taking her breath away. Then he advanced on her, kissing her again, harder, deeper, and every time she tried to change the tempo, set the tone, he took it a different way, and it felt so good, she wasn't going to argue.

His grip was rough, exciting, and she matched him, following him and taking it all. Every kiss, every lick. Every bite. His hold was bruising and it made her feel alive. His body was so hot and hard and strong above her and it reminded her that she could feel something that wasn't bad. That she could feel more than just okay. She could feel amazing. She wasn't a woman who needed to be protected. She wasn't a woman who needed to be rescued. She was a woman who knew her own body, and knew how to get her own orgasms.

But damn it all, what a relief to not have to do any of it.

To have a man who was so big and strong he could hold her; to have a man whose touch was so skilled, that he could bring her to the edge in minutes; to have a man who could show her new avenues to pleasure, who could make her feel like things were new and exciting and wonderful, rather than a broken dream she had to make do with.

It was sex. She knew that. Sex wasn't feelings. And it wasn't necessarily transformative.

But maybe it was. Because it sure felt like it.

And when he surged inside her, so big and thick and decisive, her orgasm rocked her to her core.

It never seemed to stop. The waves of pleasure. Satisfaction.

And when he came, his growl reverberated in her, and it healed something that had broken inside that she hadn't even really known was shattered.

And while she lay there, staring at Ethan's ceiling, basking in the glow of the first truly enjoyable morning sex she'd ever had in her life, she remembered.

You never needed me to fix anything for you.

Yeah. Well. You never seemed like the kind of guy who could fix things for me.

She could fix things for herself. And part of that was because she'd had to. She *liked* to, sure. She was who she was. She wasn't a damsel in distress.

But the items on her to-do list were firmly on *her* to-do list, and Ryan sure as hell had never been about to do a single one. He had an idea of his own importance; Ethan was right about that.

That surgeon/God complex that suggested he was more important, that he mattered more. He had shifted that on to her. Made it somehow about how she didn't need him enough.

He had just wanted someone easier. That was all.

Because he hadn't known what to do with her.

And okay, one intensely satisfying sex session with a man like Ethan wasn't enough to make her declare that he did.

But it had definitely put certain things into perspective for her.

"You are amazing," he said, rolling over and kissing her.

"I'm amazing?"

"Hell yeah."

"I don't… Thank you. I have not felt amazing for a long time."

"You are."

She cleared her throat. "Do you want to…? Do you want to do this again?"

He grinned at her. "Sure."

"What, like right now?"

"Yes," he said.

Her eyes widened. "You really could?"

"Give me five minutes."

"That right there is why you want to date a younger man," she said, laughing. Except she was serious.

"But to answer your question more seriously. Yes."

She trailed a fingertip across his bare shoulder. "Should we also see if we have things in common?"

"We do," he said.

"How do you know that?"

"I have watched you give impassioned speeches at town council meetings for years. I think I also watched you give an impassioned speech to your parents one night at the family barbecue. You were making a case for extending your curfew."

"You remember that?"

"I'm going to confess something, and you have to promise not to freak out."

"I make no such promises, Ethan," she said, tossing her hair as best she could while lying down. "You get what you get. If what you say freaks me out, I'm going to freak out. But since I would have to run out of here naked because my clothes are in your living room, I probably won't run off."

"You were definitely my first sexual fantasy. Teenage Jenna pushed *all* my buttons."

She blinked. "Really?"

"Does that gross you out?"

"No. I always knew I was the main character. Thank you for supporting my narcissism."

"I aim to please."

"I feel like you really do." She had to take a shift at the store before she went to get the kids. "Five minutes, you said?"

"Only three now."

"How quick can you get me there?"

"Very, *very* quickly."

Ethan was a man of his word.

38

Afterburn

Alex

IT WAS BARREN out there. The ground was still charred.
And it sent a shiver down her spine. There was something
eerie about it. The ground was black, some trees around them
standing, others reduced to nothing.

The farmhouse that had once been there was gone. Completely. The fire had burned so hot, it had been an apocalypse
of flame. The wind had been merciless and the ground might
as well have been tinder. It was the perfect storm, ready to
enact destruction so swift and so horrific nothing could have
stopped it.

Then there was the randomness of it. That was what she
had always found so terrifying.

The houses that had been burned. The houses that had
been spared.

The people that had been burned.

The people that had been spared.

She was one of the saved ones, she supposed. Except... It was hard to think of herself that way. She must've been close enough to the flames to be burned, but she couldn't remember them. She just remembered the pain. The paramedic shining a light in her eyes and asking her questions. Her first memory. After a long run of nothing.

"You okay?"

"Yes," she said.

Cody reached his hand out to her, and she took it. He held on to her while they walked across the charred black ground. There were darker streaks, like malicious, poisoned threads spidering across the ground, giving suggestions of how the flames had moved. And there was one spot that looked altogether different. Carried the suggestion of a burst of flames.

"The ignition point," he said, standing at the center and turning a slow circle.

"*Fuck,*" she said. "I..." She felt nausea rise up in her gut. She took a deep, steadying breath, but the air tasted acrid.

"Are you okay?"

"No." She put her hands on her knees and took another deep breath, leaning forward and touching her forehead. It felt clammy.

"I just... I don't... I wasn't prepared. But it's okay."

Just like that, she felt like she gathered herself.

This was where the fire had started.

The fire that had burned down her whole life.

So much of her life was tied to this place. Was that a co-incidence?

Like this was all about you?

Still, she couldn't help the memories it triggered. She couldn't help but remember being here with Cody.

And she'd spent too long without him. He would probably leave when this was over.

When this was over.

It would never be over, would it?

People were dead.

The question was who would go to prison for it?

She swallowed hard, moving a shaking hand to hold her purse close to her body. That was where she had the locket.

"About two months after my mom left, it was like Paul noticed that I was sad. That I wasn't myself."

"That was when you were meeting secretly with me," he said.

She nodded. She and Cody, they had met here in the woods. Had drinks. She had never been an underage drinker, not until then. It had been friendship between the two of them. Until it hadn't been.

"I remember when you kissed me. The first time. I really wanted... I wanted more, but I was afraid. And also, a little scared of having sex outdoors."

He laughed. "I mean, how can you not want to get it on out here?"

"It was like I was paralyzed," she said, once her laughter had subsided slightly. "By what had happened. And you made me feel like I was racing toward something. Something new. And for a while it excited me. But then... Then Paul started to show an interest. And he felt safe."

"Safe," he repeated.

"I was in love with you," she said. "And I was afraid. Because I was a snob. Because your family wasn't like mine." Tears filled her eyes. She felt ashamed, sick, saying this now. "I was overwhelmed by it, and by you. And I was afraid. Afraid of what being with you would look like. But I knew what being with Paul would look like. My dad's a doctor. And I knew that I could have the same kind of life. A chance at a do-over. And it was like I was…desperate for something that felt familiar. You terrified me, Cody." The tears slid down her cheek. "That night in the woods that we… That we came the closest… I lost control. Do you remember?"

"Yeah. I do."

He'd stripped her clothes off her, and she'd been desperate, kissing him, riding his lap, his jeans still on.

She'd had her first orgasm with another person right then. And when that had subsided…she'd run away.

"I lost my head. And Paul had been pursuing me. And I knew that he had decided he wanted me, and part of me has always wondered if he knew. If he knew that I was with you and he wanted to see if he could take me. And I actually knew that what he wanted was to win me more than he actually wanted to have me. Do you know what I mean?"

He nodded slowly, his expression grim.

"So I let him. I didn't mean to get pregnant."

"Did you come?"

She should be mad at him for asking that. But she wasn't. "No. I didn't."

"Right."

"I didn't want him like I wanted you." The honesty scraped her throat raw. This was the first time she'd ever told the truth about this. Even to herself. "I wanted the life I figured that choice would get me. That was what I wanted. I wanted something easier."

"Was it?"

"It was a life." It sounded so bleak. "And you know, it was pretty easy. The kind of life that was so easy, actually, that I figured out how to ignore all the pieces that didn't quite fit. And it was great. We moved back here a few years after med school, and I got to be near Jenna again, and coming back somehow felt easier, like maybe I'd changed. We were like this golden couple when we returned home. We were…"

"Was it worth it?"

"You can't ask me if twenty-five years and two kids is worth it. I can't imagine my life without those kids."

"Did you love him?"

She nodded slowly. "Sometimes. I thought about you a lot. And yeah, sometimes I wished that I had been braver. Because if I had been, I could have been with you. I wasn't brave. But I was really pretty. And I was perfect." She looked up at Cody. "That was why he wanted me. And that was how he loved me. He treated me really well. He treated all of his possessions really well."

The words made her feel cold, but she realized just how true they were when she said them.

They were the golden couple.

She was beautiful.

He wouldn't have wanted it any other way.

"Alex," Cody said, his voice rough. "I'm leaving when I'm done here. And I have the life that I have. I'd like to promise you things that I don't think I can. But no matter what, I want to know you. I want to know more about what happened then, and what's happened since."

She felt like she was staring into a very dark abyss. One she'd intentionally not looked into for all these years. "I wanted him to save me," she whispered. "And sometimes I think he wanted me for the same reason. But you know, I never knew he needed saving."

"I won't ask you to try to save me."

"Why?"

He smiled, but it wasn't happy. "I'm not going to ask you to be the patron saint of lost causes, Alex."

"Why does it have to be hard?"

"I think the reasons you didn't want to be with me back then were probably good. Yeah. I wanted to be your hero. Marry you, raise his kid like she was mine. But I'm not eighteen now. And I get that I'm not the hero I thought I was. Ironically, getting into the FBI made me realize the limits of what I could do. And now I'm a long way down a very dark path." He looked away. "This kind of work changes you."

"All these years change anybody."

He nodded slowly. "Yeah. I want to fix this for you, Alex. Identify your husband. Get you some answers. All the unidentified remains are still in custody. I've got a specialized lab running some additional testing. It is very tough to extract DNA from bones that have undergone that much heat. Dental records would obviously be easier. But in many cases, the remains were not intact enough. Or we couldn't find teeth." He winced. "Sorry. I forget it's… I told you. The job changes you."

She swallowed. "It's fine."

It wasn't. But she understood. This was a job to him, even if it was about his hometown. About people he knew.

People he'd hated.

But no matter the unsettling realizations she was having about her marriage, it didn't change that they were talking about her husband. And it hurt.

"Anyway. I don't know." He looked around. "I looked at pictures. Of the scene. But I just can't get a picture of it." He walked ten paces away from her, and stood right there, where the black lines spidered out in all directions. "We're just missing too many pieces of the picture."

Fire.

Her mom.

Paul's eyes.

The locket.

"I wish I could help."

39

Morgan

SHE WAS READY to go out, but tonight she would have Lily with her. She had put her in the cutest little pink outfit, but was nervous about her making it through a meal.

Cody probably hadn't thought about that when he'd told her to bring her along.

Cody didn't have kids.

That made her want to laugh. Because in that way, she had more life experience than her uncle did.

Her heart squeezed as she buttoned up Lily's floral coat. It was adorable. She had money to buy clothes for Lily, thanks to Marjorie. She was doing better than her mom had. When she walked into the restaurant, she could see Cody behind the server, already seated.

He was wearing one of those FBI suits.

"Do you need a high chair?" the hostess asked.

"Yes," she said. "Thank you."

She walked up to the table, and he glanced up. "You made it."

"Sorry. It takes…forever. To get her ready. I'm still figuring that out. Also, I never really go anywhere except work. And it's just downstairs from where I live. So…"

"Yeah." He looked back down at the menu.

"Are you okay?"

"Yeah," he said. "I'm good."

"You seem… I don't know. I don't know that I can actually comment much on your moods."

There was a time when he had been unquestionably her favorite person in her life. But ultimately, she hadn't seen him all that often.

The waitress came with the high chair and set it up against the side of the table, and she stood up, working Lily out of her little coat and putting her in the seat, buckling her tight. She took some crackers out of her bag and stuck them in front of her.

"Parenting skills," he said.

"Just self-preservation."

She looked at the table next to them and saw a woman who was probably her age, sitting with a man who was also her age. They didn't have kids. They were just enjoying having a meal together. She'd never even had a boyfriend before Ryan. Had never been on a real date. And he'd never really taken her on a date, either.

And she'd been so…lost. In that moment, that fantasy, when everything had exploded into something bright and wonderful. But it had been the most perfect moment, and after that…

"What did you do today?" he asked.

"Oh. Work. That's all. You, too?"

"I went to the ignition site. With Alex—Alex Coleman? I don't know if you know her."

"She's Paul's wife."

"She was," he said, his voice tight. The reaction was such that she… Well, she wondered if Alex was the complication from his past.

"Did you find anything?"

"Just ghosts. Going back over there is a lot."

"I haven't been. Since the fire."

She was afraid. Like she might find Ryan's body or something. The house had burned so hot, there had been nothing left. Metal had melted.

She wondered if he'd gone back there. It haunted her.

"I don't blame you. It's the first time I've actually wished that I had gone back to the house at least once over the years."

She was happy to have things redirected to Cody's life. "What happened? Between you and Marjorie. To make you leave. To make you not even come back for her funeral."

"It wasn't any one thing," he said. "It was just years of… She always thought the worst of me. And she blamed me for the worst in her life. When I was a teenager, it was especially bad. Like she was just done with me."

"I never got that feeling."

He looked at her and there was something in his eyes she couldn't read. "You didn't?"

"No. She was pretty proud of you, actually."

He laughed. "After I left. That sounds about right."

"No. I think maybe she realized she didn't do a good job with you or my mom. But you managed to make something of yourself, anyway. And I think she was impressed."

"Well, that's a better view of it than I've ever had."

"What did she do to my mom? I mean, why was my mom…? Do you know why she was the way she was?"

"Do I know why she was an addict?"

"Yes."

"I don't know. I mean, not specifically. I can't tell you exactly when it started, but I can tell you what she said to me one time."

"What?"

"She told me not to start. She said she wished she hadn't. And she said that for a long time, it made her feel like her choices didn't hurt quite so much. She could soften the edges around everything. And it was better at first. But she said it didn't really change her choices. It just made it so even when she wanted to be, she couldn't be part of her life. I've thought about that ever since. I was probably sixteen when she said that. I made my choices. I don't know that they were right. But they were mine. And I can't change them. And I've made a decision not to soften the edges of my choices. Sometimes you just have to sit in it. Because maybe you didn't do the best thing. But you did what you did. I didn't forgive her. We didn't reconcile. That was my choice. I walked away from here, chose a different life. And I have to live with that. For the most part, I'm happy enough with it."

The words hit her, sharp and hard.

Sometimes you have to sit in it...

She'd tried standing in endless defiance of the consequences of her choices. Staring down the sister of her dead lover and saying she didn't regret what had happened between them. But the truth was she did. She regretted it all the time. She regretted that she lived with this immeasurable grief. She regretted that in the end, it hardly felt worth it because she had all this pain, all this responsibility, and the guilt on top of it. She regretted that she felt sorry for herself, because she was just so damned tired of her self-pity. And somewhere in there...was Lily.

And the knowledge now that her own mother had been a bad one because there had been choices in her own life that she couldn't come to terms with.

"I've made so many mistakes," she said.

"Are you talking about Ryan?"

"Well, just for starters."

"It's not a crime to be naive."

"I wrote myself a story. I wanted so badly for it to be a romance that I didn't care about all the inconvenient parts. And yes, part of that was being naive. But now I can't be. Not anymore. I can't afford to ever be that stupid again. I have a kid. And my mom never got it together for me. I have to be better than that for her. I am trying to be better."

"You know, there's nothing wrong with being better than that for you," he said.

"But I don't feel like I deserve anything." She put her elbows on the table, her fists over her eyes. "And I just want to be… Want to be done with that. With this feeling. I can't even just leave here and pretend it didn't happen."

"No, you can't pretend. It is what it is. But she doesn't deserve to be treated like a consequence, either."

"I love her," she said. "But I worry I'm not doing the right things. All the time, I worry I'm not doing a good job. I don't know how to be a mom. I don't know how to do any of this."

"I'm not exactly the most well-adjusted person. And I don't actually have anyone in my life on a real, permanent basis. In that way, you are leagues ahead of me, kid. But I know what fucks people up. And I know you don't want that. Not for her."

"So what's the right thing to do?"

"I think a place to start is to quit feeling sorry for yourself and to start feeling sorry for the people who got hurt."

"Well, Jenna hates me. And probably doesn't ever want me to talk to her."

"Yeah. Good point. Maybe she doesn't want to talk to you. Maybe it will do more harm than good. Anyway, the person that really owes her an apology is dead."

She nodded. "Unless he's not. Unless he left."

"Do you think he did?"

"I wonder. I always thought it was weird that he agreed to leave her for me. Sure, I told myself that he loved me. That we were a great love story. Star-crossed and all of that. Separated by his marriage and our age, and it defied reason, and that made it special. But when I found out I was pregnant, that was when I really had to face it. I was just a woman he had an affair with. He didn't respect what I had to say about anything. He looked at me and saw a kid, but for some reason it was fine to sleep with me. Now I... I don't think he loved me." She said that, and it was like opening up a festering wound. Admitting to the thing that had scared her the most, because if she admitted that what they'd had had been a lie, then her justifications for it began to crumble. "He didn't love me. I was just a Band-Aid for some shit he was going through. I didn't realize that at the time."

She shook her head. "I do now. I started to realize that as it went on. So do I think that maybe he just chose to run away? From all of his responsibilities? Yeah. I was just a way out. I wasn't special. I was just someone who needed to believe they were enough so that I would take what he was offering without looking into it too deeply."

"Well, maybe that's why they never found his body. Maybe you're right. Maybe that's exactly what he did."

"I hope not. Because I like to believe that... Even if I was wrong, I wasn't completely wrong about him."

"Yeah. Sometimes we're wrong about people."

"Are you?"

"Not usually."

"Somehow, I didn't think so."

"And I'm not wrong about you, either. I spent a long time sending you birthday cards, remember? Because I believe in you. You're not your mom."

"I know," she said, except she didn't.

"My mom passed pain on to me, on to your mom. Your mom passed it to you. You passed it to Jenna. Don't pass it to Lily, too."

That terrified her. And made her feel resolute all at once. He wasn't wrong. She had been hurt and she'd chosen to pass that to someone else. To decide her own happiness in the moment mattered more. But she hadn't passed it on forever. It had been fleeting, and now she was back where she'd started, with all the same wounds she'd ever had. But this time with a child.

She couldn't keep passing on the pain.

She had to start trying to heal it.

40

Afterburn

Jenna

JENNA WAS FEELING FANTASTIC. Really fantastic. Honestly, you couldn't have that many orgasms and not feel great.

This was starting fresh.

She was moving into the new house, and her friends were due to come over and help out. She had movers bring the big stuff, and that was all settled. But this was sort of a housewarming. And tomorrow they'd be doing the same for Chelsea, who had been elusive in the group text, and downright evasive when questioned on why.

The new place was incredible. She had chosen all gold kitchen fixtures, and had gone with white cabinets and countertops, a contrast to the black that she'd had before. Because she was starting fresh.

She looked at her brand-new bed and her brand-new bedroom. And imagined Ethan tying her to the bedposts. She clenched her teeth and pressed her thighs together. He had said something about that. Being into that. She genuinely didn't care if her sudden interest in bondage made her a cliché. A woman exploring a little soft kink in her post-divorce, midlife freedom quest.

It was really fun. Clichés be damned.

She was going to let the extremely hot, extremely tall, extremely sexy younger man show her how it was.

She jerked the door open when she heard a car pull in, and saw Chelsea with a rather shell-shocked look on her face.

"What's wrong?"

"Mark is back in town."

"Oh shit, honey. Is he wanting to sell the house?"

"No. He wants to…date me."

"What?"

And she stared at Chelsea for a long moment while her friend stared at her.

"How do you do it?" Chelsea asked, standing in the middle of her driveway, not moving. "How do you make it so obvious what you want? How do you know what you want?"

Jenna frowned. "How do you…not know?"

"Because I don't know anything. Because my marriage is a mess, and it has been for so long and I just…somehow, years ago, I started believing lies, and I built lies on lies, and Mark has his own lies and now I don't—" And suddenly, Chelsea put her hand over her mouth. "Jen, what do you do if you don't even know if your husband is a good person and you still want him?"

Jenna was, for the first time in memory, speechless. It took her a moment, but she finally found some words.

"Do you want to have your mental breakdown in my new living room instead of in my driveway?"

"I don't know. I don't know what I want."

"Well, I would like you to come into the house. Because the neighbors are going to stare."

"Do I care?"

"You probably do. I wouldn't. But you probably do. Come on," she said, ushering Chelsea in and sort of standing next to her with her hands fluttering up and down. If she had a blanket, she would wrap her in it. "So he wants to date."

"Because he says we don't know each other. He's not wrong. But what I realized is that I don't really know myself."

"Okay. I thought you wanted a divorce?"

"I don't. I love him. I told him I don't want a divorce. I asked him if he did. And I hadn't been brave enough to do that before, because I was afraid his answer would be yes. So there's that."

"Good."

She heard another car and saw Alex. She was in Paul's old muscle car.

"Wow," Jenna said. "I didn't realize that today was…going to be a whole day."

She opened the door. "Look at you," she said.

"I was feeling…nostalgic today."

"Oh…"

She appraised Alex as she walked into the house. Alex, who looked radiant. And wasn't wearing makeup.

"You had sex with Cody."

"No, I didn't."

"Yes, you did. That's why you're driving Paul's car. Some weird thing that you're doing because you were with another man."

She might have looked at her wedding photos this morning. Wedding photos that she had uploaded to the cloud a long time ago, so when everything had burned up in the house, those had not burned. Kind of ironic all things considered.

But it had been like a weird goodbye to some of that pain. A reconciliation of that union.

So she sort of understood.

It was also why she didn't bring up Alex's words about it all being too soon. It was one thing to tease; it was another to be living through this constant radical confusion that was trying to have a new life.

"Okay. I did."

Chelsea looked over at Alex with wide eyes. "You really did."

"Yeah. Well. I…" And she spelled out a story about her and Cody. The whole story.

"Wow."

"I'm going to pour wine." She went into the kitchen, and Alex and Chelsea followed. "This is gorgeous," Chelsea said. "I know this has nothing to do with anything that's happening right now, but it is a really good kitchen."

"Thank you. I am particularly thrilled with myself. Because it is what I wanted, and Ryan would've hated it."

"I need to move," Alex said. "I don't like living in the house that Paul and I lived in. I don't like not knowing what was going to happen between us. But I'm trying to put things in their place."

"Me, too."

"Mark is back," Chelsea said to Alex.

"Oh…"

"We're going to date."

"That's good?" Alex asked.

"No," Jenna said. "It's bad because Chelsea doesn't know what she wants."

"I do know what I want. I want to be married to him. But married to him in the way that I imagine it could be, and not the way that it's been. Does that make sense?"

"It does," Jenna said.

They talked and had wine and moved knickknacks around and very thoroughly warmed the house, and it had been a couple hours before Jenna had realized they hadn't asked how her date with Ethan had gone. But she didn't feel the need to tell them. She had planned on it. She had planned on crowing about her exploits. But suddenly, she just…didn't need to. Chelsea and Alex had things going on. And they needed to talk about it. And she was all right with letting them. Without running anyone over.

Anyway, what was happening with Ethan was… Yeah, she could tell herself it was her getting her groove back or whatever. Her having a *Fifty Shades* reenactment or whatever. But…it wasn't. There was something deeper happening there. Not just between the two of them, but in what it was making her think about herself. And maybe she could just sit with that quietly for a minute. It was funny to have Chelsea say that Jen always knew what she wanted. She often did. Or at least… She knew one thing she wanted. And she was very good at hyperfocusing on that one thing and letting it eclipse everything else. So good at that, in fact, that it allowed her to ignore any and all blind spots she might have about herself and the people around her.

An uncomfortable thought hit her.

Had her marriage been great, or was she good at ignoring what she didn't want to see? Was she good at talking over it and planning over it and having meetings over it?

The three of them were good at hiding, she realized. Alex was suddenly sharing, Chelsea was talking about her marriage, and those were marked differences. Jenna *not* talking was different, too.

Normally, she'd want to give advice or contribute. Anything not to feel invisible.

But as she sat there and listened to Alex and Chelsea, she didn't feel invisible at all. They'd loved her enough, trusted her enough, to come to her house when they had something to share.

And above all else, that mattered.

It really did.

41

Afterburn

Alex

THEY HAD GONE back to the ignition point. It was a brighter, clearer day than they'd had recently, and she was squinting in the sun like a mole that had been dragged out of its burrow. The sun was aggressively bright. The sky overhead a washed sort of blue.

She turned to look at Cody, but he wasn't there. And the air around her was so hot. There was wind, but it didn't do anything to cool it down. It was a strong, hot wind that made her hair swirl around her, blowing the skirt of her dress up around her thighs. She looked down at the ground. But it wasn't black. It was dry and brown. The dirt was cracked and bleached like the sky.

It was the scene where she was with her mother again.

But she was standing where her mother normally stood in the dream, and she was…

It hadn't been her mother.

It was Alex all along.

She turned slowly and saw Paul standing behind her. And then she turned back toward the dry expanse of ground and the white farmhouse in front of her.

It was on fire.

And it was then she realized she was holding something in her hands.

It was a book of matches.

Alex sat up in bed, gasping for air. And this time, when she looked for Cody, he was there.

She had spent the night at his apartment. Not entirely on purpose, but she had wound up there for dinner, and dinner had turned into sex on the living room floor, which had turned into sex in his room.

Her heart was still thundering hard, her skin clammy.

She tried to replay the dream over again.

She could still feel the matchbook in her hand, slick and shiny, with that chalky stripe on the back. For starting a fire.

It was a dream.

But she couldn't get Paul's face out of her head.

The way he'd looked at her.

His blue eyes were so cold, and the fire was so hot.

It wasn't a memory. It couldn't be. Why would either of them have been there?

She let out a distressed sound, and Cody stirred beside her.

He sat up. "Are you okay?"

His gaze was sharp. Even in the dark, she could see that.

"I just... I had a bad dream."

He reached out and gathered her close, pulled her against his chest, and she buried her head there.

She tried to get her breathing to slow down. To normalize. She wasn't there. She hadn't seen that. It wasn't real.

She was in Cody's apartment. Cody, after all this time. Cody, after all these years. She was finally with him.

And she knew that it wouldn't last forever. He'd said that. That he'd made his choices, that he'd lived his life. Well, she made her choices, too. But she was really glad that their choices had brought them here for at least a little while.

It felt good to be in his arms again. She had never, in all the years since, felt the sort of comfort with anyone else that she did with Cody.

"What happened with your mother?" Talking about him felt like it might help. Like it might soothe the fear rioting through her.

"What do you mean?" he asked.

"I mean, you weren't speaking to her at all. Why?"

"I blame her for a lot of things. Things I probably shouldn't have in hindsight. But the situation was Julie. My sister. I blamed her for that. For cutting her off. That's one reason I reached out to Morgan the way I did. I didn't feel like... My mom helped with Morgan sometimes." He cleared his throat. "I didn't help. I felt like I was a young guy that..."

"Morgan is younger than my daughter," Alex said.

"Yeah. I know. You were also barely eighteen when you had her."

"I know. I'm just saying."

"Maybe I should have helped. Instead, I got bitter at my mom. It wasn't just that, though. Something changed with her. She was always kind of distant and strange, but something changed. I stayed for you. And, well, because I wanted to join the FBI. And I knew I needed to finish school so that I could get into college. I did. I did what I needed to do. I'm glad about that. But she told me the only good thing I ever brought into her life was my dad's money."

"Why would she say that? You were an easy kid, especially compared to your sister."

"There was a man that she wanted to be with. He didn't want to deal with a teenage boy with an attitude. My mom resented me for it. I just don't think she was ever in the right place to raise kids. I think she felt guilty. I think that's why she brought Morgan into her life toward the end of things. Plus… Julie couldn't take care of her, and I would've just hired someone else to do it."

"I'm sorry. You know, maybe it is easier if your parent just abandons you. I'm serious. If they don't want to be part of your lives, at least there is no gray area. It seemed mean to me that you didn't come back for her. I couldn't understand it. And I did think about it. Trust me. Mostly, I wish that you would've come back for Paul's funeral. I… I get it. She might not have left, but it might've been a kindness if she had. At least then it would just be…"

"I'm sorry," he said. "Still. About your mom."

"Me, too. But your mother died without ever telling you… Without ever giving you a way to understand why she did things the way she did. And I bet she never apologized to you."

"Sure as hell not."

"So I guess, in that way… I don't have closure. Neither do you. We are not that different. It isn't that different. It's just crap. That's the thing. All of this is just crap. And we have to deal with it, whether we want to or not. I had Paul and my kids. My dad. His wife, Lucy, who has been just the best grandmother to the kids, and really a good friend to me. What have you had, Cody? After all these years?"

"My career. Which isn't so bad. I've had my career. I did what I set out to do with it, and…that's that."

"You really never had anyone in your life?"

"Coworkers. You bond over the stuff that happens during a

case. Over the fact that you're the only people you know who see the kinds of messed-up things you do. So yeah. I mean, I have work friends."

"That seems lonely."

"Maybe. But I chose it."

She lay back down, snuggling beneath the covers.

"What did you dream about?"

She stared up at the ceiling. "I have a reoccurring nightmare about finding out my mom is gone. Just reliving that."

And she didn't know why she'd lied to him. Because her dream was just a dream. Maybe it was because she didn't want to talk about Paul. Except…she'd just said his name a moment ago.

There was no reason not to tell Cody. Because it was just a dream.

But beneath the covers, she rubbed the burns on her arms, and she had a very hard time falling back asleep.

Fire.

Her.

Paul.

And a matchbook.

42

Kindling

Morgan

"I'M SORRY ABOUT THAT. She should never have done that to you. She shouldn't have yelled at you like that. And she definitely shouldn't have gone accusing you of anything. She's crazy. She's lost her fucking mind."

"Has she?" Morgan was sitting on the couch in the living room, looking down at her rounded stomach. Was Jenna crazy? Or was she just… Morgan had proven herself to be the least trustworthy person there. Along with being new.

Was Jenna crazy? Or was it just…logical?

She hadn't considered herself a villain. Not all this time. She had fallen in love. Deeply. Truly. For the first time in her life. She was having a baby, and she was so happy about that. And it was so easy to just pretend that there had been no consequences to it. But there were. Jenna—her pain, the anger that had been directed at Morgan tonight—that was the consequence.

"I'm the new person," she said. "If money has never gone missing before, it isn't crazy of her to think it's me."

"It is crazy," he said. "She isn't doing it because you're new. She's doing it because she's mad at me."

Crazy. He could call the woman he'd been married to for that many years *crazy*?

Crazy. When he was the one who'd lied.

He was the one who'd proved he couldn't be trusted.

"Well, I didn't take it, Ryan. So they aren't going to find anything. The police are welcome to search my bank account. There is nothing exciting in it."

She looked at Ryan for a long moment, and for the first time she felt the seed of disquiet. If the police looked at her bank account, she knew what they would find. What about if they looked in his? She wouldn't ask that. She wouldn't.

How could she?

He had uprooted his entire life for her. It was no use feeling guilty about any of it now. That was the thing. Ryan had done what pretty much no man ever really did. He had left his wife for her.

She might have jumped into this whole thing being willfully naive, but part of her had been aware of the fact that it was quite possible—likely, even—that he wasn't going to commit to her. That he was just going to get what he wanted from a younger woman and stay with his wife.

A part of her was realistic about the fact that whatever he told her—that it was the first time he had ever been with someone other than Jenna—that he was probably lying.

That he might have lots of much younger girlfriends, but he just kept them all secret.

Yeah. She knew that. She did. So she had actually been

surprised when he hadn't told her to get an abortion when she found out about the baby. She was even more surprised he had decided to move in with her. To publicly out himself.

So how could she ask him now whether part of why he was so upset about Jenna's accusation was that he had taken the money?

It made her uncomfortable to examine him, to examine herself, and admit that she could believe it in part because of what they had done. Because if he was willing to betray his wife, his marriage vows, she had to genuinely ask herself what else he might be able to make excuses for.

And if he was smart, he would ask himself the same thing about her. Because hadn't she found all kinds of creative ways to bend moral boundaries and truths? To convince herself that she deserved Ryan? That she deserved some happiness? That if he was offering it, it wasn't up to her to reject it?

She wanted to curl in on herself and weep. Truly.

"I'd look at Tom," Ryan said suddenly.

"Tom?"

"He's the chair of the town council. His wife had a big medical event a few years ago. Required surgery. He had to declare medical bankruptcy eventually. Obviously, I'm not supposed to tell anybody about that. But… I wonder. I wonder if he maybe couldn't ever dig out of it."

"And you think he would just…steal all that money?"

"Look, I have to give Jenna credit. When she sets her mind to something, she does it big. She never goes halfway. She raised so much money with this charity dinner. I don't think there's ever been that much cash sitting in the bank account. It might have just been a temptation he couldn't resist."

She didn't know if she was relieved he had an answer to that, or if…

If it made her suspicious that he had an explanation.

An excuse.

Another suspect that wasn't him.

"I don't think we should go to the town council meetings anymore," she said.

"I kind of have to. The doctors go as a group."

"Yeah, I know you have a group. But I shouldn't go. And I know that my grandmother… I'm sorry. But she's going to die any day now. And I'm just going to have to disappoint her."

"Hey," he said. "You're not going to disappoint her. I'm sure she has more important things on her mind. You'd think that asshole Cody could come back and see his mother."

"I haven't been able to get a hold of him. He doesn't keep the same phone. He sent me birthday cards every year, but through work or something. Never with a return address. I never know how to find him."

"How long has it been since you've seen him?"

"I was probably like fourteen?" She shrugged. "So like… five years?"

She noticed a slight bit of tension in Ryan's face when she did that math. It made her want to hit him. Because it wasn't like he hadn't known how old she was. He acted bothered by it sometimes.

She wanted to ask him why he only had occasional bouts of self-awareness.

Why her age made him a god sometimes and a cliché others.

"Still. You'd think that he…" Ryan looked out the window. "We used to run all over this place. We didn't really come inside. I guess… Marjorie wasn't really all that into having us hang out. But yeah… I have good memories of this place."

"My grandma wants to see you," she said. Suddenly, she remembered the conversation she'd had with her the other day. It had been completely wiped out by the drama of the meeting.

Marjorie was more supportive of the whole thing than Morgan had a right to expect.

Love is complicated.

That was all she'd said.

"Oh yeah?"

"Yeah. She wants to talk to you about something. She probably wants to tell you to marry me or something."

She laughed, and then realized that she probably sounded desperate. "You don't have to."

"Well. I need to not be married to someone else first."

He said that in a slightly more self-deprecating tone than he should have, and it was about the only thing that redeemed him in that moment.

"Well, you can make sure to tell my grandma that when you see her."

"Yeah. I will."

43

Alex

ALEX WAS STILL spacey the next day when she went to the bakery. She tried to focus on baking, and thankfully, all of her signature recipes resided in muscle memory, not requiring deep thought to accomplish them. They were meeting again this morning so that Jenna could go over the particulars of the upcoming Harvest Festival.

She finished the pumpkin streusel and muffins and took the day's cinnamon rolls out of the oven.

She let them cool for just long enough and then put home-made cream cheese frosting on them. And got everything out to the front bakery case just as they officially opened, and just as her friends and her employee arrived.

She decided on the cinnamon roll this morning and brought it to the table along with a drink.

She took a notebook out of her bag, and it caught the edge of the locket.

She sat there and stared at it, down in the bottom of her bag.

Then she straightened and set her notebook on the table.

She didn't know what to do about the locket.

She didn't know what it meant.

If her mother was alive or...

She decided, resolutely, to put all of this, her fraying thoughts and every doubt, into its own box. She had to, or she wouldn't be able to be in the present at all.

She would still be hung up on her dream.

The first thing she noticed was that Jenna looked...tired. Which was extremely unusual. Jenna could stay up all night writing a proposal for the Main Street Business Association and not look tired. Jenna could go through finding out her husband was having an affair, get left and still triumphantly organize a charity event without looking tired.

Jenna's looking tired was one of the signs of the apocalypse. For sure.

Chelsea was even quieter than usual, contemplative, but Alex knew why that was. With Mark being back in town...

Alex had to wonder, if Paul were still here, if they could start over, would she have *wanted* to date him again?

She'd chosen to sleep with Cody. She was reasonably sure Paul was gone, but if he walked back through that door, which man would she want?

She'd chosen Paul once.

But it hadn't been because her feelings for Cody were lacking.

She and Cody weren't dating. They were...exploring something they hadn't been able to when they were younger. It wouldn't have been this much fun then, either.

This was truly the first time she had ever gloried in her aging self.

She wasn't comparing to her prechildbirth, tight-bodied younger self. Because her younger self would not have known what to do. Not with this man.

He was relentless, unrestrained—filthy, really. And she didn't have inhibitions of any kind. She was more than up to the task of giving as good as he gave. More than up to the task of everything that happened between them.

It was glorious. And seventeen-year-old Alex would have been overwhelmed by it. She would not have been able to cope.

The woman she was now... She was fully able to grab on with both hands and ride them both to satisfaction.

It was a beautiful thing.

The idea of dating, though... That was less appealing. And would she want to go back and date her husband all over again?

She had never dated him in the first place.

He had never had to win her. Not really. He had caught her in a terrified, vulnerable moment, and she had decided to make a decision she couldn't take back, because she knew that it would force her off the precipice she'd been standing on with Cody.

She hadn't meant to get pregnant at seventeen.

But she'd chosen to marry Paul. She'd chosen it. But...

If they were where Mark and Chelsea were now...

She wouldn't have said yes.

The dream came back to her. Hard and horrible, and she pushed it aside.

"Why do you look tired?" she decided to ask Jenna, because Jenna would have asked any of them.

And she'd done a couple things recently that felt Jenna-inspired.

Jenna, at least, was never uncertain.

Sometimes Alex felt like uncertain was 90 percent of who she was.

Jenna looked up from the three planners that were stacked in front of her. "Would you believe multiorgasmic sex with a younger man?"

"Are we…*supposed* to believe it?" Chelsea asked, blinking. "Because I would like to believe it."

"Well. That is what it is. But see, I have to have sex with him in the morning, while the kids are in school. And so I'm staying up late doing work things. Because there's only so many hours in the day."

"And you didn't *say anything*?" Chelsea said. "*You, Jenna*, did not say anything?"

"I was going to. Believe me. I had a speech prepared. I was going to recite epic poetry about the man's cock. But then you guys came with real, serious things."

"*This* isn't serious?"

Jenna blinked and looked spacey for a moment, and Alex could honestly say she didn't recall her friend ever looking spacey before. "I don't think so. I mean, how serious can it be? He's…" She lapsed off. "Wonderful. He's wonderful. I can't even say anything degrading about his age. He's such a nice guy. And…literally the best sex I've ever had."

"Wow," Chelsea said.

"You know when you've been eating chain restaurant hamburgers for years. Years and years. And it gets the job done. And it is a hamburger. But then you go to some gourmet hipster place and you have one there. And it's like, oh, right. *That's* how good it can be. He is a gourmet hipster hamburger."

"Wow. Apt," Chelsea said.

"And I like him. I really like him. And I wasn't supposed to."

"Why not?" Alex asked.

"Because how am I going to explain that to my kids? They lost their dad, their dad who they were mad at, in a terrible fire. And he was dating somebody improbably younger than him…"

"Hey, even if he would have been a young dad, Ethan could have actually fathered your children," Chelsea said. "Not shared a preschool class with one of them."

Jenna snorted. "Yes. I'm less ridiculous. I'm also not married. So. There's that. It's just…"

"What's the real issue?" Chelsea asked softly.

"I wanted a new life, not a retread of the old one," Jenna said. "Can you imagine? My kids are… They're almost grown up. He's thirty-five years old. He doesn't have kids. Will he want kids?"

Something stirred inside Alex. Because the same was true for Cody. Of course, Cody wasn't thirty-five. And they'd already discussed the fact that there was no possibility of permanence between the two of them. But that was the first thing that made her think maybe Chelsea wasn't crazy. Because Jenna had a point. Starting over now? That seemed impossible. It seemed exhausting. All right, maybe her marriage to Paul hadn't been perfect, but it had been twenty-six years of being a couple, twenty-five of those married, and they'd had their kids and they were empty-nesters. And yeah, what she had with Cody was exciting. More exciting than anything had been in… Well, since Cody. That was how exciting it was. But the starting over…

It was a good thing that all she was doing was sleeping with him.

"Have you actually talked to him about that?" Chelsea asked.

"No. Because he would start hiding the neighborhood bunnies for fear that I would boil them. All he has offered me is sex. Except, we talk also, and I just… I can't go bringing up future things like that now. But the problem is… The problem is I'm forty-three years old. I don't have that kind of endless patience of youths."

"You're eight years older than him. You can take it down a notch."

"It isn't just the age. It's the *life*. I was married for a thousand years. My husband had an affair. I've raised two kids. Mostly. And… I don't want to waste his time. If he's just messing around, I'm happy to mess around. But if he's looking for more… I don't know. I might end up just hurting myself, because he's just a lovely guy."

"He's gorgeous," Alex said. Because she wasn't blind. He was massively tall and muscular. Straight out of a fantasy.

"Anyway." Jenna picked up her pen and tapped it on the side of the table. Her lid popped off and she bent down in a hurry to retrieve it. She popped back up and set her pen down again. "I'm trying to just enjoy the moment. But I'm bad at that. I always want to plan."

"Do you bring your planners to bed?" Chelsea asked.

"No. Because if I did, he would tear them up. Because he is…" Jenna closed her eyes and let out a slow breath. "He is *in charge*. In the bedroom."

Chelsea and Alex exchanged a look. "And you… Are you into that?" Chelsea asked.

"Oh yes. I didn't think I would be. But for a couple of hours every day, he is completely in charge. Of everything I feel, everything I do… And it is like the biggest weight has been lifted off my shoulders. And also, I have so many orgasms. *So many.*"

"I don't know," Chelsea said. "I think I'd marry him. I don't even have a uterus anymore, and I would still try to have his babies."

"Somehow, I don't think that's true," Jenna said, shooting narrow eyes at Chelsea. "Given that you are literally dating your own husband."

"Yeah. We are going out tonight."

"And you're not sleeping with him?"

"No," Chelsea said. "We have agreed that it would confuse things."

"Do you want to sleep with him?"

Chelsea looked lost for a second. "Yes. But I want a lot of other things. I want to fix us. Because I know that when we're having sex, it's always good sex. We didn't quit having sex because it wasn't good. It was the other stuff. The distance. The things we can't seem to sort out. So yeah. We could have sex if we wanted to. But it would just put us back in the same place we were before we separated."

"I suggest bondage," Jenna said.

"I'm not opposed," Chelsea said. "But I've also done it before."

"Really?" Alex asked.

"Yes. First of all, Mark is not the only man I've ever slept with. Second of all, he is...proficient in *many* things. But it's the talking. The talking is the problem."

"Another reason to avoid a relationship," Jenna said. "I'm *tired* of talking."

Alex was lying to the man she was sleeping with. So... That was its own issue.

"What about you?" Jenna asked. "How are things with Cody?"

"Well, I don't have any of the time constraints that you do. I'm just spending the night with him when I feel like it."

"And it's going well?"

"There's not a *going well*. Cody and I never said goodbye. I... He and I got very close after my mom disappeared. I told you that. And then we started, you know… We were teenagers. We were fooling around. Not having sex, because I was emotional, and I was a virgin and I was scared. And I was in love with him but…he terrified me. I was trying to figure out what my life looked like without my mom, and Cody just had me. I think Paul knew. And there was an idea that he and I would always eventually get together. At least there had been. And I departed from that so that I could…have this moment in time when I thought maybe I would just burn everything to the ground." The words fell heavily from her tongue, and she saw that picture again. Her hands. Matches.

Paul's eyes.

And how could she explain that look in his eyes?

He had always treated her well.

Paul Coleman was proud of his house. His car. His wife. His kids. He treated everything that belonged to him with care.

Each and every one of his possessions.

"But I got scared. We always hung out in a group, and I knew Paul was…interested enough in me, even though I hadn't really returned the interest. But for the next couple weeks when the group would separate after hanging out, I didn't try to avoid it being just me and Paul who were left. One night Paul drove me home from a football game. He parked the car on a rural road. He started kissing me. I… I didn't say no. We had sex. And I got pregnant."

"You didn't say no?" Jenna asked, looking at her hard.

"No. I didn't."

"Did you say yes?"

Pressure built at the backs of her eyes. "It doesn't matter. I knew what I was doing."

"The first time I was with Ryan, I dragged him into the backseat of his dad's car and literally climbed on top of him."

"Well, I didn't do that, Jenna. I just let him take the lead. It was so much easier to just…not say no. I told Cody no. That I wasn't ready. I just thought with Paul it would be easier… It would be easier if I did it. Because then… I could tell Cody. And he wouldn't want me. And it would be broken and…"

Jenna put her hand over Alex's. "I'm sorry I didn't know."

"How could you know?" she whispered. "I didn't know. I'm figuring it all out now. Why I ran from Cody. Why I… ended up in that car with Paul. I didn't have words for it then. I just knew what felt easy and what felt impossible."

"Are we going to discuss the new and improved Harvest Festival?" Chelsea asked, abruptly changing the subject, her eyes bright.

Alex's gaze caught hers and held.

Chelsea tried to smile. "I'm sorry. I just, I have an appointment in a half hour, so if we have planning to do, we need to start."

"Yes," Jenna said definitively. "I have everything written in my planner. And I got Ethan to agree to build some new booths. He's very handy. And very strong."

"I like this on you," Chelsea said.

"What?"

"It's…subtly different, but I feel like you are with someone who's giving help rather than being… I don't know. Enlisted?"

"Yeah," Jenna said. "I guess that's true."

Alex looked down at her arm, at the burn there. The rough patch that wouldn't go away. And suddenly, it was like she could feel it. The fire. Touching her skin. Suddenly, it was like she was there.

And she looked through the flames, and saw Ryan standing there.

Ryan.

And just like that, the flash of memory was gone but the panic it left behind remained.

"I'm getting more cake," she said. "You guys want more?"

"You still have a cinnamon roll," Jenna pointed out.

"I just want some variety. I own a bakery. So why not?"

"Right. Live your life."

"That's what I'm doing," she said.

And she got up and went back toward the kitchen, and when she was there, she grabbed the edge of the counter and braced herself.

She really wanted to believe her dream was only a dream. But the fact of the matter was… Ryan hadn't been in her dream. And he was suddenly in her mind. Right there. As clear as day.

Standing in front of the farmhouse. Surrounded by fire.

And the matches were still in Alex's hand.

44

Chelsea

SHE MET MARK at the restaurant. She couldn't remember how long it had been since she'd been out to a decent dinner.

She'd felt off balance after the coffee with Alex and Jenna today. Alex's story about what had happened with Paul…

She felt cut open by it. It was so heavy. Thinking of how she'd been toward Alex in high school because Alex had hooked up with Paul… She was such a bitch.

So she tried to focus on the moment. This moment felt nice. Because Mark was here.

There wasn't a single man in here she would rather be sitting with. When it came to looks, she would choose her husband again every time. She felt smug sitting there with him. This man she had known since they were in their twenties. She'd seen the kind of good-looking he was then, and she knew the kind of good-looking he was now.

And he hadn't been with anyone else.

He told her that. And she believed him.

He hadn't asked her the same question. And she couldn't decide if it was because he didn't want to know the answer, or if it was because he didn't think she would... Or didn't think she could.

So right then, before the waiter even came to pour the water, she decided to say it. Because even though this was a date, it wasn't their first date. And she was going to start saying things. Because there was nothing to defend. Nothing to protect. If they didn't start going in with their swords drawn, all of this was over, anyway. Silence hadn't worked.

"I haven't been with anyone else, either. Since the split."

"Thank you," he said. "For that."

"Would it bother you?" she asked.

"Yeah. It would. But...we were separated."

"Why didn't you sleep with anyone else?" He could have. Hell, she could have, too. If there was one thing she'd learned recently, it was that sex appeared to be available everywhere.

She hadn't wanted anyone but him.

"I wasn't separated from you because I wanted something else. I thought maybe things would improve with distance."

"They didn't," she said.

"No. Because distance is the problem, isn't it?"

"When did we finish having all easy conversations, Mark? It's like there was a certain number of years where we got to talk about all these fun and easy things. And all that was left was...stuff we didn't want to talk about. So we didn't."

The waiter came by and took their drink order, and she took a moment to look at the menu. It really did feel like a date. But a date with a heaviness to it. Weight. Not a bad weight necessarily. It was just that there was no undoing the history of what was behind them. Their history.

It was work.

That was the thing.

They were out of easy conversations.

They had hard things. Things they'd decided not to talk about. The words that got stuck in their throats every time.

It was all that was left.

"If this was a real first date, you would ask me what I like. But I bet that you could actually order off this menu for me. Unerringly."

"I wouldn't assume," he said.

"Oh, go on. Assume."

"You want the filet."

"You're right. That's annoying."

He laughed. There was humor in his dark eyes, and she loved that. It had been too long. But there was an edge to this. An edge of excitement and possibility. So strange after so many years of things just being...unspoken.

"All right. I like steak. That isn't actually that big of a revelation."

"You also love it when the steak is done more than it should be. You're going to ask the chef to cook it to death. You'll get the mashed potatoes on the side. You don't like your food to touch on the plate. You like sunsets, and you've never liked sunrises because you don't like getting up early. You don't like morning sex. But you do like being woken up in the middle of the night. You like it when I kiss my way down your body. You really like for me to go down on you."

She was starting to feel flushed. A revival of something that had been extinguished almost two years ago.

You don't deserve it.

She shook that off.

"That is just...most women."

"No. Not like you do. And you're the only one I ever think of when I want that."

"Good answer. You were always good at that."

They didn't want to be apart. They wanted to be together. Wasn't that what mattered?

And maybe... Maybe the foundation wasn't irretrievably cracked. Maybe they weren't built on something impossible. Maybe the fire was a reminder. A reset. Maybe it had burned away everything that could have destroyed them.

And it had left...her.

Maybe it was enough. Maybe it would be enough.

If she could fix herself, maybe that would be enough. If she could keep taking steps forward, maybe they didn't have to go back.

"We shouldn't have sex," she said.

"No?"

They were interrupted by the waiter, and she quickly ordered her severely cooked filet mignon with mashed potatoes on the side.

"No. We're taking this slow."

"I remember the last time," he said, his voice pitched lower.

So did she. And she didn't want to think about it. But he didn't understand that.

"In the shower. I joined you and...it was just like it always was."

Yeah. She remembered it well. Right before he left for Germany. It had been over a month since they'd made love before that. And they had already decided they were going to be apart, and there had been something desperate about that last time.

It made her feel skinned alive just thinking about it. He didn't know, but she had cried after. Sobbed her guts out for an hour, but in the closet so that he couldn't see.

"I remember. Everything."

"You're my girl, Chelsea. You always were. You always have been. Do you know how many times I wanted to come back here? How many times I wanted to... But I wanted to give you what you needed, too."

"I know."

And as much as she was enjoying the honesty, she suddenly didn't want to talk. She wanted to embrace this moment. This electricity. Their food came, and while they ate, she reached across the table and feathered her fingertips over his hand. Beneath the table, she touched his thigh and found that he gripped hers in return, his hold firm.

She wanted to cry. Because she wanted this so bad. Because she wanted to forget everything and just be with him. Like there was no baggage.

Her feelings for him hadn't changed. That had never been the issue. She was never disconnected from him. She was disconnected from herself. And had been for such a long time, and then...there had been that moment, and it had just... It hadn't been a slow undoing like she let herself imagine. The threads had been loose, and one day a well-placed reminder had torn them completely. And she hadn't been able to find her way back from that. It made her feel afraid. And dirty.

But the life she had worked so hard to make, the reality she had worked so hard to cultivate, wasn't what she wanted it to be.

But she did not think about that now. She wanted to shrink it down to this moment. To let that weight go.

Because he was the sexiest man in here, and even if she'd never known him, he would be the one that she wanted.

Mark would always be the one that she wanted.

He was.

He was the one she would choose over and over and over again, and she knew that. She did.

Maybe they could start fresh. Maybe they could start new.

"Do you want some dessert?"

"No, thank you," Mark said, looking at her, his gaze knowing. And it thrilled her.

Because he did know what she wanted. And he knew what she liked. But there was something different about tonight. An edge to it. Because they hadn't been with each other for so long. Because neither of them had been with anyone for so long. And they had memories and needs and desires, and they were rising to the surface.

She could have this.

That was what fire was for. It burned everything away and left the ground bare. Left you able to start over.

That was what she should've done back then. When he had come back to see her. She should have taken hold of it then.

It had been foolish not to. She knew better now.

He didn't take her back to the house; he took her back to his hotel. And that was somehow better.

It wasn't a christening of the new house, or anything half as deep. Just married strangers giving in to temptation in a hotel room. And it felt like a reclaiming of what they were. Of what they could be.

And he did everything he promised, his mouth insistent and wicked, his body familiar and new all at once.

She didn't take her dress off, didn't take off her high heels; she wrapped her legs around his back as he drove them both wild.

And she tried to hold her emotions back when they finished. She tried to let go of everything except the way that her body felt.

But this was why she pulled away from him. Physically.

Not because she didn't feel enough. But because she felt too much.

She was shaking. And he put his arms around her and held her close, and didn't ask why.

"I should go home," she said.

"You don't have to," he said.

"But I should. That's the point, right? Anyway, that's the fantasy."

That wasn't it at all. She didn't care about a fantasy. Not now. She wanted to stay with him and wanted to let him hold her all night.

She wanted to believe the lie that she was spitting to herself about the two of them. About new beginnings, and what she owed him and what she didn't.

She wanted to believe it, but she couldn't. So when she found her underwear and her coat and took herself back down to her car, she sat in the driveway for a long time while reality crashed in on her.

She wanted to have it both ways. She wanted to have honesty over the silence that had consumed them for these past years.

She wanted to start over on common ground, but it would still be a lie.

She wanted so much to be able to keep lying. To be able to keep secrets.

She wanted to blame her mother, and blame Ryan and blame all of the feelings. And not the secret she'd been keeping from him for the past twenty years.

She had no right to hold tightly to him saying he didn't want a divorce. Not when he didn't know her. Not really.

And she was going to have to tell him the truth.

45

Jenna

JENNA WAS STANDING behind the counter in the store when she walked in.

She'd imagined any number of confrontations with her. This small-looking, pale creature who crept into the store like a mouse about to stand in front of a cat. And part of her thought *well, bitch, as it should be.*

Except she wasn't the temptress she'd built up in her mind, or a predator, or siren of any kind.

She was a twenty-year-old single mother who had been nineteen when she'd met Jenna's husband. Nineteen.

Chloe, her daughter, was seventeen now, and the idea of a man in his forties…

Well, Jenna would kill him.

And suddenly, she only saw a sad kid. She couldn't believe she'd come into her shop. And she would like to be mad about it. She *liked* to be filled with self-righteous indignation and rage. It gave her fuel for her daily life. It was part of her balanced breakfast.

But she just couldn't be.

The reasoning of that was so tangled up she couldn't get her head around it, and she could really only compare it to the moment you actually saw the monster in the horror movie.

When you saw it all for what it was, it was so much less horrifying than what your mind conjured up.

Seeing her now, she didn't see a woman who'd proudly worn her lover's necklace in the presence of his wife. She saw an idiot girl who probably didn't even think of it. She probably just wore her boyfriend's present because it was the nicest thing she had.

She had given an awful lot of credit to this pale creature, for being a manipulative mastermind or a home wrecker. She didn't look like either at the moment.

Suddenly, Jenna looked at her and saw...herself.

She might not have taken up with a married man ever, but she knew what it was like to feel alone. Jenna had tried to make the community a Band-Aid to go over the wound left by her parents' neglect. She'd used Ryan to help with that, too.

If Jenna had moved to a new town at eighteen, and Ryan had showered her with attention, with care...

She would have clung to it. And she knew it.

She could see it had taken strength for Morgan to walk in here. But she was more floored by the realization of her own vulnerability, and how much it made her empathize.

"I just...thought it was time we talked. I... I'm trying to be better. To be the best mother I can be for Lily, and I just... I know I need to talk to you so I can do that."

"Okay," Jenna said, pushing back on the counter.

Her instinct was always to jump right in. To launch into invectives or accusations.

But right now she wanted to listen. To hear what she had to say, even if it did erase her momentary nonhomicidal will.

"I'm sorry. And I don't have any right to ask you to forgive me, but I just wanted you to know that I… I do know that what I did was wrong. And you weren't crazy for being mad. And you weren't mean. And you—"

"Wait. Who said I was crazy?" Probably the wrong thing to focus on. Morgan looked away. "Ah. My husband?"

"I'm sorry."

Jenna had to laugh. "No. No. He… I didn't know him in that last year and a half. I wondered if I ever did. Nice to know he rewrote what he knew about me to you. That seems on brand for his breakdown."

"I bought into it. All the way. I met him and he was… He was so good," Morgan said. "And I'm sorry…" And to Jenna's overwhelming horror, Morgan started to cry. "He was the first person to ever treat me like he loved me. And I'm sorry. I'm sorry for what it cost."

This hurt. It was too sharp and Jenna wanted to lash out, because it was always so much easier to just…strike first.

But why? Everything had already burned to the ground. Jenna's personal scorched earth would be a bit much.

"The truth is if a man with a wedding ring comes on to you, you should probably walk away, especially when his wife is in the room." She looked down at her hands, where there was no ring, not anymore. "But he should never have walked up to you in the first place."

Morgan nodded. "I just wanted… For once in my life, I wanted to be the girl who got picked, and I wanted it so badly I didn't care who did it, or what he already had." She wiped a tear from her cheek. "So he left or…or he's dead. Neither of us got him in the end. He either left or died alone, because he wasn't with me that morning."

"He wasn't?"

She shook her head. "No. I went into labor. That's why I wasn't at the farmhouse. It's what saved me. But Ryan wasn't there when I woke up."

"I thought… I kind of thought maybe he died because he was there. Because he left me."

Morgan shook her head. "I never saw him that day. I don't know where he was. Somewhere in the path of the fire. Or he left me. If he'd been home, he could've gone to the hospital with me, and if he had, he would've lived. It's why I lived. Because she was born early. Maybe he was cheating on me, too. And I would deserve that. Because I didn't deserve to trust him, did I?"

Jenna closed her eyes. "It doesn't matter. It just doesn't matter anymore. Because nothing is going to bring him back. And nothing going to change what happened." She swallowed hard and, for one moment she let herself feel the sadness. "I loved him, you know. I really loved him. Whatever he said to you. Whatever he… I loved him. For all those years."

Morgan looked up at her, her eyes still glassy. "So did I. For a few months I really thought he was the only person in the world who had ever loved me. And I wanted to believe that so badly."

"You know, Morgan, you are closer to my daughter's age than you are to me. You're barely three years older than Chloe and you're twenty-three years younger than me. And I wanted to make you my enemy but you aren't, are you? You're just a casualty of the whole thing."

"I made my decision," Morgan said softly. "I'm not innocent."

"No. I know you aren't innocent," Jenna said, feeling tired.

Drained. "But you aren't evil, either. There's more to life and people than that. And Ryan certainly doesn't deserve to have any of my anger deflected off him. Why were there sides to this whole thing? Because it is so easy to convince people a woman is crazy, especially a woman like me, and he did a damned good job of that. With anyone who'd ever had a disagreement with me. Because it can't just be that I have strong opinions I stand by. No. Every annoying, wrong, pushy thing I ever did got amplified, and all his bullshit was forever minimized because people just wanted to look at him and see a hero. One of Tenmile High's football stars. Go Tigers. A doctor. A man who could claim to be six feet tall in the right shoes. I mean, hell, what sin can't that cover?" She laughed. "I'm over that."

And she was over him. Which was the biggest thing. She couldn't be sorry anymore that the marriage had ended.

She had discovered new things about herself since having to stand on her own. She had discovered something new about herself when it came to the kind of man she was interested in being with now, versus the kind of man she had chosen to be with at sixteen.

She wouldn't trade that self-discovery.

She could hate this woman forever. But why? She only had so much energy, and while it was great energy, with brilliant focus, it was a waste to use it on this child who had her own vulnerabilities, her own issues. Maybe this woman had exploited some deficit in her husband; that strange need that he had to take care of soft and fragile things; that need that he claimed she had never allowed him to fill with her.

Or maybe he had taken advantage of something in her. The need to be cared for when no one had offered it before.

Maybe it was both.

Maybe she would never really know which it was. Maybe it

didn't matter. Really, at the end of all things, maybe it didn't matter. It was a mystery she wasn't going to solve.

And it wasn't one she needed to solve.

Her gift was that she had freedom. From all this.

From needing to be needed by him, and maybe by anyone else.

She could just be.

And she needed to accept that.

"I don't want to be angry at you," Jenna said. "I really don't. And... I was really hurt. I was devastated. That was my whole life. That was our whole life. But if he didn't want to be in it anymore, there's nothing you or I could do about that. He would've found a way out one way or another. And believe me, Morgan, ask anyone here. I'm not the bigger person. Not in any scenario. Not for the sake of it. What happened was bullshit. But then, what's happening now is kind of bullshit, too. I'm sorry that you're by yourself with a baby. I'm sorry... I don't know. I guess I'm just sorry about all of it. That it ever happened. But you can't change it. All we can do is keep living. Because we are alive. And that is the thing. Ryan is the only person who can tell me why our marriage fell apart, and he's gone. He didn't have the conversation with me while he was alive, and he can't have it with me now. You don't have the answers I want."

Morgan looked down at her hands. "No. But I can tell you why I did it. I really wanted it to be real. And I decided that you didn't matter because you had a house and money, and you were beautiful, and you had kids, and friends and all these things that I didn't have. And I let every small, petty part of me decide it was okay if I had your husband. Because you were better than me. In every other way. And you wouldn't miss the one thing. It was a whole lot of justifying things that couldn't be justified. I understand that. What I did was wrong and—"

"He was really something when he set his mind to getting what he wanted," Jenna said. "Handsome and compelling, and just the nicest guy. There's a reason people loved him. There's a reason you fell in love with him so easily. The same reason I did. Because even at sixteen, that's who he was."

Jenna was never the bigger person. She liked her axes ground down to a fine powder. But she had to care deeply about the cause. And the greatest gift she'd gotten from this moment was realizing that while she might mourn Ryan's loss because of the pain it caused her kids, she did not mourn their marriage.

He hadn't changed.

This had just shone a light on who he was.

And she couldn't love that man.

Couldn't miss him.

Couldn't wish they could go back, because she didn't want to live with someone who was pretending to be someone they weren't.

He was immature. And he'd missed the way he was admired in high school. So he'd chosen a girl who was just fresh out of high school to relive his glory days.

"Where's your baby?" she asked.

"Oh. I… With your…ex-mother-in-law."

Jenna laughed. She couldn't help it. "Oh. Wow."

"Yeah. She really wants to be involved."

"Well, my kids still visit her. She's a pain in the ass, though." She cleared her throat. "Maybe they can visit at the same time."

Morgan looked shocked. "That would be…"

"The kids lost their dad. Maybe they should… I don't know. Maybe it would be good if they had each other."

It was the only olive branch worth extending in Jenna's opinion.

"Okay. I'll ask Melinda to keep me posted on when your kids are coming over."

She forced a smile. "Sounds good."

Morgan gave a half wave and turned, walking back out of the shop. This whole past two years had uncovered a lot of hidden monsters.

But Jenna felt like she'd just looked one more full in the face.

And it had lost its power over her.

Which made her feel like she'd reclaimed that much more of her own.

46

Morgan

SHE'D NEVER REALLY gotten to know Alex Coleman.
It wasn't a mystery why, at least, not really. Alex was friends
with Jenna, so of course she wouldn't be friendly with Morgan.

Morgan hoped she'd done the right thing by going and
talking to Jenna. But after her dinner with Cody, she'd felt...
resolved.

She wanted to fix things, as best she could, anyway.

Still, Alex's presence in the yarn store was a surprise. She
was looking around like she wanted to be anywhere else.

Morgan studied her. She was a beautiful woman. Morgan
could only hope to be half as pretty in twenty years. Her skin
was clear, her eyes bright. She was extremely thin, though,
and there were burn scars on her arms. She'd heard something
about that. In a litany of horror one of the older women had

dropped on her about the fire and its aftereffects. She'd tried to tune them out.

She didn't want to hear about Alex's burns. About Tom from the town council disappearing. About the young man at the gas station who'd been blown up.

She had been so focused on her own loss, and on Lily and her recovery, and she hadn't paid much attention to the way the fire had affected everyone around her. For fair enough reasons, she had thought.

But that was the problem with her.

The real problem.

Her struggles had made her small and selfish, and she'd left no room for other people.

"Welcome in," Morgan said, going ahead and operating on the assumption that Alex must be here to buy yarn. Because it wasn't like they had anything personal to say to each other.

"Thanks," Alex said.

She started to walk around the room slowly, touching different skeins of yarn. Then she stopped and looked at Morgan. "Do you know where Ryan was?"

Morgan felt like Alex had put her hand on her and physically pushed her. "What?"

"Do you know where he was? The day of the fire?"

The day of the fire...

"I... No. I was in the hospital."

"Right. Of course. But was he with you before that?"

"No," she said. "It was early. It was early and he was already gone. I thought maybe he was on call."

There was something desperate and strange in the other woman's face. "That could be. I can verify that with the hospital. But...the hospital would've surely already verified that."

"Why?"

"I think Ryan was there," Alex said.

"Where?" Morgan asked, her heart thundering.

"At the ignition point. The place where the fire started. I went there with Cody a couple days ago."

"With my uncle Cody?"

"Yes," she said, looking back and forth. "Your uncle Cody. He took me there. And that was when I had the dream. And then today I was standing in the bakery, and I saw more of it. And it makes me feel like it's a memory. Not a dream."

She had no idea what Alex was talking about. The other woman had looked fragile for the past year—hell, who hadn't?—but now it was clear she was unraveling.

The look she gave Morgan was beseeching. "If you could tell me that you knew Ryan was somewhere else, that you saw Ryan somewhere else… That would mean it's not a memory."

Why didn't she know? None of it made sense, and Alex didn't seem interested in making it make sense.

"I can't tell you that. Because I don't know. I woke up that morning and I was by myself. It wasn't normal. It was very early, and the only reason I woke up was because I was having contractions. We'd lived together for four months. In the farmhouse. And he always slept with me. All night. The only time that wasn't true was if he got called in to the hospital. But I usually knew to expect that."

"Right." She nodded. "Right. Morgan, do you know anything else about that day? Anything the rest of us might not know?"

"I have no way of knowing that."

"Would you consider meeting with us? All of us…"

"I've already been talking to Chelsea. And there hasn't been…anything new to discuss. She's just been visiting Lily. She's her aunt, so it makes sense that she'd talk to me a little. I'm…worried Jenna may have reached capacity with me. She just… She already had a conversation with me."

"Jenna is more than capable of saying if she doesn't want to do something. Let Jenna worry about Jenna. I feel like there's something that we're missing. I know there's something I'm missing." She looked around, like she was looking for answers, then she met Morgan's eyes again. "Did Ryan ever talk to you about my marriage?"

She recognized something in Alex's gaze. She felt alone. Right then, she felt alone in whatever was causing her pain. And Morgan knew what that was like.

Cody had said she could try to be better, just for herself.

Maybe she could try to be better, stronger, for the people around her, too.

Morgan frowned. "No. Why would he?"

She looked at a loss. "Sometimes I don't think I knew Paul. I have no concrete reason for thinking that. It's nothing but a feeling. But it's a feeling that scares me."

Morgan bit her lip. "I don't know. Paul always seemed…"

Alex's gaze sharpened. "You *knew* him?"

Morgan took a step back. "A little bit. He came over for dinner a couple of times."

She could see that that surprised Alex. And Morgan realized…that of course he wouldn't have told her that. She wouldn't have approved.

"Did he talk about…me? Us?"

A pit opened up in the bottom of Morgan's stomach and started to expand. "He didn't talk about you. I mean, it was just sports and the hospital and things like that."

Morgan had learned to keep herself safe. With bouts of homelessness and her mother's penchant for bringing home men who were using her for something, Morgan had learned to listen to her feelings when it came to her safety.

Paul Coleman had given her a cold feeling.

He was handsome. Beautiful, even.

But something was off.

"What about our kids?" Alex pressed.

"I don't know your kids' names."

She nodded. "Right. Right. I don't… I don't know if I knew anything about my own life."

"I didn't *know* Paul, not really. But I knew what Ryan thought of Paul. He thought he was…the best. The greatest. He was always trying to impress him. Show off, I think. Sometimes I felt like… Sometimes I felt like that was half of why he was with me. He had something Paul didn't."

"Paul didn't have a girlfriend?" Alex asked.

"If he did, I didn't know about it and Ryan didn't tell me."

She nodded slowly and walked out of the shop.

Morgan had been convinced when she'd moved here that these women had everything. More than she had. That if she'd taken Ryan from Jenna, Jenna at least had everything else. But she'd been wrong.

All those beautiful houses were concealing a lot of pain.

The fire had just taken away the walls it hid behind.

47

Alex

SHE FELT GUILTY that she hadn't talked to Cody yet. But she needed to get everything straight in her head. And then she could talk to Cody about it. She still wasn't sure what she was remembering, and what she was dreaming.

She had been at the ignition point that day. She was almost certain.

That terrified her, but she couldn't hide from it. This was all coming to find her. The locket was somehow connected with that, with what she couldn't remember. With the truth.

It would come for her if she didn't come for it first.

She needed to talk to Cody. Today.

She didn't bother to text first; she just showed up at his door.

He was there, wearing a shirt unbuttoned down to the center of his chest, his hair a mess. She wondered if he had slept the night before. She hadn't.

"Sorry. Been in the middle of looking at a bunch of re-ports."

"It's okay. I was…dealing with some things."

"I probably shouldn't have taken you out to the burn site. I'm sorry."

"Is that why you think I was avoiding you?"

"Kind of. That and whatever happened last night."

"A bad dream. And yeah, it was also a little that I was avoid-ing you. But I want to go back."

"Why?"

"I want to go back because I want to see…" She was lying. Lying to Cody. He was investigating this and she was afraid. Afraid that she was the one who had started the fire. Because in her dream, and her memory, she saw herself holding the matches. And if that was true… If it was true, she was respon-sible for the deaths of so many people. For the destruction.

What if she had done it?

She had no idea why she would have, except…that look on Paul's face in her memory. That cold, blank disdain.

She'd ignored it. For twenty-six years, she'd ignored that. What if she'd stopped ignoring it?

What if that day she'd let him know what she'd seen?

"What if I was there? At the ignition point. I don't remem-ber where I was. That's the thing. So now I'm wondering… What if I was there? And if I was there, what does that mean? And maybe if I go back…"

"What makes you think you were there?"

"I lied to you, Cody. The dream that I had? It was about being there. I want to go back, and I want to see if it triggers something."

He dragged her inside, his hand hard on her arm. "Why did you lie to me?"

"Because you're an FBI agent, and I genuinely don't know

what happened. I really don't. You could give me a lie detector test and it wouldn't tell you anything."

"This is complicated," he said.

"I know that. We're sleeping together, and I might have been there. A witness or—"

"It's not just us sleeping together. It would've been complicated before that."

"Can you please take me out there?"

"Yeah. I will. Just...give me a minute."

And she felt like they had taken a step back in intimacy, because he left the room to go get dressed and straighten himself up, and came back looking every inch the fully put together FBI man. She was completely rattled. By everything.

They walked down the stairs of the apartment in grim silence, and she got into his car with more of the same.

She buckled and looked out the window as the rebuilt parts of town gave way to charred, blighted sections that were still damaged. That were still twisted and grim.

Out to that area of land just out past the farm.

"Is Morgan going to rebuild?"

He was silent for a moment. "Eventually. I think she was waiting to see..." He shook his head. "I don't actually know. I haven't been as involved in her life as I should be."

"*Should* doesn't fix anything," she said, keeping her eyes focused on the view out the window.

"No," he said. "I guess not."

They got out of the car, and she looked around.

She tried to see where she was standing in her memory. There was the ignition point. That was where she had been. She had a strong impression about that, and now she knew why. It was a memory; it made perfect sense.

Because if she had been here...she would know. Somewhere inside herself, she would know. Her heart was thundering, heavy in her ears, and she could hardly think past it. It made her dizzy.

"I don't remember anything," she said.

"Just give it a minute," he said. The lines around his mouth were deep grooves. And she was sorry that she was part of making those lines deeper. She was sorry she'd brought more stress into his life.

That made her want to laugh. Because honestly, she and Cody White had been bringing stress into each other's lives since the bad old days. Somehow, it felt inevitable. That he would be sent here to investigate, and she would somehow get tangled up in it.

Paul was at the ignition site.

She was sure. It was the strangest thing. The most bizarre thing.

She started to walk in a circle that got wider, ever wider. Spiraling out through the area, breathing in deeply as she went. She stopped and looked at Cody. "I don't know. I don't know what I was thinking. I don't know what I want. I don't—" She stared at him, the broad expanse of ground between them, and she wondered if they would be able to cross it again. If there was even a chance she had something to do with this, could they keep on as though she didn't? Could they continue sleeping together? If he was just going to leave when this was over, did it even matter all that much? But of course, it did matter. It had to. It mattered everything to her, to finally be with him. Because whatever steps they had taken in all the years since they had come here to kiss and talk and share secrets… This was where they had started. And it was what mattered.

She had never forgotten him.

And she had carried feelings for him that had never been surpassed by anyone else. Ever.

She closed her eyes and tried to remember. Something. Anything.

"Hey," he said, then he started to close the distance between them, taking his jacket off before draping it over her shoulders. And that was when she noticed she had started shaking. She looked up at him, and she felt like she was in high school again. Young and uncertain and hurt. Wounded. He lowered his head and he kissed her. Just a brush of his lips against hers. But it was an answer to a question that had been burning a hole inside her soul.

"Cody…"

"Alex. We'll figure this out."

"I don't want to get you in trouble."

"You spend your whole life fighting for justice in a general sense when you're in a job like mine. At least, if you're one of the good guys, that's what you hope you're doing. I stood for that, all these years. And I will stand for justice here, too. But you have to understand, for me, that will always be standing with you. Whatever that means."

"I don't know that you can call that justice."

"After all these years? Getting to kiss you? That feels like justice."

"That doesn't sound temporary to me," she said.

"Let's cross those bridges when we come to them, okay?"

She felt sure then, cemented. Held together in a way she hadn't anticipated. Held together by him.

She touched his face. "Was I ever there for you? Or did I just torture you? You were so good to me…"

"You don't remember?"

"No. I remember all the things you did for me. I remember realizing my mom wasn't coming back, throwing a rock at your bedroom window. And you met me out here. With a blanket. I remember you sitting with me and talking for hours. I remember the first time you held my hand. I remember the first time you kissed me. The way it escalated… And how you became the first guy I really thought about… sleeping with. But you know what I remember even more? I remember you holding me that night. All night. Until the morning, when we were both freezing, and you kissed my temple. I remember that in my lowest moment, you kept me safe, Cody. For myself, from everything. And I don't know that there's anything that I ever could have done for you that would've matched that."

"You don't remember how the football team was pushing me around, and you punched Paul in the shoulder and told him to leave me the hell alone?"

"No. When was that?"

"Middle school. Way before we all started hanging out. You always said hi to me. You treated me like a human being. When I was just that kid… That kid who lived in the run-down farmhouse, who nobody talked to. That kid with the druggie sister."

"But it isn't hard to be nice. It wasn't hard to be nice to you."

"It was for a lot of other people. Maybe it shouldn't have been radical, but it was. I fell in love with you then."

"What?"

"You know, he knew. He knew that I loved you. He couldn't stand it."

A chill swept over her. Down her spine.

Her throat went tight. Her chest heavy.

"This one time, Ruth fell," she said. "She fell and she hit her head on the corner of the coffee table. And she started to bleed. She was screaming hysterically. I was panicking. Paul had this look on his face that was just blank. Hollow. And I have told myself ever since that it was a weird reaction to the moment, because it was stressful. But he was never stressed, not once in all the years I knew him. He was always perfectly calm and perfectly in control of every situation. As long as no one ever told him he was wrong. That was the only thing that ever got a rise out of him." She looked at the trees. They were still. There was no wind at all. "It's not that I wanted him to panic over Ruth being injured. That wouldn't have been helpful. And he's a doctor. He was in medical school at the time, and it wasn't like he wasn't used to that kind of thing. But there was no concern at all. No fear."

Cody was looking at her, and his eyes weren't blank. They were a novel of emotion she couldn't read fast enough.

"I tried not to think about it," she said. "I didn't tell anyone. What can you say? My husband *did* all the right things. He said the right things. But I don't think he felt them. I'd look at him sometimes, in those key moments, and what I saw didn't match what he did. I couldn't see care or concern or love when I expected to. He acted accordingly. He did what a concerned father should've done. But he didn't look like a concerned father."

Cody didn't speak for a moment. "How was Paul with the kids? How do you think he…felt about them?"

"I've always thought he loved them. But I keep thinking about everything in a different way now and the truth is…he is very proud of them. He *was*. They're overachievers, both of them. And I think for Paul, they were mirrors that reflected how wonderful he was back to himself, back to the world. I mean, first of all, when he married me everyone thought that made him so wonderful. So he always had that. That even though he'd been such a young father he had done spectacular things in spite of it. But there was more than that. They got into good schools. And he was proud of that. Everything good they did, he was happy to take credit for. But he was like that with me, too. It's like we were all part of his collection. His possessions."

She blinked. And felt an immediate sense of guilt. These were dark thoughts she'd kept shoved down. Dark thoughts that always led to a loop that ended with dismissal.

Paul was good to her. He was good to the kids. She was putting too much significance on these little tiny things. There was no point to it.

"You know, that's exactly what I always saw in him," Cody said. His jaw was set firm. "A man who collected people like things. Sometimes I wondered if he just wanted to take you away from me."

Panic started to tighten in her chest, making it hard to breathe.

She'd love to say Paul wouldn't do that.

To say it wasn't like him.

She couldn't.

She went toward the woods, toward where she and Cody had gone together, and she tripped over a mound of dirt, her toes disturbing it.

And then she screamed.

"Cody!"

She looked down, at the skeletal hand she had just unearthed, and her vision fractured, then turned to nothing.

48

Jenna

SHE COULD WATCH Ethan swing a hammer all day. And maybe it was shallow, but it felt good to be a little bit shallow for a minute. He was helping her with the booths, and he was doing an amazing job. The whole area for the Harvest Festival was looking brilliant. Old Town had never looked cheerier. There were scarecrows out front, and some had taken the total harvest direction while some had opted for something more spooky, and Jenna was here for all of it. She was wandering around, supervising the different stations, wearing a witch hat, which she was aware was potentially on the nose, but she didn't really care.

Tomorrow they would have the carnival, and it was just so different from last year, when they'd had nothing, and everything had been hollowed out and sad, and people had been mourning. And the year before when her marriage had been splintering apart, and she hadn't even known it.

This year she had a— Was he her boyfriend?

That made her want to giggle.

Surely, women her age didn't have *boyfriends*. He was her *lover*. Her younger *paramour*.

And maybe her boyfriend.

She smiled.

She went over and surveyed the booth that he had just finished assembling.

"You, sir, are very good with your hands."

"I thought you already knew that?"

"True," she said.

She snuck a furtive glance around, and he leaned in, looking directly at her. "What's the problem?"

"There… There are people."

"Yes. But you are the sexiest witch I've ever seen, so if you're expecting me to behave myself…"

"I haven't told my kids."

He let out a breath and leaned back. All right. She had managed to get him there.

"Okay. Fair enough."

"I'm not ashamed of you. Just so we're clear. But this has been a very strange, transitional point in my life. And I really… You're inconvenient, do you know that? Because I was kind of just going to do the whole on-my-own thing. And I was going to explore my sexuality. And you were supposed to be a very convenient himbo."

"A himbo?"

"Yes. You know—"

"I know what that means. I'm just struggling to figure out exactly how you thought that about me."

"Because you're so hot," she said. "And younger than me.

And I admit that I was prejudiced against you for that reason. But that isn't what it is. I really like you." She laughed. "I really like you. And I feel like I'm in high school. I do. Because I just like you, Ethan. So much. And I don't want to screw it up. You make me...weird and giddy. And I love it when you help me with things. You make me feel like all this stuff I've been carrying for the last twenty-five years is lighter. Because you know exactly the right things to say and do. And that can't be good."

This wasn't her usual word vomit. Not born out of anxiety or a need for control of the moment. She just wanted him to know how she felt. And it made her feel exposed.

"Isn't that a relationship? Shouldn't the person you're with make things feel a little lighter?"

"That's not my specific experience of what a relationship is. And honestly, it is very strange to me that this thing that was supposed to be a fling is getting closer to something I didn't even know I wanted. Something I didn't even know I needed. Something more than my very long marriage ever was. And I don't know how to deal with this with the kids. Because they've been through so much. And... Yeah. I'm just kind of a mess. So if you could have been slightly less amazing that would've been great. But you're you. I want to figure out the right way to handle this. The best way. Because you're such a great guy."

"Don't say it like that," he said. "It makes it sound like you pity me."

"Well, I don't mean it like that. At all. I don't pity you. And I don't pity me. This just isn't at all where I thought my life would end up. And I am a planner. I always think I can fight tooth and nail and make what I want to have happen, happen, and you're showing me that sometimes being out of control is okay. And that I can trust another person to hold on to things and tell me that they've got it. And I've never had that experience. Not once in my life. So you have to bear with me. You have to bear with me because I don't know what to do. And I was not going to subject Chloe and Aiden to…the embarrassment."

He laughed. "I'll try to not be offended that you think your kids will find me to be an embarrassment."

"Not you. The fact that their mother has a sex drive."

"I think I'm more than an outlet for your sex drive, Jenna. Don't you?"

"Yeah. Well. Even so…"

"I don't think it's a bad thing for your kids to know that you're a woman. That you like to have somebody in your life who isn't dependent on you. That helps you with things. That wants to be there for you. I don't think there's anything wrong with that at all."

"You make it sound so rational," she said, looking up into his eyes. They really were such beautiful eyes.

"I am rational. Not a *himbo*."

"Yeah. Well. I'm going to talk with them. I want to talk with them about this and see where we get. Because you're right. This might actually be one of the healthiest relationships I've ever had. Okay, it is. Except for the sneaking around."

"So let's stop sneaking."

"Okay."

And she had to let go. She had to accept the fact that she didn't know what was going to happen, and that was okay. She didn't know if they were going to end up together, if they were going to end up having to break up because he wanted kids and… She wasn't actually sure if she would say no to that.

Oh, Lord. She was falling for him. She was falling in love with this man who supported her without trying to minimize her. Who thought she was just right, and not too much at all.

She let out a hard breath. That was very inconvenient. And she couldn't even compare it to the last time she'd been in love, because when she had fallen in love with Ryan, she had been sixteen. And they had to stay together, and they had melted together, and they had a life, and a whole lot of it had been good. They had entrenched into specific versions of themselves, and they hadn't really bent around each other the way they ought to have.

But that conversation with Morgan actually made her stop caring quite so much. She had stopped wondering if they could have fixed things if they'd talked. Because she didn't care.

And it was that last little bit of caring that had dissolved and left her free to feel all this.

This was infinitely better than caring about a man who hadn't loved her like he should have.

Infinitely better than clinging to anger that was hotter and stronger than he deserved.

He didn't deserve a corner of her heart. Not even the smallest one.

Her kids, her friends, Ethan.

They deserved that.

"Yeah, okay. The Harvest Festival. Let's do this. Together."

"Great."

He leaned in and kissed her, just quickly, but she was breathless when he pulled away.

She turned around and started to sing. Just to herself. And she didn't even mind that she was wandering down the streets of town in a witch hat, singing to herself.

49

Chelsea

"DEVON SAID THAT he's like, 10 percent Brazilian, and he had no idea."

"That's interesting," Chelsea said, listening to her son download at the end of the school day. It didn't really matter what he said; she was just glad that he still said it.

Sean was such a good kid. He was compassionate, and he was warm. He was so very much like Mark.

Mark was such a great father. He had raised him to be the kind of man that he was, and Chelsea was so grateful for it.

"And I guess Lucas's family did it, and his mom found a half sister he didn't know about."

The hair on the back of her neck prickled. "That's interesting."

She opened the fridge and got out some steaks wrapped in white butcher paper.

"Interesting? It's crazy. It turns out her dad got up to a

whole lot of stuff when he was a traveling salesman years ago. But now people can get caught doing that stuff. So nuts." He reached into the bowl at the center of the counter and grabbed a chip, crunching into it. "We should do one of those tests."

"What?"

"It would be interesting. To see what we are."

"We're Irish," she said. "And maybe English and… I don't know, German or something on your dad's side?"

"Yeah, but it's interesting to see for sure, because there's always stuff you don't know about."

"No," she said, her heart pounding just a little too hard. "No. I don't want to do that. It's creepy. The government getting your DNA."

"It's not the government, Mom."

"But it could end up with the government. And who knows what they're going to do with it."

"Don't tell me you think they're going to make an evil clone."

"Well, they could," she said, her brain spinning its wheels. "They could make a clone. They did it with the sheep."

"I don't know what you're talking about. And I think you're being paranoid."

"I'm not being paranoid. I'm just… It's one of those things, right? You don't want to find out later that your actual DNA was being used for something unethical. New things like this… We don't really know how it's all going to shake down. Or what they're going to do with it."

"Okay. Weirdo."

"Anyway. Maybe I committed a string of robberies and I have to keep my DNA out of databases."

He laughed. "Uh, that's Dad."

"All the more reason to avoid it. Anyway, how good have you been? The pills…"

"I had one bottle of pills! And I only took one. And my DNA would have nothing to do with that."

"Whatever. Just, you know, in case you commit future crimes, maybe you don't want it all out there."

"Whatever." He grabbed a handful of chips. "Let me know when dinner's ready."

"Sure," she said.

She grabbed the edge of the counter and braced herself. Home DNA tests. Of all the things. Of all the things that she had never imagined she might have to worry about. He couldn't take one.

It would confirm something she didn't want to know.

She was too afraid that she already knew the answer.

50

Jenna

JENNA WAS GOING through inventory in the store when the door opened. She turned around with her cheerful shop-keeper face on and stopped. Because it was Alex, standing there with a grim-looking Cody.

"Hi, Cody," Jenna said.

"Jenna," he responded, nodding once.

She was still wearing her witch hat. But it was festive, and she had figured it would be kind of fitting with all the dec-orations going up around town for her also to have a witch hat on. Which felt silly now that she was standing in front of a guy she had once known in high school who was now an FBI agent.

"I've matured a lot," she said, pointing to the hat.

"I have something that I need to tell you," Cody said.

"What?"

"We found a body," Cody said. "At the ignition site."

"Oh shit," she said, her heart pounding so hard she could hardly breathe. "Oh *shit*. It's Ryan, isn't it? Or Paul. Oh…"

Suddenly, she felt like she was grieving all over again but she didn't know why. It was like the world was tumbling down on her head. There had been that chance. That really small chance that said nothing good about him. Because if he had run away, then he had probably stolen all that money, and he was abandoning all the consequences of his shitty actions, and his children. But he wouldn't be dead.

The father of her children wouldn't actually be dead.

It was pain for them that killed her now.

Pain for them that outraged her.

How dare you? All your nonsense and now I have to tell your children they found your body? I have to do it. I have to do it alone.

"We don't know anything," Cody said.

Alex closed her eyes. "We really don't. Jenna…it could be Paul. I remembered something. I was at the ignition point. So was Paul. So was Ryan."

"What?"

"That's why Cody and I went back out to the site. We were walking around and suddenly, there was a body. It was outside where law enforcement had looked, a bit farther from the ignition site. I know they swept the area for evidence…but it must've gotten missed."

"Oh, Alex…"

"We have to get it tested. They're setting up a crime scene, and it's going to be sent to a forensics lab."

"Get *it* tested? Whoever that is, they aren't an *it*," she said. "I hate that. Why does somebody become an *it* when they become a body? It's like it's no longer… It's not even a person. But Paul was a person. Ryan was a person." Angry tears filled her eyes. So, so angry. "He was kind of a terrible person in the end, but he still was one. I was so angry at him. And so hurt. But he was still so much of my life. And nothing erases that many years and kids and life."

Alex broke away from where she was standing next to Cody and she pulled Jenna in for a hug. But Jenna could hardly feel it. Because she could hardly feel anything. Except for the blinding pain ripping through her.

"I always just said he was dead, and kind of…shrugged it off. But there was no body, so it wasn't real."

"We don't know," Alex said. "We don't know it's them."

"What are the odds it isn't one of them?"

"We don't know anything," Cody said. "And we won't until we get results back from forensics. So in the meantime, we just wanted to make sure that you know without hearing it through any kind of rumor mill."

She didn't know what she felt. Just felt swamped and overwhelmed by grief.

Paul and Ryan had been at the ignition point.

Alex, too.

But Alex was alive.

She couldn't make sense of it.

"Why?" Jenna asked. "Why were you there?"

"I don't know, Jen," Alex said. "I don't."

Ryan…

Oh, Ryan. She could only feel grief.

At the pointlessness of all of it. The sadness. She had been flippantly telling people that her ex-husband was dead for a year now, but there hadn't been a body, and she hadn't realized how much of herself was holding out just that tiny sliver of hope that he was actually still out there somewhere. And now she knew.

It wasn't the man she'd screamed at in parking lots she

thought of now. Not the man who had hurt her, devastated her, abused her trust.

He was the one who'd taught Chloe to ride a bike.

Who'd made Aiden the ugliest birthday cake known to man, and had looked so damned proud of it.

It was the good things. Good things she hadn't remembered—on purpose—for so long.

He'd been both. That was the problem.

If he had never been good, the bad wouldn't have hurt quite so much.

"I have calls to make," Cody said. "You stay here with Jenna."

Alex nodded. "I'll see you later."

"See you later." He leaned in and kissed Alex on the cheek.

He left, and Jenna just stood there, feeling limp and terrible. And still in the damn witch hat.

"I don't know what happened," Alex said. "I don't know."

She looked tortured, and that made Jenna feel worse. She didn't want her best friend tortured.

She laughed. Because it was just absurd. All of it. "I'm really not mature enough for this," she said when laughing turned to tears rolling down her cheeks. "I don't know how to have a dead ex-husband. I hadn't even figured out how to have an ex-husband. Oh, and his lover just came and apologized to me and I looked at her and I couldn't even be mad because she's a baby child mourning him in a way I don't want to, and can't, at this point. And my poor friend's husband is dead. And you maybe witnessed all of it, and this is really so far above my paygrade."

Alex looked dazed. "I don't know what I saw."

"You don't remember anything?"

"I wish I did."

"Why didn't you tell us? Why didn't you tell us that you didn't remember?"

"It freaked me out, Jenna. I thought I was losing my mind. I started having dreams, and I thought it was all PTSD, but then... I got something in the mail."

"What?"

"A necklace. My mother's necklace."

"What? When?"

"A few weeks ago. Paul missing, and my mom's disappear-ance...that was already a lot, and then the necklace sort of triggered all this other stuff. I started dreaming about her. I don't know what it means. If she's alive..."

"Do you think your mother burned the town down?"

"No. I don't know. I don't know anything. At first, when I dreamed I saw her, in the fire. Now I see me. But I can't tell what's a dream and what's a memory, I just know this damned necklace started it. Before this, my memory was blank. If I'd remembered anything about being at the ignition point with Ryan and Paul, I swear I would have said something."

Jenna's heart was pounding so hard she couldn't breathe. "Have you given Cody the necklace?"

She shook her head. "No."

"He might be able to swab it for prints or DNA or some-thing."

"I've been touching it for weeks. I'm sure there's no way—"

"You never know," Jenna said.

"I guess."

A wave of sadness overcame her. "I didn't realize that I was still so delusional about him being alive." She rubbed at a sore place on her chest. "I don't want him to be dead," she said. "And I really thought that I did. I thought I didn't care. But it doesn't fix anything. It just compounds the hurt. I thought

I'd accepted it. But I haven't." She sighed. "Had you accepted it? About Paul?"

Alex paused, not in the way she often did. Like she was carefully arranging words she'd already hand selected. She paused like she didn't know what to say at all.

"I'm with Cody," she said. "So I must have."

She stared at her friend for a long moment. "You and Cody might not have anything to do with that."

Alex frowned. "I don't know what you mean."

"Do you think if Cody had come back to town, and Paul were here, Cody wouldn't have mattered?"

"I wouldn't have cheated," Alex said.

"But you'd have wanted to."

Alex's eyes were hollow. "Yes."

Jenna wasn't sure if this was the time to ask this question, but then, timing had never been her strong suit, so why worry about it now? "The first time you were with Paul, you said you didn't say no. Alex, did he force himself on you?"

She shook her head slowly, her eyes getting farther and farther from the moment. "I'm almost certain he didn't."

The words sent a cold chill down Jenna's spine.

"Did he ever hurt you?"

Her vision snapped back to the moment. "No," she said. "Never. He would never hurt me."

But there was so much space for other insidious things to creep between *I didn't say no* and *he would never hurt me.*

"What aren't you telling me?"

Alex's eyes went glassy. "That's the thing, Jen. There's really nothing to tell."

Jenna had always been a pusher. And Alex was always so careful. And right now Jenna wanted to punch her own self in the face for not pushing on this before.

You didn't know there was anything wrong.

No. And now it felt like maybe everything had been wrong. "What is there to...not tell?"

Alex forced a smile. "How do you explain what you don't see in someone's eyes when they say they love you?"

Jenna swallowed hard. "You don't need to. If it felt wrong, then it was."

"I don't know about that."

Jenna could see clearly right then that it suited Paul that Alex couldn't be certain. That the space between force and uncertainty was where he shone.

You're kind of an asshole, Paul.

She'd seen him then.

He'd known it.

He thought it was funny.

"No problem," Jenna said. "I'd throw a bottle of tea at him if he was alive."

"I was happy, though. I think." She tried to smile but didn't make it. "But I don't want him to come back." She whispered that last part. "I want Cody. Or even...to be alone." She looked up at Jenna. "Jenna, what if I did something?"

She reached out and put her hand on Alex's. "You didn't. You wouldn't."

"I don't feel like I know anything right now." She rubbed her forehead.

Jenna had never seen subject changing as the better part of valor, but she was exhausted by everything, and she could see Alex was, too.

"Have you talked to Chelsea yet?"

Poor Chelsea.

"We need to," Jenna said. "Just in case."

"I wish she was at an easier spot in her life. I don't want to heap things on her plate while she's trying to...whatever it is she and Mark are trying to do."

"You think they'll make it?"

"I really hope so," Jenna said. "Because I want like hell to believe in some kind of happy ending."

"Me, too."

But she had no idea right now what happy looked like for the rest of them.

51

Kindling

Morgan

"YOU KNOW, Tom had to be involved in it," Ryan said, looking across the table at Paul, who nodded in agreement.

Morgan sat next to Ryan, not touching him.

She always felt insecure when Paul was there.

He was perfectly pleasant. But there was something about the way Ryan changed. His voice got louder and everything he did reminded her of kindergarten show-and-tell.

Including how he wanted her to hang out when Paul was there, but they didn't talk to her, really.

Maybe she was just...hormonal and it was making her weird. Or maybe it was the way time revealed things.

A moment could obscure so much. In a moment everything, anything, could feel justified.

But then you had to sit with the consequences.

The way that, at the end of the night, she could almost

feel that he wished he were at his other home. That was what he'd done before. Pretend he was on a shift, sleep with her, go home.

But now this was home.

She wasn't sure he liked it.

"I'm going to confront him about it," Ryan said.

"Don't do that," Morgan said, and felt silly when Ryan looked at her like she was being ridiculous. "I don't want you to get hurt, that's all. The police can handle it."

"What do you care, Abbott? You don't have to listen to Jenna having an aneurysm about the town council anymore, so you might as well leave it alone. Maybe Tom and Courtney stole it together. Maybe he's giving her some dick."

Ryan laughed. Like that was funny. It really wasn't. "I care because I've essentially been accused of being involved."

"No, they accused her." Paul gestured to Morgan, then tipped his beer bottle back. "Even if you'd done it, I bet you could hang around town and spend it all and people still wouldn't really think you'd done it."

"I don't know about that."

Paul smiled, and Morgan had to look away. "You're one of the favored sons of Tenmile, Ryan. You can do whatever you want and they'd still think you were a solid-gold trophy."

This was what she didn't like. The way they made her feel like she wasn't even in the room when they were together.

Her stomach felt tense.

"I'm going to talk to him," Ryan said. "He could just give the money back. Nobody needs to press charges. I doubt he's a bad guy. I think it was probably too much for him to handle."

That made her feel better. Somehow. That Ryan still wanted to do the fair thing.

"You do that, Dr. Savage," Paul said, leaning back. "Go be a hero."

52

Afterburn

Jenna

IT WAS THE day before the Harvest Festival, and Jenna was a mess. She was supposed to talk to her kids so that she and Ethan could be normal around Chloe and Aiden. Be themselves. She was supposed to make it clear that they were a couple now. Except...she had been basically nonfunctional since Alex and Cody had told her about the body. Waiting to find out if it was Ryan or not. She had gotten one of her employees to cover her shift at the store, and she was just trying to sort through everything before the actual Harvest Festival.

The doorbell to the new house rang, and she looked around, having a slight out-of-body experience over where she was. This new house. This new moment.

She got up and went to the door. And when she opened it, it was Ethan.

"Oh," she said.

"I wanted to check in with you. You said that you weren't feeling well. I brought coffee beans. And soup."

"You didn't have to do that."

"I wanted to, Jenna. I wanted to make sure that you are taken care of."

"Thank you, Ethan."

She moved away from the door and invited him in. He entered and set the soup on the table, and then immediately went looking for bowls, which he found unerringly.

"I'm not *that* kind of not well," she said.

"You want to talk about it?"

She froze. "I… No."

"Hey. Whatever you need. We can sit here and not talk, if that's what you want."

She took a breath and sat down at the table, allowing him to dish her a portion of soup. "Where did you get this?"

"From the café. They do great soup."

"They do. I try to go there for lunch at least once a week. Support local businesses and all that."

Misery welled up in her chest, and tears filled her eyes. "They found a body. At the ignition site. I think it's Ryan. It could also be Paul but I just have this feeling and—"

He didn't say a word. He got up from his chair and sat in the one right next to her, wrapping his arm around her shoulder and pulling her up against him. "I'm sorry."

"Really? Because this is ridiculous, me being this upset about my…*ex-husband*. And you certainly don't need to comfort me about it…"

"Life is complicated," he said. "If I wasn't okay with that, then there would be no hope for us at all. Because you used to babysit me."

She laughed, somehow, through her misery. "For God's sake, Ethan, I kept an eye on you while our parents had a barbecue in the backyard. You make it sound so sordid."

"When will you know?"

"I don't know. I didn't ask about…the *process*. The condition of anything. Or how identifiable or… I don't even want to know. And poor Alex. She saw it. Poor Alex. She doesn't remember what happened that day. But she told me she thinks she might have been at the ignition point. I don't understand any of this. It makes me feel like I'm losing my mind."

"Hey. If this is too much for you right now, if this is going to be too much for your kids, we don't have to do this. We don't have to tell anyone what's going on with us."

"Why are you so great?"

"I don't know that I am. But I love you, Jenna. And don't tell me it's too soon. I've known you a long time. I've admired you just as long. The truth is I've had a lot of sex."

"Hey," she said. "I don't really need to— I mean, I *assumed*, but I don't need to be certain how you got those skills."

"No, I want you to know that. Because I want you to understand I'm not inexperienced. I've done physical-only relationships. I've had a couple serious relationships. I've had a lot of not serious relationships. I know who I am. One thing that's never changed in all of that is how much I admire you. The way that I feel for you. Being with you has been fantasy fulfillment, but it's more than that. It's always been more than that. So when I tell you that I love you, it comes from really knowing me. And really knowing you."

"Thank you," she said. "That actually means…a lot more than you maybe know. Because I've heard that a lot. And said it a lot. Every day, in fact, to someone, and… I think it had lost its meaning. Only I didn't realize that until it was too late. Too late to fix it. Too late to save it. And it matters what you said. About knowing yourself. Because I don't think I knew myself. I think I was a little bit lost and… I'm a lot."

"You're just right," he said.

That meant so much. Too much. For someone who went around always feeling like they overflowed their allotted space. For a woman who'd felt big and loud and like her feelings sent people running. "I mean, thank you." She laughed. How stupid. *I love you*, and *you're just right*, and she thanked him. "I do things, and I plan things, but sometimes I forget to think about them. And think about my own feelings. I get lost in the doing. It's not my fault that Ryan cheated on me. I would *never* have done that to him. Ever. It never even entered my mind. I thought you were really hot, and I never once thought about cheating. Fantasies don't count. But I still forgot to make sure that I meant what I was saying. Or even look at myself and really ask if I knew what I was saying every day when I said *I love you* before he left for work."

"You don't need to say anything to me, just so we're clear."

"Again, thank you. Because I think I need to sit with myself for a little bit. Especially right now."

"It's okay that you love him."

"Thank you. For that. It doesn't feel okay. It feels sad. Like I just shouldn't. But thinking about the kids and all the years and—"

"It's okay."

She put her hand over his. And she didn't want to shrink; she didn't want to whisper. Because she had found someone who seemed like he could take it all. Carry it. And someday, she would tell him how much she appreciated that. Someday, when things were a little less screwed up. But not right this second.

"I still want to tell them about us. I want to go to the Harvest Festival with you."

"We can do that," he said. "We can do whatever you want."

It was amazing. To be with someone who knew when to give and when to take. When to stand strong and when to bend. Ethan just seemed to know. And it was unlike anything she'd ever experienced before. It was a miracle and so was he, and at this point in life, she didn't take miracles lightly.

"Sometimes I think I'm too old to...start over. Whatever that means. But at least at my age, I actually know what I want."

"And what is that?"

"A cheeseburger and fries." She smiled. "And the under-standing that I can be a woman who knows what she wants, and can handle everything in her life, but who can also give up that control sometimes, and have a partner she can trust to help carry the load."

"And?"

"A little bondage."

"There you go."

"You are more than welcome to tie me up...tomorrow morning."

"I thought you were going to talk to the kids about us?"

"I am still not fucking you in the room down the hall from them. Not right now."

He chuckled. "Fair."

"I'm way too loud. Which I like. I'm in no hurry to turn this into domestic, muffled lovemaking to keep the kids from being emotionally scarred."

"It doesn't ever have to be that. Not if you don't want it to be."

She nodded. "I'll figure out what I want it to be. Right now I'm happy with what it is. But I am going to tell them. It's not going to remain a secret."

"Good."

"Do you want to make me coffee?"

She smiled.

"I would love nothing more."

53

Afterburn

Jenna

OF COURSE, her vision of going to the Harvest Festival as a family was compromised when she found out that Chloe had already planned to go with a group of friends and volunteer in the booths—and she loved the volunteerism, she really did, which was why it was so difficult to be too annoyed—and Aiden was going with friends also.

"I just kind of thought that we would do things together," she said as she put on a very dark lipstick to go with her witch hat. She was wearing a long black dress, which she felt complemented her figure quite nicely. She was back and forth on that. Sometimes she was completely okay with the fact that she had a stomach that looked like it had carried two babies, and sometimes she was mystified as to why it wasn't flat. Today she was feeling hot.

"We're not avoiding you, Mom," Chloe said. "We just have other plans."

"But…"

"Mom, you're wearing a costume," Aiden said.

"Yeah, it's for Halloween," Jenna responded. "If you're not wearing a costume, you're the one that's lame."

"It's okay, Mom," Aiden said.

"Do you, like, not have anyone to hang out with?" Chloe asked, which made Jenna want to roundly defend herself by saying she had a hot boyfriend *thank you very much*.

She figured that wasn't the intro. However, it was a way in.

"I actually was planning on going with someone, *thank you*." She couldn't resist that. "But I thought that maybe we could all spend some time together. I wanted to talk to you about all that…"

"Why?" Chloe asked.

"Because I have a boyfriend," Jenna said.

"What?" Aiden asked, looking legitimately dumbfounded in that way that really only a fifteen-year-old boy could pull off.

"Yeah. And I didn't want to say anything until it was…a little more serious. But—"

Chloe looked confused. "I thought you didn't like the guy you went on a date with?"

Aiden looked the most confused. "You went on a date?"

"I *don't* like that guy," Jenna said. "But I…started seeing… a different guy. And I do like him. I like him a lot."

"What does that mean?" Chloe asked, looking deeply skeptical.

"As far as you're concerned? Maybe nothing. As in, you don't need to do anything. I just wanted to say something because I would like to walk around the Harvest Festival with him. And maybe hold his hand."

"Hold his hand?" Chloe looked at her like she was in utter disbelief.

"Well, I didn't want you guys hearing something without talking to you first. I… I'm trying to be responsible."

"Who is it?" Aiden asked.

"Ethan. Coffee roaster Ethan, of the slightly famous coffee brand."

Chloe made a very strange noise.

"What?" Jenna asked.

"Nothing. But all my friends think he's hot. Oh my gosh. When they find out that my mom…"

"He's too old for you," Jenna said, frowning.

"He's too young for you," Chloe countered.

And Jenna could not help herself. She full-on smirked. "Apparently, he's not."

"Mom," Chloe said.

"I am not asking for you to be cool with it. I'm just telling you. I would like for it to not be an issue. I love you guys, and nothing is going to come between me and you. And you know that. Because I've been with him for a while, and it hasn't affected your life. Has it?"

"I guess not," Aiden said, looking skeptical.

"Because I work everything in my life around the two of you. Not the other way. But I would like for him to come have dinner sometimes, and I would like to be able to walk down the street with him in public. So that's all. In an effort to get ahead of the rumor mill, yeah. This is how it's coming out."

"I just don't want a stepdad," Aiden said.

"You are a lot of steps ahead of me, buddy," she said. Except…was he? Because it wasn't like she hadn't thought of it. "But even if he moved in or I married him or whatever, he doesn't have to be your stepdad. You are too old to need that. And…you had a really good dad."

"Wow. That's the first time I've heard you say something nice about Dad in a long time," Aiden said.

"Well, I'm figuring it out. I'm figuring out how to separate what hurt me from the good stuff. Because there was good stuff. Particularly when it came to you guys."

Aiden seemed mollified by the discussion and went off to put on his football uniform, which Jenna shouted after him was in fact a costume when not being worn for a game or practice. So he could lighten up on the shade he had thrown at her. Chloe loitered in the kitchen.

"When you say you've been seeing him…"

"Don't ask questions you don't want the answers to," Jenna said.

"Look. Our dad got a nineteen-year-old pregnant. We already had to know our parents…have sex. At least you aren't *gross*."

Jenna grimaced. She wasn't wrong.

"I just want you to be careful," Chloe said. "Because I know that you haven't been out there dating for a long time. And people do things differently now."

"Are you lecturing me? About…safe sex?"

"Well. I want you to be…safe."

"Thank you, honey. But I'm good." She looked at her daughter, and her heart just kind of melted. Because as awkward as the discussion was, Chloe wanted to take care of her. And she shouldn't want to do that.

"I'm sorry," Jenna said. "I'm sorry that I've been such an emotional mess that you feel like you have to take care of me."

"It's not that. You've been angry, sure, but also really strong. You never fell apart. I want to be as strong as you are. That's all I want."

And right then, Jenna thought maybe she hadn't messed

everything up. Because if Chloe wanted to be like her, she must've done something right.

"Can I hold hands with my boyfriend tonight?" Jenna asked.

"Yes. You can."

"Thank you."

And she knew that there was going to be more hard stuff ahead. Adjustments. Maybe she and Ethan would break up. Or maybe in the next couple of days they would verify that it was Ryan's body, and they would all get plunged back into grief. They would have to plan a funeral. Except…she would just be attending it. She wouldn't be planning it. It would be his parents, she supposed.

What a mess.

But right now things were going okay. Right now things felt a little bit new. And that was good. Really good. Tonight she was going to go to the Harvest Festival that she had helped create, she was going to make a somewhat public declaration of her association with Ethan and she was going to let the hard stuff settle right into tomorrow. And let now be good. She had just done some very hard things over the past few days. Because she had looked her seventeen-year-old daughter in the eye while basically acknowledging she was having a sex life, and she had also talked to the woman that her husband had used as an escape hatch.

So yeah. She was owed some good things. And she was going to take them.

54

Chelsea

MARK HAD DECIDED they could go to the Harvest Festival as a date. It was a good, neutral place for them to be. The sex between them had been intense, and the aftermath had been shattering.

She was coming to terms with the fact that they were going to have to have the conversation she'd been avoiding all this time. But tonight was Jenna's harvest baby, and it had been a whole difficult and strange day.

She hadn't talked to Mark since the revelation that they'd found a body at the ignition site.

Ryan?

Paul?

Someone else?

She couldn't deal with it right now.

She let out a breath and walked to the mailbox, and she

took out a stack of envelopes, flipping through them as she walked back to the house.

The third envelope had only her address on it.

She turned it over and opened it, and a matchbook slid out and into her hand.

She stared at it for a long while. She believed Mark.

She knew he hadn't set the town on fire, as nice as it had been for her to believe for a minute, like she was lost in her own teenage drama.

That her husband had burned it all down over her. Their fire was between them, no less hot, but not literal.

She turned the matchbook over and her lips went cold.

The Fuller Hotel.

Chicago, Il.

Oh, God. God. God.

It was a prayer more than a curse. From deep inside her, but she couldn't make her lips move or her voice work.

She went inside and put the envelopes on the counter and shoved the matches into her coat pocket.

The Fuller.

Chicago.

She didn't know what that meant.

You know.

And so did only one other person.

Her costume felt ridiculous now, and Mark was going to be here in a minute so she needed to breathe.

She needed time to think.

The knock made her jump, but she did what she could to school her expression into something calm.

She'd decided to go to the festival as a punk rocker girl, because all it required was for her to put safety pins on an old denim jacket and put on two coats of her favorite lipstick. She was never that far away from the grunge nineties look of her youth. Mark obviously wasn't dressed up, and he greeted her at the door just looking like a very attractive man who worked in finance but was on his day off.

"Hi," she said, forcing a smile.

He leaned in and kissed her. She closed her eyes and let her desire for her husband wash over her. She looked at him and her heart hurt. This was the problem. She felt connected to him again, just like that. He was the man she loved. More than anything in the entire world, and she had realized that the risk of losing him was unacceptable.

But there were matches in her pocket, and they could burn down her life.

She'd spent years letting space grow between them when it could, because it had terrified her. How much she wanted him, how much she needed him. And the more she'd wanted to cling to him, the more she'd perversely wanted to let go.

And then there had been the conversation with Sean about DNA.

That was what had broken it. What had turned a slow demise on its head. And plunged her right back in the middle of the same kind of terror she'd experienced back in the early days.

Because it was easy to forget about it. She'd set the intention on how to be so long ago, that it had become a habit. She had put all the pieces of the situation into their own folders, and had made it so she didn't have to look at them again. But he had made it so she had to look at them again.

And it terrified her.

She'd hoped she could have him back without this needing to be talked about.

But the matches.

The matches.

"You okay?" he asked as they got into the car.

No. She wasn't okay.

Her brother was dead.

And...

She couldn't even think the rest through.

"Yeah. It's been... You being back has been emotional. And then Cody's arrival—I don't think you really know who Cody is. He's someone that we were friends with in high school, and he's back investigating the fire. He's in the FBI. He and Alex found a body at the ignition point the other day. And of course, they think it might be Ryan. They don't know for sure. But I've just been...sitting with that."

"I'm sorry, Chelsea."

He was so good. He was wonderful. She was the one who hadn't been. It had never been Mark. It didn't matter that he hadn't told her he'd been to prison. His secrets had never been the problem.

It was her.

And she knew that she had to tell him. She had to tell everyone what she suspected. Had to tell them everything.

But it started with Mark.

She had to tell him what she had suspected for a long time.

That Sean might not be his son.

55

Tinder

Senior Year

Cody

HE KNEW SOMETHING was wrong, because she hadn't called him or come to the house in days. And he felt sick, because maybe he had misread the situation. He knew she didn't want to go all the way, but that was fine. He could wait for her. He would never be in a hurry for Alex. He loved her. He could kiss her forever. And things had gotten a little more heated than that the last time they'd met up, and he wondered if he'd done something wrong. He walked into school hoping to see her. But he saw Ryan and Paul first. They were friends. Kind of. It was weird. Because they'd been jerks to him in middle school, and then in high school had decided they would all hang out. But it was like he was still there to catch shit. They just all went out for a burger after. He didn't really know how to describe it. Because it was weird. He'd never had the feeling Ryan meant anything by it.

He couldn't say the same for Paul. And when Paul looked at him that morning as he walked into the building, he could feel his intent.

People tended to excuse Paul. They just liked him. Cody wasn't sure why. He never had.

You hang out with them, though. Because that's how sad you are. How lonely.

You don't like it, and you still do it.

But it was how he had gotten to know Alex. Really gotten to know her. And after loving her for so many years, it was worth it.

"How's it going, White?" Paul asked, a smile on his face that didn't sit well with Cody.

"Fine. What are you guys doing?"

"We were just talking about my night last night."

He already knew he didn't want to hear the story. Because he had that look on his face that already told him it wasn't a good story.

"Great. Well, I have an early—"

"I fucked her."

"Who?"

"Alex." And he could tell by the way Paul looked at him when he said it, that he knew. He knew exactly what he was doing. Who he was telling. And he had the feeling he'd maybe only done it for this moment alone.

"It's weird that you feel the need to tell people that," he said, refusing to give him a reaction. Refusing to give them a response.

He didn't go to class. He went through the school, out to the back. Then walked straight into the woods. And puked his guts out.

56

Alex

ALEX WASN'T SURE how she had talked Cody into coming down to the Harvest Festival. Especially given he was busy trying to get the lab to give information on the body they'd found as quickly as possible. Though she had told him he could only call so many times, and finally, he seemed to take that on board.

She wanted to be at the festival to support Jenna, but she also felt compelled to be there. For something a little bit happier. A little bit better than they'd been experiencing for the past however long.

Cody had spent the night with her last night, which was… interesting. A little more serious. But then, he had essentially declared that, no matter what happened, he was committed to her. And she still hadn't told him the full truth. Not that she really knew what the full truth was, but it was probably relevant that in her memories, she saw herself holding matches.

It ate at her. Paralyzed her. Made it difficult to eat or sleep. And she had already been having difficulty with that. But maybe that was the real reason why. Maybe… Maybe she had gone after Paul to talk to him about their marriage. About him wanting to end things. Maybe she had flown off the handle, gone into a rage. Maybe she had lost her mind.

She didn't want to think about it. Not now.

"I was thinking we could drive the muscle car to the festival."

"Why?"

"I don't know. I have it. It's a cool car."

"So you said."

"Driving it with you would make him mad," she said.

Cody lifted a brow. "I'm sure me sleeping in the bed you used to share with him would make him mad."

"Probably not the sleeping as much as the other things."

"Yeah. There's been a lot of that."

"I know it's weird. All of it. We're just so…messed up with history that it's hard to see a way forward without all of it…"

"I'm starting to think I don't see much of a way forward without you. One way or the other."

"What changed that?" She wanted to know; she wanted to know even though she didn't deserve the answer. She wanted to know even though it wasn't fair of her to ask that of him, since she was still withholding information.

"Because I can pretend that it's my job that made me not settle down all this time. But it was you. Because I fell in love with you when I was a teenager, and I never fell out of love. And maybe I didn't handle everything perfectly. I should've taken you away with me. I should have asked you."

She shook her head, misery tightening her throat. "I wouldn't have been brave enough to go."

Except she didn't really know who she was now. Had she snapped? Had she set the world on fire and her husband along with it?

How had she gone from being too afraid to go with Cody to whatever she had become now? The thing her mind wouldn't let herself know.

She couldn't have planned it, though. That was the thing. She remembered the night before. She had not been planning on killing Paul. She had not been planning on setting the town on fire. Whatever had happened at three in the afternoon on the day of the fire, she had not planned it.

She'd gone to bed the night before and it had all felt normal.

Of that, she was certain.

And it was the only thing that gave her hope now.

"I still wish I would've asked. I wish I would've been brave enough to exhaust absolutely every option. Because you are worth it."

"Did you really know that much about me from making out in a forest when we were teenagers?"

"No. It was more than that. You had everything together. Always. And everybody liked you. And you never had to look outside of that to be kind to me. You just were. That's rare. You made my life here not hell."

"I'm sorry I was one of the things that hurt you."

"Someone used you to hurt me. That's different."

She hesitated for a moment, then reached into her purse and took out the necklace, which she'd put into a plastic bag after her talk with Jenna.

"I have one more thing I didn't tell you. And I promise this is the last thing." She held it out toward him.

He took it. "What's this?"

"A few weeks ago someone sent this to me, in an envelope with no handwriting and no return address. This belonged to my mother."

"Are you serious?"

"Yes."

"How can you be sure it's the same necklace?"

"I guess I'm not. But someone sent it to me intentionally."

"Shit. Do you have the envelope?"

She shook her head. "I wasn't thinking clearly. But I think it's what triggered…everything. It's what triggered my dreams, what started bringing my memories back."

"I can send it to the lab and see if we can still pull prints or DNA."

She nodded. "That's why I wanted to give it to you."

"Okay. Thank you."

"I'm sorry I didn't trust you with it sooner. I just… This made me feel crazy, like I couldn't trust myself. I've felt that way for a long time, actually." She let out a breath. "Anyway. Want to drive Paul's car?"

"I appreciate the fact that you're embracing the more petty aspect of this."

"Honestly, why not?"

"I feel like your memory of being with him is changing."

She shook her head. "It's not my memory of it. I'm tired of doubting myself. It's choosing to look at the things that I ignored. It's a funny thing. Because I was the detail-oriented person in school. The one with all the notebooks. But I did a very good job of skimming over what I didn't want to see about Paul. I accepted a lot of things he told me because I wanted to. And I don't know if I should've done that. I don't know if that was… I wanted to believe that I had made myself safe. That I made the best choice. For me and my kids. I married him when I was so young. Because I was pregnant.

And maybe I can't prove that he ever did anything awful. But it's a feeling."

I didn't say no.

The look of horror on Jenna's face when she'd asked if Paul had forced himself on her had made her conscious of how wrong it was.

There was so much space between not saying no and getting a yes.

She was beginning to realize that Paul Coleman lived his life in that space.

He was smart, and he was funny. And he was beautiful. And he did a fantastic job of making you think that he was the brightest and best in the room. He made you think that whatever he wanted was the right thing.

Because he was just that kind of guy.

And it was different. Different than Ryan's ego. He really was just a high school jock who had gotten bent out of shape about his glory days and craved attention from a younger woman because it made him feel invincible again.

At his core, Ryan was insecure.

It was why he'd needed the admiration of a girl like Morgan.

At Paul's core? There wasn't any insecurity at all.

"Fair enough. But yeah. I'd love to drive his car."

"Thank you for going with me."

"Thank you."

He wrapped his arms around her and kissed her. And she wanted to believe everything would be okay.

57

Afterburn

Jenna

ETHAN ACTUALLY STOOD with Jenna at the registration table for the event while she passed out wristbands and punch cards and greeted people as they arrived. And she knew that, to an extent, some of this was that whole new "beginning of a relationship" thing, where you didn't really want to be away from each other, but it felt like more than that, too. Because they weren't kids, so this wasn't just about being shiny and new. They were both who they were. Deeply. And there was something comforting about that. They weren't going to have personality transplants in six months.

The wind was unseasonably warm, and it blew a swirl of leaves around them. She decided to go ahead and kiss him. She had to stand on her toes to do it, even in her witch boots, and he made her feel small and protected. She'd never thought she cared about that. But it was just a really nice thing with him. He made her feel…special.

And that was another thing that made everything feel lighter. She had always been pretty convinced of her own effectiveness. Her own ability to make things happen. Her own…specialness, really. But she had often felt like she was in an uphill battle with other people to recognize it.

Ethan just did.

Paul's car pulled up to the curb. And she was aware that it was weird that she immediately thought of it as Paul's car. But he had driven that thing all through high school, and on to forever, his baby, which he arguably loved more than anyone or anything else.

Cody was driving it.

Alex got out of the passenger seat and waved, and Cody pulled away from the curb.

"He's going to find parking," Alex said, smoothing her hair and looking happy. Just really, really happy. She didn't look hollow-eyed. She didn't look exhausted.

"He's good for you," Jenna said.

"Thank you. I suspect that there are actually a lot of things about my life right now that are good for me. Better. He is definitely one of them."

She didn't want to ask Alex about the long-term prospects of being with Cody, because it would be awkward to ask that in front of Ethan. Still, she leaned her head back against Ethan's chest, and he put his hand on her hip and she reveled in the casual show of affection.

"That's a cool car," Ethan said.

"Oh, thanks," Alex said. "It's like a 1960 something, blah blah blah. It's not my thing. My late husband—it was his car. He never drove it to any of the town meetings or anything. He went to car shows out of state sometimes."

"Oh," he said. "Just really specific-looking."

"Yeah. I guess so. The green flames kind of make it stand out."

"Yeah."

Jenna looked at Ethan.

"What?"

"Nothing."

Cody appeared at the table then, and wrapped his arm around Alex. "Okay. I'm doing this small town fun thing. You better have made it amazing, Jenna."

"Please. You know me, Cody. Everything I do is amazing."

"Damn straight," Ethan said.

They gave them a roll of tickets and sent them on their way.

"Are you going to tell me now what your deal is?" she asked, looking back at him.

"It's nothing. It's a weird thing. I just… I had a dream about a car that looked just like that."

"Wow. This is getting way deeper into the male psyche than I ever wanted to go. I didn't know you guys had actual erotic dreams about cars."

"It wasn't an erotic dream. It really freaked me out. It's why I still remember it. I was a kid. I got up because I heard something and I looked out the window, and there was that car. It was stopped in the middle of the street and it was dark out. And two guys got out of the car and took something out of the middle of the road, and I suddenly realized it was…a body. I was probably—I don't know—nine at the time? I woke up the next morning and realized it couldn't have been real because that's crazy. But that was weird just now. That car made me remember it again so clearly."

A shiver went up Jenna's arms. Goose bumps.

It had to be a dream.

"Are you sure you dreamed that?"

"As sure as I can be. I don't remember going back to bed. I just remember waking up. And when I thought about it, I just thought it was weird like a dream. I couldn't piece all the steps together. You know how that is. In dreams, you don't remember how you got to the window, or went back to bed? Or how the car showed up, or what made you look…"

And she couldn't explain it, the pit of dawning horror that opened up in her stomach. But she'd learned to trust her instincts, not gloss them over as hysteria. People always wanted her to be less. To be smaller. To be quieter.

Maybe because she was often right.

"Ethan, if you could, I think you might need to try to piece all those steps together. Because I'm a little worried that wasn't a dream."

58

Morgan

MORGAN STOOD AT the edge of the Harvest Festival, holding Lily on her hip. She was dressed as a fairy, and Morgan was worried she shouldn't have come.

She was overwhelmed by emotion.

But Melinda would be here, and Chelsea had asked her to come. She'd said she wanted to see her niece enjoy it. So she'd come.

She had been here with Ryan, getting to know him, just two years ago.

Lily would never know her dad.

She looked down at her little blond head. "You'll know me, Lily. I can promise you that." Then she took a step up to the table. "Can we get tickets for the booths?"

"Sure, sweetie," said the woman manning the table. "What a cute baby!"

"Oh, thank you."

"She looks like you."

She looks like you.

Those words felt stamped on her heart as she took Lily through the booths, filled her bucket with candy.

Behind one of these booths, she'd felt like she was falling in love for the first time.

Watching Lily right now, she felt like she was falling in love again.

Bigger, brighter, deeper.

She looks like you.

It was like something shattered inside her.

And she saw herself. Not with pity, but with clarity. A little girl who had been forced to grow up without this. Without someone to take her to a Harvest Festival. To hold her. To love her.

So the first time someone looked at her with love, she had been so hungry, she'd been willing to take it. She'd needed to take it. However it came.

She could be sorry and forgive herself.

She could want Jenna to forgive her, and forgive herself.

And she would make sure that Lily was never hungry for love.

She'd never felt like she had much power in her life. But she had the power to do this.

And she would.

She looked across the field and saw Jenna, wearing a witch hat and holding hands with a tall, extremely attractive man.

Their eyes met.

Jenna smiled.

And Morgan smiled back.

59

Tinder

Nineteen Years before the fire

Chelsea

PAUL ALWAYS MADE her nervous. He was too good–look-ing. And he knew it. He made her feel sloppy and messy and just a little less.

But when they had found out they were both in town for different conventions, he had wanted to meet. She and Mark were living in Tenmile, and he and Alex were living out of state. They hadn't seen each other in a long time. For some reason he was paying attention to her tonight.

She'd been really pissed off at Mark before she'd left. They'd just moved back to Tenmile so she could buy the florist shop on Main, and he'd been moody about it ever since. He was always shut up in his home office on the phone and she just felt…invisible.

So when Paul had asked her if she wanted to have a drink,

she'd said yes, happily. It felt kind of thrilling. The object of her girlhood fantasies asking her for a drink. She wasn't going to do anything. It was just a little private, nostalgic thrill.

And Paul was funny, charming as always. Handsome... So much so she could feel everyone staring at them.

She didn't question it when she'd started feeling woozy. Or when he'd led her from the bar and put her in the same cab as him. Or took her to his room.

She didn't question it, because she should be able to trust him. Paul was her friend. He was a doctor. Everything got fuzzy and her body was heavy and when he kissed her, she couldn't tell him no. Because her mouth wouldn't make the words. It was weird. She didn't think she'd had that much to drink. But she must have. She must have gone and let herself get drunk. What a stupid thing to do. Her arms were too heavy to push him away.

She found herself spinning in and out of consciousness as the dream man of Tenmile High used her like she belonged to him.

She woke up when it was bright. And it could have been a dream except she was sore and she felt sick. Why had he kept her there all night when he'd raped her? Why had he dressed her in a soft T-shirt after he'd raped her? He *had* raped her.

She couldn't have said no.

She was sure of that.

He came out of the bathroom. "You're up."

He sounded normal. Like they'd had a romantic night. Like he hadn't taken advantage of her. She wanted to vomit.

"Paul... I didn't... I was drunk. I—" She hadn't had that much to drink. There must've been something wrong with it. He must have...

His eyes went cold. "Are you going to pretend you didn't want it?"

He was looking at her like she was crazy.

You got it all wrong…

She hadn't. She was sure she hadn't. She hadn't even been turned on. She hadn't come. She couldn't even remember it. She hadn't been able to feel her body. "I'm married."

"Yeah, me, too." He sounded so cynical. It hurt.

"What about Alex?"

"She's a big girl, Chelsea. She understands how the world works."

Like being upset about this was silly. Like fidelity was laughable. Like she was an idiot.

"I didn't want—"

"You didn't say no."

And she heard everything in that sentence. She hadn't said no. And everyone would think she was a liar. Because he was Paul Coleman and she was Chelsea Abbott and she had found a man who loved her, really and truly. And she might've wrecked it last night.

But it wasn't your fault.

But what if it was?

She heard that last question in her mother's voice.

What if it was?

She'd been pushing things again. Rebelling. She'd been basking in his attention, hadn't she? She'd had such a crush on him in high school, and she'd have killed for this back then…

Had she really just wanted to get a drink?

Or had she been asking for this?

"I need to go." She got out of bed and tried to find her clothes. "I have a flight."

"I'll get you a cab."

Like he was being chivalrous. Like he was doing a nice thing and she was an idiot.

He knew she'd never tell.

And he was right.

And she hated herself for that.

But this was the ultimate lesson. This was what happened when she was where she shouldn't be. When she read the situation wrong.

Her parents had warned her.

She hadn't listened.

And she'd paid. Dearly.

60

Chelsea

SHE WALKED ALL the way to the edge of the Harvest Festival, holding on to Mark's hand. "I have something I need to tell you."

"Okay."

"It's my fault. It's my fault we got like this. It isn't you. And it's not... It's not my mom. It's me. I did something. And I have spent the last almost twenty years afraid that you would find out. Mark, I don't think that Sean is your son."

The look on his face was everything that she had always been afraid of. It was everything she had never wanted to do to him. Not ever. Not to Mark.

She'd tried to blame his lies.

His.

But it was her lies.

Always her lies.

His lies cost her nothing.

Hers…might have cost him a whole different life. He could have had a better life.

Hers might cost him his son.

"What?"

"Something happened. A long time ago. I didn't tell you about it."

She reached into her pocket and took out the matches. She rubbed her thumb over the top of them. Matches.

That fucking bastard.

She handed the matchbook to Mark. He looked down at the logo on the front and back at her. "What is this?"

"I got them in the mail today. I think they were supposed to scare me. They did. They do. This is what's scared me for our whole marriage."

His face was like granite. "Go on."

"I've been to The Fuller. You probably don't remember. I went to a florist convention in Chicago twenty years ago, and we stayed at this hotel. We were fighting, because we'd just moved to Tenmile. You had to work and couldn't go with me, but I think maybe you were just mad at me."

"I do remember that. But I was actually working."

Of course he was. Maybe she was just trying to rewrite it. Make herself feel better.

"I met up with… I met up with Paul Coleman. He was there for a medical convention. I had a drink with him. I woke up in his hotel room. I… I don't really know what happened."

"What do you mean you don't know what happened?"

"I didn't say no." She felt bleak. Empty. Hurt. "And two years ago Sean asked me if he could do a DNA test. He was just kidding. I mean, not to find out who his parents were, but to get his nationality. Because all his friends at school were doing it. And I realized… It's like I forgot I was lying to you.

At some point it just became a habit. At some point it was just something that I was doing. Keeping this secret. And I realized it wasn't safe. That I wasn't safe."

"You slept with Paul Coleman." His words were flat. Hard.

"Yes."

"But what are you… When you say you didn't tell him no, what do you mean?"

She pressed her hands to her eyes. "I don't know what happened. I've gone over and over that night in my head until… I had to just stop thinking about it. Because it makes me sick. It makes me feel crazy. I had a drink with him at the bar, and I started not feeling well, and he took me back to his room. And I was in and out of consciousness and I didn't think I'd had enough to drink to black out, but I must have."

"Did he drug you?"

The words stabbed her. "He might have. I've definitely considered that."

"He raped you, Chelsea."

"He acted like it was fine." She ran over Mark's words. "He acted like it was so normal. And he was Ryan's best friend. And I just couldn't believe he would do that. I thought… I must've done something wrong. I must have. And then I found out I was pregnant. And I thought about… I thought about getting an abortion, because I was scared. Because I didn't know if it was his or yours. But I didn't. And I was sure we'd have other kids. And then… And then I had to get the hysterectomy and… He has blue eyes. It's the blue eyes. They scare me. Because I think… I think he's his. And when he died, part of me thought maybe we could fix this because it was really over. Because he was gone."

He held up the matchbook. "Where did these come from, then?"

She shook her head. "I'm afraid. I really am."

"Chelsea," Mark said, looking at her with ferocity in his gaze. "Fuck."

He pulled her into his arms then, and she hadn't expected that. But she clung to him, and she cried. "What are you thinking?"

"That I want to fucking kill him. If he's not dead, if he's somewhere, if he sent these I'm going to track him down and I'm going to kill him." He separated from her and held her face. "He forced himself on you."

"He made me feel like no one would believe me. Because he was acting like it was fine even then, and I thought maybe I made him think that I wanted to. And most women like him. Most women want to be with him that way, so I thought it had to be me. Do you know what I mean?"

"He's a fucking narcissist who thought everything should be his. Fuck him for taking those years from us."

"I thought maybe I had it wrong. I thought maybe it was my fault."

"It wasn't your fault."

"I… That bastard. That bastard made me doubt everything. He made me doubt you. He made me doubt us. I just… That's why, Mark. It's why. I was angry at you. And he paid attention to me and I was flattered. How disgusting is that?"

"You're human."

"I—"

"That doesn't mean you asked him for sex."

"I didn't. I didn't want it. But after… He knew, too. That's the thing. He knew about the whole thing with my dad. The way that my dad said that I was wrong. About the affair. And he used that against me."

"That's what sociopaths do," he said. "Use whatever they can against you because they know they can. He knew that you would doubt yourself, and that asshole knew that everybody else would, too. He used that against you."

"But what about Sean…?"

"He's my son. *He's my son*. That bastard didn't raise him. He doesn't love him. He never did. Fuck. How could he live in the same town as you and…"

"I should've said something. I should've told. But I was so afraid that I was going to lose the only thing that really mattered to me. And I was so afraid that… You know how it is here. Everybody thought he was God. And nobody thought I was anything."

"He doesn't matter to me. Not one bit. And he never did. But you are my life. You are everything to me. And that motherfucker doesn't get to decide what we are. He's dead. And we are not. I love you."

"We're going to need to talk to someone."

"Yeah. Probably. You probably do."

"I feel like he raped me. I felt it then, too." There had been no good truth. But she was ready to believe herself. What she'd felt then, what she still felt now. "He made me question it, just enough. And I was afraid of losing what we had. So I decided it was better if it was a secret. I decided it was safer. I don't think it was the right choice. But I didn't know what else to do. And I thought him being dead meant that it was over. But I think it's just… I have to deal with it. Even if I don't want to. It changed me, though. It made me scared. I don't want to be scared anymore."

"But he doesn't get a say in it. Not anymore. He's not in charge. Because he can't hide who he is. Not anymore."

She nodded and looked up at Mark, the man she loved. "I'm ready to tell the truth."

61

Afterburn

Alex

ALEX WAS STANDING with Cody at the ball toss when his phone rang. He frowned and took it out of his pocket. "I have to take this." He didn't offer any explanation, so she knew it had to be work.

He turned away from her and put the phone up to his ear. "Agent White. Yes. Okay. No further information at this time? Will you be forwarding it for deeper forensic analysis? Okay. Thank you."

He turned back to her. "It's not Ryan."

"What?"

"It's not Ryan. The body is too old. They have the dating of the bones between twenty-five and thirty years old. And the body is that of a woman in her forties."

And suddenly Alex's world tilted on its axis.

"A woman?"

"Yes."

"A woman. From twenty-five years ago?"

"Yes."

Alex couldn't breathe. "It's her."

62

Kindling

Ryan

RYAN HAD FUCKED UP. He knew that. He had known that for a long time. That it was going to catch up with him. That there was no running away from it. Yeah. He knew that. He had fucked up with Jenna. He had fucked up with his kids.

And Morgan... She didn't deserve to be tied up in this.

He loved her. She made him feel...like he was in high school again. Like the world was full of possibilities. She adored him.

It was that part that made him feel guilty. She looked at him like the sun shone out his ass. A lot of people did.

His wife didn't, though. She'd loved him, for sure. But she hadn't idolized him, not after twenty years.

He'd missed that.

So when Morgan had looked up at him with awe, he'd wanted to capture that. Keep it for himself.

He hadn't thought about Morgan at all. Hadn't considered what dragging her into this would mean.

There were only so many things a man could fix. Some were just past the breaking point. His marriage being one of them.

What he'd done twenty-five years ago being another.

And Marjorie knew. When she had shown him the wallet...

He got his phone out and dialed the number quickly. "We need to talk."

63

Alex

"I WAS HOLDING the matches."

"You what?"

"In my memory, I'm holding the matches. I think I did it, Cody. I think I set the fire."

"Sweetheart," Cody said, grabbing hold of her arms. "You don't know that."

"The body is my mom's, isn't it?"

"We don't know that."

"But the timeline fits. You would know if there were other missing people in the area. You would know."

She knew.

She knew.

And suddenly, her memory broke open.

64

Ignition point

Alex

SHE'D DECIDED TO follow him that morning when she heard him leave. Because she needed to know what was going on. Ryan had called in the middle of the night, and Paul had totally lost his cool, which was so unlike him.

He never did that. He never got that angry.

She hadn't been able to hear what they were talking about, but she knew that he was upset.

And so, early that morning, when he had left at five, she had decided to follow him. Because she needed to know what was going on.

Because the ice in Paul's eyes scared her.

For years, it had been quiet. Something she'd tried to ignore.

But it was wrong, and something was going even more wrong now and it had taken hold of her...

What if he'd taken the money?

And the thing was, she had no knee-jerk *he would never do that!* feeling inside her soul.

She didn't know what Paul was capable of. Or worse, maybe she did.

That was the problem.

He was headed out to Cody's old family farm. She knew the road well. Because she had met Cody out there more times than she could count. To talk to him. To kiss him. To be held by him.

She kept her distance, and when he turned onto the road that led to Cody's, she idled for a long time. For some reason she decided not to drive up to the house. She walked along the tree-lined road and as she came around the bend she saw Paul and Ryan, standing by the farmhouse. Their posture was tense, and it was clear they were arguing.

It was hot already. So hot. And the wind was warm and frightening, and the electricity that crackled between them seemed to make it worse.

Paul reached toward the side of the house and picked up a shovel that had been resting there. She noticed a red gas can by his feet.

"You're not telling anyone, we're burning all of this and we're never talking about it again."

"I can't keep it a secret anymore. I don't want to. I have to…sort all this out. Because it's messed my whole life up. This shit has ruined absolutely everything. I can't eat, I can't sleep. It doesn't get better. It gets worse."

"You think it's going to be better for you in prison?"

"I ruined my whole marriage. My whole life, because I can't… I can't deal with this."

"Where's everything Marjorie showed you?"

He shrugged. "I didn't bring it."

"You fucking what?"

"It's in the house."

Paul reached behind his back and took out a gun. A gun Alex hadn't known he'd owned. A gun he had pointed at Ryan.

Without thinking, she ran toward them, and Alex shouted. "Paul!"

That quiet ice. It hadn't been quiet at all.

And it hadn't simply been cold.

"Get it from the house, now. I'm burning it all. All of it. There won't be any evidence. And you don't have to worry about it."

"Getting rid of the evidence doesn't mean it didn't happen." Ryan didn't even look at her. Neither did Paul. It was like she wasn't even there. Like she didn't matter. Had she ever? Had she ever mattered at all? Whatever this was, whatever was happening between them now, was more than Paul had ever felt for her.

"Your conscience isn't my problem."

"I could never forget it, Paul. I could never just move on. Why do you think I messed everything up with Jenna? I can't let it go. I close my eyes and I see it. Over and over again, I see it."

"Ryan... Paul..." She was shaking.

When Paul looked at her, it was with annoyance. Like she was in the way. "Fucking hell, Alex. Couldn't you stay out of this?"

"I don't even know what's happening!"

"Get the wallet, Ryan."

"I can't do that." Ryan's tone was slow, measured. "Alex, it was an accident." He looked at her, his eyes tortured. "I swear to you, it was an accident."

Paul walked forward to the house and dumped gasoline on

the porch. Ryan ran toward him, but Paul held the gun out, pointed right at Ryan's chest.

"Paul...what are you doing? Morgan is in the house."

"It's going to burn. With or without your help."

The whole place was a tinderbox. The air hot and arid, everything around them dry. And when Paul lit the match and threw it onto the porch, it went up blistering and fast.

Paul lit more matches all around the dry ground and the wind made the flames grow, pushing them down toward town.

Paul dropped the matchbook, still holding the gun out, and she honestly wondered if he would just shoot them both.

"Alex," Ryan said. "Run."

"Ryan..."

"I have to get Morgan."

Ryan disappeared into the burning house, as the flames expanded, consuming it whole.

And Alex bent down and picked up the matches. She looked at the back of the matchbook, and then up, into her husband's familiar blue eyes.

"What have you done?"

65

Afterburn

Alex

WHEN THE MEMORY HIT, Alex was sitting in the car. And she panicked. She put her hands over her face and tried to breathe, but she couldn't. Couldn't do anything but gasp and cry.

Cody held her close.

"Paul started it. Ryan tried to stop him. And then he went to save Morgan. He went to save her. But the flames were… He was in the house, Cody."

"And you don't know what they were fighting about."

"No. I don't. Except Paul asked about a wallet. He wanted Ryan to get the wallet from the house."

"Everything burned, sweetheart. Whatever it was, it wouldn't have been there."

Alex nodded. "I know. I have a headache."

She felt so tired. Traumatized. She was still trying to piece everything together. Her mother's body...she was sure it was her mother's body they'd just found twenty yards from the ignition point. That *she'd* found.

But what did Paul and Ryan have to do with it? There had been cracks in the perfect glass facade of her life, but it was shattered now.

She remembered.

He was willing to kill Morgan. He would have killed Ryan.

She knew...if the fire hadn't exploded. If it hadn't started burning so hot, so fast, so out of control. If she hadn't run back to her car as fast as she could, her arms burned, her throat singed...

Paul would have killed her.

And he would have felt nothing.

"Let's go back home," he said.

He meant his vacation rental. Right now that felt more like home. Right now she wouldn't be able to face her home.

"I need to do something," she said.

"You need to take a breath. Please, for the love of God, Alex, let me take care of you for a minute."

They went back and he carried her to bed, and laid her down on the mattress. She told him everything she could remember. He held her until she stopped shaking, then he left her in the quiet. In the dark. She could hear him outside the door making phone calls.

An hour later he came in.

"Morgan is home from the Harvest Festival. I called her and asked if it was possible what Paul and Ryan were looking for could have been in Mom's things at the nursing home, instead of at the house."

"Ryan would have told Paul..."

"I think Ryan never intended to go along with what Paul wanted. It's entirely possible he knew it wasn't there. Or that he didn't know which things had stayed at the farmhouse, and what she'd taken to the home."

"Did Morgan say she…"

"She said she had some boxes of Marjorie's things, but she can't say for sure if she has what we're after." He sighed. "I can go alone if you need me to."

She shook her head. "No. I'm okay. I want to go. I blocked all this out, I think because I spent so many years trying to convince myself that those hollow eyes I saw sometimes were a trick of the light. Or a weird alternate persona he sometimes slipped into for a second." She looked up at Cody. "But that was the real him. The charm, the smiles…that was the fake."

Cody nodded. "I know."

"I couldn't accept it."

He moved to her, cupping her chin. "Why should you? You didn't deserve it. You didn't do anything wrong."

She wanted to argue, but she didn't have the strength. So she let him lead her back out of the apartment and to the street. They drove to Morgan's in silence.

She followed Cody up to Morgan's apartment on numb feet.

Morgan met them at the door. "I got both of my Marjorie boxes out. You're welcome to go through them. I don't know what you're going to find…"

She didn't know how much of her memory Cody had relayed to Morgan. She opened her mouth to say something, but she was all out of energy.

Cody walked across the room and bent down as he moved a few things around, and Alex was unbearably aware that this was the first time Cody was looking at his mother's possessions. He carefully took out a porcelain figurine.

His fingers lingered on it for a moment before he set it aside. He took blue latex gloves out of his pocket and put them on, before methodically sifting through the things in the box.

"Paul set the house on fire," Alex said, her voice sounding too loud in the room.

"What?" Morgan asked.

"Paul. He set the house on fire. Ryan thought you were inside." She met Morgan's eyes. "He went back in to get you."

Morgan covered her mouth, her eyes filling with tears. "I... I... I left, about an hour before the fire started. But he wasn't there. He didn't know."

"He tried to save you, Morgan. That's how he died. He went back for you." She just needed Morgan to know that. Paul had been a liar. He'd been empty inside.

Ryan had been imperfect. But he'd gone back for Morgan.

Morgan sat down on the couch, her face in her hands, a sob shaking her shoulders.

Cody grimly sifted through the boxes, silent, until finally he lifted up a slim black box and opened the top.

Inside was a wallet.

He opened it, and she saw a driver's license inside.

"Is it her?" she whispered.

He nodded slowly. "Yes."

It was a slow, rolling horror that couldn't escape. And it coated her now, entirely.

"Did Paul kill my mother?"

"I don't know," Cody said. "But I think we found the reason for the fire. And it wasn't you. It was the body, Alex."

"Ryan and Paul had something to do with it," she said, misery welling up inside her. "And Ryan wanted to make it right."

66

Ignition Point

Tom

HE COULDN'T HAVE planned it better if he'd tried. He almost wished he would have thought of it. But then, he'd never have burned down a town over a quarter of a million dollars.

It would have had to be a lot more than that.

When everything caught on fire, he ran.

And in the coming days, when he was listed as missing—possibly presumed dead—he knew he'd found a way to get away. From the medical debt. From the theft.

From the loss of his wife.

When he crossed the border into Mexico, he took a full breath for the first time in a month. Maybe even in years.

He took the fire as a sign. It burned away all the consequences, and told him to start again.

He wasn't one to argue with fate.

67

Kindling

Marjorie

TWENTY-FIVE YEARS AGO Marjorie had seen the car pull onto the property. And she recognized it. It was Paul Coleman's muscle car. Usually, all the boys went out together. But it was odd that they would be out at this hour. She had gone up the stairs and looked into Cody's room. He hadn't been there.

She'd watched from the window, barely able to make out silhouettes in the trees. So she'd sneaked downstairs and walked to the edge of the wood just as the figures were getting back in the car.

The headlight had caught Ryan Abbott's face.

If Ryan was there, Cody would be there, too.

After they'd left, she'd gone over to the site and she had found a fresh mound of dirt. She had disturbed it with her foot. And there had been a wallet there, and a shattered wristwatch.

She had picked them up.

It was later that she had realized why the woman's ID had been there. She'd held on to it, afraid that Cody and the other boys had taken it, or caused some other trouble. Only after she'd discovered she'd left town. Except she had a horrible suspicion she hadn't left town at all. What she strongly suspected was that there was a body beneath that mound of dirt. And what she could never be certain of was whether her son had had something to do with it.

She hadn't been a good mother. She knew that. Already, her daughter had gone off and destroyed her life. Given herself over to drugs and alcohol, had gone on to be an even worse mother than Marjorie herself had been.

And Morgan. That poor little thing… She didn't have anyone. She never had.

And Marjorie had known she had one responsibility. To protect Cody.

It had been worth it. Because he'd gone on to do incredible things. And maybe he had somehow been involved in the death of a local woman, but how many more had he saved with his job at the FBI?

She had difficulty speaking to him after that. Difficulty looking him in the eye. But she kept her silence.

Except…she hadn't been able to do that any longer. Knowing she was dying.

And it had seemed like fate that Morgan had fallen in love with Ryan Abbott. Oh, not so much in the way it had broken up his marriage. Not that.

But that it had brought him to her. Which was why she had asked to speak to him as her health was failing. Because she had done a great many things wrong in her life. And what she wanted was to hand some of that back. She wanted him to decide something. What he might do with what had happened. Because she had wondered… She had wondered if it had really been justice. What she had done.

She had thought about the woman often. And had wondered if she had been a better mother than Marjorie. And if her daughter missed her very much.

"Hello, Ryan," she said when he came into the room.

She missed the farmhouse. She wished she were still living there, rather than this nursing home, but she figured the point of it was that she wouldn't be here much longer.

"Hi, Marjorie," he said.

She could still see the boy he'd been underneath the lines on his face. He was still handsome.

She wondered if Morgan made him feel like that boy. Men were like that. Always using women to try to feel something.

"I want you to bring me that box," she said, pointing to a black box on the dresser. "And look inside it."

He brought it over to her and set it on the bed. She opened it up. The wallet was in there. Just as it had been. And a watch.

The wallet. She opened it up, and inside was the driver's license. Expired now for more than twenty years.

His face went white. And she knew. That she'd been right about it. All of it.

"I saw you that night," she said. "You and Paul. And Cody."

Ryan let out a hard breath and pushed his hand through his hair. "Why didn't you say anything?"

"Because. I was protecting my son. I kept this, just in case. I thought I might need it."

"To hold over our heads?"

"If it came down to it. I did a bad job at protecting Cody otherwise. But I felt like I needed to protect him in this."

"And what's changed?"

"I'm dying. And maybe there's a karmic debt to be paid. At this point Cody is going to have to figure out whether he ought to pay for it. Just like I figure you have to figure out whether you should pay for it. And same for Paul."

"Morgan and I are having a baby."

"I know."

"But you still want me to confess to this?"

"I told you. I'm just giving this to you. Letting you know that someone else knew."

"Cody wasn't involved." He swallowed. "Just so you know."

Marjorie felt like she had been hit.

"He wasn't?"

"No. And it was an accident. Just… Just to be very clear. It was an accident."

"Cody wasn't with you?"

"No. He wasn't."

"Why did you come to the farm?"

Ryan looked lost then. "It was where Paul wanted to go. He said…"

"Was it in case she was found? Did he think…?"

"Yeah," he said. "He figured everybody would suspect Cody because his old man was a violent bastard."

"So everybody would suspect my son, and so did I. And he had nothing to do with it?"

"Fuck. Marjorie. What am I supposed to do? I need to be there for Morgan. For the baby."

"Nothing has changed in all these years. You could leave it the same."

He stared straight ahead. "I don't know if I can. We never really left it behind. At least I didn't. It was never that easy for me."

"And for Paul?"

That was when Ryan looked truly afraid. "I don't think it matters to him. Not at all. She was Alex's mother. He… He married Alex after that. Like he was her hero. When he was the one who hurt her."

Marjorie had been a small, selfish woman for most of her life. Here on death's door, asking someone else to be selfless seemed unfair.

But life had never been fair.

"Do you really think this is the only horrible thing he's done? Do you think he won't just do more horrible things?"

Ryan looked at her with resolve, but to do what, she wasn't sure.

She didn't know if she'd live to find out how it all ended.

But she hoped that she'd finally done something right.

After he was gone, she picked up her phone and called Cody.

It went to voice mail.

She hung up.

68

Afterburn

Alex

IN THE FOLLOWING days they confirmed through dental records that the body was in fact Alex's mother. She hadn't left her family.

Her injuries were consistent with someone who'd been struck by a moving vehicle. Ethan's story of seeing two men lifting a body out of the street in front of his house—his house that was across the road from Alex's—helped put the pieces together from that night. But there were so many unanswered questions.

Chelsea came over the next morning, with Mark.

She told them everything. About the rape. About Sean.

"I've wondered for years…" Chelsea swallowed hard. "If I slept with your husband, Alex. Or if he raped me, and I could never decide if I blamed him or myself. I felt like it had to be my fault."

Alex felt like she'd done a lot of digging. And like her memories from the fire coming back had brought others in, too, sharp and clear. Things she'd denied for a long time. Things she'd covered up.

"Paul was good at that," Alex said. "It was how he got away with being a sociopathic narcissist for so many years without anyone noticing."

Mark and Cody looked at each other.

"He showed his hand to certain people," Cody said.

"And he manipulated people he knew were vulnerable," Chelsea said. "He knew that I was so aware of who he was. He knew how insecure I was. He knew my own brother idolized him, that my mother did. He knew I'd had a crush on him, and he knew all those things would make it easy for him. To make me question myself. To make me wonder if I was wrong about what had happened." She held a matchbook out toward Alex. "I think he's alive. I think he sent this to me."

Alex stared at the matchbook. "He sent me my mother's necklace." She looked up at Chelsea. "He still wants us to be scared. He had to run away. He had to start over but he couldn't let go of that power trip."

Within twenty-four hours they'd processed the matchbook and necklace for fingerprints, and while there were several sets on both, they were able to pull partials for Paul's.

"That asshole built his own gallows," Cody said. "I'm happy to hang him on it."

Alex almost couldn't believe he'd made such a big mistake except...

Of course he had.

They were nothing but things to him. Possessions.

He'd raped Chelsea, confident in the fact she'd never tell on him. And how many other women had he done that to?

You. He did it to you.

There was freedom in admitting it, fully.

And also in knowing they were going to stop him. End him. Expose him.

He never thought the women he'd hurt were strong enough, smart enough, *enough* to touch him.

But they were going to destroy him.

She thought about the matchbook.

The Fuller.

Chicago, Il.

"Cody, I think he might have gone to Chicago."

"Why?"

"He sent Chelsea the matchbook from the hotel. That was where he raped her."

"He might not be there anymore."

"But I bet he was."

"Finding him in Chicago won't be easy."

"I hear you're the FBI."

"That's true. I am the FBI."

69

Afterburn

Alex

IT TOOK TWO MONTHS, but they found Paul in Chicago living under an assumed name. When he was arrested and taken into the police station in Tenmile, Alex didn't go in to see him.

She'd thought about it. Thought about showing up and demanding answers.

She already knew nothing would ever make him feel shame.

She knew that sending her the locket had been his way of keeping a hold on her.

She knew the best thing she could do was fight him exactly how you fought a fire.

She had to deprive him of oxygen.

Let him suffocate on the rage that he couldn't reach her anymore.

It was after Paul was arrested that she finally went to see Chelsea alone.

"I'm sorry."

Chelsea frowned. "You don't have anything to be sorry for. All these years I felt like I'd betrayed you, Alex. It's why I couldn't…deal with you. It had nothing to do with all that petty high school stuff."

Alex shook her head. "No. He did it to me first. And I didn't say anything."

"That isn't fair to you. He left red flags wherever he went. But no one wanted to see them," said Chelsea. "I have spent years wondering if it was me. If I caused it, because I was angry at Mark. Because I was asking for it. Because why else would I meet with him? And at the end of all things, I just… I didn't trust myself enough. And that was because of him. That was what he wanted. From you, for me."

Alex nodded. "He wanted both of us to not be able to trust ourselves. It's why he sent me the locket. Why he sent you the matches. He couldn't let go of us. He couldn't let go of the game. He still had to try and keep us questioning ourselves. What we knew. What was real. That isn't our fault. It's his."

She felt that, that deep conviction, burning inside her.

Paul had lived a life of deception. His looks had shielded him from so many things. So much scrutiny.

He had been able to act charming. He was the perfect sociopath. He thought he was so much smarter than everybody around him, and he had thought nothing of twisting every moment, every doubt, to his advantage.

"He didn't want us to talk to each other. He was happy to be the reason we didn't." Chelsea frowned. "What if Sean…"

"He's Mark's son," said Alex.

Chelsea nodded. "Yes. He is."

"I'm sorry that we both had to live through him," Alex said, finally.

"But now no one ever will again," Chelsea said. "Because we finally started talking."

Later that night Alex sat on the porch swing with Cody. They'd bought a house outside town, up on a hill that over-looked the whole valley. It was amazing what new perspective could do for you.

"I'm glad there's going to be justice. I'm glad he isn't dead. If he'd died, I'd feel like he'd gotten away with something." Alex sighed and leaned against Cody.

This had been harder than the fire. Dealing with the fall-out of it all. The kids were devastated. But then…they'd had their own stories, too.

It had hurt to hear them. Their own doubts. How Paul had manipulated and undermined them, too.

That was what Paul did. He made you feel uncertain, so he could always control the story.

But he didn't get to do that now.

"It doesn't make me feel less like I wasted a whole lot of my life, though," she said.

"You didn't waste your life. You have great kids."

She smiled. "You don't know my kids yet."

"Not yet. But they're your kids. So I assume they're great. And you have great friends. An amazing business. And I loved you the whole time."

She turned to him, her heart feeling full. Feeling tender and bruised. "I loved you the whole time, too."

"That counts for something."

"I guess you can't bring back what's been burned away. You can just plant something new."

"That's all we can do."

"That's what I want. I love you."

"I love you, too."

"So," Alex said, "let's make something new."

70

Afterburn

Cody

WATCHING HIS NIECE'S grief over losing Ryan had been one of the most difficult things he'd ever been through. But that, he supposed, was having connections. Real connections.

He'd been there when any number of strangers had gotten bad news. But not people he loved.

And he did love Morgan. He loved her daughter, Lily.

He loved Alex.

Love was a painful, messy experience as far as he could tell. He'd run from it for a long time. And now he was standing in it. A lot of it.

Tenmile had burned to the ground, but in some ways it had made things clearer.

Buildings burned. People did, too.

But the love stayed.

It was love that made Morgan cry like that. But love that

made her look at him with hope, deep and bright like he'd never seen.

"He died trying to save me?"

"Yes," Cody said. "He did. And if you'd been in the house, you wouldn't have made it."

"He did love me."

"Yes. He did. And someone else will again."

She rested her cheek on Lily's head. "Someone already does."

71

Restoration

Jenna

PAUL COLEMAN HAD been driving the car that had struck Alex's mother while she crossed a residential street late at night. She'd been coming home from dinner with friends. Paul was drunk, and shouldn't have been driving at all.

Ryan had been the passenger, but he'd helped Paul cover up the death.

And Ryan had felt eaten up by it for all those years. He should have. He deserved it.

And he had gotten himself killed trying to stop Paul. He had gotten himself killed because he was going to confess. And he had gotten himself killed trying to save Morgan and the baby.

"You bastard," Jenna said as she stood there at the ignition point, looking at the scorched ground. "You got your character arc after all. Good for you."

Ryan Abbott could rest in peace as a complicated figure. Just another person that had been in awe of Paul Coleman. And then afraid of him.

Paul. Who was actually the bad guy.

Alex was having a hard time with that. But thankfully, she had Cody. When Chelsea had told Alex about what had happened between herself and Paul, Jenna had been afraid it would send Alex into a full-blown breakdown. But really, finding out that your husband had actually killed your mother, and that he had possibly pursued you for that reason… Well. Alex couldn't be more disgusted with him. But again, she had Cody. Who was absolutely everything he had always appeared to be, and more.

He quit the Bureau to move back to Tenmile to be with Alex. Through the good, the bad and the messy.

God knew they had a whole bunch of messy.

All this time they had been looking for the fire starter. The fire wasn't the issue, so much as the fuel. And that had been in place a long time ago. Way before September 8, 2022. It had been the perfect tinderbox. So when the spark had hit it, it had been primed to burn everything to the ground.

Ethan put his arm around her. "You okay?"

"Yeah. I mean, I'm sorry about everything. About the whole mess. About the fact that my husband was involved in vehicular homicide that killed the mother of one of my best friends. But you know, I'm glad he's not a monster. He just made bad decisions. But he tried, in the end, to do the right thing. It just wasn't enough."

"Yeah. Well. I have a feeling we'll be sorting through all of this for a long time."

"Yeah. You sound tired."

"I'm not," Ethan said. "I'm up for it."

"I love you," she said. Because she might as well just go ahead and say it.

"Really?"

"Yeah. I do."

"It's not too complicated of a time or…"

"No. It is extremely complicated. And as a result, I think it's the best time to say that. Because… Well, you're still here. All this, and you're still here."

"I love you, too, Jenna. If that wasn't clear."

"You've actually made that really clear."

They walked away from the ignition site together and drove into town. They went to the coffee shop, and Chloe and Aiden were there, holding baby Lily, with Morgan sitting at a table over next to Edna and her grandson Tyler, who was wearing what looked to be a freshly knitted green sweater. And everybody looked happy, in spite of everything.

"Hey, guys," she said. "Have you had a good afternoon?"

"Yeah," Chloe said, kissing Lily on the head. "It's been great."

"That's good." She looked at Morgan. "How are you?"

She didn't think she was hallucinating the slight glance that Morgan gave Tyler. "Good." She smiled. "Doing good."

And Jenna was surprised to realize that she was genuinely pleased to hear it.

72

Restoration

Chelsea

HER MOTHER HAD finally left her father. She'd lived with Chelsea and Mark for a while. Mark was working to recast the way he felt about his mother-in-law, considering that the real problem had been Chelsea's dad.

That was the thing.

And it was ultimately the decision they all made. Jenna and Morgan were never going to be best friends, and that was fine. No one expected them to be.

But over wine and a cheese board, Jenna had made a pronouncement to Chelsea and Alex, in the months following all the revelations.

"It was the men. All along. It was your father," she said, directing that at Chelsea. "It was Paul. Most of all, it was Paul. But it was Ryan, too. And I'm not going to let the patriarchy have this. I'm going to keep telling the truth. Because that's what they hate. I'm going to say it louder. I'm not going to hate another woman for the rest of my life because my husband couldn't keep it in his pants."

They all raised a glass to that.

"To confident women," said Alex. "Loud women. Women who don't stay quiet to make people comfortable. Women who don't ignore that feeling in their gut."

"Women who believe themselves and each other," added Chelsea.

"To us," said Jenna.

"To us."

★ ★ ★ ★ ★